*If You've Ever Loved a Horse
or Loved a Cowboy*

Put Your Boots On, Missy

Ann Cofield

Put Your Boots On, Missy

To: Leeda

"The journey of a thousand miles begins with but a single step."
– Chinese Proverb

Ann Cofield

Don't forget your boots!

Ann Cofield

BOOKLOGIX®
Alpharetta, Georgia

ISBN: 978-1-61005-208-5

Library of Congress Control Number: 2012911495

Printed in the United States of America

♾This paper meets the requirements of ANSI/NISO Z39.48-1992 (Permanence of Paper)

Dedicated to the Pickneyville Writers Group
who made the journey with me
as we shared the adventures of the Cherry Valley riders;
and to my horses Timex, retired,
and Firecracker, who has gone to greener pastures.
They enriched my life beyond measure.

Acknowledgements

Thanks to all the endurance riders, here, there, and yonder who inspired this book—and to our horses, whose spirit and heart help us live our dreams.

Thanks also, to Ron, The Computer Guy and his wife Amy, who pulled me out of the weeds more than one time as my computer "stalked" me!

To Randy and Deinna Jones, who keep my horses and watch my back—always a step ahead of my life!

To the Casey family who helped me bring the Riding School from a dream to reality, which provides me with extra income and is a joy in my life!

To the Clarke family who are are woven into the fabric of my life.

To my friends in Buford: Andy Jensen, Tara Ammons, and Brittany Sikes who printed pages each week for me to take to my writing group!

To Cleon for keeping my trailer on the road, and Mildred who always listens.

To my running buddies—Cindy, Karen, and Suzanne—who inspire me everyday.

To the American Endurance Ride Conference (A.E.R.C.), for supplying information when needed. Many thanks!

To my family, who encouraged me in this endeavor! Enjoy the book!

To the staff at BookLogix who provide me with professional care and have an understanding of my goals with the book...

I am lucky that Caroline, my editor, has a horse background! Also, she understands the "mindset" of my target audience! No matter how many times I needed to make changes in the manuscript, or struggled with the technology, she helped me move on with the task. Thanks, Caroline for your encouragement and patience!

Sara, who did the book cover design, layout, and all other, learned more about horses than she ever wanted to know. We looked through hundreds of Arabian pictures before we found the cover picture. She was surprised that horses have expressions, too! Thanks, Sara, for letting me change the cover...beyond the last minute!

Thanks to Ahmad, "the captain of the ship," who has guided me on this journey and to my destination!

A special thanks to all my friends who kept asking, "Are you finished with the book?" reminding me that, *To Finish is to Win!*

Chapter One

How *ow could this have happened to me? I just wanted to* *learn to ski!* Moria winced as the doctor straightened her leg and probed the swollen knee.

"Well, Ms. Harris the x-ray didn't show any broken bones. Looks like you have some ligament damage. You'll need a support brace when the swelling goes down. Stay off your feet and maybe you can avoid surgery. The nurse will be in with some instructions." He turned to leave.

Moria clutched his coat sleeve as if this would make her well. "Wait! Don't go. Surely it can't be that serious!"

"You better take care of yourself. Skiers," she heard the doctor mutter as he slid his arm away and left the room.

Sitting up stiffly, she waited for the nurse to bring a pair of crutches. Tears tracked down her wind-burned cheeks as she looked at the new ski outfit crumpled in the chair. *Doctors get so carried away sometimes! Maybe the swelling will go down and I can ski tomorrow. It can't be as bad as he says!* The throbbing pain in Moria's knee said otherwise. Gripping the edge of the table, she tried to hold back the tears.

How can I do my job? What about my students? Their fourth grade faces swam before her eyes and a wave of helplessness swept over her. *I want to go home, to my farm, my friends and my life! But, most of all, I miss the horses. I can't expect Maxine to take care them indefinitely. She has her own farm and a classroom of students, too. What will happen to me?*

She sniffed, reaching for a tissue. Like the proverbial hamster on the wheel, her mind raced around and around, remembering Fredrick. *How could you have abandoned me? I need you!* A tiny voice whispered, *maybe he needed you, too.* Moria closed her ears to the voice—her thoughts spinning into the past. Shreds of memories floated through her mind. *Why? Why? What am I going to do?* The door to the examining room opened, bringing her to the moment and the painful reality of her plight.

The nurse and Moria's daughter, Sarah, entered the room— a thankful distraction from her dark thoughts. Anxious, but trying to seem casual, Sarah said, "Well, Mom, Looks like you're going to get a chance to catch up your reading." The nurse adjusted the crutches. Moria blew her nose and handed Sarah the ski clothes.

"Yeah. Maybe a book on how to ski!" she said with a sigh, struggling to balance on the crutches.

At their suite in the ski lodge, Sarah built up a fire and settled Moria on the couch. The scent of fresh pine boughs on the mantle mingled with wood smoke added to the winter experience. Moria did not notice. Her mind was far away, already home.

"Sarah, I've got to call Maxine and let her know what's happened. Maybe she'll know someone who can help me." Just then, the clock chimed ten. "I can't call her now! It's midnight at home. Guess I'll have to wait until tomorrow. What could Maxine do now, anyway? I'm too tired to think about this anymore."

Sarah helped Moria out of the chair and to the bedroom. "I've got an idea. I have a few days left before I have to go back to college. I'll come home and help you. Maybe we can find someone in the neighborhood to do the barn work."

"Honey, that would be great if it's not too much trouble."

"Mom, I was your trouble for eighteen years! It's the least I can do. You're so independent. You never want anybody's help."

Moria smiled a thanks to Sarah, *It's better that way.* Then, spent a restless night trying to plan how she would manage these next few weeks. Maxine could give her rides to work but who would take care of the horses?

Christmas Day in the Colorado mountains presented a glorious gift of deep blue shadows and golden shafts of sunlight sifting through snow-laden evergreens. Looking out the window early that morning Moria sighed, *Maybe I can ski today. I probably just need to stretch my leg.* She unwrapped the Ace bandage and tried to walk to the bathroom, took a step, and fell. Pain shot through her leg and the injured knee felt like stretched elastic.

Hearing Moria fall, Sarah came running to the bedroom. "Mom, oh, jeez!" The girl quickly observed the disarray scattered about the room. The crutches had fallen from the chair when Moria tried to catch herself. The Ace bandage lay in a tangled web at her feet, sending a stark message about the futility of this effort. Sarah, feeling overwhelmed by Moria's frustration, helped her to a chair and handed her the phone saying, "This might be a good time to call Maxine."

The phone rang several times in Maxine's Georgia farm house before she answered. Her cheerful greeting brought a catch to Moria's voice.

"Hey, it's me."

"What's the matter? You don't sound like you're having much fun."

"I'm not."

"Oh my God! What's happened?"

"Well, I had an accident."

"I'm not even surprised! I told you this was a bad idea!" Then her voice softened. "I'm sorry. Tell me what happened."

"I'll give you the short version. Some people got in my way and I hit an icy patch on a mogul. They called for help and waited with me. The ski patrol arrived, braced my leg, lifted me onto the sled and took me down to the first aid station. I felt a terrible pain in my knee and knew something really bad had happened..."

"Let me guess. Your bindings didn't release."

"How did you know?"

"Been there." Maxine replied.

"I didn't know you'd had a ski accident."

"Long story. Go ahead. Tell me the rest."

"The doctor says I have to stay off my feet for several weeks. I didn't think it was a big deal but now I guess it is." Moria stopped talking. Unshed tears filled the silence.

"Hey, don't worry. We'll work this out. Your knee is a long way from your heart. I'll start looking around for some help. The horses are fine and so are the other critters. When are Dixie's puppies due?"

"Dr. Barr said any day now. Do you think it's going to happen before I get back?"

"Don't worry. Just get yourself fixed. Keep in touch. Looks like we might have an ice storm toward the end of the week. You'd better plan to come home before, or after, so you won't get stranded."

Moria disconnected the call and covered her face with her hands.

* * *

Christmas Day Moria and Sarah visited the neighborhood church. Moria prayed, "Dear God if you can find it in your heart to send me a cowboy, now is the time! I know we're not always on the same page...but I could surely use some help! Amen."

The traditional Christmas service progressed but Moria barely noticed the kaleidoscope of colors reflecting from the stained glass windows. "Silent Night" played softly in the background but she did not hear.

Even the words of the Lord's Prayer did not register until she heard herself say, "Thy will be done, on Earth as it is in Heaven." Moria thought, *Maybe this is Thy will, but what does it mean? Am I supposed to learn something from this?* Jumbled thoughts pounded in her head. *I just can't think about this right now.*

Later, Sarah settled Moria in the back seat of the car and drove to the ski lodge. Fatigue, pain and worry etched lines across Moria's face. She stared, unseeing, out the window, then closed her eyes. Pictures of home and the horses intruded into her mind. *How will I manage? I've got to go home!* Her throat tightened with anxiety.

Monday morning Moria hobbled into the ski lodge kitchen. Her tousled auburn hair and the dark circles under usually bright green eyes caused her daughter to reach quickly for the coffeepot.

Sarah handed her mom a steaming cup and said, "Well, I'm not going to ask how you slept. Guess you would have called if you needed me."

Moria laid the crutches on the floor and eased into the chair—aching muscles complaining of her misadventure.

She stirred her coffee and took the toasted bagel Sarah offered. "Sorry. I know my accident has ruined your vacation, too."

"Don't worry. I can ski later this winter. More important, I just watched the weather report. Maxine was right. If we don't leave tonight the Atlanta airport will probably be closed by tomorrow evening. I know we need to go home."

Home. Moria looked ruefully at the bandaged knee. "I really did enjoy our time together—except for this. I hate it when I'm not in control!"

Trying to cheer her mom Sarah said, "Somewhere I heard, 'Man plans—God laughs'... well, maybe He didn't laugh this time," seeing the look on Moria's strickened face she added, "Sorry. You're right. Most of it was fun. Don't worry. We'll get through this. I hate to bring up an unpleasant subject, but it's almost time for your appointment. What's the worst thing that can happen?"

Moria laughed, "Guess I'll have my wings clipped for a while. I really need a cowboy!"

Sarah looked sideways at her mom. "Oh, yeah. Just what you need—a cowboy!"

In the waiting room, Moria looked around. Every chair was filled with casualties from the weekend.

A young girl and her mom sat next to Moria. She sensed the child looking at her and glanced over, meeting the youngster's bright blue eyes.

Seeing that she had Moria's attention, she asked, "Did you have a horse accident?"

Startled, Moria said, "Excuse me?"

"I see you're wearing a horse sweater and horse earrings."

"No, I had a ski accident," Moria smiled and said. "But, I like horses. In fact, I love them."

"Me, too." The child answered, delighted to find a kindred soul.

"Do you have a horse?"

The girl's eyes danced. "We have a few horses on our ranch. My pony's name is Tiger," she giggled, "But he's a pony!"

Moria smiled for a moment, forgetting the reason for being in her predicament.

"What's your name?" she asked.

"Jessie, spelled with 'ie' because I'm a girl!"

The child's mother said, "Jessie, leave this lady alone. Can't you see she's hurt?"

Moria laughed. "Your daughter's good entertainment. It's okay."

The mother offered her hand. "I'm Ruth. Hope your injury's not too serious."

"As my friend said, my knee's a long way from my heart. So, in her opinion I'll get over it!"

Ruth asked, "What kind of riding do you do?"

Happy to talk about her passion, Moria said, "I do endurance riding."

Ruth leaned forward with interest. "There are some people in our neighborhood who do that sport. We love trail riding and have wanted to talk to them and find out more about endurance. Looks like it takes a lot of time."

"Once you get the horses conditioned you can do maintenance riding," Moria said, hoping to encourage them but knowing a whole new life style would consume the family if they went down this path.

Moria searched in her purse for a pen and paper. "Here is the web site for the American Endurance Ride Conference. It's AERC.org. You'll find lots of information about getting started."

Ruth jotted down Moria's e-mail address. "Keep in touch and let me know if this is the sport for you. Maybe I'll see you all at a ride someday!"

"I'll check into it when we get home. We're from southern California, and came up here to ski, except I ran over my husband's foot with the car. So our trip is over."

Jessie reassured Moria. "She's really a good mom!"

"I know, honey. Accidents happen."

Just then, Moria heard her name called. She struggled up and thumped down the long corridor behind the nurse. The image of Jessie's family trotting down the trail into a pink and gold sunrise disappeared as she entered the exam room.

Later, getting into the car and grimacing with pain from the cumbersome brace, she wailed, "I just can't live this way!"

"I know you're miserable. Why don't you take a pain pill, or two?" Sarah said, handing her mom a pill pack and water bottle.

Moria looked out the window, digging her fingernails into the palms of her hands. Finally, she said, "Got it I'm done with whining," and reached for her daughter's offering. "Guess I've got a lot of character building ahead of me."

Sarah looked over at Moria and smiled. "I told you, we'll get through this. Sorry if I upset you."

That evening at the Denver airport while waiting for departure, Moria stared at the weather channel tracking the snowstorm heading for the southeast, then looked out the window at the sleek jet which would soon whisk them homeward bound.

The long, uncomfortable journey came to an end as the plane landed in Atlanta. The pilot reported heavy clouds, freezing temperatures, and warned of the approaching storm. Moria and Sarah looked wordlessly at each other as they deplaned.

The two women began the drive home and the radio announcer gave dire predictions about "the storm of the century."

They laughed and Sarah said, "That's what they always say."

As they drove into the village of Cherry Valley, Moria said, "Maybe we had better get a few groceries. You just never know!"

While her daughter was in the store, Moria took a minute to call Maxine. "Hi, it's me. We're back. How's everything at the farm?"

"Thank goodness you're here. I turned on the heat and lights in your house when I fed the horses. You've got plenty of feed and hay for them and I plugged in the water de-icers. If the power stays on, we'll be okay."

"Maxine, thanks so much! I'm really glad to be back but I feel so...handicapped!"

"Don't worry. Remember what you always say, 'hard times build character.'"

"So I've heard!"

"See you in the morning."

Moria and Sarah left the lights of the village and crossed the ancient iron bridge then the road narrowed into two lanes. Trees closed in on either side, forming an arc of black lace against the threatening sky. Sarah drove rapidly, familiar with the road's dips and curves. Moria rested her head against the seat and closed her eyes. Almost home!

The farm was only a mile on the other side of the river. Soon the car slowed for the turn into the driveway. The entrance, flanked by two giant cedar trees, sheltered the farm sign, Peace in the Valley. Her lovely restored Victorian cottage stood at the end of the drive. The house, painted light blue with white gingerbread trim, called a welcome from the lighted windows. The security light cast a protective glow through the bare branches of the maple trees, spreading shadowed patterns on the wide front porch.

Sarah helped her mom out of the car and began to unload the luggage and groceries. Moria stood perfectly still, breathing the comforting smell of the cedars, pines, and wet leaves. Sarah paused in her efforts and said, "I know, Mom, you want to go to the barn."

"Do you mind? I'll rest better when I've seen the horses."

"Just wait a minute! I don't want to call 911 tonight. I'll go with you."

Assisted by Sarah, Moria began her precarious journey down the rutted path to the stable. The horses scrambled to alertness as they approached the dark structure. Motion detector lights came on, illuminating a neatly-kept shed row barn. Three horses looked out of their stalls, blinking in the sudden light and whinnied surprised greetings.

"Oh, I am so glad to see you guys!" They could hear Dixie scuffling around in the tack room and opened the door to be greeted by an exuberant Weimaraner with a full belly of pups.

"Hey, girl. My, you're getting big! Not much longer now," Moria said, leaning over awkwardly to scratch the dog's ears. On the crutches again, she moved from stall to stall, rubbing each furry face while Sarah gave the horses extra hay and checked the water buckets.

The gray Welch was Sarah's first show pony. He would always have a home at Peace in the Valley.

Next, stood a black and white Paint mare rescued from an abandoned farm. Animal control was glad for Moria to take the half-starved mare, knowing this would be a good home for her. A year later, the horse was in excellent condition and bred to a fine Arabian stallion. Now a foal was expected soon.

The last stall sheltered Moria's endurance horse, Rainbow Chaser. The chestnut Arabian gelding tossed his head and nickered softly. Moria pressed her face against his warm neck and whispered, "I've missed you most of all." Moria hobbled away thinking, *I am so lucky!* and began her labored progress back to the house. The night lights went off at the barn and she and Sarah proceeded in the darkness, knowing each step from memory.

Tiny pellets of sleet stung her face. Moria ducked her head against the rising wind. Cold, invigorating air helped center her thoughts. *There are people who have to walk on crutches their whole lives. I can do this. It's only for a few weeks.*

When they reached the porch, Moria said, "If it's not too much trouble, will you bring the camping gear in from the horse trailer, in case the power does go off?"

"Better to get it tonight than in the morning! Maybe we won't need it," Sarah answered.

They sat for a few minutes at the kitchen table, enjoying the warmth and comfort of home. The two house cats, Pounce and Pandora, were ecstatic to have company. Purring loudly, they jumped onto the forbidden table. Moria laughed and scooped up the cats. "How naughty you are, but I've missed you!"

Sarah ruffled Pandora's fur and said, "Bed time for me. I think we're looking at a long day tomorrow!"

Moria hugged her daughter. "You sleep well, Sweetie. See you in the morning."

Soon after, Moria climbed gratefully between the flannel sheets and pulled the comforter under her chin. Once she was settled, the cats leapt upon the bed, taking their respective places at her feet, like tiny furry sentinels. As Moria dozed off, the sound of sleet stopped and she could hear the wind swishing snow against the windows.

Chapter Two

*J*ust before dawn Moria awoke. She lay still and listened. Outside the wind blew steadily. Peering through the gloom at the electric clock's dark face and missing the usual hum of the refrigerator, Moria said aloud to the cats, "Well, some things never change. What fun is a winter storm with power, anyway?" She stretched as best she could with her stiff knee, throwing back the covers and making an effort to get up. The cats fell to the floor and scurried under the bed, knowing all was not right in their world.

The ordeal of getting dressed in a heavy shirt, wool socks and sweat pants—one leg ripped to accommodate the brace—made Moria decide to sit down on the bed and rest. She raised the blinds to look out on a changed landscape.

The sun's first rays spun bright gold from beneath low gray clouds hovering on the horizon. Sparkling points of light reflected off the snow crystals, casting a shining blanket of white over the farm. Moria leaned her head against the window for a moment, appreciating nature's offering. Then turned away, wondering what surprises would be in store for her today.

"Where are my crutches?" she exclaimed, coming back to the moment. The smell of coffee brought her fully awake. As Moria thumped into the kitchen, Sarah greeted her.

"Hi Mom, I knew you'd be awake soon. I couldn't sleep either. I am getting ready to go feed the horses."

"What a blessing you are! Now I know why people have children," Moria responded with a laugh. Sarah had filled a large thermos with hot coffee and a pan of water stood on the camp stove, ready to be heated for instant grits. A fire blazed in the double-sided stone fireplace, warming the kitchen and sitting room.

Even with no electricity, the home was inviting. Moria was glad she had taken the time and expense to decorate it as she pleased. Maxine jokingly called it "the magazine house." Moria stretched out on the couch, dreading the long, uncomfortable day that lay ahead.

Sarah returned, bringing Dixie, who bounded into the house. The dog bounded into the room. Sarah, out of breath and laughing, said "Dixie seemed restless and the heat light was off. Maybe she'll have the pups today. Anyway, I didn't want her to be in the cold! "Dixie greeted Moria with excited barking, sniffed the brace, and began her search for Pounce and Pandora chasing them to the loft.

Barking to announce Maxine's arrival, Dixie forgot the cats and ran to the window. Sarah opened the door to find their neighbor bringing the week's mail and a pot of fresh vegetable soup. "Oh, you didn't have to do that!" Moria exclaimed.

"If I can't ride, I might as well cook. Made this last night. I see your power's off, too. You've got a tree down on the driveway - that old dead pine you've been wanting to get rid of. Guess it's divine intervention!" Maxine gave Sarah a hug. "Good to see you again. I'm glad you're going be here for a day or two. Maxine stopped for a breath and sat down in the recliner. Dixie settled at Moria's feet for a nap.

Sarah began putting on her outdoor clothes again. "I want to turn the horses out so they can go to the creek for water and

I'm going down to the store and put up a notice for some barn help. I think we should try to get someone in the neighborhood before we post on the internet."

"Good idea. Can't be too careful. The jeep's parked down on the road if you want to take it," Maxine volunteered.

"Thanks. I would probably end up in a ditch! The walk will do me good."

Moria and Maxine settled down to visit and catch up on what had been going on in each other's lives. Moria retold the ski accident in detail and then recounted her meeting with Ruth and Jessie and their endurance discussion. "Remind me to send some Endurance News magazines to Jessie's family. I think they're interested in our sport." Moria said, smiling, as she remembered the child's bright eyes when they talked about the horses.

"You know," Maxine said, changing the subject, "Our endurance clinic at the Horse Fair is coming up soon. There are a few details to finish up. We have a room reserved for our presentation and we can have the indoor arena for thirty minutes. This should be plenty of time to showcase our sport. You can talk about how safe endurance riding is compared to skiing!"

Moria looked glum at this possibility. "Just kidding!" Maxine said quickly. Sarah returned, to see the two friends with horse catalogues choosing items they 'needed' to order.

"Well, I put up the ad. We'll see what happens." Sarah said as she looked at the stack of catalogues and commented, "You two are dangerous when you're left alone, ordering all this stuff! By the way, who's staying over at the Rutherford place? I saw a truck and trailer in the driveway and some horses I didn't recognize."

Maxine answered, "Oh, I meant to tell you. Some guy, he's the Rutherford's house sitter while they're gone to Europe. I think he's living in the guest house. Wonder what kind of horses he has? Maybe we should pay him a visit when the weather breaks."

Moria looked at her injured leg and said, "I'll be doing good to get to school, much less go visiting!"

"Sarah, I'll be back to help you feed tonight. See you then," Maxine said, stuffing her black curls under a red knit cap and pulling on her boots.

Mother and daughter settled down for a long afternoon. Moria began to grade some school papers. She noticed Sarah pacing restlessly from room to room, then walking over to poke around in the fire.

Suddenly Sarah blurted out, "Mom, did you love Dad?"

Moria looked startled, and tried to gather her thoughts. She put the papers down and pulled the afghan tighter around her shoulders. A shiver ran over her, knowing she must be honest, and yet say the right things. "I tried to love him," she began. Her throat closed, remembering their mismatched existence. Moria took a deep breath and continued, "I didn't know how. Now it seems like we were poles apart in every way. It's a wonder we lasted as long as we did. I wanted to be the perfect wife and mother. Growing up and getting married was serious business for me."

Sarah picked up Moria and Fredrick's wedding picture from the mantle and studied it. "Look at this. No one was even smiling."

"Like I said, being a grownup was serious business. And then, there were the normal issues that married couples face...but we didn't handle them very well. That just made matters worse."

"What about when you guys were dating?" Sarah asked, coming over to sit on the couch.

"We had dreams and plans but no idea of the challenges we would face. It seemed as though our lives would unfold like a movie. All the pieces would fit into place and we would live happily ever after."

Not wanting to interrupt Moria's stream of memories, Sarah sat statue-still beside her mom...waiting.

Moria seemed to have forgotten all about her daughter.

Staring into the fire, she continued, "If today were yesterday, maybe I could do a better job."

"Why, Mom?" Sarah asked, puzzled.

"If I had been older and perhaps wiser... maybe I could have been more understanding of Fredrick's personality and I could have been more... fun." She paused, thinking of what to say next.

Sarah said, "I never knew anything was wrong until the divorce since Dad traveled and we just went on with our lives when he was away. You never fought, at least not in front of me, anyway. I knew he drank a lot but some my friends parents did, too."

Moria met Sarah's level gaze. "How did you know about the drinking? You were so young."

"I can remember a few things, like the smell of stale beer, and not understanding why you wouldn't let me recycle the beer cans at school."

"Honey, I'm so sorry we've never really talked about this. Explaining a grown-up world to a child was more than I could deal with at the time, and then you seemed okay, so I just left well enough alone. I'm glad you and your dad stay in touch and that he does pay for your schooling."

Sarah picked up Pandora, who had jumped into her lap and held the cat close, saying, "I did some research at school last year and talked to the counselor. I understand drinking problems better now. She answered a lot of my questions. But she couldn't answer the question I really want to know. Did you love Dad?"

"Did I love your father? Yes. Did he love us? Yes, I believe he did. But, sometimes love is not enough." Moria looked at Sarah and saw tears in her daughter's eyes. "Honey, I'm sorry. I didn't mean to upset you."

Sarah wiped her eyes on her sleeve, "I just want you to have a normal life."

Moria laughed. "I don't think I would like a normal life. I have you, the rest of our family, friends, a meaningful job, the farm, the horses...and memories of the good times."

"You had some good times?"

"Yes we did, and one of them was having you for our daughter. Sometimes we traveled, did projects around the house, visited with friends and enjoyed each other's company. It was those other times that were so hard. I do still miss him," she ended honestly, surprising herself with these words.

The two sat silently for a minute then Sarah asked, "Mom, what if you met someone else...your soul mate?"

Moria hesitated. "I don't know. Committing to another relationship is a huge risk. What if I failed again?"

"Does this sound familiar?" Sarah asked, stepping into the kitchen, removing a magnet from the refrigerator and reading aloud: 'Only those who risk going too far will ever know how far they can go,' and handed it to her mom.

Moria rubbed her fingers over the words, saying, "What about, 'better safe, than sorry'?"

"Mom! Find your true self!"

Moria laughed, "Maybe I will someday. Ah, the innocence of youth. You know, I read an article relating the fear of falling off horses to the fear of abandonment...I thought that was just a bunch of psychobabble...but maybe not." Moria unwrapped herself form the afghan, stood up and stretched. Smiling at her daughter, she said, "You're the best! Maybe I just need to get over myself. Will you come see me in the hospital if I fall off Rainbow Chaser?"

"Oh, Mom! Enough already!" Sensing that her mom had tried to answer questions as best she could, Sarah knew it was time to stop. Getting up from the couch, she gave Moria a hug and said, "Let's go check on the horses."

During the night Moria stirred in her sleep as the security light came on and the house purred to wakefulness. Having the power on lifted everyone's spirits but the snow lay deep and did not appear to be melting.

Moria struggled into the kitchen, propped the crutches against the counter, and looked out the window. She could see Sarah dumping the frozen water buckets upside down, leaving a cluster of tiny igloos. The horses raced up from the creek and skidded to a stop, eyeing the "invaders" suspiciously. They pranced, snorted, and whirled indignantly seeing these strangers in their pasture. White fans of snow flew out behind them as they dashed away.

In the few moments of watching the horses, Moria forgot her plight and the ever present pain of lugging the brace around while supporting her weight on the crutches. Her arms, back, and other leg ached constantly from this effort. "This too, shall pass," she said aloud, to no one in particular.

Sarah returned from the barn saying. "I took Dixie back to the barn since the heat light's on now.

Moria sighed, "I wish she'd hurry and have those puppies. I can't wait to see them! See you in a few minutes. I'm going to clean up."

Sarah busied herself with starting breakfast when suddenly she heard the roar of a motorcycle in the long driveway. She hurried to the front of the house and looked out. At the end of the driveway she could see a guy pushing his motorcycle around the fallen tree. She watched in amazement as he mounted again and continued through the snow drifts toward the house.

As he drew closer she noticed he was wearing a cowboy hat instead of a helmet. The stranger approached the house, casting a long shadow onto the porch. He stepped up and knocked on the door. Sarah called as quietly as possible, "Hey Mom, I think your cowboy's here..."

She opened the door part way and said cautiously, "May I help you?"

The stranger looked at Sarah with appraising eyes, "No, darlin.' I've come to help you! Are you the lady of the house?"

"No, I'm the daughter."

"Well, is your momma as pretty as you?" He flashed Sarah an engaging smile and took off his hat, revealing dark hair, flecked with gray. By now the man had propped one foot on the threshold and his hand rested on the door jam. Sarah realized she couldn't just close the door on his fingers and really shouldn't leave him out in the cold.

"You're answering the ad at the store?" she finally asked.

"Yes ma'am. May I come in?"

Sarah could hear Moria coming from the bedroom and said grudgingly, "Okay."

Just as the cowboy entered, Moria came in, dressed in her robe and traveling carefully on the crutches.

"Jackson Durant from Wyoming." he announced, reaching out to shake Moria's hand. "I do believe you could use some help and that's why I'm here." She teetered on the crutches but managed the handshake without falling. Jackson quickly steadied her. Moria felt uncomfortable with his closeness and backed away.

"I'm staying over at the Rutherford place while they're gone to Europe, just to keep an eye on things and take a little time to rest up in the sunny South."

He glanced out the window, "Maybe I came a little too early in the year."

Moria stared in disbelief at this rugged, attractive man, a sure enough cowboy. *Thank you, God.* She breathed a silent, grateful prayer.

Recovering from her surprise, she said, "Let me take your coat." Laying it on a nearby chair she smiled, "Thanks for taking the time to come by."

Jackson smiled and looked directly into Moria's eyes. "Well, I don't have much to do at the farm, with it being winter and all. Helping out a neighbor passes the time."

She smiled back, but not with her eyes. "Let's talk about the job," she answered, ignoring Sarah's frown and trying to stay on track. "I'll tell you what we need and see if this will work for you."

The two women sat down on one of the love seats near the fire. Moria waited for Jackson to sit across from them on the other couch. Instead, he reached for a wooden straight-backed chair from the kitchen table and tipped it forward without so much as looking at the sleeping cat who occupied it. Pandora slid unceremoniously to the floor and stalked away. Jackson turned the chair around, straddled it, and propped his arms on the back. He looked approvingly around the room as he waited comfortably for the conversation to continue.

His presence filled the room with a captivating sense of cowboy persona. Moria quickly decided this might be worse than dealing with her fourth graders. At least she could send them to time out if they misbehaved.

"You must not like cats," she said, trying not to show her displeasure.

"No, cats belong in barns." Jackson said firmly.

"Well, that's a matter of opinion. Let's talk about the job."

Determined to be business-like, Moria began to discuss the daily chores and how she wanted them done. "The horses are fed twice a day. We've cut down on their grain since they're not being worked right now. They have free choice hay and there's plenty in the barn. The stalls need to be cleaned daily and fresh water put in their buckets. The routine is to put them up at night and turn them out during the day unless the weather is bad."

She paused, as it appeared Jackson was not paying attention. His eyes continued to rove around the room, but always coming back to rest on Sarah and her. She restrained herself from saying, "Excuse me, did you hear what I said?"

As she waited, he said, "Is that all?"

Startled, Moria replied, "Will you take the job?" Suddenly she remembered they had not even discussed the pay. By now the interview was taking on a life of its own. "We didn't talk about how much you'll charge," she continued.

"I really don't need the money. It's worth helping out just to meet my neighbor. I'm planning to be around awhile." Jackson rose from the chair, began to put on his coat and said to Sarah, "If you have time, show me the barn and I can meet the horses," ending his request with a charming smile.

Moria had never felt so helpless. A stranger had just come

into their house, made himself at home and now he was taking her daughter right out the door! Moria saw Sarah's questioning look as they stood at the door. "Don't be long," she called, thinking of nothing else to say. Then quickly, "Here Sarah, take the two-way radio in case there are some questions." Moria leaned back and took a deep breath.

Shortly, she heard static on the radio. She answered immediately, to hear Sarah's excited voice. "Mom, Dixie's puppies are here! I think there's nine. She's cleaned them up and they're all alive."

Moria sighed with relief, forgetting all about Jackson for a minute. "Do you think we need to call the vet?"

"No, she's licking the pups and they're starting to nurse. I'm going to show Jackson around and we'll be back in a few minutes."

As the radio fell silent, Moria tried to envision the barn, the horses and Sarah and Jackson in her place. Even cleaning stalls seemed like a pleasant activity at this point! During the anxious moments as she waited their return, it seemed that life was continuing on without her. The injured knee was always there, a painful reminder of life's twists and turns whether on the ski slope or at the farm. *I can do this. It's not forever!*

Moria tried to appear nonchalant as the two returned from the barn. Somehow the image didn't fit as she was dressed in her robe and wearing sweat pants. Sarah's animated conversation told Moria that her daughter was no longer worried about this cowboy who had suddenly come into their lives. *How could he have so completely won me over in just a few minutes?*

"Jackson, would you like some coffee?" Moria asked, reaching deep down for her Southern hospitality.

"No thanks. Sarah found the chain saw and I'm going to cut away the downed tree before I go."

"Oh, you don't have to do that," Moria exclaimed.

Jackson looked at her with a disconcerting gaze, "Then who will?"

"Uh, thanks, I appreciate it."

Jackson smiled at her as he prepared to leave, and a feeling Moria couldn't quite describe crept into her already tangled emotions. How could she feel drawn to this man she hardly knew? Was it lust? Was she bored? Was it time to emerge from her fragile shell of being single? She sent a little prayer out the door with the charismatic stranger. "Dear God, if he's the ONE let me know soon, before I get into trouble or get hurt." Perhaps God smiled and said, "You'll know." Moria heard no answer. The chain saw buzzed in the distance. Moria watched out the window wondering what the future would hold.

Sarah interrupted her thoughts. "Well, Mom, what do you think?"

"I'm not sure. Guess we'll just have to wait and see...see if he gets the job done."

Sarah came to sit down at the kitchen table with Moria. "Mom, if you feel all right, I need to get back. I have a date for New Year's Eve. Maxine said she'd take me to the airport."

"Sure, Honey. I'll be fine and Maxine's close by. You've been a wonderful help. Thanks, more than I can say."

As Sarah left the room to pack she said, "I can always come on the weekends if I need to."

Moria laughed. "Maybe you can bring your 'friend' to help!"

Soon Maxine came to take Sarah to the airport. Moria, left alone, still sat at the kitchen table, chin in hands. She thought about New Year's Eves in the past when Maxine, Moria, and the neighborhood horse people partied at the local bar, the Juniper Tree.

The group of endurance riders lived in the same community, socialized, did training rides together and were generally supportive of each other's efforts in the sport. Obsessive about the care of the horses, the riders were on a constant search for the right stuff, whether it be tack, shoeing techniques, trailers, new places to ride, feeding programs...the list of common interests was endless and bonded the group together. As usual, a certain amount of gossip kept things lively!

Dancing at the Juniper Tree seemed a faraway dream. Looking at her trophy shelf brought back memories. Gold and silver lights danced brightly off the awards, reminding her of the "thrill of success, the agony of defeat," each ride a new and exciting adventure. Dancing gold and silver lights, dancing at the Juniper Tree...Through a blur of tears, the room, lights and colors began to swim before her eyes. Moria rested her head on the table in the crook of her arm for a few moments.

Then she picked up her ever-present calendar from the table and looked at the ride schedule for the coming season. *How many rides will I miss?* She sat up and wiped the tears from her face, and began to study the ride list. *The Ridge and Valley ride—it's three months away. That's my goal. I can do that!*

Chapter Three

New Year's Eve Day brought strong winds and bright skies. Remaining snow dripped from the roof. Small white patches hid beneath the shrubs and shaded corners of the yard. The path to the barn was a muddy trail and Jackson's boot tracks were the only sign that the horses were being cared for, although she could see his truck come and go each day. Moria begged Maxine to check on the horses, which she did, reporting that all was well. Moria didn't know whether to feel better, or worse.

In the evening streaked flames of sunset hovered over the horizon, silhouetting the stark branches of the surrounding trees. The taillights of Jackson's truck, tiny pinpoints of light, grew smaller in the distance as he left the farm. A terrible sense of loneliness crept into her heart. Not tears for Fredrick, but for a life not yet lived, perhaps a life that would always be lonely—fraught with dangers of the unknown. She reached for the phone.

"Maxine, it's me. Are you busy?"

"No, just catching up on some paper work. Remember, we

do have to go back to school soon. How are you doing?" She already knew the answer.

"Not too good. What are you doing tonight?"

Well, I was thinking about going over to the Juniper Tree. You want to go? Don't give me that bull shit about not having anything to wear. What about that long denim skirt with the matching vest and those gorgeous silver earrings? One boot and one wool sock for your feet, how's that for an outfit?" Maxine paused to get Moria's reaction.

Moria laughed and said, "I can see you've been thinking about this. I guess I might as well be miserable at the Juniper Tree as at home."

Maxine smiled to herself.

"Tell me what time and I'll be ready."

Moria began the slow process of dressing. She put the finishing touches on her make-up, fastened her earrings, and took one last look in the mirror. Still thinking about Jackson's indifference, she said aloud to the image of the woman looking back at her, "You'd think he might come to the house once in a while to report on the horses and Dixie's pups since I can't get to the barn in this mud...and maybe see if I need anything!"

Maxine and Moria drove to the Juniper Tree over two-lane back roads illuminated by a full moon. Two deer stared at the headlights and then scampered into the undergrowth. Moria sighed. "I can't wait to ride again! Just a few more weeks and my leg will be well. I'm planning to go to the Ridge and Valley Ride."

Maxine said, "I don't want to be discouraging, but it'll still take time for your knee to get back to full use. Don't hurt yourself again."

Moria's thoughts turned to the endurance clinic coming up the next weekend. "Maxine, you've done a great job with the last minute details for the clinic. I'm glad you're inviting the forest ranger to speak. He'll love to tell us about the environmental issues and make some suggestions on trail maintenance."

Maxine replied, "Well, it's almost like preaching to the choir, but having him there is a good PR move for horseback riders, so he'll know we care about what happens to the trails. Maybe he won't be so quick to close them off if he knows we're willing to help repair the problems.

"Changing the subject," Maxine continued, "What about your cowboy?"

"He's not my cowboy! Jeez! I hardly know him. He never comes to the house!"

"That's a problem?"

"You'd think he'd check on me to see how I'm doing!"

Maxine laughed. "Have you asked him in?"

"Well, no."

"It seems to me if you want him in, you'll have to ask him."

Moria considered this possibility. "I don't want him to think I'm...forward."

Maxine laughed again. "Are you?"

Moria smiled, contemplating the possibilities. "It could happen!"

They turned into the gravel parking lot. Trucks of all makes and colors announced the presence of their owners. "Drive around. Let's see who's here before we go in," Moria suggested. The two women made a slow pass through the parking area. "Looks like we're not missing many of the regulars," Maxine observed. "There's Jada's truck. Wonder what she'll be up to tonight?"

A mental picture of Jada flashed through Moria's mind. She could see cute, petite Jada, her pony tail swinging side to side as she raced on the trail. And, much to Moria's chagrin, this was the view she always remembered. Countless times they'd ridden down the trail in endurance competitions and in the last mile Jada would race to the finish, leaving Moria in the dust, afraid to run. Fear of falling at the finish line if the horse spooked or tripped overcame her desire to win.

Pushing these thoughts away, she heard Maxine say, "I'll let you out and find a parking space," They reached the front of the building and Jeremy, the bouncer, opened the truck door.

"What have we got here? I heard you got hurt. You should'a stuck to horses."

"There's a lot more to skiing than I thought," Moria said as he helped her into the building. "Jeremy, don't you just love this place?"

The smells of stale smoke and beer, old musty carpets, mingled with the sickening odor of restroom deodorizer met them at the door.

Jeremy's answer was left unspoken as the two reached the table unofficially reserved for Moria and her friends. Two of the guys jumped up to help her get seated. The waitress brought her favorite drink, a White Russian. By the time Maxine arrived, Moria had given the short version of the ski accident and the conversation moved back to the horses, their never-ending source of interest.

Moria was on her second drink when Jackson arrived. He looked so western standing in the doorway, surveying the room. His well-worn jeans, boots and denim shirt created the image of a man accustomed to a casual lifestyle. Seemingly satisfied with his surroundings, Jackson pulled his doeskin hat low on his forehead and walked to the bar for a drink. Then, doing that "guy thing," he propped up against the wall and gazed out across the room. His hat brim shadowed dark eyes and guarded his personal space.

In one electrified second Jada's eyes widened and the inevitable question was out. "Who is that gorgeous hunk?'

"Jackson Durant." Moria answered reluctantly.

"Do you know him?" Jada probed. Moria didn't answer.

Maxine chimed in, "He's helping take care of Moria's horses until her knee is well."

"To be so lucky," Jada sighed. In a few minutes she said, "Excuse me, I need to go to the restroom."

"Sure you do," Maxine muttered under her breath.

In a carefully scripted move, Jada approached Jackson and after a brief conversation they were on the dance floor.

Moria watched for a moment, turned her back and ordered another drink. Soon the minx had guided Jackson to a table across the room. *Which was worse, to look or not to look?* Finally, curiosity won. Glancing over her shoulder through the dim light, Moria could see their chairs pulled close together. She knew Jada's well-practiced web had caught its prey.

During the evening Moria chatted with others at the table, but continued to be distracted, knowing Jada had Jackson's undivided attention. When the band took a break, Jackson came over to the table and pulled a chair up beside Moria. "Hey, Miss Moria. I didn't know you'd be here. I could have come by and given you a ride."

Moria tensed at his closeness but smiled and said, "Maxine brought me over, but thanks anyway. Are you having a good time?" Jackson looked steadily into her eyes holding her gaze, "It's better than spending New Year's Eve alone. Too bad you're injured. We could be dancing." With this statement, he rose to leave. Looking down at her, he gave a wink, squeezed her shoulder gently, and said, "See you in the morning." As Jackson walked away, Moria called to the waitress. "Bring me another drink, please."

The old year ended to the familiar strains of Auld Lange Syne. Everyone got up to dance, leaving Moria alone. Even Maxine and Jeremy danced away the old year, wrapped in each other's arms. The waitress came over and gave Moria a hug. "Don't worry, Honey. It's a brand new year. At least they didn't amputate your leg."

Moria smiled through her tears and accepted a glass of champagne. Her eyes searched through the throng of dancers and even though the floor was crowded, she knew Jada and Jackson were gone.

The two women drove to Peace in the Valley Farm in silence. Moria leaned against the window, asleep. Silver moonlight sifted down through the dark pines lining the road, flashing shadows on their faces.

Maxine helped her friend out of the truck and as they reached the steps, she heard Moria's slurred words, "I want to see the horses and wish them a Happy New Year."

"I knew it! I almost had you in the house. Okay. Let's go. No point in arguing about this." Maxine steadied Moria at every step. They made slow progress due to Moria's drinks, the crutches and the rough terrain and mud. Their uneven steps created spectral shadows on the moonlit trail.

They reached the barn and Moria lurched forward to grab the gatepost. "Look!" She pointed across the pasture to the Rutherford's property. They watched Jackson's truck turn in the driveway and stop at the guest house. He turned off the headlights. Even with the bright moon, the two women could not see if there were one or two people getting out.

"This is making me crazy!" Moria's voice shook with hysterical laughter.

Maxine began to laugh, with relief. This was not a good time or place for a crying jag. "Laughing is better than crying," she finally said. "Why don't we take a look at the pups while we're down here?" hoping to distract Moria from having a meltdown.

As they continued a few more steps to the barn, the horses greeted them with friendly whinnies, hoping for a treat. "Hey, you guys, Happy New Year." Moria sang a few lines from Auld Lang Syne and collapsed on a hay bale outside Rainbow Chaser's stall. The horse sniffed and blew gently through his nostrils to be sure this was his person and then settled contentedly, with his head over the stall door and his nose close to her face. "I'll put my money on the horses anytime," she announced, smiling into the dark. "Who cares if Jada and Jackson screw each other's eyeballs out!" Just then, the light went out in the guest house.

Moria looked across the meadow, toppled sideways, and fell off the hay bale. "Oh my God!" she exclaimed, "I've fallen and I can't get up!"

"Bedtime for you," Maxine announced. "Jeremy is on his way over to my house right now and I need to be out of here."

"Wait! I need to see the pups."

Maxine turned on the tack room light and said, "See. There they are...all awake. We'll take another look tomorrow." She pulled Moria away, closing the door.

* * *

Peaceful sleep eluded Moria as dreams came, unbidden in the night. The pain and fright of the ski accident mingled with imagined falls from racing Rainbow Chaser. Then Fredrick reached out to her. She could see his lips move but no voice came. Jackson's face was in shadows as he stood outside her door, knocking, knocking, knocking. Suddenly Moria woke up. There was someone at the door! Bright sun shone in the window and she could see Jackson's truck in the driveway.

"Oh my God, I'm a wreck!" she said, struggling out of bed. Looks forgotten, her head spun as she lurched for the bedpost. Her sleep-swollen face and tangled hair gave testament to her evening of fragmented celebration. Staggering to the door, one hand covering her eyes against the sun beaming through kitchen windows, she managed to say through the closed door, "You're up early."

She could hear him clearly through the door saying, "It's ten o'clock. I hope the horses don't mind being fed a little late today. What about some coffee when I'm finished?"

Moria thought quickly, *Don't panic. This could be a new adventure—or misadventure.*

She answered, "Sure, come on back when you're done. Don't hurry, I just got up." She got the coffee started, cleared off the table, set out two red and white checked place mats and dark blue mugs on the pine table.

"I need to take a shower," she said aloud. Freeing herself of the brace, she stepped carefully into the shower stall and turned the water on full force. Soap and shampoo flowed over her body waking her to the day and the promise of a man in her life. What am I thinking? He only wants a cup of coffee. Reluctantly, she rinsed and got out, awkwardly drying herself, impeded by her stiff knee. The usual outfit of ripped sweat pants, a flannel shirt and wool socks would have to do. Natural color highlighted her cheeks as she anticipated Jackson's arrival. The shower had definitely helped her headache, or was it Jackson's unexpected visit? She hobbled back to the kitchen and poured herself a cup of coffee.

Jackson knocked at the door. "Come on in," Moria called. As he entered she noticed he held his hat protectively to his chest. With a few steps across the kitchen he set his offering on the table. Nestled inside were two of Dixie's puppies. Moria scooped the pups up to her face, kissed them and snuggled them to her neck. "Oh, what a surprise! Aren't they adorable?" The soft wiggly balls of grey opened their tiny brown eyes, looked around and settled peacefully in her arms.

She set them carefully in her lap and stroked their backs with her fingertips. "Have some coffee. I hope you don't mind getting it for yourself. This is the first time I've seen the pups since I can't get to the barn," she lied, remembering her midnight trip the night before.

Jackson began to fix his coffee and said, "I thought I saw a light over there last night. I started to come and check on things, but when I looked again, it was dark."

Yes, when did you look again? When you were finished with Jada? "Oh, When Maxine brought me home I asked her to look in on the horses since we heard fireworks in the neighborhood. We wanted to be sure they weren't upset." Moria was anxious to change the subject. "Tell me about your horses."

"The ones at Rutherford's are from my best rodeo string. They needed a rest. Some of them are pretty banged up."

"I can imagine. Is that your job? Rodeoing?"

"Well, for now it is."

She waited for him to continue. No other information was forthcoming so she said, "Tell me about Wyoming."

"You'll have to see it for yourself someday." He flashed her an innocent and charming smile. Moria caught her breath and for some reason, thought about the time out corner in her classroom.

Then Jackson asked, "Did you have a good time last night?"

"Sure, for somebody who's lame. How was your evening?"

He hesitated before answering, reached for one of the pups and his hand brushed her leg. She felt her body grow warm with an electric shiver.

"How was my evening? Good question." She could see he was stalling for time. "When you're the new kid on the block you have to make friends any way you can. Going to a bar is a pretty level playground. That Jada, she's a piece of work."

"She's married. Her husband travels a lot. In fact, he's gone now."

"Is that right? You'd never know." Jackson seemed totally at ease with this revelation. "Jada is going to help me find a suitable horse for endurance riding. I've decided to take up the sport."

"No, that's a very bad idea!" Moria leaned forward quickly and in her excitement mashed the pup who squealed indignantly.

Jackson looked truly surprised at this turn in the conversation but said, "Why is that?"

"Jada is a hot shoes rider and doesn't begin to know about endurance training. She's just been lucky."

"She's hot, all right," he commented.

Moria gave an exasperated sigh. "No doubt she's hot! That's not what I meant. Sometimes people get caught up in the moment and over-ride their horses. Then, the vet pulls them. It rarely happens to Jada because she's is so small her horse runs wide open like he's in the race without a rider." She paused, her face flushed with annoyance. "You'll be sorry if you hook up with her."

"Are you finished?" Jackson asked. Moria didn't answer.

He jumped up from the couch and began pacing back and forth, "I know something about endurance riding. I crewed for a friend of mine at a couple of rides. I can do this. I just need a good horse. Jada is going to help me find the right one but I was planning to ask you to help me with the training when you can ride again. It will take some time to find the right horse. We talked about the clinic and I'm going to come so I can get off to a good start. Now, Missy, is that all right?"

Moria thought about Jada and Jackson driving all over the countryside day after day looking for horses while she was trapped in school. She frowned and said, "Just let me know when you think you've found the right horse. I would like to take a look at it. I'm glad you'll come to the clinic. And yes, I'll help you."

Jackson gathered up the puppies. "Guess I'll go. We can talk more later."

As soon as Jackson's truck pulled onto the main road, Moria picked up the phone to call Maxine. Her friend answered, to hear Moria's agitated voice. "You'll never guess what's happened now!"

Maxine said, "No, I can't guess, but it must involve Jackson. Tell me."

"Well, now he thinks he's going to start endurance riding and Jada's going to help him find a horse! He thinks he knows something about endurance riding because he crewed for a friend in Wyoming. "

"Hummm," Maxine replied. "Is there more?"

"Yes. He wants me to help him with the training."

"That's a bad thing?"

Moria hesitated. "I guess not. I just don't want them off looking at horses all day when I'm in school!"

Maxine waited a moment. "So you want to be in charge and Jada is in the way?" She paused. "And you want Jackson all to yourself?"

Moria blew out her breath in frustration. "To tell the truth, yes."

"Don't go borrowing trouble. I'm sure he'll keep the horse at your barn since you'll help with training and then you'll have him all to yourself!"

Moria sighed, "Jeez! This is more than I can handle. I'm going to start looking on the Internet. Maybe I can find him a horse."

"There are some really great finds out there. It just takes patience. Good luck. See you tomorrow."

As they hung up Moria headed straight for her computer.

Early Monday morning Maxine stopped by to give Moria a ride to school. The effort of getting into the truck left Moria breathless.

"When I get home today I'm going to try driving. My knee feels better. I think I can do it and I'll still have the brace."

Maxine looked concerned and said, "Why don't you let me drive you for a few days. Making it through the day may be harder than you think. Besides, this is the only time we have to catch up on things. How did your computer search go?"

"Very slowly. You're right. It takes a lot of patience! There are good horses for sale all over the country, and abroad."

This reminded Moria of the e-mail from Jessie, the young girl she'd met in the doctor's office. "Jessie and her family are making great headway with their endurance riding plans."

"Who? Have I missed something here?"

"Remember? The family I told you about who wanted to get started in endurance? The ones I met in the doctor's office in Colorado."

"Oh yeah. What are they up to?"

"They bought a three horse trailer with living quarters. Sounds fancy, with a real bathroom, and a full kitchen. Also, the dad got a new horse. The mom's and Jessie's horses are okay for the sport. Doris Weaver is helping them get started. They're lucky she lives close by."

"Talk about starting at the top. Doris is the best. Good for them!"

Moria laughed, "I imagine we'll see some rising stars this year."

By now they had reached the school. Cherry Valley Elementary sat back from the road, surrounded by large old elm trees. Over time, the red brick had taken on a soft patina and the windows were filled with children's artwork. The two women entered the building and were greeted by the other teachers. In this small town, everyone already knew about the accident so Moria did not have to tell the story again.

In the classroom Moria looked over the class roll and the children's faces and names came back to her. It seemed so long ago that she bade them good bye for winter vacation. So much had happened since then.

Waiting for her students to arrive, she looked around the room at the colorful posters, book shelves, and tables filled with art supplies—her world Thoughts of the horses and Jackson slowly faded as she heard the roar of the buses and screeching brakes. The schoolhouse door clanged open announcing the children's arrival. Their high-pitched, excited voices made her heart beat faster.

The children came in and stopped short, seeing Moria standing in front of the room on the crutches. She smiled to put them at ease, and then they all began to talk at once. "I'll tell you all about it as soon as everyone is here," she said.

The children were eager to open the doors, get her lunch, and for once, they were quiet and attentive during class. I bet this won't last, Moria thought.

During their planning time Maxine looked in to see how the day was going.

"You were right. I am exhausted, just from moving around in the room. I can't teach sitting at my desk. Going down the hall to lunch and the restroom is making my arms hurt worse than my leg. Maybe I need a wheel chair."

Maxine thought for a moment. "Why don't you take some of your sick days?"

"Then how could I use my sick days to go on endurance rides?"

Maxine smiled, "Yeah. How could I ever think we would use the sick days when we were sick or injured?"

Just then Moria had a call over the intercom asking her to come to the office during planning.

"Oh, Jeez. It's Mr. Baldwin. What could I have done now? I've only been here a few hours!"

On the way down the hall Moria reviewed the problems that could possibly have occurred. *One of the students did have low grades and I hadn't notified the parents yet. Or was it about the two boys who got into a fight? Or maybe the girl who had teased one of the younger children.*

The principal greeted her at his office door and she searched his face, trying to be prepared for what was to come. "Well, young lady, I see you've been out on a new adventure."

Moria tried to relax and gave a little laugh. "I don't think skiing is my sport."

Her mind whirled, *Get on with whatever I'm here for.*

Mr. Baldwin handed her a slip of paper and said, "Michael's mom called today and wants him tutored in Math. She asked that you do this, and of course she'll pay the going rate for tutoring." He smiled expectantly. "I told her I was sure you could, and you would getin touch."

Moria thought quickly. *This is my least favorite parent. She is always causing some difficulty, like the last time she just showed up to sit in the class and had Michael in tears. Well, I could use the money and I can't do much else right now.*

"Sure, I'll call her tonight. I'm not certain tutoring is the answer. Remember when I wanted to have some testing done on him and the parents refused?"

Mr. Baldwin nodded. "I do. But go ahead and give it a try." She could see he had solved his problem by giving it to her.

That evening Moria tried to settle into the routine of grading papers and planning for the next day. Soon, she was fast asleep on the couch.

Was someone knocking at the door? She sat up quickly, looking through the glass to see Jackson standing outside. "Come in," she called.

The rush of cold air and Jackson's sudden presence brought her fully awake.

"Are the horses okay?"

"Oh sure. I've got something to show you. Jada and I went horse-hunting today. We may be in luck and have found one already. The owner sent this video and I want you to see it."

"Does Jada know you're here?"

Jackson looked puzzled. "No, I guess not. What difference does it make?"

"Well, not any, really. Let's see what you've got."

Without asking, Jackson threw a few logs on the fire and started the video. Then he sat on the couch next to Moria and leaned forward, turning slightly toward her. "Just wait! You'll love this guy!"

My gosh, he's like a little kid on Christmas morning.

A gorgeous gray Arabian trotted and cantered through his paces as the video played. Looking at Jackson's delighted face, Moria knew it would be hard to get him to search for any more horses.

"Tell me what his owner said about him," Moria asked as they played the video for the second time.

"He's six-years-old, green broke, and sound."

"Why are they selling him?"

"They said they had too many horses and they would give me a really good deal."

"That's what they all say. Maybe you should get Dr. Barr to do a pre-purchase exam. Why don't you look at some more horses first?"

Jackson slumped down on the couch and continued to watch the video. "This is the horse I want."

At least he won't be running off with Jada every day.

"I guess you can always sell him if it doesn't work out."

Jackson smiled his boyish grin, picked up the remote,

settled back on the couch, put his arm around Moria and said, "Let's watch the video again. I'm going back and get him tomorrow." She didn't move. Her heart pounded as he pulled her closer.

"This is going to be the greatest horse yet!" He looked right into Moria's eyes.

"Aren't you excited?"

"Oh, sure!" she answered, hardly daring to breathe.

Just then, the phone rang. Reluctantly Moria reached to answer it.

"Hi Mom. I just called to see how you're doing with the horses, school and all. How is that guy Jackson working out?"

"Honey, thanks for calling to check on me." As Sarah and Moria continued their conversation, Jackson turned off the video and picked up a set of the student's math papers lying on the coffee table in front of him. He flipped idly through them, picked up a red pen and started to grade one of the papers. Moria frowned and shook her head at him, mouthing, "No." Jackson continued to mark the paper and then began to draw in the margin.

"Sarah, I'll call you back tomorrow when we can talk longer. Someone's on the other line. Thanks for calling."

Jackson laughed. "Liar. Why didn't you just tell her I was in your business?"

"Jeez, you're driving me crazy!" Her cheeks felt hot, but she couldn't help laughing. "Give me that paper. Let me see what you've done." In the margin Jackson had drawn three sets of blocks in four rows. Then he drew an arrow over to the incorrect answer. Michael's paper showed the problem 3 x 4 = 7.

All the multiplication problems showed addition answers.

"This kid just doesn't seem to get it. What's his deal?" Jackson asked, seeming genuinely interested.

"Well, something is really wrong. He reads on grade level, it's just his math. His parents refuse to get him tested. They feel it's a reflection on them if he doesn't do well. I am going to tutor him for a while and see if one-on-one teaching will make a difference." Moria reached protectively for the other papers and held them in her lap.

"I can help you grade these papers. I'm not in a hurry to go anywhere."

Moria looked doubtful. "Where did you go to school?"

"University of Wyoming."

Moria raised her eyebrows in disbelief. "And majored in what, fourth grade math?"

"No, environmental law."

Moria's eyes widened in surprise. "What are you doing here, pretending to be a rodeo guy?"

"I am a rodeo guy...now."

"What does that mean, exactly?"

"It means I didn't want to be a lawyer, and besides it's none of your business, Missy."

Jackson glanced toward the backdoor, "What's that scratching sound?"

"It's the cats. Will you let them in?"

Jackson stalked to the door, opened it, and watched the cats scurry into the bedroom. "Maybe we should go check on them," he suggested.

Maybe we could if I wasn't so handicapped! But she said, "Jackson, just come help me grade these papers."

They settled down to work and Jackson continued to draw explanations in the margins. Before she knew it, they were finished. "Thanks for your help."

"No problem."

"So what are your plans for tomorrow?" Moria asked.

"Jada and I are going to pick up Silver Dollar, that's his name. I'm keeping him at Jada's for a while. It saves time to have the horses together when we do training rides."

I am going to be riding very soon! "Are you sure you'll still have time to take care of my horses?"

"Of course." Jackson turned toward Moria and took her hands in his. "Don't you worry about that for one minute."

Then he smiled. "I'll even grade some more papers if you think I'm qualified."

Moria lay in bed that night, thinking about Jackson and wondering what his life had been like in Wyoming. *Is he really who he says he is? Maxine's pretty good on the Internet. I'll bet she can find out.* For the first time in many days, she slept peacefully.

On the way to school the next morning Moria brought up her plan to check on Jackson's personal life. "Will you try to find out something about him?"

Maxine said, "Why are you so interested in this guy? Sure he's cute but he's here today and gone tomorrow. He even said he'll be going back out west in the fall. Don't tell me you are thinking about trying to reel him in, long term?"

Moria looked out the window at the winter landscape while trying to sort out her thoughts. Finally she answered, "He's a pretty high maintenance guy. I think keeping him occupied would be a full-time job. I feel kind of like I'm at a crossroads. I can let the bars down or back off."

Maxine looked sideways at Moria. "So who's in charge of this game?"

"Sometimes I think I am and then I know I'm not. Maybe he is. I don't know!"

"Well, just go to bed with him and see if sparks fly. If they do, go for it. Who knows? Maybe you'll move to Wyoming."

Moria leaned her head against the window. "I'm getting a headache. Do you have any Tylenol?" Maxine fumbled in her purse and handed Moria the bottle. "Give it back before lunch. I'll need it by then."

The morning passed in a blur as Moria tried to concentrate on her restless students. *Somehow, these rascals can tell when they don't have my attention. I've got to get well so I can think better!*

On the way home Maxine reminded Moria about the endurance clinic scheduled for the weekend. "If it's okay, I'll come over this evening and we'll make the final plans. That is, if you're not busy grading math papers with your helper," she laughed.

"Oh, gosh, the clinic! What is it we still have to do?"

"Don't worry. I'll bring you a list. See you tonight."

Once at home, Moria looked through the mail, watched the news and soon fell asleep on the couch. She did not hear Jackson come or go when feeding the horses, nor did she see him look in through the glass-topped door smile, and walk away.

Chapter Four

C old, brisk winds and bright sunshine greeted the endurance riders early on Saturday morning as they gathered for the clinic. The Agriculture Center bustled with activity as equine enthusiasts from all parts of the southeast region gathered to share and gain more knowledge about their passion, the horses, and the sport of endurance. Booths were set up representing the different breeds and vendors selling horse products were highly visible and busy.

Maxine carried in the needed supplies and arranged the table with handouts to help the new people. Participants began to assemble, hurrying to the coffee pot and warming themselves by the large stone fireplace.

Moria looked around for Jackson. Most of the local riders had come to help out, including Jada. *Well, at least Jada's not piled up in bed with Jackson this morning. Wonder if she was last night? Enough of this!* She noticed the new people were looking a little lost, and she quickly called the first session to order.

"Thank you for coming out on such a cold day to learn more about this exciting equine sport," she began. "I can certainly tell you that endurance riding is much safer than skiing!" The audience laughed and seemed to appreciate her predicament.

Moria propped herself on the crutches and held up several nationally circulated horse magazines. "Endurance riding is a fairly new horse activity, only recognized since the early 70's. In the beginning, there were few rules, and frequently horses would die in the races. Over the years, due to public pressure and outrage from responsible horse owners, safeguards for the horses are now in place." Moria's years in the classroom helped her judge the attentiveness of the group. She scanned the audience with a quick glance, confident that they were following along.

"Our sport is now governed by a national organization, The American Endurance Ride Conference. Regional and state groups manage rides according to these rules. By the end of the day we hope you'll have a plan and plenty of information to get you started in this sport. I have always thought of endurance riding as an equine marathon over a marked and measured trail. It is a timed event, but in Limited Distance the first horse across the finish line is not automatically the winner. You'll learn more about these differences later today."

Moria held up a shiny belt buckle. "Sometimes you do win," She said, smiling. "Sometimes you finish." She held up a tee-shirt completion award. "And," she paused, held up a vet card to show the record of the horse's progress throughout the ride, ripped it up and said, "Sometimes you lose or even go home with an empty trailer." There was silence as the people realized what she meant. By now, she had everyone's attention.

At that moment, Jackson appeared in the doorway. He leaned against the door jamb, tipped his hat back just a little and winked at her. Every head turned as Moria stopped talking and looked toward the door.

Maxine, who was sitting next to Moria, said, "Well, here's one of our newest endurance riders, Jackson Durant. Come in and have a seat."

Instead of sitting down quietly, Jackson waved to the group and said, "Hi, y'all. Yep. I've got the fastest horse in the county. Better look out!"

The seasoned riders looked at each other, frowning and muttering among themselves.

"Who does he think he is?"

"He'll learn the hard way."

"What a jerk!" they commented in low voices. Even Jada bit her lip in annoyance.

Moria struggled to regain her composure "As I was saying..."

Jada grabbed Jackson's arm and pulled him down onto the chair beside her. After a few whispered words in Jackson's ear, she gave Moria a bright smile, as if to say, "I've got him under control."

Maxine could see the distress on Moria's face, so she said, "We'll stop for a minute, get acquainted, and have another cup of coffee." Maxine introduced the experienced riders who were available to answer questions. The new people introduced themselves and each one told a little about how they had become interested in the sport.

Moria sorted through her notes. As everyone settled down, she announced, "Our first topic is 'A Horse! A Horse! My Kingdom for a Horse!' One of the first things you will want to know before you start endurance riding is whether you can use the horse you own now. In most cases, yes. Some breeds perform better than others, but consistent training can offset some of the problems which might occur. Dr. Barr and some of our members will have a session to describe the pros and cons of each breed and give helpful tips on conditioning your horse."

Moria could see anxious looks on some of the participant's faces and realized they were distracted by the questions they wanted to ask. She smiled and said, "I know you are bursting with questions. You'll get a chance shortly. Remember, consistent training, a diet recommended specifically for endurance horses and balanced shoeing will help improve your chances of success. I would advise you to start with the horse you have, and plan on riding to finish until you know how it responds to training, camping and traveling."

Several hands went up and Moria paused to answer their questions.

She laid the crutches aside and sat on the corner of the table. The most often asked question related to care of the horses at camp. "Some great endurance prospects don't eat or drink well in strange places. Without enough intake of food and water, they won't go very far. We call it 'running out of gas.' You'll know when it happens. You'll be trotting or cantering down the trail and your horse will go slower, slower and finally stop. What to do? Let the horse graze and drink along the trail and lead him back to camp. Always have the horse checked by the vet in case there is something else going on and if you really like the horse, don't give up until you have attended several rides."

"If the problem continues..."

Jackson, who did not appear to be paying attention, suddenly interrupted, "Sell that sucker!"

By now, Moria had had enough. "Jackson." She gave him her 'school teacher look' and said firmly, "Go to timeout."

Everyone laughed and Jackson, in good humor, answered, "Yes ma'am."

Moria continued. "As Jackson said, sell your horse and look for another prospect. Sometimes you have to try several different horses before you find the right one." *And just when you've found the right one he gets sick, injured or lame,* but she did not voice this discouraging thought.

"Let's take a short break. Our members are wearing blue name tags and will be open for questions. You'll find out soon enough, endurance riders have strong opinions!" Moria looked around for Jackson and noticed he and Jada were standing away from the others, engaged in animated conversation.

Once everyone was seated again Maxine introduced the guest speaker. "Today we are fortunate to have Dr. Stanley

Barr share some time and advice with us. Many of you already know him from his visits to your farms. Dr. Barr brings his expertise to many of our rides. Also, his services are in demand in other regions, where he gains additional experience and shares his knowledge with us."

She looked out over the audience, her gaze coming to rest on Jackson and said, "Listen and learn!" Then, turning toward the vet she announced with a flourish, "Presenting Dr. Stanley Barr!"

The group applauded as Dr. Barr unwound his lanky frame from the chair, pushed back a lock of brown hair, put on his glasses, stood and turned toward the audience. Thanking Maxine, he began to talk.

"I know you have more questions. I'll answer those first and then give you information about proper care for your horses. Now, I want to talk about feeding programs." Even the experienced riders never tired of hearing more about the best nourishment for their horses.

The discussion was lengthy but informative. Dr. Barr had brought various types of feed and supplement samples provided by the local feed store. These were displayed on a table at the back of the room. At the conclusion of his talk, the vet suggested that the riders take a look at the products and stretch their legs, knowing horseback riders couldn't sit still very long.

The vet approached the topic of shoeing and said, "I'll give you some handouts to look at later, as some of what I say will be pretty technical. The most important thing to remember is to use a farrier who will at least listen to your concerns and be willing to consult with a vet if there is a problem. Most endurance horses do require certain techniques to be applied to the shoeing process, due to the various types of terrain they have to cover. On the other hand, it's wise to listen to your farrier's advice with an open mind, since that's his expertise.

He smiled and said, "Farriers are a pretty independent breed. You will lie awake at night agonizing over whether to change shoers." The new people looked at him in disbelief but the experienced riders nodded as if to say, "Just wait!" Dr. Barr ended his talk by reminding the audience that the shoeing of your horse was not a place to look for bargains. "I will welcome your further inquiries and those of your farrier. Let's keep these horses sound." The riders responded with enthusiastic applause, letting the vet know they appreciated his time and efforts.

Then Moria announced, "After lunch we'll do a demonstration in the arena and you will have an opportunity to see the horses tacked up and also see what the riders wear. Our comfort is important, too!"

As people were leaving, Jackson approached Stanley Barr. Moria stood by the table, slowly gathering her papers, hoping to hear the conversation. *Now what other stupid things is he going to say?*

To her utter amazement, Jackson shook hands with Stanley in a professional manner. "Dr. Barr I'm new to this sport and have just bought an Arabian gelding from Camelot Farm. His name's Silver Dollar and he's over at Jada's right now. I'd like for you to come and take a look at him. I guess we'll have to call it the post-purchase exam," he joked.

Dr. Barr smiled and said, "I know the horse. I helped with the foaling and have watched his development over the past six years. He's an excellent prospect. With good training he should go right to the top. I'll come by and have a look at him. Call my office and set up an appointment." As an afterthought he said, "You're training with Jada?"

"Only until Moria gets back in the saddle. Then we'll train together," Jackson replied.

Dr. Barr looked relieved and said, "That sounds like a good plan. Be patient. Moria knows what she's doing." Just then the doctor's pager went off. Excuse me. Guess I'd better go. See you in a few days."

Jada's husband, Richard, sat in the announcer's booth, ready to give information about the riders and their horses during the demonstration. With great effort, Moria managed to climb the stairs and Jackson, uninvited, followed.

When she reached the booth, Moria said, "Hi, Richard. Hope you don't mind some company."

Looking over her shoulder at Jackson she said, "This is Jackson Durant. He's house-sitting for the Rutherfords and is thinking about becoming an endurance rider."

"Hi Jackson. Glad to have the company." Richard laughed and added, "Hope you have some deep pockets if you're going to get into endurance."

"I have some resources. If I run out of money, guess I'll have to marry a rich cowgirl," He winked at Moria.

Richard raised his eyebrows at her, as if to ask, how did you get mixed up with this guy? Changing the subject he said to Moria, "Stay around. I may need some help with these Arabian names."

The arena darkened and a spotlight focused on the entrance. One by one, twenty endurance riders entered, leaving enough space between themselves for Richard to announce each rider's name, horse's name, and list their accomplishments. The house lights came up and he began the presentation, giving some general background of the sport and describing opportunities for people to get involved. During the thirty-minute event the horses continued to trot around the arena. The lights gleamed off their coats. Dark bays, grays, and chestnuts, palominos, spotted coats, duns, and sorrels all showed the conditioning, grooming, and training they received.

The riders, dressed for a day on the trail, complimented the elegant horses and all the riders wore helmets.

Richard explained that riders can wear whatever is comfortable for them, adding with a chuckle, "Sometimes it takes a few tries to get it right. Many riders wear tennis shoes with a heel. These shoes are made especially for endurance riders as some of them will run or walk beside the horses when they need to. You can get a close-up look at wearing apparel and horses' tack in a minute.

They will remain in the ring to answer questions. The afternoon sessions will begin in twenty minutes."

The presentation ended with the riders reversing and cantering around the ring to one of Moria's favorite songs, "The Wind Beneath My Wings."

Tears of happiness and pride welled up in her eyes as she watched the riders leave the ring. *This is my life; the horses, my friends, all the places we go and the things we do.* With a little sniff, she turned to leave, forgetting all about Jackson.

"Excuse me, ma'am. Would you like some help down the steps? Bet you didn't think about how you were going to get down?" Moria looked down the steep steps and then at Jackson. Without a word picked her up, carrying her like she was a small child. Speechless, Moria was afraid to struggle, for fear they would fall. The spectators filing past the announcer's booth and laughed and cheered as Jackson descended the steps. Depositing her on the ground, he said, "Well, Missy, how's that for a fast ride?"

Moria didn't know whether to laugh or cry. She reached for the crutches she had left at the bottom of the stairs. "I ought to hit you with these!" she said indignantly, "But I won't." With those words, she reached up, pulled his head to hers and gave him a kiss he would not forget. Now the crowd, which had stopped to watch, gave another resounding cheer. Moria smiled, hooked the crutches under her arms and limped away without a backward look.

Moria and Maxine drove home later, discussing the apparent success of the clinic, noticing most of the new people had joined the endurance club. Some of the spectators who watched the arena presentation attended the afternoon session.

The two women re-hashed Jackson's disruptive appearance and behavior, now seeing the humor in that moment.

"So what did you think of Jackson's kiss?" Maxine asked.

"It was my kiss," Moria replied.

"So what did you think?"

"Ask him,"

Jackson's truck was parked in the drive. "I guess he's down feeding the horses. Let's go and help," Moria suggested.

Just as they started down the path to the barn, Jackson came running toward them with something cupped in his hands. Breathless, he managed to say, "One of the pups fell in a bucket with some icy water in the bottom. I found him unconscious. He may not be dead... maybe it's hypothermia." The pup lay in his hands like a lump of wet, gray clay.

Moria and Maxine stared in horror. "Quick, unlock the door." Moria dug in her purse and handed the keys to Maxine. Maxine and Jackson bounded up the steps and into the house. Moria followed more slowly. By the time she reached the door Maxine was already on the phone to Dr. Barr and Jackson sat on the couch trying to briskly rub the puppy back to consciousness.

"Do you have some whiskey?" Jackson asked.

"For you?" Moria looked incredulous.

"No, for the puppy. If you do, mix it with some warm milk. His heart is still beating. Do you have a medicine dropper?"

"I have some rum. Will that do?"

"Sure. Hurry."

"And I think I have a medicine dropper somewhere around," Moria said as she began to rummage through the kitchen drawer.

Maxine turned from the phone. "Dr. Barr says immerse him in warm water ten minutes at a time. Keep massaging, and the whiskey and milk is a good idea. We're to call him back if the pup isn't reviving and bring him to the clinic."

With shaking hands Moria put the rum and milk on to heat and ran to the bathroom to search further for the medicine dropper. Maxine filled the sink and Jackson carefully placed the tiny dog in the warm water, cradling him in his hands. The pup lay still. His head lolled over to one side, with no sign of life.

"Are you sure his heart is still beating?" Moria questioned, coming back in with the dropper and a towel to wrap the pup in.

Jackson checked and nodded his head. "Just barely."

Moria held the pup gently, propping him up, hoping he wouldn't choke as Maxine squeezed a dropper full of warm liquid down his throat. The little pup coughed, spewing the mixture all over them.

"Try again," Jackson said in a quiet voice. Soon they got a couple of droppers of liquid down the little guy and then gave him another trip back to the sink. Suddenly the pup began to struggle in the water and opened his tiny brown eyes, blinking in the light.

The three rescuers smiled at each other triumphantly.

Moria dried the dog with care and gave him a kiss on his soft gray face. Then the pup settled contentedly into the warm towel to rest from his ordeal.

Moria leaned back on the couch with relief and announced, "If there's any rum left, I think we've earned some hot rum and apple cider." No one disagreed and Maxine mixed the drinks for everyone. Then they sat around discussing the dog's close call and watching the pup peek out from under the towel at his amazing new world.

"Why don't I take him home tonight to be sure he's okay?" Jackson suggested. Moria held the puppy closer, frowning with indecision.

Jackson added, "You're not going to be able to take care of him very well tonight. You'll probably fall and hurt yourself."

"Well, okay. But bring him back first thing in the morning," she finally agreed.

"I won't fall and hurt myself," Moria said as an afterthought, looking Jackson straight in the eye.

"Just to be on the safe side," he said with a smile.

Maxine began to put on her coat. "Guess I'd better go. My horses need to be fed."

"And Jeremy's coming over?" Moria asked, knowing the answer.

"Could be." Maxine laughed as she left.

Moria and Jackson looked at each other. "Your horses are

fed and mine have plenty of hay until I get there," Jackson said as he stroked the pup's head. "What about another drink? We need to watch this little guy for a while, don't you think?"

Moria answered by handing him her mug. She found herself glad for the company. Jackson returned with their drinks and threw another log on the fire.

They settled down on the couch with the puppy snuggled between them.

To break the silence, Moria said, "He needs a name."

Jackson thought a minute. "What about Lucky?"

"That's so ordinary. Let's think of something more heroic."

"How does Hero sound? Jackson asked.

"Hero. I like that." Moria touched the puppy softly on the head with her fingertip and announced, "I christen thee Sir Hero."

"Sir Hero it is, forevermore," Jackson agreed, picking the puppy up and placing it gently on his lap. It crossed Moria's mind that her ownership of this particular puppy would be short-lived.

The fire crackled and sparks flew up the chimney, reminding her of sparks flying from the horse's hooves as they raced over the rocky trails. Jackson stared into the flames, comfortable in the silence.

Moria, relaxed by the warmth and rum said, "Can I ask you a personal question?"

"I won't promise to answer," Jackson replied, looking sideways at her.

She continued, "When you ride broncs and bulls are you afraid? Afraid of falling?"

Moria felt Jackson would choose his answer carefully, sensing this was not a time to joke around. Silence. *He's not going to talk about this.*

Then, Jackson said, almost to himself, "Yes, sometimes I'm afraid. I know I'm always going to fall, the question is, how hard? And, will I be able to ride again or will I have an irreparable injury?" He paused. "Does that answer your question?"

"Sort of. But what do you do? How do you keep riding?"

"Sometimes I don't."

"What do you do?"

"I walk away for a while but something always draws me back."

Moria hesitated, then asked, "Is that why you're here?" She felt Jackson tense and shift uneasily.

"Maybe. Or maybe I'm just here to meet a pretty girl." He put his arm around Moria and she did not pull away.

"Hey, why all the questions?" he asked in a light tone.

Moria took a deep breath. "I'm afraid to race Rainbow Chaser because I have a terrible fear of falling. I just wondered how you managed. When I went to Colorado to learn to ski I thought maybe I could get over the fear by being successful at another dangerous sport." She laughed, looking down at her brace. "I didn't have time to find out."

Jackson put his arm around her and said, "You can do this. Don't walk away. We'll be riding together soon and we'll be a great team. You'll see."

He began to quote softly, "Tiger, tiger burning bright, in the forests of the night..."

"What immortal hand or eye..." Moria continued, "Could frame thy fearful symmetry?"

They sat in silence, each chased by their own bright tigers, trapped in the middle of an obsessive circle to succeed with their horse endeavors.

William Blake's prophetic words and Jackson's haunting dark brown eyes pierced through Moria's worried thoughts. "I can do this," she said, with much more confidence than she felt.

"Atta girl," Jackson encouraged. Getting up from the couch, he handed Moria the puppy. "Be right back. Need anything?"

"Could you bring the clothes from the dryer? It's easier to fold them here."

Jackson returned shortly with the clothes and dropped them on the opposite couch. He stood behind Moria with his hands on her shoulders, leaned over and whispered in her ear, "Need anything else?"

"Now that you mention it, could you clean the cat box? It's really a hard job for me."

To her alarm, Jackson took hold of her head and tipped it back so that she was looking at him upside down. Her eyes grew wide as he leaned over close to her and said in measured tones, "I have waited on you hand and foot, fed the horses, cleaned stalls, brought in the mail, tuned your truck, repaired the fences, unfroze the pump..." He paused for a breath. "No. Hell no! I will not clean the cat box!"

With those words, Jackson snatched the pup from Moria's lap, grabbed his coat and headed for the door. Speechless, she stared at Jackson's retreating back. He reached the door, jerked it open and slammed it hard. The glass upper half of the door shattered and fell in all directions.

Moria struggled up from the couch and limped rapidly toward the door. Just then Jackson's startled face appeared, framed in the broken glass, as the last shards clinked to the floor. "Oh my God! I am so sorry. So sorry! I'll fix it right now."

"No. No you won't," Moria screamed. "Get out. Just get out! Give me the puppy!"

Jackson turned and walked away, not looking back or responding to Moria's angry tirade. She stood helplessly, watching the truck taillights fade into the distance.

"Tiger, tiger burning bright in the forests of the night..." she whispered and reached for the phone.

"Maxine," Moria said in a quavering voice, "Hey, I hate to bother you so late. Can you come over with a large piece of cardboard and some duct tape? It's an emergency."

"A Jackson emergency?" she asked.

"Well, sort of...I guess." And then Moria burst into tears. "Hurry."

Soon she heard Maxine's truck in the driveway.

Her friend's voice came clearly through the open space in the door. "Looks like you two had a fight."

Moria sniffed and looked at Maxine through swollen, red-rimmed eyes. She held both cats in her arms for fear they would step in the glass. "I guess that's about the size of it. Would you please put the cats out before they get cut so I don't have a vet bill on top of everything else?"

Maxine set the cats outside and then began to sweep up the glass. "Jeez! What a train wreck! Did he hit you?"

Moria began to cry again. "No. But he yelled at me and he took the puppy."

Maxine burst out laughing. "Something else must have happened."

"I just asked him to clean the cat box."

"And?"

"I think he had other things on his mind."

Maxine stopped sweeping and said, "Sit. We need to talk."

Moria reluctantly pulled a chair out from the kitchen table, sat down, and began to bite her fingernails.

"Don't do that," Maxine said, frowning. "Now I'm going to say this only one time. Don't tease this guy or you're going to find yourself in a shit pot of trouble."

"I haven't teased him!" Moria answered indignantly.

"Excuse me. What about the kiss?"

"Oh. That."

"If that wasn't a tease I don't know what is. What do you think he expected when he stayed on after I left?"

"More of the same?"

"More, much more. What were you thinking?"

"I do like Jackson but I'm afraid if we get in a relationship..." Moria ran her fingers through her hair. "I know he's going to leave..." *and I'll be alone again* was her unvoiced thought.

Maxine finished taping the cardboard. "You could move to Wyoming."

"No," was Moria's adamant reply.

Maxine let the cats in and said, "It's late. Why don't we talk about this tomorrow? See you in the morning. By the way, you better turn the heat up! It's a little cold in here!"

Later, Moria tossed and turned with a restless dream. It felt so real. Jackson and Silver Dollar galloped just ahead of her on the trail and every time she caught up, the cowboy and horse disappeared around a bend. A heavy mist crept into the woods, blanketing the path. Its soft elusive fingers seemed to hold her in its invisible grip.

She tried to call out, but had no voice.

The alarm sounded all too soon and Moria awoke, exhausted and with a splitting headache. "Damn you Jackson Durant. You have turned my life upside down." Then she paused and said softly, "No, I let you do this to me." She smiled and addressed the cats who sat attentively at the foot of the bed, "Well, this is a brand new day. Look out Mister Jackson Durant!"

Moria struggled into Maxine's truck for the trip to school, and said cheerfully, "I can't believe the doctor is going to release me today."

"Well, I have some more good news. Jackson is rich!" Maxine announced.

"What? What did you say?"

"I couldn't sleep after I got home last night so I took a few minutes to browse the Internet. It's pretty amazing how much information is available on people if you just know where to look. I can tell you this, Durant and Durant is an internationally known firm, specializing in environmental law. Jackson is the second half of Durant. He did graduate from the University of Wyoming, top five percent of his class."

Maxine paused for her friend's reaction.

"Oh, my gosh! I guess he is qualified to help me grade papers. But why is he a rodeo guy when he could be so much more?"

"Maybe you'll find out, if you're really interested. And why do you think Jeremy's a bouncer when he has an MBA?"

"Maybe it's a guy thing. Not our problem." Then Moria smiled. "But Jackson is my problem. He just doesn't know he's met his match!"

"Watch yourself. Maxine answered. "He's a pretty smart dude."

"So are my fourth graders. See you this afternoon."

After school Maxine drove Moria to the doctor's office. "See you in about an hour. I'm going to the feed store."

Maxine returned to find Moria in the lobby. Moria's grim expression signaled that all was not well.

"Humm, you don't look too happy. What's the matter?" Maxine ventured.

"My leg is bent and won't straighten out! The doctor says I have to go to therapy to get the muscles and ligaments working again. I told him if my leg isn't okay, I'm suing that other doctor in Colorado."

"Get a grip. Look on the bright side. At least you're rid of the brace."

Moria did not respond but stared out the window which reflected a troubled face, full of uncertainty.

When they turned into the driveway, Moria's expression changed to one of anticipation. "Jackson's here feeding. I'm going down to help him."

Maxine said, "No emergencies after nine o'clock. I'm going to bed early."

Moria laughed. "No emergencies. Thanks for the ride. I believe I can drive tomorrow. See you at school."

As Moria entered the house she noticed new glass in the door. "Well, Mr. Jackson Durant, I see you've been busy today," she said to herself.

Changing into jeans, she felt like her old self, but even better. "Soon I'll be able to ride and take care of the horses myself. Maybe Jackson can move Silver Dollar over here now, away from Jada," she announced to her mirror image and was pleased to see the sparkle in her eyes and headed for the barn.

When Moria opened the gate her steps slowed, confidence wavering. She had turned to go back when she heard Jackson's voice. "Hey, wait!" he called.

Moria stopped and felt her heart pounding. *What's the matter with me?* Jackson hesitated at the gate and Moria felt his gaze search her face.

"I'm sorry about last night," she blurted out. Jackson's intense look held her in place. He put his hand over hers on the gate. Static electricity shocked them, breaking the moment.

They both jumped back. Their eyes locked in that unguarded instant, sparking the air with a far greater shock. Jackson opened the gate and said, "Wow, some powerful force must be at work!" Continuing, he said, "I'm sorry, too. I was out of line. I'm surprised you didn't call 911."

"No, I called Maxine," and they both laughed.

"I came down to help you feed. I've really missed the horses."

"I see you've got the brace off. Bet that's a relief. I'm almost done but you can give them hay and I'll fill the water buckets."

The two finished their tasks in comfortable silence and Jackson said, "I've got to go down and close the gate into the other pasture. Be back in a minute."

Moria sat down on a bale of hay, leaned her head against the barn and closed her eyes. Soon she sensed Jackson's presence and opened her eyes to see him standing nearby.

"I thought you were asleep," he said.

"No, just enjoying being myself again."

"Mind if I sit down?" She moved over and Jackson settled down beside her.

The setting sun streaked through high cirrus clouds, turning them into pink and gold feathers. An evening wind blew winter leaves across the field. Dixie's puppies dashed after the leaves and the mother dog came and sat watchfully beside Moria, her head on her mistress's knee.

Jackson called the puppies to him and picked up Hero. "He's going to be a fine dog," Moria could hear the longing in his voice, the voice of a little boy, long ago.

"Did you have a dog when you were little?" she asked.

"We had work dogs on the ranch but I never had a dog of my own."

"Well, now you do. Hero is yours."

"Moria, I can't take your dog. These pups are worth a lot of money."

"You have helped me more than I can say. I don't know how I would have managed these past few weeks. Consider Hero payment for your help." She paused, "Even if you wouldn't clean the cat box."

Jackson glanced quickly at Moria to see if she was joking. Seeing the twinkle in her eyes, he put his arm around her and said simply, "Thanks."

Moria leaned her head on Jackson's shoulder, enjoying the rough wool of his jacket against her face. Who needs silk? The smells of leather, hay and horses soothed her senses. Lost in the moment, she closed her eyes again, feeling suspended between the past and the future. Is this is peace? Peace in the Valley? her drowsy thoughts questioned.

Moria shivered, disoriented and cold. The sky had turned to lavender and the clouds to icy white. "What time is it? I didn't mean to fall asleep."

"Time for you to come on over to the house for a good steak dinner," answered Jackson.

Moria pulled her coat closer, feeling chilled and hungry. *What could it hurt to go over for a little while?*

"You can cook?" she asked, surprised.

"Cowboy cooking. Come on, you'll like it."

Moria made awkward progress on the path to the house, but Jackson lent a steady arm and her heart felt light.

As his truck stopped in front of the guesthouse, she had second thoughts. What had she always told Sarah? "Think twice before you go into a man's house or apartment. This makes you fair game for unwelcome attention." *But, what if it was welcomed? Did Sarah heed my advice? Am I going to heed my own words?*

Jackson opened the door and helped her out. He seemed perfectly at ease as they made their way up the brick walk. "Have you ever seen the Rutherford's guest house?" he asked. "Come on, I'll give you a tour." They stepped into a stone entryway leading to thick carpets of desert gold. "Here's where we take off our boots." He gently removed Moria's boots and began to rub her feet. "Your feet are cold. Come on over by the fire."

Moria didn't move. Her knees felt weak. This was her last chance to leave gracefully—but she turned and made her way to the soft brown leather couch with bright Navajo blankets folded over the back. Colorful Western prints hung on the walls and lanterns along the way gave off a soft light. The gray, smooth driftwood wood tables held Indian pottery and horse and farm magazines.

Jackson threw some wood on the fire and sat down beside her. "Well, you can take the tour from here. To the right is the bedroom. To the left are the kitchen, laundry and bath. This is a great place."

"Looks cozy," Moria answered. *Oh my God! Was that a suggestive statement?*

Jackson looked her straight in the eye. "Two people could make it cozy." She glanced away, not responding.

He continued, "What about a beer or a glass of wine?"

"Sure. Wine would be great."

Jackson returned shortly with a cup of hot mulled cider. "You'll like this."

Moria sipped the drink. "Umm. Very good. Is this a cowboy drink?"

"No, it's a cowgirl's drink. Here, have some more." He filled her mug to the top again. Then placed his beer on the table and sat on the floor on front of her.

"Let me rub your feet again. They must still be cold."

"No, They're fine." Looking around the room for some distraction, she noticed the bookcases flanking the fireplace. "I love books. Are these yours?"

"Most of 'em." Jackson answered and got up from the floor. "I'll start dinner."

"Need some help?" she asked.

"I've got it covered. You can keep me company though. Give me a minute to go out and feed the horses. Be right back."

When Jackson left the room Moria walked over to the shelves to get a better look at the books and perhaps learn more about this charismatic man.

The usual assortment of horse books one would expect, rodeo how-to books, books on horse care and horse-related fiction filled the shelves. A dog-eared copy of The Black Stallion, one of her favorites, told her more about Jackson than he could ever tell her about himself. She could imagine him, a gangly teen-age boy sitting among the hay bales, lost in Walter Farley's magical world of horses.

Looking at the next shelf, she was startled to see several books on hypnotism. She had just begun to study the titles when Jackson returned. As he walked in the door she said, "These are your books, too? The hypnotism books?"

He gave her a look of surprise and answered, "Yep."

"How did you get interested in this? I've always been curious to know more about how and if it works."

"Why?" he questioned.

She hesitated, trying to think of just how to ask her questions. After a moment she said, "Remember when I told you about my fear of falling off Rainbow Chaser?"

Jackson nodded, "Come out here so we can talk."

Moria wrapped her coat around her shoulders and stepped out onto the patio. Stars shone in the dark sky and Moria felt as if she were far away...maybe in Arizona in a Western hideaway with her cowboy. *What am I thinking?* She mentally shook herself. "Have you ever been hypnotized?"

"We fooled around with it some when I was at college. To answer your next question before you ask, no you cannot be hypnotized against your will."

Moria laughed. "So you're a mind reader, too?"

Jackson flipped the steaks and said under his breath, "You'd be surprised."

After dinner they settled down in the living room again. Jackson said, "I'll bet you'd like to see my rodeo scrapbooks."

"Sure," replied Moria, surprised at first that Jackson would reveal so much about his personal life and then remembering, *He's got that cowboy ego.* Jackson brought a couple of scrapbooks from the shelf and slowly turned the pages. He became again the young cowboy in the pictures. His rodeo stories were barely believable, laced with the names of cowboys, their horses, and their wondrous feats.

The shared passion of the horses, even though their sports were different, gave Moria a feeling of closeness to Jackson. Did Jackson feel the same way, or was this his plan to get her into bed?

Two scrapbooks later, Jackson stopped his journey into the past and made coffee, which they both agreed did not keep them awake. "I want to know some more about hypnotism," Moria said, as she curled her legs underneath and sat facing Jackson.

He reached in the end table drawer and got out a quartz prism-shaped crystal on a chain. "This is how it works," he began. "You have to let your mind go free. But most of all you have to want this to happen. Now, let's think about Rainbow Chaser. We're going inside his head."

Moria was staring into Jackson's dark eyes. "Don't look at me. Look at the crystal." Moria's eyes shifted to the crystal and followed its gently swinging motion on the chain. She began to feel distant from reality as she heard Jackson's voice. "Rainbow Chaser is going to speak to you."

"Trust me, Moria. I won't hurt you." Her eyes glanced away from the crystal to Jackson's face. Confused, she tried to gain control of her senses. Jackson's steady gaze held her in its grip as he said, "Look only at the crystal. Rainbow will speak. Close your eyes...close your eyes..." his voice droned on, "You are not afraid. The horse is afraid. Give him confidence..." By now Moria's eyes were closed, her chin dropped to her chest and her breathing became slow and relaxed.

Jackson's voice changed to a lower tone, "Moria, this is Rainbow Chaser. You can help me. Look through my eyes and help me understand about those spooky things on the trail. Give me courage through your hands and legs to be brave and go forward. You know my instinct is to flee from danger." Moria sat quietly, eyes closed, hands folded in her lap. "Can you help me be brave?" the voice continued. After a few moments of silence, she lifted her hand, as if to stroke Rainbow's face. "Yes, yes I can help you."

Suddenly Moria awoke. Morning light streamed through the window and she was not at home. Jumping up from the couch, she tried to get her bearings. *I'm still at Jackson's! I slept in my clothes! What time is it? I'll be late for school!* She scrambled around on the floor, looking for her shoes. *Oh, my God, What if we had sex? What if Jackson tricked me?*

Shoes in hand, she ran to the bedroom, banging open the door and hearing pictures crash to the floor. Jackson sat up with a start, blinking in the bright sunlight. "You are a terrible person," Moria shrieked, throwing the shoes at him. Jackson began to laugh, swung his legs over the bed and stood up, revealing his naked body.

Transfixed, Moria stared as Jackson put his hands on his hips and said, "Excuse me, Missy. Did I miss something here?"

"I doubt it," Moria retorted. "Get some clothes on."

"Yes, ma'am!"

Moria stalked out of the bedroom slamming the door to punctuate her statement. Jackson called through he closed door, "Hey, before you go, have some coffee. It should be ready by now." She stopped, regaining some composure. The coffee did smell good. She checked her watch and realized it wasn't as late as she thought. Without answering, she went into the kitchen and poured herself that first great cup of morning coffee. Then she started to laugh. "This scene would have made a great commercial," she called to Jackson.

Coming into the kitchen, barefoot, shirt tail out and his usually smooth hair rumpled from the night, he said, "We could have a whole series of fight scenes, starting with your back door. By the way, are you going to fix these pictures? Some are probably broken." Pouring his coffee, he joined her at the breakfast bar. "I know what you're going to ask, did we have sex? No, Moria, it takes two. I would never take advantage of a woman." Moria felt young and naïve, hearing his sincere voice, and maybe felt a little disappointed.

"So what does that mean?" she asked. "Are we going to have sex?" *Jeez, I am really losing it!*

He tipped her chin up and kissed the tip of her nose. "It's your call," he answered lifting her off the barstool. "But right now, I suggest you hurry or you'll be late for school. I'll go over and feed the horses. If it's still okay, I'll bring Silver Dollar on over to your barn later today. We can put Sarah's pony in my pasture so we'll have room for Silver."

By the time Moria pulled into the parking lot at school she felt ready to face her restless charges. *I really need to pay attention today. Those standardized tests are coming up soon and I've still got a lot of ground to cover.* As she walked through the school house door, the five minute warning bell rang. A peaceful, secure feeling swept over her. The familiar sounds of children's voices, lockers banging and scuffling feet gave her day a frame and she felt in control.

Maxine stopped Moria in the hall. "Good morning! How was your evening?"

"You don't miss much, do you?"

"Well, I stopped by, and called a few times. You were never around. I didn't think you were spending the night in the barn."

"I slept on Jackson's couch."

"Is it a fold out?"

"Nooo. Let's eat lunch in the room so we can talk. See you then."

Chapter Five

*T*he rest of Moria's week passed in a blur of school, tutoring Michael, and going for swimming therapy. Jackson continued to feed the horses and called each night to report on the horses and dogs. He always had some entertaining story about the animal's activities and assured her he would wait until the weekend to ride. Moria tried not to think about Jada lurking close by with too much time on her hands.

Moria and Maxine left school on Friday afternoon going out into the crisp winter air. Blue sky and bright sun promised ideal weather for an outdoor weekend. Moria's eyes sparkled with excitement when she thought about taking Jackson on his first training ride.

Maxine interrupted her thoughts. "Are you ready for a night out at the Juniper Tree?"

"Maybe next week. I am doing better. Swimming laps is helping, but riding will be the best therapy of all."

"Why don't we just go to dinner?"

"Sounds good. See you in a little while."

Later, as the two women drove past the Juniper Tree, Moria couldn't keep her eyes off the parking lot. "There's Jackson's truck!"

"Do you want to go in?"

"No."

"Do you want to look for Jada's truck?"

"No. Keep going. I feel the need for a great, big, juicy steak!"

Maxine drove Moria home several hours later. "You be careful! " Maxine called out the window as she drove away.

Still standing in the yard, she paused to breathe the cold air and looked skyward. Bare winter branches reached up into the star-studded sky and tiny night creatures rustled in the leaves.

"I've got to see the horses," she said aloud and started toward the barn. At the gate, Dixie and the puppies tumbled out of the tack room to greet her. "Hey, little guys! How you doin?" The fat little dogs rolled over each other, jumping and playing at her feet. Dixie sat nearby, the ever-watchful mother. Moria glanced across the field to Jackson's house. No lights shone from the guest house windows.

She turned her attention to the horses, whose heads appeared at the stall doors as they looked in her direction. "No treats tonight, just hugs." Upon reaching Silver Dollar's stall, she stopped to look closely at his face. His large, dark brown eyes held a glint of kindness and yet a spark of mischief. She scratched behind his ears and laughed, "I'll bet you're going to give your cowboy the ride of his life!" The gray gelding snorted and pawed the ground, as if understanding her prediction.

Rainbow Chaser whinnied as she approached his stall. "Get ready for a run tomorrow, good boy. I've missed you." Rainbow stretched out his neck to meet her and gave a soft whickering sound. Moria stepped closer and stopped. A lightheaded feeling swept over her. Some elusive thought began to surface. She closed her eyes and stood still. Rainbow whinnied again. He seemed to say, "I am afraid. You can help me. Give me confidence with your hands and legs so I will move forward, past the spooky things." Moria's eyes flew open. She stroked Rainbow's neck and said, "Of course! I know you spook when you see strange things. I need to look through your eyes and anticipate the bad 'horse getters.' That's when I need to help you with my hands and legs. Why didn't I think of this before?"

The next morning Moria met Jackson in the driveway. "What a great day for a ride," he said, flashing her a heart-melting smile.

Moria took a deep breath. "I've already fed the horses. Let's go. I can't wait for you to see my back yard. Our mountains may not be so high, but the beauty of winter in these woods will make up for it."

"You don't have to sell me on Georgia. Great place, great people!"

Did he see Jada last night?

By now they had reached the barn and the familiar sounds and smells comforted Moria. The two riders fastened the horses in the crossties and began to curry and brush their coats. The horses moved about nervously. Moria tried to relax, knowing Rainbow Chaser sensed her anxious feeling. *Going out to ride with Jackson for the first time and having my first ride since the ski accident is enough to make anyone crazy,* Moria thought. She reached for a hoof pick and lifted each of Rainbow's feet to clean them.

Out of the corner of her eye she noticed Jackson bringing his saddle from the tack room. "What do you think you're doing? That saddle is way too heavy for Silver Dollar! Didn't you learn anything at the clinic? Has Jada been letting you ride in that thing? It must weigh fifty pounds!" She paused for a breath.

Jackson threw the saddle on Silver's back and then fastened two large, leather saddle bags behind the saddle. He attached the breast collar to the saddle and turned to her. "Are you finished, Missy?"

Moria began to have second thoughts about her outburst. "Well, yes, for now. But..."

"Now I have a little lesson for you." He grabbed Moria's arm and spun her around to face him. His grim expression stopped Moria in her tracks. She flinched and tried to pull away as Jackson held her arm with one hand and reached into his saddle bag with the other. He pulled out a thin leather strap and dangled it in her face, letting go of her arm. He laughed. "Did you think I was going to hit you?"

Moria reached for her cell phone. "You might hit me once but after that, you can count on your ass being in jail!"

"Hey lady, take it easy!" he said, giving her a devilish grin.

Moria looked suspiciously at the strap. "What's that for?"

"You'll see. Now it's time for your physics lesson. I'm going to be the teacher and you're the pupil." He fastened the strap around Rainbow Chaser's neck. "This is your insurance for staying topside on the horse."

She looked at the strap and then at Jackson. Relieved that he wasn't going to hurt her, she focused his next words.

"Hold the reins in one hand and the neck strap with the other. When he spooks, you'll be able to keep your upper body from lurching over. As long as you can keep your center of gravity perpendicular to his, you'll stay on the horse, at least enough to recover yourself." Jackson began to draw a picture in the dirt to emphasize his point. "So what do you think?"

"Is this a cowboy thing?"

"Actually it is."

"Then why do cowboys fall off the horses?"

"You tell me."

"They lose their center of gravity?"

"Hey, you might get the hang of this yet!"

Moria did not reply, silently saddling her horse and thinking about what Jackson had said. It does make sense, she thought. "You know, I've been thinking. I believe Rainbow needs more confidence in me as a rider. I'm going to concentrate on using my hands and legs to move him forward when he's afraid."

"Good idea," said Jackson. Moria did not see the cowboy turn his head to hide a smile. "Need some help?" he asked.

"Just hold the horse and I'm going to stand on this hay bale."

The two riders started down the trail at the back of the farm, Moria breathed a sigh of relief and said a little prayer. *This is the first day of the rest of my life. Thank you God, for this beautiful day, my wonderful horse and a cowboy, even if he's not mine for keeps.*

"We need to ride ten miles today," Moria announced. Jackson adjusted the reins, pulled his hat brim down, and nodded. "When we get to the top of Rocky Ridge, we'll do a pulse check on the horses. Did Jada teach you how to use a stethoscope?"

"No, we just rode."

"I'm not surprised."

"We always had fun, and the horses did great."

"Jackson, you don't know if the horses did great, or not. Y'all probably thought they were okay if they weren't lame, bleeding or falling down. That's Jada's style!"

"Well, none of those things happened," he answered.

"Never mind. We're going to trot for five minute stretches and walk for three minutes, to let them recover. Each time we ride, we'll increase the trot time and shorten the walk."

"What about cantering?"

"No cantering until the horses have a strong conditioning base."

Jackson frowned, but said nothing.

The riders came out of the woods and onto a dirt road. Rainbow Chaser, in the lead, picked up an energetic trot, eager to leave Silver Dollar behind.

Moria said over her shoulder, "One of the best traits of an endurance horse is to freely leave the herd." *You would be a great racer, if I would just let you go!*

"What about Silver Dollar?"

"We don't know yet. Time will tell. The first thing you have to do is get him ready. Then we'll see what he's got. If you try too soon, you'll never know because he'll probably get injured." The riders trotted on in silence.

Moria checked her watch and pulled Rainbow Chaser down to a walk. "We're turning onto the mountain trail in a couple of minutes. Then we'll be in part of the National Forest."

"So who lives up here?"

"The forest ranger, Kam Bryson, lives up at the top of the mountain. He's super about helping us connect old trails and put in new ones. There used to be several communities in this forest, years ago."

"What happened to them?" Jackson asked, now truly interested.

"Well, it's not a pretty story. Years ago, Cherokee Indians lived in these mountains and were moved westward. You know about the Trail of Tears, I'm sure. Time passed and people began to settle here and clear the land for small farms. You'll see evidence of them as we ride."

Moria looked at her watch again. "Time to trot. Let Silver Dollar lead this time." The trail became steep and loose rocks rolled under the horses' feet. Moria called to Jackson, "Stay off his back!" *What a cute butt!*

The horses scrambled onto a rocky ledge and stood, breathing hard. "Keep going," Moria said. "They can recover at a slow trot. It's better for their muscles." She could see rivulets of sweat dripping from under Jackson's hat band and hear his heavy breathing.

Jackson called back to her, "I hope you are going to check my pulse!"

Moria laughed, "We never check the riders!"

The trail leveled out and the riders slowed to a walk. Leaves crunched under the horses' hooves and squirrels ran rampant in the woods, scattering from the intruders. A red tailed hawk soared overhead. Blue jays and crows called an alarm from their safe treetop perches.

"So where are the farms?" Jackson asked.

Well, in the 1930's the government took this land through eminent domain for a national forest and the people had to move. They were paid small amounts for their farms but the worst part for them was leaving land that had been in their families for years. Most of them were so angry, they burned their farms to the ground or sold all the wood and even the stone foundations."

"Sure is a lot of interesting stuff not in the history books. Tell me more."

"Not now. Time to trot again, let's go." By now the horses were warmed up and doing a big extended trot. They were puffing and blowing back and forth to each other and Moria knew Rainbow Chaser was telling Silver Dollar about the big 'horse getter' just around the bend.

Suddenly, Jackson's horse went spraddle-legged in the middle of the trail, and whirled around, slinging the cowboy off onto the ground. With practiced agility, Jackson landed on his feet, with the reins still in his hand.

He stood facing Moria, eyes ablaze. "If you're trying to take me down a notch, you're going to need a bigger ax than this!" He looked over at the uprooted tree, which had spooked the horse. "I'm sure you knew what was going to happen. The horses did. I expected something, but not this!" He leapt back on the horse and galloped away, leaving Moria speechless and regretting the trick.

She twisted the horse's mane between her fingers, whispering, "I just wanted to see if he was really as good a rider as he said. No, I wanted him to learn a lesson. No, I want to be in charge." Tears rolled down her cheeks. "Why am I having such a hard time?" A gentle wind blew through the trees, as if to say, "You are afraid."

Moria sniffed and rode on up the trail after Jackson. Around the next bend she came upon them. Jackson was off the horse adjusting the saddle. He looked at her, but did not speak.

Moria looked straight into his dark eyes and said, "I'm sorry. I don't know what I was thinking."

"Get off the horse," he said. Moria dismounted.

"Come over here. We need to have an understanding." She walked closer and Jackson held out his hand. She put her hand in his and felt the warmth reaching right to her heart. "You know," he said, "We could get along really well if you would just get this chip off your shoulder. I'm talking about really well."

The horses stood quietly, glad for a rest. Jackson drew Moria to him and held her close. "Just relax and be yourself. I want to be more than your friend. This can be a special time for us, no matter how long it lasts; we'll always have great memories. We won't even call it a relationship... we'll just call it a 'thing.'"

Moria gave a sigh, shivering in the cool air.

Jackson held her closer and she buried her face on his shoulder. His hands reached under her jacket and around her waist. He began to rub her back and she leaned into him. Time seemed to stand still. Is this love—or lust? Jackson lifted her chin and gave her a soft inquiring kiss. Her arms went around his neck responding to his touch. He stepped away. "I want you to come over to the house tonight."

Moria smiled. "I'll be there. Come on, let's finish this ride."

The trail wound up the side of the mountain, in a serpentine pattern to prevent erosion. The riders climbed steadily. Unspoken thoughts and expectations distracted Moria from her training mode and even the scenic beauty of the valley below failed to get her attention.

At last Jackson said, "You're mighty quiet. Change your mind?"

"No, just trying to get myself back together. I feel like I'm standing at the end of a high diving board."

"Take the leap of faith. You'll be fine. Now what about this pulse taking thing?" The riders dismounted and tied the horses to nearby trees. Moria got out a stethoscope from the small pack attached to the front of her saddle. "The horses pulse needs to be at sixty beats per minute for Limited Distance to get into the vet check. Sometimes the heartbeat is hard to find. Just move the stethoscope around on his side right here."

She pointed to a spot on the horse's side just behind the elbow. With the stethoscope in place, she located the heartbeat. Looking at her watch, she began to count. At the end of sixty seconds she stopped counting. "Silver's pulse is at sixty.

Jackson tried, and quickly caught on to the technique. "Maybe there is more to this than I thought," he admitted. Winking at Moria, he added, "Education's not a bad thing when you have the right teacher."

The trail followed the ridge for some distance and then descended into Cherry Valley. Jackson began to sing. "On top of old Smoky, all covered with leaves I found my true lover, and courtin's a breeze!"

Moria laughed, thinking of the evening to come. The riders continued the trot five, walk three where terrain permitted until the last mile and walked in the rest of the way. They stopped at the creek to water the horses. Looking down at the water swirling over the rocks made Moria dizzy, or was it Jackson's hopeful smile when he said, "See you tonight."

After the horses were put away, Moria walked to the house in deep thought. *What am I going to wear tonight? Not too dressy, not to casual. Jeans, for sure. My favorite shirt? The dark blue one with the silver threads, then I could wear those great silver earrings. And...I'll wear my silver endurance buckle. Thank goodness, I have lots of perfume from my kids' Christmas gifts.*

By now Moria had reached the house. What to do? Too early to dress, not enough time to start a project. Grade papers? No. I'll check e-mail. A long message from Jessie gave detailed and humorous accounts of her training rides with Doris Weaver. Moria answered the message, bringing the young rider up to date on the happenings in Georgia and when the first rides are scheduled. She mentioned a new rider at her barn, Jackson Durant, who was starting endurance riding and how much she likes his horse, Silver Dollar.

Then Moria surfed some of the horse web sites, with one eye on the clock. When all else fails, take a nap. She set the clock and fell sound to sleep. The two cats, Pounce and Pandora, leapt on the bed and snuggled down beside her, surprised to have company for their afternoon snooze.

Moria awoke just before the alarm went off and hurried to the shower, muttering to herself, "I've got to remember to shave my legs. Where is that razor?" Just as she started to dress, the biggest decision of all loomed before her. *What about underwear?* Rummaging through the drawer, she came upon a set of black, lacy panties, and bra. Remembering with bitter sweetness these were a gift from Fredrick, she stuffed them back in the drawer. *I surely can't wear those! I don't think Jackson will care, anyway.* Finally, she chose the newest of her regular underwear. *I need to go shopping soon, or maybe not. This might be a one night stand.* At last, she was ready. The phone rang.

"Hey, sweet thing. I can hardly wait to see you...hurry on over."

Moria blurted out, "I'm so nervous."

"Do you want me to come get you?"

"No, I'm on the way."

Jackson met her at the door and took her hand. "I was afraid you would back out."

"No, I'm good for my word."

He laughed. "Well, let's hope this is not an ordeal!"

They stopped talking and looked at each other. The moment of truth; not one, but two hearts were racing. Without a word, Jackson took Moria into his arms and held her. He began to kiss her softly at first, and then with more intensity as he caressed her with a gentle, meaningful touch. She responded, feeling her knees weaken and her head spin.

Stars flashed before her eyes, which were tightly closed. Jackson stopped kissing her. "You can open your eyes now."

"Wow! Was that a cowboy kiss?"

"There's more, or we can have dinner first." Moria looked startled and Jackson continued, "I guess this is a no brainer. Twenty steps to the bedroom. Don't break any pictures this time." With his arm around her, they walked into the bedroom. Moria began to cry. Jackson led her to the bed and sat down beside her. He held her close and handed her a handkerchief. Looking worried, he asked, "What's the matter?"

"I feel half-married, like this is not okay."

"You're not half-married, you're only half of a marriage that's not anymore."

"I guess if Fredrick cared, he would be here."

"Look Moria, I'm not going to play games. I really like you and I definitely want to get to know you better, preferably in bed."

"That's not all."

"What else?" Jackson began to unbutton his shirt.

"I've never slept with anyone but Fredrick."

"Hey, it's just like riding a bicycle. You never forget how. Here, see if this will help." Jackson reached down beside the bed and picked up Rainbow's neck strap. He put it around his neck, took Moria's hand and placed it on the strap. "It's your call."

Moria laughed and pulled Jackson to her saying, "You are going to take off your boots, aren't you?" Jackson laughed as he kicked them into the corner. Moria shivered with uncertainty.

"Now what?" Jackson asked, becoming perplexed. "Have you changed your mind?"

"No. Just cold."

"We can fix that." He pulled the covers down and turned off the bedside lamp. Only the soft glow of the outside security light filled the room. Moria stood up and Jackson took her in his arms again, with the urgency of desire, too long waiting. She lifted the leather strap from around Jackson's neck and dropped it to the floor. Then, as if in a dream, unfastened her belt and unzipped her jeans. The abandoned clothing lay in a heap on the floor along with any reservations she had about this moment. She rubbed her fingers over Jackson's rodeo buckle, unsnapped it, and unzipped his jeans, feeling Jackson sling them off his feet. Moria leaned into Jackson. His heavy breathing filled the room with anticipation as she began to rub her leg against his. He unbuttoned her shirt with practiced fingers, slid it off her arms, and threw it aside.

By now, Moria began to feel the power of being a woman and realized she had Jackson's undivided attention. He whispered, "I don't think I could have waited one more day to hold you."

Smoothing the hairs at his open collar, she encouraged him. "You won't be sorry." On a whim, she took hold of his shirt with two hands and ripped it open.

Buttons scattered over the room, airborne missiles of Moria's intent. Jackson took a look at his shirt and Moria's delighted expression and announced, "Let the games begin!"

Laughing like a naughty child, she said, "I've always wanted to do that," and began to run her hands over his chest.

Jackson shrugged out of his ripped shirt. "Maybe there's some more things you've always wanted to do, honey. This is your chance."

Two shadows on the wall melted into one and two silver belt buckles on the floor reflected dancing spots of light on the ceiling. Outside, the horses stamped and whinnied, but no one heard them. The wind blew through the meadow with a soft, wistful sigh. The windows in Jackson's room fogged over and Moria delighted in his pleasure. He seemed to read her like a book, from experience or instinct, she didn't care.

In this moment, she knew happiness. Her world became this room and the cowboy beside her, a precious treasure. I can never let you go. But in her heart, she knew the time would come to say good bye. Waylon Jenning's song played softly on the radio. "Cowboys ain't easy to love and they're harder to hold..."

Moria awoke several hours later, sat up and looked around, remembering with great pleasure, those earlier moments of the evening. Jackson stirred but did not awaken. She quietly made her way to the bathroom. Wide-awake now, Moria decided to leave. *I'll rest better in my own bed.*

While she was dressing, Jackson awoke. "Where are you going?"

"Home."

"Didn't you have a good time?"

She stopped dressing and sat back down on the bed. "I had a great time, the best ever." *Although I don't have much to compare it with.*

"Don't leave."

Moria hesitated. Her stomach began to growl.

"Oh my God! I'll bet you're hungry. We never had supper. Actually, I didn't fix anything," he admitted.

She laughed and leaned over to kiss him. "Well, I don't think food was a high priority! Anyway, I want to sleep in my own bed."

"We could go to the Waffle House before you go home. What about it?" Jackson asked, pulling her closer.

"If I don't get up, it looks like food won't be an option, again. Besides, I can't go to the Waffle House at three in the morning with a cowboy."

"Why not?"

"It just wouldn't look right."

"To who?"

"The people in Cherry Valley—the kid's parents—this is a small town, remember? They all know me. What would they think?"

"Probably that you are out having a good time. Besides, if they're out at three in the morning, they're going about their own business and won't worry much about you."

Still not convinced, she answered, "This is not a good idea."

Jackson thought a minute. "We could go over to Drapersville. It's only fifteen miles away."

The idea of some hot coffee and a good breakfast did sound appealing. "Well, okay. I really am hungry."

When they walked outside, Moria started toward Jackson's truck.

"No, honey. I've got a better idea." Jackson handed her a motorcycle helmet from his bike, parked nearby. Moria stopped and stared at the helmet and then at the bike.

"No, noo, noo. I'm not getting on that thing!"

Jackson reached in his pocket and pulled out Rainbow Chaser's neck strap, placing it around his neck. "Now will you go?"

Moria couldn't help but laugh. "Why not?" Fastening the helmet, she noticed it was a small size. *Humm, wonder who else has worn this?* But she didn't ask. "Show me where to put my feet," she said, climbing on behind him.

She straddled the bike, putting her legs close to his and her arms around his waist. *No wonder I see so many women on guy's motorcycles.* Dark rain clouds hovered on the gray horizon and the wind blew dust from the driveway into their faces as they prepared to leave. To Moria's surprise, the motorcycle purred quietly to life. I guess that's what money can buy. She smiled and leaned closer to Jackson, trying to picture him in another life, a high dollar "suit guy" in the legal world.

There were few customers in the restaurant, and no one she knew. Relieved, she relaxed, enjoying Jackson's admiring gaze. She smiled to herself. *Maybe inexperience isn't such a bad thing, after all!*

While working through her favorite cheese-eggs breakfast, Moria's thoughts turned to the horses and the training plan. "We need to make a long range plan and decide which will be our first ride. Silver Dollar needs some LSD."

Jackson interrupted, "The horses take drugs?!"

Moria laughed, remembering Jackson had a lot to learn.

"No, for endurance riders LSD means long, slow, distance and your horse needs plenty of it. Why don't you ride some during the week while I'm at school?"

"Great idea. I have to do some work on the Rutherford's farm but I'll still have plenty of time. Maybe Jada can ride with me."

Moria shrieked inwardly, *Stupid me.* Regrouping, she took a deep breath and said, "Why don't you call Jeremy? He has time to ride during the day and he's a consistent finisher. You can really learn a lot from him."

Jackson nodded in response but said, "You're not worried about Jada, are you?"

Thinking quickly, she asked, "Should I be?"

Jackson reached for the check. "Let's go. Don't start giving me any grief."

Moria's heart pounded as they climbed back on the motorcycle. *Don't let me screw up now!* A cold wind took her breath away as they pulled out of the parking lot and sleet pellets began to sting her face and hands. Worried and miserably cold, she leaned her head to the side, against Jackson's back. *Soon I'll be in my warm bed and...tomorrow's another day.*

By the time the two reached Jackson's house, sleet covered the roads. "We got back just in time. Come on in and get dried off. No need to get sick."

Moria looked at her cold, ice-coated truck and then at the warm, inviting glow from the guest house windows. "Sounds good. Thanks."

Jackson added wood to the fire and mixed two hot buttered rums. "Nobody can resist these." He handed her the drink and a blanket.

She dropped her wet clothes to the tile floor, wrapped up and gratefully accepted the drink. Jackson stripped and wrapped himself in another blanket, propped his feet on the coffee table and put his arm around her. "There's only a couple of things better than this. What about a hot shower?"

"Together?"

"Your choice."

Moria took another sip of her drink and studied its contents, as if finding her answer in the bottom of the cup. She felt Jackson's inquiring gaze but did not look at him. *Well, I had sex with a man I've known two months, ridden a motorcycle for the first time and stayed up all night and now I'm sitting here naked under this blanket! Why not?* "Sure. Sounds like fun."

"Let me guess. You've never taken a shower with anybody." He grinned and pulled her close. The blanket dropped away but Moria didn't notice. Jackson took her hand. "Come on. You'll love this!"

Hot water and apple-scented soap suds washed over her. She closed her eyes and relaxed as Jackson's hands roved up and down her body. "Stop!"

Jackson wiped the water from his face but not the look of surprise. "What?"

"Stop...my knees are weak!"

"Oh my God! What next? Anyway, it's your turn to wash me."

Moria began to rub over Jackson's body with tentative strokes.

"Hey, just wash me like you would Rainbow Chaser." Moria delighted in her new-found skill.

Jackson said under his breath, "Damn, you're good." He continued, "Did you notice? We've used up most of the hot water."

Reluctantly they emerged from the shower to find the steamy room illuminated by early morning sunlight. The golden steam swirled around them as Jackson took Moria in his arms and whispered, "Imagine what could happen if you practiced!"

Laughing, she reached for a towel. "Playtime is over. I'm exhausted. I've got to go home." Jackson began to nuzzle her neck.

"Well, maybe in a little while..." sighing, she put her arms around his neck, savoring his touch again.

By the time she left, the sun had melted the ice from her truck. A sharp wind blew down from the mountains, bending the trees and scattering the few remaining leaves across the driveway. Moria smiled, reliving Jackson's comforting, yet exciting style of love-making. Or, was it just sex?

Whatever it is, or was...I wouldn't have missed it for anything!

After feeding the horses, she tumbled into bed, but did not sleep long. The ringing phone startled her awake. Answering, she heard Maxine's voice.

"Hi, glad to see you finally got home."

"How did you know I wasn't here?"

"Check your phone. I left you a bunch of messages... yesterday. Did you and Jackson have fun?"

Moria took a deep breath. "I'm in love."

Silence. "Maybe you're just in lust. It's a lot easier to deal with."

"What am I going to do?"

Maxine's voice smiled as she said, "Enjoy it. The reason I called, Jeremy and I are going to ride that new trail we're working on. Want to come along?"

Moria shook herself to reality. "Sure. I'll call Jackson and see if he wants to go. See you in about an hour." She dialed Jackson's number. "Hi, would you like to go riding?"

"Absolutely." The tone of his voice left no doubt about his expectations.

"Ride the horses. Jeez, you have a one track mind!"

When Jackson reached the barn, he gave Moria a hug. "Hey, sweetie. How're you doing?"

Grateful for Jackson's lighthearted greeting, she put the night into her precious memories file and concentrated on grooming Rainbow Chaser. As she fastened the tie down from the horse's halter bridle to the girth she said, "I wish you would ditch those heavy saddlebags. You know the horse doesn't need that extra weight."

Jackson continued to tack up Silver Dollar and strapped the saddle bags down just as if she hadn't spoken. They mounted up and trotted down the dirt road to meet Maxine and Jeremy.

The four riders reached the mountain trail at an extended trot. Sparks flew from steel-shod hooves and white clouds of breath exploded from the horses' nostrils. The four rode silently, concentrating on keeping a steady pace and watching for the spooky "horse getters." A strangely shaped rock, moss covered log or sudden puff of wind could send the horses into a frenzy—especially on a cold, windy day. After a couple of miles, they slowed to a walk.

"Let's show Jackson the covered bridge," Jeremy suggested. The riders agreed and followed him down a steep trail toward the river. Rocks scattered under the horses' hooves and underbrush tugged at their legs. The riders ducked, avoiding the low branches, as the horses slid the last few feet to the river trail.

"Reminds me of home," Jackson commented. "Maybe we can take a trip to Wyoming sometime this spring."

Moria replied, "Why not? Just order the corporate jet and we'll start packing."

Jackson laughed, "Don't be surprised."

Maxine and Jeremy looked at each other with raised eyebrows and said nothing.

The four made their way slowly along the overgrown path. The rushing creek dashed over the rocks, daring those who thought to cross. Soon the riders reached the covered bridge. Jeremy dismounted to test the footing inside. Returning, he announced. "No way. It's coated with ice from last night, besides there are some rotted boards." The sides of the deep ravine and dense growth of mountain laurel shadowed the bridge, as shafts of weak winter sun struggled to melt the ice.

Maxine said, "We could go back up to the road. Jeremy and I need to do some interval training and the road seems like the best place."

Jackson's face brightened. "We're going to run the horses?"

Moria frowned. "No. We're going to stay on the river trail. Remember the long, slow distance?"

Jackson's envious eyes followed Maxine and Jeremy as they turned to leave. "Jackson, I know you want to race Silver Dollar but he's got a lot of serious training to do before you can turn him loose to run."

Fear gripped her as she thought of racing down the gravel road. *What is the matter with me?*

Jackson looked at her with concern. "Are you cold?"

"It does seem colder, now that we've stopped for a few minutes."

"I've got a great idea! What about some more hot buttered rum?"

"So is that what's in your saddle bags?"

"No," he smiled invitingly. "We have to go home. I don't want you to get sick."

Moria thought for a minute. The setting sun cast long shadows across the hilltops and it would soon be dark. "If we crossed the bridge, we could take a short cut back to the farm. But it's way too dangerous."

Jackson gazed down into the swirling, icy water. "Can we ford the creek here?"

Moria looked doubtful. "We always cross in the water when the weather's warm, to cool the horses. I don't know about now. It would save about five miles if we went this way."

The cowboy took matters into his own hands as he urged Silver over the rocks and into the water. Moria watched the two wade out deeper, until water covered the horse's legs. Jackson took his feet out of the stirrups and pulled his legs up so his knees were level with the saddle horn. The gray gelding scrambled up the muddy bank and stood, dripping and shivering in the cold wind. Jackson called across the stream, "Come on in. The water's great!"

Rainbow Chaser, eager to follow Silver Dollar, plunged willingly into the stream, slipping on the rocks in his haste to cross. "Whoa, boy! Slow down!" Moria commanded the horse as he struggled to get his footing. Keeping her feet in the stirrups, she felt the cold water fill her boots.

Rainbow Chaser lunged up the bank and then fell back into the creek. Jackson yelled, "His leg's caught in the tie down!" Just then, the chestnut's head went under the water. As the horse struggled to free himself, Moria lost her balance and fell off of him into the creek. Still holding the reins, she righted herself and fought to unfasten the tie down. Seconds passed as she felt under water for the snap release, praying she would not be caught in between the thrashing hooves.

"Get his bridle off!" Jackson came running along the bank, lasso in hand.

Moria reached between Rainbow Chaser's ears, grasped the headstall of the bridle and pulled. Desperate, the horse pulled back and the bridle came off. Falling backward into the stream, Rainbow stood in chest deep water, disoriented. Wild-eyed, he plunged away, downstream, ignoring Moria's frantic cries.

Still in the water, she watched helplessly as the horse disappeared around the bend, stumbling and floundering on the rocky creek bottom. Moria covered her face and began to cry, from fear, and exhaustion. Suddenly she heard the whirr of Jackson's lasso and felt it settle over her shaking body.

"Hold onto the rope. Don't worry. We'll catch up with Rainbow in a few minutes. He's not going far." Jackson helped Moria up the bank, coiled the lasso, attached it to the saddle and opened the saddle bags. "Now, Missy, you may have a different opinion about saddle bags." Saying this, he pulled out a fleece- lined poncho and put it gently around her.

"Come here, honey. Everything's going to be ok." Jackson hugged Moria for both warmth and comfort. Moria pushed him away. "We've got to find Rainbow!"

Silver Dollar's ears pricked forward and he whinnied softly. The couple looked down the trail to see Rainbow, muddy but bright-eyed, trotting eagerly toward the group, his broken bridle trailing behind him. He stopped right next to them. Jackson reached into his saddlebag and pulled out some pieces of rawhide.

"Lucky he climbed out on our side of the river. Hmm...look what I found in my saddle bag." Jackson reached in and produced a flask of brandy. Moria couldn't help but laugh. Reaching for it, she asked "You don't happen to have a towel in there, do you?"

"Why, yes, I believe do," and handed her a towel. Moria began to wipe Rainbow Chaser down and check him for injuries while Jackson repaired the bridle. "This'll get us home. Let's go."

The horses climbed steadily up the side of the ravine. Moria held onto Rainbow's thick mane and looked over his ears at Jackson and Silver Dollar. A chill of fear and cold shook her body. *What if I had been alone?*

The riders reached the ridge and stopped to let the horses catch their breath. Moria looked down on Cherry Valley. She could see the winding black top road far below, the old iron bridge and the churning river. Just across the river bare gray elms sheltered the school. *Was I there only two days ago? It seems like a lifetime!* The sun slanted bright orange rays of light across the valley. "Hey, I didn't come prepared to camp tonight," Jackson laughed. "Let's go." The ridge line provided excellent footing for the horses and the riders made good time for the next few minutes. Moria began to feel warm under the poncho but cold water squished in her boots. *This too, shall pass.*

The two riders made a slow descent on the other side of the ridge. Frozen ground had thawed during the day, causing the chestnut and the gray to slide and scramble for footing. Reaching the road, the horses picked up the pace, sensing they were almost home.

Walking the horses the last mile to cool them, Jackson glanced at Moria.

"How're you doin'?

Her smile trembled at the thought of nearly losing her horse. "Okay." Tears welled in her eyes. *I'm not going to cry!*

He reached back in the saddle bag for the brandy flask and handed it to her. Moria took a welcome sip and handed it back. Now they rode side by side, stirrups touching. Jackson's closeness sent a surge of heat through her body. She unbuttoned the neck of the poncho.

"Getting hot?"

"What do you think?" She took her foot out of the stirrup and rubbed his leg. *Oh my God! Is this me?* She looked sideways at Jackson. Surprise flickered over his face and he smiled.

When they reached the barn and dismounted, Dixie and the pups scampered up and down the aisle. The horses stepped carefully, accustomed to the pups antics.

Jackson reached down and picked up Hero. "Just look at him. He's the greatest."

Moria smiled. "He's old enough for you to take home if you want to." *Lucky dog!*

"I'll take him tomorrow and see how he does."

The familiar routine of putting the horses away helped steady Moria's emotions. Without a question, Jackson began to clean Silver Dollar, brushing the mud and dried sweat from his coat.

Grateful for the companionable silence, Moria worked on Rainbow's coat until it shone like burnished copper.

"They'll need extra grain tonight and some beet pulp," she said, opening Rainbow's stall door, turning him in, and removing his halter.

Jackson leaned around the feed room door. "Some what?"

"Beet pulp. Here, let me show you." She opened a barrel and they peered inside. The feed looked like shredded gray bark. He sifted it through his fingers.

"Is this a Southern thing?"

"No, we use it for the endurance horses, especially during the ride season. It's dehydrated sugar beets."

"Why is it so good?"

"It's nutritious, adds fiber and helps hold moisture in the gut. We think it helps prevent colic. Watch." She emptied the feed scoop of beet pulp into a bucket and went to the sink. Covering the pulp with hot water she said, "Now look at what happens." The beet pulp began to swell and fill the bucket.

"Looks like oatmeal," he commented.

"The horses love it." They mixed the beet pulp with grain and divided it between their nickering customers.

By now dark settled over the farm. Moria turned off the barn lights. As they walked toward the house arm and arm, she said, "I'll be glad to make some coffee and sandwiches."

"Sounds great. What kind?"

"Well, I have peanut butter and jelly or peanut butter and banana or..."

"Don't you cook?"

"No. Come to think of it, I do have some bacon."

"Bacon and peanut butter?"

Moria laughed, "No, I have some eggs if they aren't too old. We'll have bacon and egg sandwiches."

Reaching the house, Moria turned up the thermostat and started the coffee. "I'm going to get out of these wet clothes," noticing Jackson had disappeared into the bedroom.

He called back to her, "What about a shower?"

"Two showers in a day? Sounds good to me." She walked into the bathroom and dropped her muddy clothes, expecting Jackson to follow. The bathroom mirror reflected Jackson sitting on the bed, removing his boots. She heard his voice. Thinking he was speaking to her, she paused, looking in the mirror.

The gray cat sat on the dresser, staring at Jackson through slitted green eyes. "What?" he said, giving Pounce a startled look.

Moria covered her mouth with her hand to keep from laughing out loud. Jackson stared back at the cat, which began to lick his long, soft fur. "Look at him, waiting to jump on me when I'm not...paying attention!"

Moria walked into the bedroom and crawled across the bed behind Jackson. Still on her knees, she put her arms around him. Momentarily forgetting about the cat, he turned around and they fell back on the bed, laughing.

"Come on. Pounce, out you go." She picked up the struggling cat and pushed him into the hallway, closing the door. Turning to Jackson, she asked, "Now can you pay attention? And, what about our shower?" she teased, ruffling his hair.

Chapter Six

$\mathcal{M}$uch later, Moria lay relaxed beside Jackson, who had dozed off. Reaching for the comforter, she pulled it over them and snuggled up to Jackson's warm sleeping body. She felt lonely. *Enjoy the moment. But I can't. What will happen? Am I in in love or in lust?* Finally, Moria slept, unaccustomed to Jackson's presence or her feelings of pleasure and fear.

She awoke to the smell of coffee. *Is it morning already?* she thought, hearing movement in the kitchen. Looking for the clock which had fallen to the floor, she focused her sleep-bleary eyes on the dial. *Five o'clock...I've got plenty of time to get to school.* In the bathroom she glanced in the mirror. What a wreck! Quickly brushing her teeth and putting on a dash of lipstick, she grabbed a tee shirt from the drawer, pulled it over her head, brushed out her tousled auburn hair and walked into the kitchen.

Jackson sat at the table putting on his boots. Pounce lay in a nearby chair washing his coat again. Not seeing Moria,

Jackson stared at the cat's pink tongue darting in and out. "Too bad your tongue is so small. You missed a good time," he smirked.

"Jackson! How perverted... leave Pounce alone."

"Well, who would you choose to sleep with?"

"Don't ask," she laughed, pouring a cup of coffee, *At least Pounce is going to stay around.*

As Jackson stood at the door to leave, he said, "I'll go on down to feed the horses and turn them out. Silver Dollar might need a day of rest. Maybe Jeremy and I'll ride later in the week."

Moria nodded absently, searching for her school bag. "Remember the long, slow distance."

Jackson folded her in his arms and said, "There's something about endurance riders and the long, slow distance. Maybe it's just a way of dragging out a good thing!"

Chanting under his breath, "Long slow distance, long slow distance..." as he departed"

Moria smiled. "See you later."

Realizing she hadn't checked e-mail all weekend, Moria sat down at the computer. She scanned the messages, saving the ones to be answered and deleting the others. *Doris Weaver? Oh my gosh! I've got a message from her?* I hope Jessie's okay.

Moria quickly opened the message and read:

Hi Moria,

Jessie and her family are doing very well in their training. She told me Jackson D. is at your barn. You'd better watch out for that two-timing weasel, scumbag, womanizer! He'll use you for his own pleasure and fool you into lovin' it!

See ya, Doris Weaver

Moria felt the blood drain from her face and re-read the message. Pandora jumped on the computer desk and settled her furry golden body for a nap, totally unconcerned. Moria scooped up the cat and buried her face in the warm fur. "Oh no!" she cried. Then, dropping the cat to the floor, she hit the delete key and said, "Eat your heart out, Doris Weaver!" *What if she's right? He is irresistible. Should I tell him about the e-mail? If what she said is true, he'll probably lie. I hate liars. This just can't be....*But driving to school, she had second thoughts—Yes, it could be.

The intercom crackled. The children paused in their self-absorbed world, automatically coming to attention for the Pledge of Allegiance and the announcements. During the day Moria's students needed her constant attention. Disconnected thoughts swirled through her head as she tried to focus on her job. "Miz Harris, I need to go to the bathroom." And then another, "I lost my homework." And from the back of the room, "Johnny's ripping up my math book."

The day dragged by as Moria watched the sun move shadows across the room. For self-preservation, she had given the children a social studies assignment that involved lots of drawing.

Moria avoided Maxine during the day, afraid of falling apart and upsetting every one. After school they walked to the parking lot and Moria said, "Are you in a hurry?"

Maxine laughed, "Nope, am I ever, except on the trail? What's going on? Another Jackson emergency?" Moria burst into tears.

"Want to stop by for coffee?" Maxine asked, throwing her book bag onto the backseat of her truck.

"See you in a few minutes," Moria sniffed, wiping her eyes on her sleeve.

Moria followed Maxine up the driveway and looked out at the bright green fields of winter rye. Shining white fences bordered the driveway leading to a white, two-story farm house with a blue roof and blue trim. She thought briefly about Maxine and Jeremy. *Their relationship seems to cruise along, uninterrupted by crisis. How do they do it?*

The two women settled down at the kitchen table with their coffee and Maxine said, "Well?"

Moria hesitated, thinking about how to begin. "I got a message from Doris Weaver."

"What?" Maxine's coffee sloshed over the edge of the cup. "Is Jessie okay?"

"Uumm. It's Jackson. Doris knows him. She thinks he's a..." Moria began to cry again.

"Ladies' man?" Maxine asked.

"Well, that's not exactly how she put it. She called him a... scumbag!"

"Sounds like he gave Doris a rough time."

"That's what I'm worried about. I don't want a rough time." Moria began to bite her fingernails.

"Don't do that. You know, for all your whining, underneath you're as tough as—"

"I don't feel tough," Moria said, rubbing her face in despair. "What am I going to do?"

"Just watch your backside, or let Jackson watch it when you walk away," Maxine said with a wink.

Moria thought for a moment. "I don't want to walk away. He'll have to do the walking."

"Man, you've really got it bad!" Maxine got up and went over to the refrigerator. "Remember when I gave you one of these?" She removed a round ceramic magnet from the fridge and read aloud, "Only those who risk going too far will ever know how far they can go."

"This is worse than being afraid to race Rainbow Chaser!"

"No, it's not. It's all the same. Now 'lace up your boots' and let's not have this conversation again," Maxine said, giving her friend a hug.

As Moria drove home, she thought about her own brave words, but deep in her heart she knew a page had been torn from her book of dreams; the page titled Trust. Her head pounded. Between the e-mail, her stressful day and the conversation with Maxine, she wanted nothing more than to go home to bed.

Turning into her driveway, she saw Jackson's truck parked by the house. He must be feeding the horses. *I can't see him right now.* Before Moria reached the door, Jackson came up from the barn. Hero followed at his heels.

"Hey, look at this little guy!" Jackson scooped the puppy up and held him close, rubbing the soft gray ears. "You need some help grading papers?"

Moria shifted the heavy book bag to the other shoulder and said, "I'm probably not going to grade papers tonight. I had a pretty hard day."

Jackson laughed. "I bet those little boogers can get to you. Sure you don't need some help? The relaxin' kind?"

Moria cringed. Opening the door she said, "Thanks anyway. I'm going to bed early." *Alone.* Even the disappointed look on Jackson's face did not sway her resolve to be in control of the relationship. *Was that what Maxine meant?*

Jackson gave Moria a long look. "See you tomorrow?" He lifted Hero onto the seat of the truck and drove away. Moria opened the door to the house, not answering.

She searched for the headache medicine, fed the cats, and went to bed. *I could lose weight like this. Maybe I could package him...the Jackson Diet!"*

Early the next morning Jackson called. "Moria, something's going on. You were fine, and now you're not. Is it something I've done?"

Jackson's earnest voice brought tears to her eyes. "No, I just need some time. Things are moving too fast."

Silence. "Honey, I really care about you." The e-mail flashed through her mind. *Scumbag, womanizer...and he'll have you lovin' it.*

"Jackson, I've got to go. I'm going to be late for school."

The following week dragged by. Each day Moria's thoughts hop-scotched back and forth. *Continue the 'thing' with Jackson for as long as it lasts, or stop before I get hurt? Even Maxine's optimistic outlook can't help me this time.*

Moria went to swim therapy most afternoons, avoiding Jackson at feeding time. At night, she fell into bed, exhausted, knowing she was getting behind in her school work.

"I'm a wreck!" she said to her early morning reflection in the bathroom mirror. Dark circles ringed her eyes and tense lines of worry formed around her mouth. "Maybe Jackson should take Silver Dollar back to Jada's barn." Her reflection blurred through tears of uncertainty.

As Moria hurried across the parking lot at school, Maxine caught up with her. "Hey, I've hardly seen you all week!" Seeing Moria's strained look, she said, "You still having trouble with that Doris Weaver thing?"

"I can't talk about it right now. I don't want to go into school all upset."

"You're right. Especially not on Valentine's Day."

Moria gave Maxine a wordless look of distress as she opened the schoolhouse door.

At the end of the day the two teachers sat in the empty lounge, drinking cokes and trying to look busy with their planning notes.

Moria dropped her pencil on the table and closed the book. "I don't think I have the energy to swim today. I'm just going home to bed. All this chaos with the children, parents, Valentines, cookies, and trying to wear my 'be nice' face all day is too much! Don't try to help me right now. I'll work it out."

Maxine and Moria walked through the silent hall and into the sunlight of a February afternoon, soft with the promise of spring.

"See you this weekend?" Maxine said.

"Maybe." Moria slid across the seat and into the comfort and security of her truck, looking forward to her bed and the oblivion of sleep. As she drove the familiar streets toward home, her mind drifted. *I wish I'd never met him!* Then she remembered her total relaxation and happiness when they made love. *What's the real story behind Doris Weaver's e-mail? If I ask Jackson, will he lie? What about our plans for the endurance training and competitions?*

Glancing up at a nearby billboard as she stopped for a traffic light, Moria gripped the steering wheel and stared. Go for the Gusto! the sign proclaimed. *Is that a message for me? Would God send me a message on a beer sign? Or, maybe this is what I want to see.* A grinding headache became the result of this prophetic ad.

Jackson was waiting for her on the steps when she arrived home. With no plan of action, she gathered up her book bag and numerous boxes of candy. "Hi, you're early today."

Jackson opened the door for her. "I came to check on the mare. I think she's going to foal in the next few hours. Come on down and take a look."

Alarm for her mare washed away all thoughts of the 'Jackson problem.' "She's not due to foal yet. I'd better call Dr. Barr." Dropping the bag and candy on the steps, Moria hurried inside. Over her shoulder she called, "Have some candy!"

By the time Moria returned, Jackson had finished a small box of chocolate and was licking his fingers. A quick thought intruded on Moria's worry about the mare. *How can he be so sexy, just licking chocolate off his fingers?*

Without a word, they started for the barn. Jackson reached for Moria's hand. "Don't worry. I've helped birth early foals and most of them do well. It's that first few days of care that really count."

"This is my first baby. It will break my heart if it dies. And the poor mom, she's already had a hard life, being a rescue horse." Dr. Barr's truck turned into the driveway. Moria opened the barn gate. "Thank goodness he was nearby. Sometimes it's hours before he can get here."

Jackson answered, "You'll see. The mare will be fine and no doubt have an amazing foal."

For a moment, Moria forgot Jackson's deceptive ways, thankful for his support.

Dr. Barr examined the mare, "Well, she could foal tonight or might be a couple of days. I know that's not much help, but it's hard to tell since we don't know the mare's history.

She'll need to be monitored every couple of hours, around the clock and will probably have it between the times you check on her. They usually do. Don't worry, but call if things don't look good. I'll need to see them anyway, after the birth."

Moria stroked the mare's neck. "What should we be doing for her now?"

"Clean the stall, bed it with fresh straw. Be sure she has water, hay, and a small amount of bran mash. If she doesn't foal tonight, turn her out during the day if the weather's okay."

"Thanks for coming by so quickly. I'm really starting to get nervous," Moria said, twisting a strand of the mare's black and white mane around her fingers.

"You've got Jackson to help you. Call me if you need to. I'll be in the area."

Dr. Barr drove away and Jackson took the paint mare from her stall.

"What are you doing?" Moria snapped.

"Excuse me, I thought the vet said clean the stall and bed it with straw." Jackson handed the lead rope to her, went to the end of the barn for the wheelbarrow and pitchfork and began to clean the stall. "If you don't mind me staying over until the foal is born I can check on her during the night since you'll have to go to school."

"I could take a sick day but I'm trying to save them for the rides." Moria felt as if she were on a roller coaster, poised at the top for the plunge. *I have to ask him now.*

"Jackson, we have to talk. Something's come up and it's bothering me." She stopped, waiting for his response. He pulled the wheelbarrow out of the stall and wiped the sweat from his forehead.

"What?" Jackson answered, occupied with the heavy load.

Moria knew she did not have his attention. *Well, here goes.* "I had an e-mail from Doris Weaver. I guess she's not a fan of yours."

Startled, Jackson whirled around, tipping the wheel-barrow over. "Doris? You know her? What did she say?" Then he grabbed the pitchfork and began to shovel the manure back into the wheelbarrow, not meeting her eyes.

"Never mind that I know who she is. She said you were a...womanizer and called you some more stuff." She waited.

"She is a lyin'..."

Moria faced Jackson, her face flushed and voice shaking "Just tell me the truth, if you know how."

"What's that supposed to mean? Maybe it's none of your business!"

"You are my business now, Jackson, as long as we have a thing going!"

Jackson slapped his forehead in disgust. "Oh my God! Is that a girl answer?"

"You need to leave! Just leave! I can handle this!" She turned the mare loose and snatched the pitchfork from his hands.

"Maybe you can handle this, but I don't want you to." He stepped closer and took the pitchfork back, leaning it against the wall.

"Come here, let's sit down and I'll try to tell you what happened." Concern in his voice and intensity in his eyes swayed her resolve to be done with him.

"Okay. Let's hear it."

Jackson cleared his throat and sat down on the feed room steps. She sat on the next step, but turned to see his face. He did not touch her, but stared out into the field for a few moments.

"Doris and I were engaged a couple of years ago when she lived in Wyoming. She wouldn't sign a prenuptial agreement and my family pitched a fit, especially my Dad. I was having second thoughts, because money seemed to be the most important part of our relationship. I got the feeling that the marriage wasn't going to last and she planned to walk away—a rich woman."

Jackson paused, gathering his thoughts. Moria looked up at his earnest face and said, "So?"

"One day, during those rocky weeks, I caught her having sex with a mutual friend of ours out in the barn at our ranch. I grabbed the guy and beat the shit out of him. Doris screamed, snatched her clothes and ran." He gave a chuckle. "I guess she got dressed somewhere between the barn and the car."

As Moria listened, she tried to sort out the two stories. *What does it really matter? He'll be gone in the fall, anyway.*

"Then what happened?"

"I went straight to her house. She wouldn't let me in and we called the whole thing off. The end."

"So you left?"

"I did. Our business is chock full of attorneys. They didn't need me, at least not right then. So I went on the rodeo circuit. I do have to go back to work this fall. They're making some changes and I need to be involved." Then, he added, "Doris is the one I crewed for at the endurance rides. She's living somewhere in southern California now.

Moria buried her face in her hands. "I know where she lives—she's Jessie's trainer. Why didn't you tell me this before?"

"Wait a minute. Who's Jessie?"

"A junior rider from California. Doris is getting her started in endurance. Never mind about that...why didn't you tell me all this before?"

Jackson said softly, "I just didn't want to spoil what we've got going."

Moria sat very still, not meeting Jackson's eyes. *At least I know the story, or maybe not. Can I live with this for a while? Can this relationship be a stepping stone to a more permanent relationship maybe with someone else? If I just hadn't fallen in love, yes, it would be okay. Is it now? I don't know.*

"Moria?" Jackson put his hand on her shoulder, "Moria, look at me."

She opened her eyes, remembering Maxine's ceramic magnet, Only those who risk going too far will ever know how far they can go.

"I don't want to talk about this anymore. I'm going to take your word as the truth. Please stay. I'd appreciate the help in case Phoenix foals tonight." At least she had made a decision for the immediate future.

Jackson went home to feed his horses. Moria went to the house. When she opened the door, Pounce and Pandora leapt off the kitchen table. She sat on the couch and the cats jumped up beside her. She began to stroke their soft fur. "Well, guys, I guess Jackson is back in our lives again. Or, maybe he never left." She paused, "Just don't jump on him when he's... busy." The cats looked at her through unblinking, inscrutable eyes and made no promises.

Moria fed the cats, put in a load of laundry, then sat down to watch her favorite station, the weather channel.

Soon Jackson knocked on the door. "I brought a pizza. This might be a long night. Somehow, I didn't think there would be a meal on the table when I returned."

Moria couldn't help but smile. "You catch on fast."

As they sat down to eat, Moria said, "I've never seen a foal born, much less helped with the birth. I have done some reading and watched a couple of videos..." her voice trailed off as she watched his face.

Jackson took her hands in his. "Millions of horses have foals. Usually it's not a big deal. If it gets to be, we'll call Dr. Barr."

Moria did not withdraw her hands. Jackson continued, "More than likely, she'll foal during the night. I'll go and check every couple of hours." He began to run his fingers up and down her arm. Their eyes locked. All thoughts of the impending birth disappeared.

"Why don't we relax awhile?" he suggested with a wink.

"I haven't fed the horses."

Jackson took her in his arms.

"But maybe they'll be okay for a..." He covered her mouth with his. Moria leaned into Jackson and closed her eyes. The circle of his arms became her world. Her body flushed with warmth as she kicked off her shoes and began to unbutton his shirt.

Jackson laughed, "You're not going to rip my shirt again?"

Moria looked startled. "Oh, well, I could!" He crushed her to him and kissed her again.

The cats looked on with interest at the trail of castoff clothes leading toward the bedroom. As the door closed, the two cats looked at each other. *Maybe next time they'll forget to shut the door,* Pounce whined, lashing his tail back and forth.

Darkness enveloped the two sleeping figures as they lay in each other's arms, bedcovers pushed to the floor.

Dixie began to bark with urgency. Moria and Jackson scrambled out of bed, falling over each other to get to the door. Without a word, the two ran into the living room searching for their clothes.

"Do you think it's time?" Moria asked as she struggled into her jeans and grabbed her shirt and shoes. Jackson was already at the door, dressed only in jeans and boots. He stopped and looked at his watch. "It's only been a couple hours since we were at the barn. The dogs could have been barking at anything. Let's just ease down there and not frighten the mare. Besides, it's time to feed the other horses." Dixie's frantic bark continued.

As they went out the door Moria asked, "What can I do to help?"

"Well, you could boil some water," Jackson said with a straight face.

"Oh you!" she laughed, pushing him off the path.

The pastured horses cantered up to the gate. Dixie and the barking pups joined them. "So much for being quiet," Moria said, as they pushed their way through the animals and headed on into the barn. Moria started toward the mare's stall, but Jackson took hold of her arm. "Wait, let me show you something in the tack room."

"Jackson, we don't have time for sex," she scolded, pulling her arm away.

"Now you're the one with a one track mind," he laughed. "No, it's something else."

She followed him in, watching as he went to the wall beside the mare's stall. He reached up and unlatched a tiny window. "Now we can look in without making her nervous."

"How clever!" Moria said as she climbed onto an overturned bucket to peek in at the mare. "Oh my God, she's lying down!" Jackson caught her as she fell from the bucket. Moria got her balance and Jackson took a look. He watched for several minutes. "It'll be a while yet," he predicted. "Why don't we get comfortable? No, never mind, go on to the house. Get to bed so you can make it to school tomorrow."

"Are you kidding?" said Moria, "You think I would leave now? I need to be here."

"You will just get in the way," he answered. "I've got my phone. I'll call Dr. Barr if things don't look good."

"I'm staying."

Jackson gave up. "All right. Why don't you make us some coffee and bring our jackets and a blanket." Moria raised her eyebrows.

"It's going to get cold," he reminded her.

Soon they were settled in the tack room. Jackson pulled down some hay bales and spread a horse blanket over them. Moria set the coffee thermos and food on a tack trunk then heaped Jackson's plate with ham sandwiches and chips. "Here. I don't want you to get weak."

"I'll bet," he laughed.

"Jackson, we've got serious business tonight," she answered, but couldn't help laughing with him.

By midnight Moria had fallen asleep. She roused up, reaching to pull the blanket closer and noticed that Jackson was gone. She climbed on the overturned bucket and looked down into the stall. Jackson was standing beside the mare with his hand on her side. Moria could see him timing the contractions.

He would have made a great husband. She briefly imagined Jackson by her bedside when Sarah was born.

Bringing herself to the moment, Moria put those thoughts behind her, wishing they would stay there. "How are things going?" she whispered.

"You don't have to whisper. She's doing fine. Is this her first foal?"

"I don't know. Remember, she was a rescue mare."

Jackson came out of the stall. "Why don't we get some fresh air? I thought you were going to keep me company," he teased.

"I am now." Moria looked longingly at the warm blanket, but being in Jackson's presence gave her comfort. The blanket would always be there but one day Jackson would be gone.

"Come on, let's walk down to the creek," he suggested taking her hand. Moria took a deep breath of the winter air. Wood smoke and wet leaves mixed with the earthen smell of plowed ground brought a sigh of contentment.

Jackson asked, "Are you tired?"

"Oh no!"

"Why the big sigh?"

"I was just thinking about how much I love the farm and all the animals, even though it's hard work. Will you miss being here...when you go?"

Jackson hesitated. "I don't know since I haven't gone yet. This place can grow on you. It's not just the place. The people are great." He squeezed her hand. "Especially one."

How can he do this to me?

By now they had reached the creek. Moonlight danced on the rushing water and night animals scurried away as they approached. "If you're not too cold, let's sit here a few minutes," Jackson suggested. He helped Moria down the bank to a flat rock and put his arm around her. She leaned her head against his shoulder. They sat in silence for a few moments.

Jackson took Moria's chin in his hand and gently turned her face toward his.

He's going to kiss me.

But instead Jackson said, "Would you ever live in Wyoming?"

Without even hesitating, she said, "I could never leave Cherry Valley."

"Why?"

"My life is here, my friends, my job..." tears welled in her eyes.

"And memories of Fredrick?"

Is that why I can't leave? How pathetic!

"No, I just can't leave. Would you move here?"

Dixie began to bark. Without answering, he helped Moria up from the rock. The two hurried to the barn and looked into the mare's stall. She was down and they could see the foal's two front feet emerging.

Moria gasped, "We need to help her!"

"No," said Jackson, "Let her do her job."

The mare, focused on the birthing event, seemed oblivious of the two people standing at the door. They continued to watch as the head appeared, and then with one final groan and push the foal came into its brand new world. "Oh she's beautiful!" Moria exclaimed.

"How do you know it's a filly?" Jackson asked in a puzzled voice.

"Why, look at her precious face. I know it's a girl!"

Jackson laughed. "That's a new one for me, telling the sex of a horse by its 'precious' face! Give her a few minutes and I'll go in and check for sure."

Moria and Jackson returned to the tack room to warm themselves with coffee. As they sat on the hay bales, with the blanket over them, Jackson asked, "What's the mare's history?"

"I don't know her background. I call her Phoenix since she rose from the ashes of neglect to become a beautiful mare, and now a mother."

"Good choice. What about the 'filly'?

"I'm going to call her Promise. I hope she'll have a future in endurance."

Jackson handed Moria his cup and threw the blanket aside. "Well, we'll see if you've got yourself a filly." He went into the stall. The mare looked at him but did not offer to kick.

"Hey, let me see your baby." Phoenix moved to the back of the stall, placing herself between Jackson and the foal. He waited, then moved forward a few steps. She laid her ears back and refused to move.

He looked at Moria, her face framed in the tiny window. "Bring me a little grain. Maybe we can distract her."

The mare munched on the grain, and the foal came around her mother on wobbly legs, looking at them with curiosity. Moria stood still in the corner, so grateful that the foal was healthy and that Jackson was there to help.

Jackson reached in his pocket for a small bottle of iodine and a soft cloth. He handed them to Moria. "Give these to me when I say so." With caution, he approached the foal and placed his arm over its back. He held his hand out and she handed him the soaked cloth. Jackson reached underneath with his other hand, felt around and then treated the umbilical cord nub with the iodine. The foal jumped from the sting.

Jackson let go. "You were right. You've got a little filly. She's a beauty and okay as far as I can tell. We'll have Dr. Barr come by later. Now get the pitchfork and scoop up the afterbirth."

"The what?"

"That bloody stuff in the straw. Dr. Bar will need to see it. If all the afterbirth's not expelled, Phoenix can get sick. Put it in the wheelbarrow, cover it with an empty feed bag and put it in one of the stalls so the dogs won't eat it."

Moria stood transfixed. "Oh yeah, the afterbirth." Slowly she went to get the pitchfork.

"You asked what you could do to help," Jackson grinned.

Orange and purple streaks of a dawning sky greeted the two as they left the barn They walked up the path to the house, arms around each other, as if Doris Weaver had never entered their lives or their budding relationship.

The crunch of tires on gravel announced Maxine's arrival. She stopped her truck, waiting for them.

"Guess what?" Moria asked.

"You have a new baby at the barn," Maxine answered.

"How did you know?"

"Well, unless you and Jackson spent the night at the barn for fun, I figured you all were attending the birth. I saw the lights when I went into town last night, but it was too cold to come out unless you needed me. Is it a colt or filly?"

Trembling with excitement and exhaustion, Moria replied, "A perfect filly! Come on down and see!"

"I can't right now. I'm still in my pajamas. Are you going to school today?"

Moria looked at Jackson. He answered, "Yes, she's going. I'll stay around and have Dr. Barr come by later and check on our baby."

Maxine raised her eyebrows as if to say, 'so he's in charge'? Moria just smiled. "I need to hurry. See you at school."

Later that day Moria and Maxine had lunch in Moria's room. She told Maxine about the filly's birth. "I learned more about birthing a foal than I ever wanted to know. Jackson made me clean up the afterbirth!"

Maxine laughed. "Guess he just wanted to see if you're a real cowgirl."

"Maybe so, but there's something else."

"Am I even surprised? Tell me."

"Jackson wants me to move to Wyoming."

"What?" Maxine shrieked, turning over her tea. They both jumped up, grabbing paper towels. As they mopped, Maxine continued. "Are you going? Did he ask you to marry him?"

"No, to both questions."

"What did you say?"

"I told him my life is here. Wyoming seems like a foreign country. I wouldn't know anybody."

"How many more excuses can you think of?" Maxine asked, crossing her arms and leaning back in the chair.

"Did you tell him you can't commit to a real relationship because of your issues with Fredrick? He isn't coming back. You...?"

"No, I didn't tell him anything. I guess he's figured it out by now. Why can't I move on?" Anxiety spoke volumes as she ripped her napkin into shreds and threw it into the trash. Just then, the bell rang. She sniffed, "Will you bring my kids back from lunch? I need to go to the restroom."

Maxine hugged Moria. "Don't worry. We'll go out for a ride this afternoon. You can talk, or not. I'll get the kids. Take your time."

During the afternoon, Moria found herself frequently staring out the window. Her students worked independently on their assignments and required little help from her.

Jackson's crystal on its silver chain lay on her desk. Early spring sunshine glinted on its prism surface, reflecting a rainbow of colors onto the ceiling. She quickly picked it up so the shimmering colors would not distract the children.

Holding the prism, she tried to center her emotions. *I am okay. I am happy. I do not have to go to Wyoming.* A still, small voice questioned, *Are you really okay?* Moria dropped the crystal into the pocket of her blazer.

Focusing on the rest of her day, she asked, "Michael, are you staying for tutoring?"

"Yes ma'am."

"Go ahead and get your book while the others are packing up." Soon the room was quiet. Moria and Michael settled down to work again on the concept of multiplication. She got a box of colorful number blocks off the shelf.

Michael sat attentively, waiting for directions. Moria looked at his face. *This is a very bright kid. What's going on with him?*

For several minutes Michael laid out different amounts of blocks in patterns, three sets of four, six sets of two, three sets of five. He could look at them immediately and tell her the values. Moria glanced at the clock. Half their time had passed.

"Now, Michael, let's put these ideas on paper."

He frowned. "I can't"

Exasperated, Moria said, "You can't or you won't?" She waited.

"I wo... can't"

"Let's try."

Michael began to write.

Moria took the crystal out of her pocket to put it back on the desk.

"What's that?" Michael asked.

"Well...it's a...magic crystal!" *Maybe this will work,* she thought and began to swing the crystal back and forth. Michael watched for a few moments.

"So what does it do?"

"It helps you remember how to do multiplication!"

"Huh?"

"Just watch the crystal and listen to my voice." She began to swing the crystal on its silver chain. Michael stared.

"Michael, say these words, I can do multiplication."

The boy continued to stare at the shining crystal. Moria watched in fascination as rainbow colors swam across his face. Suddenly, the classroom door flew open, crashing against the wall. Moria and Michael jumped up, scattering the blocks to the floor.

"What's the meaning of this?" screamed Michael's mother.

Over the irate parent's shoulder, Moria could see Mr. Baldwin's pale face, horrified eyes and open mouth, but no words came. The mother dashed into the room, snatched Michael by the arm, and dragged him toward the door. The child's frightened look seared his teacher's heart.

"Wait! Wait! I can explain!" Moria called, running toward the door.

The classroom door slammed. That was her answer.

Mr. Baldwin opened the door, stepped into the classroom, clearing his throat. "Ms. Harris, what's going on here?"

Silence filled the room. Moria sat down and looked at Mr.

Baldwin's face. Grim and unyielding features replaced his usual smile. "I don't know where to begin," she replied.

"At the beginning. Get your story straight. No doubt we're going to hear from the Dexters' attorney in the morning."

Moria took a deep breath. "Remember a few weeks ago when I first began to tutor Michael? I told you then something was wrong."

Mr. Baldwin nodded. "Go ahead."

"He needs to be tested so we can get to the bottom of his problem."

The principal frowned. "His mother says nothing is wrong with him."

Moria ran her fingers through her hair. "Maybe he is okay at home, or maybe..."

He finished her statement. "She's lying?"

Surprised, she said, "Well, yes. Or maybe they don't have issues at home because she doesn't push him to do unpleasant tasks."

Mr. Baldwin looked thoughtful. Moria waited. Dust motes danced in the last rays of sunlight. She could hear the night cleaners begin to vacuum. Bright spots of pink appeared on the man's cheeks as he spoke. "Moria, you may be right. Nevertheless, we must deal with the immediate issue."

"Does that mean you're going to support me?"

"Let's see what their attorney has to say, talk to our school attorney and then make a plan. Now, tell me about the crystal."

"I know this may sound strange. Someone gave it to me. It was in my pocket and I started to put it on the desk. Michael saw it and wanted to know what it was."

Mr. Baldwin picked up the prism and examined it. In the harsh classroom lights, its beauty had faded. "Ms. Harris, have you been practicing hypnotism?"

"No, no sir. I was curious about hypnotism. My friend explained how it works and gave me the crystal."

Moria leaned forward, placing her folded arms on the table. Mr. Baldwin looked at her intently. "Just be sure your private life doesn't interfere with your school life."

"Yes sir."

"Tell me what happened."

She continued, "To me it was a 'teachable moment.' I was desperate for anything to help Michael break through this learning barrier."

Mr. Baldwin placed the stone on the desk between them. "I see. Unfortunately, this was an unorthodox approach to the problem. We'll talk tomorrow and see what we have to do."

Tears sprang to Moria's eyes. "Will I have to go on administrative leave?"

"It's doubtful. But you should be prepared. Let's not jump to conclusions."

The two walked down the hall in silence and the principal released the security system to let them out. They said goodbye in the gathering dusk. A light wind blew stray papers across the deserted parking lot. *Just like my life; blowing away like a few old papers.*

Moria turned and looked back at the school. *I don't want to lose my job. I know was put on this earth to teach.* She said a quick prayer. *Dear God, your hand is on my shoulder. Help me know your will. Amen.*

Moria drove away from the campus and reached for her phone. A message from Maxine and one from Jackson appeared on the screen.

She smiled as she heard Maxine's voice. "Hey, where are you? I thought we were going riding. I came back by the school and saw your truck and Mr. Baldwin's car. Don't tell me y'all are having an affair! Ha! Ha! Call me."

Jackson's message followed. "Hey, where are you? I've fed the horses and I'm getting ready to cook steaks. Maxine and Jeremy are already here. Are you okay? Call me."

Moria laid the phone on the seat and tried to gather her thoughts. *I just want to go home and to bed. I'll tell them I'm sick. It wouldn't be a lie. I am sick at heart. But, they're going to find out anyway. These are my best friends. I need to go.* She picked up the phone and returned their calls.

Moria parked in Jackson's driveway. Before she could get out, Jackson hurried from the house and opened the truck door. Taking her in his arms and holding her close he said, "We've been worried about you! Come on in. Looks like you could use a drink."

"Thanks. I've had a really bad day."

Settled in front of the fire with Jackson's 'cowgirl drink,' she relaxed. "You're not going to believe this..." she began. When she finished her distressing story, they all sat in silence for a few moments.

Then Maxine said, "Jeez, I'm really sorry. You know I'll back you up. Michael's in two of my classes. It's evident he has some unknown learning difficulties. Math just seems to be the subject he's focused on as being the hardest."

Moria handed her glass to Jackson for a refill. His hand covered hers for a lingering touch. Warmth spread through her and with it, strength to endure whatever followed. Their eyes met. He smiled and said, "You could always move."

Looking directly at Jackson and then at the others, she said, "I'm not moving. I may not win, but I won't give up--not yet."

To break the tension, Jeremy said in a joking tone, "We could always use another bartender at the Juniper Tree, just in case you need a job."

Jackson added, "Speaking of the Juniper Tree, maybe we should all go dancin' this weekend."

"Good idea," Maxine answered.

Moria frowned, thinking of New Year's Eve and Jada's skill at spiriting Jackson away before her very eyes. *This time it will be different,* she vowed.

Jackson caught her eye and winked, then said to Jeremy, "Let's get these steaks on the grill."

Maxine looked around the dining area as the two began to set the table. "This place is gorgeous." The western motif carried through from the living room. Gray stone tile covered the floor and a desert mural decorated one wall.

The cabinets held western artifacts and art objects. "Look at this! I'll bet this statue is an original Remington!"

Moria came over to look into the cabinet. "Don't open the door! We might break something."

Maxine laughed. "Yep. Then we'd both be working at the Juniper Tree to pay for being so nosy. Jackson was lucky to find this place. Guess they really trust him to take care of things."

Moria reminded her, "If his dad hadn't known the Rutherford's and that they were going off to Europe for six months, Jackson would probably still be on the rodeo circuit, getting bucked off horses every day."

Maxine laughed. "I just don't get it. How can Jackson be an environmental lawyer and not want to do his job?"

Moria said, "He won't talk about it. And look at Jeremy. He's a bouncer and he has an MBA! Go figure."

At dinner, the four stayed away from discussing Moria's plight. Jackson brought them up to date on the new foal's progress and then the conversation turned to the upcoming endurance ride. For the moment, Moria forgot her uncertain future.

Jeremy asked, "Now where is it we're going for the ride?"

"We have two choices," Moria answered, putting down her fork. "If we go south, or east toward the coast, it will probably be warmer. But the footing will be sandy. I don't think the horses are conditioned this early in the season for sand. It's too hard on their muscles and they can get leg cramps."

Jeremy rubbed his thighs and winced. "Us, too," he laughed.

Jackson asked. "So what's our other choice?

Moria continued. "If we go north, it's more mountainous. But our horses train in the mountains, so that helps. The Ridge and Valley Ride is only fifty miles from here. The south ride is almost two hundred miles away."

She looked at Maxine. "I'd say the Ridge ride."

Maxine nodded. "Well, let's make a plan. At least we won't have to take a personal day. The guys can pull the trailers to the ride that morning and you and I can drive up in the afternoon. That will give them time to get set up."

Jeremy and Jackson looked at each other. Jeremy laughed, "Looks like this is a conspiracy."

Jackson frowned with concern. "So, what does 'set up' mean?

Jeremy answered, "It is a 'set up.' We do all the work and when the girls get there, they can relax!"

"Well, not exactly," Maxine laughed, "Jeremy knows the drill. We'll send all the stuff."

"Stuff?" Jackson asked.

"You know, like what you would take to a rodeo."

"My bedroll and horse feed?"

She smiled. "A little more than that." Moria could see that Jackson had heard enough for now. "Don't worry. I'll give you a list."

Jackson stood up and pulled Moria's chair back. "Let's have some coffee and talk about doing a training ride. Maybe we can all go tomorrow afternoon. That is, if Moria's not in jail."

He gave her a hug and she answered, laughing, "You might be taking care of the horses for a long time!"

Moria drove home later in the evening thinking about the coming ride season. *Now I don't have to just worry about Rainbow Chaser and me, I've got to keep an eye on Jackson and Silver Dollar. That guy is such a loose cannon. He says he'll take it easy, but I know he'll get caught up in the competition...it happens.*

Her thoughts continued as she turned in the driveway. *I could ride Limited Distance, with him to help with the pacing, but I need to do fifty miles with Rainbow Chaser for the points. It's going to be a really competitive year for the longer distance riders. Managing Jackson will be like taking care of a junior rider! Humm, wonder how Jessie is doing? I need to touch base with her and see how her training is coming along. I guess Doris Weaver's only redeeming feature is being an excellent trainer. Too bad Jessie doesn't live here.*

Dixie and the pups ran to meet the truck. "Hey you guys! Let's go check on the horses." At the barn Moria walked quietly to the mare's stall and looked over the divided door. The mare and foal were lying down. Phoenix scrambled to her feet. With a burst of energy, the youngster struggled to her feet and began to nurse. Moria knew all was well. She stepped into the stall and gave Phoenix a hug, burying her face in the coarse mane. "You're a great mom," she whispered, then closing the door and moving next to Rainbow Chaser's stall.

His watchful eyes looked out into the night, self-appointed guardian of the barn. "Hey, big guy. Sorry to disturb you." She stroked Rainbow's neck and the gelding turned his head into the crook of her arm. "I know, you want your head scratched. What a baby! Well, you better get ready to rock and roll, mister. We've got a busy ride season ahead."

Chapter Seven

*L*ater Moria lay awake, thinking about the day's events. *What if I lose my job? Maybe I could live in Wyoming. Worse than that could happen. If I stayed here, who knows where I might be working?*

She finally fell asleep, only to be awakened by a scratching sound outside the window. The cats, sleeping at the foot of the bed, crept over to the window and pawed at the blinds. "Settle down, you guys, it's only branches scraping against the screen." The cats continued trying to peer outside. She turned over and pushed them off the bed with her foot. The scratching continued, and then a voice.

"Moria! Moria! Wake up!"

She threw the covers aside, crawled to the foot of the bed and raised the blinds.

"Jackson!" She opened the window. "What are you doing here? Is something wrong?"

He laughed. "No, I'm lonely. Need some company?"

"No, it's four o'clock. I need some sleep. Why didn't you come to the door?"

"I didn't want to ring the doorbell and scare you."

"So you scratched on my window instead?" Smiling, she propped her elbows on the window sill and cupped her chin in her hands.

"Hey, it's really cold out here! Little girl, little girl, let me come in."

"So, what's it worth to you, big bad wolf?"

"A kiss and a peck and a hug around the neck. Besides, my nose is froze, among other things." He grinned. "Last chance."

"Now that I'm wide awake, why not?"

Jackson came in through the kitchen door, dropping his coat and hat in the nearest chair. Hugging her, he said, "Man, you are a hard case!"

Unfastening his belt, she answered, "And you're a nut case! Besides making my knees weak." She put her arms around him and slid slowly down his body. Looking up, she laughed, "Now, you're the hard case."

He took her hands, "Come on, we can fix that." Soon the two were lost in their own private, intense world. Moria had left the bedroom door open.

Pounce crept into the room. He sat for a few moments, watching and listening. Then he jumped onto the dresser. Now, he could see Jackson's bare back, a perfect target. The cat waited patiently for the right moment. *How hard can this be?* Twitching the end of his tail and crouching to spring, he leapt over onto the 'enemy', digging his claws in for a firm grip.

Howling, Jackson fell over, grabbing for the cat. Pounce dug in tighter. Jackson snatched the startled offender by his fur and flung him to the floor. Pounce slammed against the dresser and lay still.

Moria shrieked, "Oh my God! Look what you've done!" Climbing over Jackson, she knelt on the floor beside the injured cat. Crying, she scooped the limp cat into her arms and laid him on the bed. Grabbing her robe and slipping into it, she sat down beside Pounce and stroked his head.

Reaching around to feel his back, Jackson yelled, "What about me? I'm bleeding!"

"You have killed my cat. Go. Just go!"

Their fragile relationship wavered in the early morning light. A flash of lightning illuminated Jackson's anger and Moria's distress. Thunder crashed and rain began to fall. Pounce opened his eyes.

Jackson laughed. "He's tougher that you think. Guess he still has eight more lives."

"Jackson, this is not funny." She hugged the cat to her. "You're lucky he didn't die. I've had Pounce since he was a tiny baby. He's precious to me. You wouldn't understand."

"Maybe not, but I'd hate for a cat to come between us."

Pounce jumped out of Moria's arms to the floor, and stalked away, his gray tail held high, as if nothing had happened.

Silence. Moria watched the cat leave then turned to Jackson. "I'm so sorry. I know you don't like cats but I don't think you understand. My animals are my life. They give me unconditional love and are a great comfort."

Jackson sat down beside Moria. "Look at me." She lifted tearful eyes to his face. "I do understand about unconditional love. I just haven't found it yet. Maybe I can be more patient with the cats and you can be more patient with me." He waited.

"You're right." She took a deep breath. "I know I have some trust issues, mainly because of my life with Fredrick." Running her hands through her disheveled hair, she said, "Enough of this. I'm going to be late for school if I don't hurry." She turned him around to look at his injuries. "Jeez, your back's a mess. Let's get in the shower."

Jackson winced, "Oh yeah, I bet a shower will really help."

Pounce sat in the doorway licking his paw and washing his satisfied face.

Jackson's shouts of pain pleased him. *Serves him right, he doesn't belong here.*

Moria drove to school in the pouring rain. Swishing windshield wipers seemed to say, 'choose me, choose me.' *Choose Jackson? Choose her animals and a life she could depend on?* She pulled into the parking lot. *We'll get it figured out.* Remembering Jackson's face at the window, she smiled. *I'll close the bedroom door next time.*

Moria went straight to Mr. Baldwin's office. He was on the phone, but with a wave of his hand motioned her to come in. She lowered her book bag to the floor and sat down. Looking out the window behind the principal's desk, she watched rain drip from the eves, blurring the images of the yellow buses and the children dressed in colorful rain gear. She began to bite her fingernails.

Mr. Baldwin put down the phone. "Good morning, Ms. Harris. I hope you had a restful weekend. I didn't. Mr. Dexter called me at home several times, pushing to have you fired." Mr. Baldwin looked at his notes. "We have a meeting set for Friday if it fits everyone's schedule. Maybe the Dexter's will have cooled off. In the meantime, you'll meet with our attorney, the school counselor and Dr. Brant, our county psychologist, to prepare your defense." The principal managed an encouraging smile and stood, signaling the end of the meeting. "Gather any documentation you think might be helpful."

Moria stood also. "Yes sir. Let me know when those other meetings will be." She picked up her book bag and hurried to class.

The children had already arrived. Maxine stood in the doorway between the two rooms to maintain order. "Thanks for watching them, Maxine. See you at lunch and I'll catch you up on the latest drama." Maxine gave a thumbs up and closed the door.

Moria took the attendance and noticed Michael was absent. Just before lunch he came in and handed her a late pass. She looked at his tear-streaked face.

"Michael, what's the matter?" She already knew.

"My Mom says you're mad at me because I caused trouble."

She longed to hug him. "Oh no. You didn't cause trouble. Remember, Michael. It's not your fault. I'm the one who caused the trouble."

He would not meet her eyes. "Yes ma'am," he mumbled and turned away.

At lunch Moria brought Maxine up to date on what Mr. Baldwin had said about the upcoming meetings.

Maxine frowned. "What a mess! I'll help you get some stuff together and we'll go over everything before your meetings. Why don't we work on it tomorrow night?"

Moria nodded. "I've saved a lot of his papers and my notes. We can start with that."

Maxine glanced out the window. "It's stopped raining. We can ride this afternoon and clear our heads."

Moria's face brightened. "That's what we need to do, clear our heads. Maybe Jackson and Jeremy can go. I feel better already."

After school the four riders met on the dirt road behind Moria's farm. The horses danced in place, snorting and blowing puffs of mist into the air. "Jeremy, why don't you lead?" Moria suggested. His sixteen-hand gray, Arctic Cat, pawed and twirled around, anxious to be away. Maxine followed on Star Shine, a feisty half-Arabian Palomino, then Jackson on Silver Dollar and last, Moria on Rainbow Chaser.

The horses took off at a big trot. Gravel and mud flew up behind them as Jeremy set a steady pace. In a couple of miles, he slowed down to a walk. The riders loosened their reins to let the horses stretch their necks. Jeremy turned to Moria. "How's your leg doing?"

"It's much better. Actually, riding's not too hard because I can brace my knee against the saddle. Ask me again after I've ridden fifty miles!"

By now they had reached the path leading up the mountain to the ridge trail. Maxine took the lead and Jeremy dropped back. As Jackson moved up, he looked over his shoulder at Moria and pointed toward Rainbow Chaser's neck. She smiled, remembering her 'physics lesson' and took hold of the neck strap.

Maxine and Star Shine led the group at a brisk pace, only walking to go around some deadfall on the path. Calling over her shoulder, "I'll bet Kam Bryson's going to be calling us to do some trail work soon."

Jackson asked, "Y'all volunteer to come out and clear the trails?"

"If we want to keep them open, we have to help maintain them. The rangers will take out the big trees. Stick around long enough and you too, can be a trailblazer."

"I was a Boy Scout," he laughed.

"Okay, Jackson, it's your lead." Maxine said, moving off the trail to let him pass.

Jackson and Silver Dollar brought the riders to the ridge trail and stopped. "Time for a pulse check." He winked at Moria. "Thought I'd forget didn't you?"

"Did you bring your stethoscope?"

"Oh, shit! Can I borrow yours?"

"Why don't you just leave your stethoscope in your enormous saddle bags? You've got to get rid of those things."

"Ha! You didn't think that when you fell in the river and I had everything I needed to save your cold, soaking wet butt."

"Nevertheless," Moria answered, defending her position, "You need to get rid of them. He doesn't need all that weight banging on his sides."

Maxine had finished checking Star Shine. "Pulse sixty-four," she announced, distracting the two riders from their argument.

Jeremy checked Arctic Cat. "Seventy."

"Rainbow's at sixty-eight. What about Silver Dollar?"

Jackson took the stethoscope from around his neck and handed it back to Moria. "He's at seventy, too. Now what is it they have to be?"

Jeremy laughed. "Sixty or sixty-four. Get it tattooed on your hand like I did."

Jackson looked at Maxine. "He did?"

"Yep, he did. Okay, folks, let's ride."

The riders mounted and walked their horses. Shadows lengthened in the woods, casting moving patterns across the trail. Jackson turned Silver Dollar toward the back of the line. When he passed Moria, he said under his breath, "Okay,

Missy, have at it. Time to rock and roll." She looked down the darkening path. *I can do this.*

Gathering up the reins, she took hold of the neck strap, and the horse began to trot. She remembered Rainbow Chaser's words in her dream. *Give me confidence with your hands and legs when I am afraid.*

"Move on out," Maxine called. Rainbow Chaser began to canter. Moria could hear the hoof beats of the others close behind. *If I fall...no, I'm not going to fall.* Now the horses were galloping. Moria knew the 'horse- getter' tree stump was just around the bend. The other riders backed off, giving her space, knowing Rainbow Chaser would spook. A fleeting thought crossed her mind. *Guess nobody wants to be in a horse wreck!*

Just then, the uprooted tree stump came into view. Rainbow spooked hard, jumping into the bushes. Moria lurched to one side, struggling to maintain her balance. Clutching the neck strap in one hand and the reins in the other, she righted herself and guided the horse back onto the trail.

"Nice save!" Jackson called.

"Wow!" Maxine said. "Want to stop for a minute?"

"No, I'm okay," Moria answered, pulling loose leaves from her hair. "We need to head for home." She patted Rainbow Chaser's neck and an unwelcome thought crossed her mind. *Is he too much horse for me?*

The riders continued to where the trail split. Dusk had fallen but the familiar trail was easy for the four to follow as their eyes adjusted to the fading light.

Jackson called out, "Hey, I've got a game for us! It's called Maggot." The riders stopped to listen, looking at each other. Moria said, "What did you say?"

"A game, Maggot. Here's the way it works. Close your eyes and ride. The first one to open them is a maggot."

Silence.

"So it's a trust game, trusting the horse? Have you ever done this?" Maxine asked.

"Sure. Lots of times when we had long night rides to round up cattle."

"Well, I'm not going in front. One scare per ride is enough for me!" Moria answered.

"So how do you know if someone looks?" Maxine questioned.

"Honor system. If you look, call out Maggot!"

"I'll go first," said Jeremy. Maxine followed, then Moria and last, Jackson. The horses walked on down the trail, oblivious of their riders' whims. Several minutes passed.

Suddenly, Rainbow Chaser stumbled. Moria's eyes flew open. "Maggot!" she called out, her call echoed by three other voices, instinct forcing them to look.

The game continued as the riders made their way down the mountain. They stopped where the trail met the dirt road. Jeremy commented, "We did get better. I guess it is a trust thing, just in case any of us ever ride a hundred miles."

Moria's eyes sparkled as she said, "Let's make a pact! A year from now we'll do a hundred mile ride."

"I'm in," answered Maxine.

"Me too," said Jeremy.

Jackson offered, "Maybe we can do our ride in Wyoming."

The rest of the way home they talked about the possibilities and logistics of riding out west and closer to home, how they would travel to the Ridge and Valley Ride.

"In the meantime," Moria reminded them, "That ride's coming up in two weeks." Soon they parted company, Maxine and Jeremy continuing to her farm, Moria and Jackson turning toward the pasture gate.

After they had finished the barn chores and started up the path to the house, Jackson hugged Moria and said, "Looks like you need an early night. If you walk any slower, I'll have to carry you!"

"Thanks. I need to make some notes about the 'incident' so I'll be prepared for the meeting. No scratching on my window,

I might have to sic the cats on you!" But she smiled, remembering his nocturnal visit.

Moria sat on the couch, staring into the fire. The cats curled up on each side of her, purring contentedly. Aloud she said, "I just can't do another thing tonight. I'll get up early in the morning."

Sleep eluded her. Like a thief in the night, the clock stole the minutes away. Pounce and Pandora took up their watchful positions on either side of the pillow, waiting for her to settle. Their soft purring finally brought the relief of sleep. Moria dreamed she was riding down the trail the riders had covered that afternoon, but she rode alone. A violent wind blew through the trees. Leaves and pine cones pelted her face. She let go of the neck strap and put her arm up to protect herself. Jackson's voice called out, "Trust! You must trust!" Rainbow Chaser spooked. The ground rushed up to meet her.

Moria awoke on the floor. The cats fled the room with frightened whines. For a long time she sat on the floor slumped against the bed. The cats crept back to the door and peered in. Moria had to laugh. "Come on, guys. Let's try this again." Exhausted, she finally fell sleep, with the yellow and gray guardians by her side.

During the remainder of the week, Moria and Maxine worked on the plan. "Just tell it like it happened," Maxine finally suggested, after the two had spent long hours trying to figure out the best approach for her defense.

Moria pushed her chair back and began to pace around in her small kitchen. "Want some more coffee?" she asked Maxine.

"No thanks. I need to go."

"Why don't you write a narrative account of what happened and bring it to school in the morning? We'll look at it one more time. Remember, when you're under pressure, it's easier to tell the truth!"

Moria walked Maxine to the door and gave her a heartfelt hug. "Thanks, more than I can say. I owe you one."

"Not in this category, I hope!"

Later that evening, Moria stared at the blank computer screen as if she could will the right words to appear. An hour later she had written her account of the events. She pushed the print button, This is 'the truth, the whole truth and nothing but the truth....The printer growled out her statement. And, sometimes the truth really is stranger than fiction.

On Friday after school, Moria and Maxine walked down the hall to the conference room. At the far end of the hall Mr. Baldwin ushered Mr. and Mrs. Dexter toward them.

Maxine whispered, "Doesn't this remind you of *High Noon*?"

Moria burst into nervous laughter. "Don't do this to me!"

Hang in there. Remember, we're going dancing at the Juniper Tree tonight."

For a moment, Moria imagined Jackson's protective arms around her as they swayed to one of her favorites, "Stand By Me." This comforting thought was interrupted as she walked through the conference room door, followed by Maxine, Mr. Baldwin and the Dexters. The attorneys, counselor, and psychologist were already seated.

Mr. Baldwin introduced everyone and spoke first. "It is my hope that this issue can be resolved today. Each of you will have an opportunity to express your concerns. Let us all remember that our goal, as educators, professionals, and parents, is to reach a solution that is in Michael's best interest." Mr. Baldwin peered over his glasses at the group.

Moria nodded in agreement. Out of the corner of her eye she saw Maxine do the same. The two attorneys, glancing at each other, nodded also. Mr. Dexter sat, staring straight ahead.

Mrs. Dexter blurted out, "Let's get on with this! We need to talk about Michael!"

Mr. Dexter jumped, as if pinched, and grabbed his wife's arm. She scowled and jerked away.

Disconcerted, Mr. Baldwin continued, "Yes, let's move on." He glanced at his notes. "Ms. Harris will present her version of the incident. I believe everyone has already received a copy of Ms. Harris's report." Mr. Baldwin nodded to Moria.

She stood, and in a clear voice, read from her paper, pausing from time to time to scan her audience. Mrs. Dexter frowned, leaning back with crossed arms.

Mr. Dexter stared straight ahead.

When she finished and sat down, Mr. Baldwin looked at the attorneys. "First we'll hear from Mr. Boyce, representing the Dexters."

The attorney rose and addressed the group, stating that Michael suffered 'grievous mental anguish' due to Ms. Harris's peculiar approach to teaching Math. He elaborated on the Dexter's statements that Michael suffered from sleepless nights, cried frequently, and threw up after each meal. Moria made a note that throwing up had not been observed at school and passed this information to her attorney.

"In conclusion," he stated, "On behalf of Michael Dexter's parents, I plan to file a suit against the Cherry Valley School System for one million dollars and against Ms. Harris for the same amount." No one seemed surprised.

Moria's attorney had discussed several possible outcomes, this one being expected. She remembered his words. "Your case is the least of the worst we've had to deal with in a long time. Don't worry. Just tell the truth. Don't forget, you've got a million dollar liability policy through the school system, and we're covered. Remember, we need to win, not just because of the money. We don't want parents thinking they can sue us and we'll roll over and pay. Unless, of course, it's a legitimate case."

The school attorney, Mr. Rice, stood to speak. Before he could begin, Mr. Dexter leapt to his feet, banging his hands on the table. Shocked faces turned to his, as Michael's father shouted, "Something is wrong with my boy!"

Mrs. Dexter's eyes blazed, "Shut up you fool!"

Moria smiled to herself. *Yes, and the truth shall set you free.*

Mr. Baldwin spoke quickly to Mr. Boyce. "Would you like a moment with your clients? You can step into the hallway."

They did so, and while the others waited, Mr. Baldwin announced to the group, "It's possible we'll not be able to continue today, or we will proceed without the Dexters."

Soon the trio returned to the room. Mrs. Dexter jerked her chair back and scraped it across the floor as she pulled up to the table. Mr. Dexter glared at her and seated himself. Mr. Boyce said, "We're ready to continue."

Mr. Baldwin said, "Let me remind everyone, we are here today to get everybody's story and begin to make a workable plan for Michael. This is not a trial. Now, we'll hear from Dr. Brant, our school psychologist."

Speaking without notes, Dr. Brant stood at ease to give his input. "Mr. and Mrs. Dexter, I haven't met Michael. I only know who he is from the request Ms. Harris turned in to have him evaluated." He glanced down at the papers before him. "I believe you all refused to sign a release to begin the process?" He raised questioning eyebrows and handed the paper to the parents. "Is this the paper you all signed, refusing to let the school move forward with the evaluation?"

Mr. Dexter looked at the paper. "Yes, it is. We think..."

Dr. Brant raised his hand. "We all have opinions at this point. The only way we can have definitive information is to go ahead with an evaluation of his abilities."

Mr. Boyce stood and spoke to the group. "The Dexter's do not wish to have Michael tested. I informed them of the law that says the success or failure of their son's education is now in their hands. They understand his education will continue with no modifications or tutoring. These interventions would only be provided after an evaluation."

Moria began to doodle in the margin of her notes. She had sat through many such meetings and knew the script by heart. Even with her job at stake, her mind drifted to Jackson and going dancing at the Juniper Tree. She looked at Maxine who gave her an encouraging smile.

Dr. Brant spoke again. "I would like to add a possibility to consider. I understand, Mr. and Mrs. Dexter, that you all are in the process of seeking a divorce."

A hostile look passed between the Dexter's. "If you only knew..." Mrs. Dexter began in a strident voice.

Mr. Dexter yelled, "Our private life is none of your business!"

"Nevertheless," Dr. Brant continued, as if the outburst had not occurred. "Family issues do affect a child's ability to concentrate. Many times in divorce cases the child feels he is to blame. Guilt and fear of abandonment can paralyze a child's mind. This can manifest itself in other ways. Sometimes guilt transfers into a fear of failure and can interfere with learning school subjects. Or even fear of falling when learning to ride a bike. Abandonment is a child's worst fear and imagined guilt can have far-reaching consequences."

And abandonment can be an adult's worst fear, thought Moria. *No wonder I'm afraid of falling off of Rainbow Chaser. Failure, abandonment, fear...it's all Fredrick's fault.*

Her thoughts were interrupted by Mr. Dexter's agitated voice. "We've heard enough!" He took Mrs. Dexter by the arm. "We're leaving. It was your job to teach our son, not traumatize him. If you can't teach him," he looked directly at Moria, "We will."

Mr. Boyce addressed the group. "I'll have a written communication to the school as soon as my clients have reached a decision" With those words, he and the Dexters left the room. Mr. Baldwin looked at his watch. "We've done all we can do for today. I'll let everyone know when we get a response."

Moria and Maxine walked in silence until they reached the parking lot. Moria let out a sigh. "You know, it's all Fredrick's fault that I have so many problems, being afraid of falling off the horse, afraid of getting into a relationship..." her voice trailed off. Maxine didn't respond.

Moria continued, "Don't you think it's his fault?"

Maxine grabbed Moria's arm and said, "Don't you ever watch Dr. Phil? He would be rolling his eyes for sure. What do you think he would say?"

Moria laughed. "You can't choose the circumstances, but you can choose how you react to them. Or something like that."

"Tattoo that on your hand. Come on. Let's go dancing. By the way, I think the fear of falling off a horse is a pretty healthy fear."

That night at the Juniper Tree the neighborhood horse people sat at their usual table. "Well, here comes our latest source of gossip," Jada announced in a loud voice as Moria and Jackson approached the table. *You can choose how you react,* flashed through Moria's mind before she answered, "Maybe I should clear up the gossip with a first-hand account?"

Laughter from around the table greeted her answer. The two sat down and ordered drinks. People took up their various conversations again and the band began to play.

Jada reached across the table for Jackson's hand, "Come on, cowboy, let's dance." Jackson raised a questioning eyebrow at Moria.

She winked and said, "Don't go too far away." After the first song, Jackson returned Jada to the table and to Richard. Moria watched as Jada smiled up at Jackson but his gaze was already searching Moria's face.

As Jackson sat down she said, "I don't think Richard even noticed she was gone. No wonder he can't keep up with her."

Jackson took Moria's hand. "I'm glad you're not the jealous type." He looked at her palm. "What's this written on your hand?" He peered closely in the dim light.

She smiled. "It says, my choice."

"So it's your choice not to be jealous?"

"Well...to a point! I'm learning."

Jackson put his arm around her. Moria leaned into him when she saw Jada's unsteady approach toward them.

Jada held out her hand to Jackson. "What about another dance?"

Moria began to rub the inside of Jackson's thigh.

He answered, "Maybe later." She frowned and walked away, cruising around the table for another likely prospect.

"Come on, Missy, I hear your favorite song." Jackson said, and they walked arm in arm to the dance floor.

She put her arms around his neck and head on his shoulder, taking a deep breath as they swayed to "Stand By Me." "Mmm, you smell good."

"It's all for you, baby."

"Pounce will be jealous."

"Serves him right," Jackson laughed.

Soon Maxine came in. Moria made a place for her as Maxine pulled up a chair. "Jeremy's off duty at nine. He had the first shift." Looking around she said, "I see Jada's is here. No doubt up to her old tricks."

Jackson smiled. "I guess she found out things have changed since I was here last time..." Taking Moria's hand, Jackson moved the two out onto the floor again and into the swarm of dancers.

Moria became lost in the moment. They danced close to the huge speakers set near the edge of the stage. Vibrating beats from the music engulfed her. Flashing strobe lights, the crowded dance floor, and a few beers had made her knees weak. She held tighter to Jackson and dug her fingernails into his back.

He tipped her face up to his. "Hey, you must be ready for bed!"

She looked startled. "What?"

"Your fingernails."

"Oh, sorry. I wasn't thinking."

"Maybe you were thinking," he grinned.

When they returned to the table, the conversation had turned to the upcoming endurance rides. Everyone had an opinion on the great debate: which was better, mountainous or flat rides?

Jackson listened for a while and then whispered to Moria, "Have you ever noticed endurance riders always have a strong opinion, whether it's right or wrong?"

"Well, you know what? We listen to each other and then do exactly what we meant to do in the first place! Seriously, we do learn from each other, the good and the bad.

Not to change the subject but I'm hungry. Who wants to go to the Waffle House?" The four left and were soon settled in a booth, ordering their food.

The waitress left and Moria said, "I've got to make a list so Jackson will know what he needs to do to get ready." She looked across the booth at Maxine and Jeremy. "You two have these trips down to a fine science."

Maxine laughed. "Jeremy had a list when he started traveling with me, didn't you, honey?"

"List? It was more like a manual!"

"At least we have everything we need when we get to the ride."

Moria looked at Jackson, "Well, I haven't even made the list yet. I'll try to keep it short," she laughed.

Soon their food arrived. The waitress placed the plates on the table and Maxine lifted her coffee mug, "A toast to the ride; may we all finish with sound horses!"

The four lifted their mugs. "Amen!"

Jackson raised his mug. "And may I not lose the list before I'm finished shopping!"

Jeremy cautioned, "You better hope everything's on it. Or, you'll be making a trip to Walmart from the ride site. Sometimes it's twenty or thirty miles."

"Why wouldn't Moria go?"

"Because she made the list. Isn't that perfect female logic?"

Maxine gave Jeremy a kick under the table.

"Hey, woman, you might make me lame, then you'd have to jog my horse at the vet check! But guess I won't see you since you'll be riding the fifty. I've decided to ride the Limited Distance with Jackson."

The cowboy frowned. "I don't need a babysitter. How hard can this be?"

The other three laughed and said in unison, "You'll see!"

Silence fell over the table for several minutes as they began to eat. Maxine set down her cup and said, "Why don't we talk about our ride strategies?"

Jeremy spoke up, "I think Arctic Cat needs some more miles on him before he does the longer distance. Jackson and I have done a lot of training together, so a short ride ought to work for both of us."

Jackson nodded in agreement, "Well, that probably is a good idea for Silver Dollar and me. I can keep you company on the trail...this time," he added. "What about you two?"

Moria answered, "We're going to ride slow." Maxine agreed.

"Umhum. That's what you always say," Jeremy laughed.

The waitress brought the check and the group left. In the parking lot they stopped to make a plan to ride Saturday afternoon. Moria and Jackson waved goodbye. "See you all tomorrow," she called.

When they reached Peace in the Valley Farm, the two decided to walk down to the barn and check on the horses. A full moon shone through the trees lighting the path. They walked arm and arm toward the barn and Moria thought back to New Year's Eve at the Juniper Tree when Jada spirited Jackson away.

She remembered later that same night...Maxine had walked her to the barn to wish the horses Happy New Year...How could she forget...sitting on the hay bale, laughing and crying hysterically and falling to the ground when she saw lights in Jackson's house. *Now I know what 'knee-walking drunk' really means! I wonder if Jada was there that night? Guess I'll never know.*

The horses blinked sleepy eyes and greeted the two with expectant whinnies. "Guess I'd better get them some treats," Moria said, opening the tack room door. Dixie and the puppies spilled out of the room, bouncing around with joyous barks.

"I'm taking four of the puppies to the ride for their new owners. I'll miss them. Why don't you bring Hero? This can be his first camping experience."

"I'll do that." He opened the door to the living quarters. "Smells good. Like cedar."

"That's what the cabinets are made of—makes the living quarters smell fresh. I keep the door to the stall area closed. That's where I put all the wet, dirty clothes and shoes, in the first stall. The other two are for the horses. A shower's in the back, too."

"Fancy. You even have a sink." Jackson commented as he stepped on the bench and climbed up onto the bed. He smiled. "Come on up."

"What?"

"We need to check it out, see if we'll both fit up here." He held out his hand. "Jackson, we can't both sleep in this trailer at the ride."

"Why? Because somebody might notice you're having a good time? These are not your school parents, need I remind you? And, where did you think I'd sleep, in the bed of the truck or with Maxine and Jeremy? Maxine doesn't seem to have a problem with the sleeping arrangements and she's a teacher. Is that what this is all about? The endurance riders don't give a rat's ass what your job is, from what I've observed."

Ignoring Jackson's opinion, Moria sighed. "I didn't think about where you'd sleep."

"Just so your trailer gets to the ride. Is that right?"

"Well, yes. I guess so."

Jackson took off his hat and ran his fingers through his hair. "Get up here, Missy." Moria climbed up without a word and sat beside him.

"Now we need to get something straight. I don't have to sleep with you. I can pull my own damn trailer. You can get yours there the best way you can."

"No!" she said in alarm.

"No, what? There's nobody else to pull your trailer?"

"No, I'm sorry I didn't think things through." She sniffed and wiped her eyes on the back of her hand.

Jackson looked out the window. Silence filled the trailer. Moria reached over and took his hand. "I'm sorry." Jackson turned back to look at her. Moria began to unbutton her shirt. "I think we'll both fit up here just fine."

"You minx!" he laughed, and he took her in his arms.

Chapter Eight

S aturday morning Moria woke early. A soft, pre-dawn light shone around the edges of the blinds. She pulled them up and looked out over the farm. Mist swirled in ragged streaks across the yard. Tiny drops of moisture clung to bushes and trees.

The silent, gray world waited for the first streaks of light to break over the horizon. She smiled. *I am happy and so, so lucky.*

Moria made coffee, took the afghan off the back of the couch and went out onto the porch. Sitting in the swing, wrapped in the afghan and sipping from the warm mug, she began to think about the coming day.

One more training ride and then, the first ride of the season. Wonder if Jackson will keep it together? Men! They're so competitive. I've got to remember to ride the plan, one ride at a time...pick up the pace at each ride until I'm racing. By September I should be riding in the top ten and ready for the championship in October.

Fear crept over her, a silent presence. *What if I fall?* Her thoughts were interrupted by Jackson's arrival. Jackson bounded up the steps. "Ready to ride?"

"Oh man, I didn't think you'd be up so early."

"Who did you think was going to feed the horses?"

She smiled, "Well, I'm thinking about it."

"Yeah? Why don't you get dressed while I feed?"

Jackson left for the barn and Moria hurried in for a quick shower. By the time she finished, Jackson had hooked up the trailer and was sitting in the kitchen leafing through the latest Endurance News magazine. He closed the magazine and took the cup of coffee she offered.

Moria joined him at the table. "We need to stop at McDonald's for breakfast," she announced.

He laughed, "I know that. Why would I think you might cook?"

"It just takes too much time. Besides, I hate to cook."

"Did you cook when you were married?"

"Yes, I had to. I didn't like it."

"Did Fredrick like your cooking?"

Moria pushed her chair back with force. "I don't want to talk about my past. Let's go."

As they climbed into the truck, Moria said, "We're going to do the lake loop today. You'll like it. It's really pretty, lots of stuff grows along the banks, cattails and exotic weeds."

"Now I've heard everything! Exotic weeds?"

"That's what we call them since we don't know what they are! I need to tell you ahead of time, this is a fast and spooky loop. Fish jump out of the water and critters lurk in the brush. Deer leap onto the road..." Her voice trailed off.

Jackson put his arm across the back seat. "Come over here."

She scooted over beside him and looked out the window without speaking.

"Just remember what Rainbow Chaser told you: 'I am afraid. Give me the courage with your hands and legs.'"

Moria nodded silently and laid her head on Jackson's shoulder.

Soon they pulled into the parking area. Maxine and Jeremy were already there, the horses tacked up. Before long, the four riders started down the trail, walking the horses for a few minutes to warm them up.

The sun cast gold streaks through the trees. Mist on the lake absorbed the golden glow, spilling it over onto the gently lapping waves. Moisture dripped from the overhanging branches, full with new spring leaves. Enjoying the smell of wet pine needles, sweat from the horses, and a whiff of Jackson's after shave, Moria thought, *It can't get any better than this*. Her heart kept rhythm with Rainbow Chaser's hoof beats.

An unbidden thought came to Moria on the light morning breeze. *What would I be doing now if Fredrick had stayed in my life?* A bright red cardinal flew across her path. *How ironic*—reminded that cardinals mate for life.

The riders reached a stretch of the lake which had a low bank and a rocky shoreline. The horses turned onto the beach to get a drink.

While the riders waited, Jackson commented, "Looks like good fishing."

Jeremy laughed. "Might be. I've never been here except on the back of a horse. Maybe I'll fish here someday...when I'm too old to ride."

Jackson laughed. "Well said."

The riders continued on, walking and trotting down the red clay road. As they reached the last quarter mile, Maxine said, "Let's sprint to the end." She looked at Moria. "You can do it."

The horses picked up a trot, faster, faster, then into a canter. Soon they were galloping. Dirt clods flew up in Moria's face. She remembered Maxine's favorite phrase, "No dirt if you're in front!" Rainbow ran faster still, passing the others. Moria shortened the reins, and took a better hold of the neck strap. She knew he would not stop, not now that he was in front.

Suddenly, a rabbit scampered across the trail. Rainbow took a mighty leap, landed, and raced on. She heard yells of encouragement from behind. "Oh my God, I stayed on!" she shouted.

The horses slowed around the last bend in the road, knowing that this is where the riders would dismount and they would walk in to cool down. Back at the trailers, while the horses and riders rested, they talked about Rainbow's incredible leap.

Reaching in the cooler, Moria pulled out a water bottle and handed some to the others. Uncapping the bottle and sinking down against the nearest tree she said, "My knees are still weak!" Deep in her heart, she knew she was very, very lucky.

After the horses rested, the riders loaded up and headed for home, grateful for a joyous ride and a safe day.

*   *   *

On Monday morning Moria walked up the steps to the school. An early March breeze ruffled her hair. *Sure hope this weather holds for the weekend.* She remembered the cold, rainy rides when she would say, "I'm never doing this again!" Moria laughed out loud, knowing she would go again, no matter the weather.

In the hallway Moria met Maxine coming out of the teacher's lounge. Maxine handed her a large stack of folders. "Here's your fund raiser stuff. One more thing to fool with that's not in our job description!"

Moria took the packets and said, "I agree. Who knows? I might not even have a job if this Michael thing gets any worse. I'm going to stop by Mr. Baldwin's office on the way to class. I'll let you know the latest."

Mr. Baldwin motioned Moria to a chair. "Well, Ms. Harris, it seems as though you have been spared a costly law suit and the loss of your job, as far as we know." Moria held her breath, clutching the sides of the chair.

"What happened?"

"Mr. Dexter came in earlier this morning and withdrew his son from school. He and Michael are moving to Texas. Mr. Dexter mentioned possibly home schooling him."

Moria breathed a sigh of relief "What about Mrs. Dexter?"

"Apparently, they're getting a divorce. I understand she's

giving him full custody. I think Mr. Dexter works from home. They'll have to figure it out. Now that Michael's not in our school, I don't think we'll hear further from them."

Moria slumped in her chair, suddenly realizing she hadn't really won at all. "I'm so sorry. I wasn't able to help Michael and caused trouble for you and the school. What will become of him?"

"This is not a new story as you know. Some parents move their kids frequently to avoid facing the possibility that there might be something wrong. The child never stays in one place long enough to get help. Nevertheless, please prepare Michael's records in case there is a request for them." Mr. Baldwin stood to dismiss Moria. "Unfortunately, this incident will have to go in your file. Let's hope you stick to approved teaching methods from now on. I will have some paperwork for you to sign in a few days. Ms. Harris, you're a good teacher. I don't want to lose you. Please consider your actions carefully from now on."

"Yes sir, I will. Thanks so much for your support." Moria shook Mr. Baldwin's hand and left for class.

When Moria reached the classroom she saw that Maxine had opened the divider and had the children busy with morning work. Maxine motioned Moria over to her desk and whispered, "Well, what's the latest?"

"Good news and bad news," Moria replied. "Mr. Dexter withdrew Michael from school and they're moving to Texas. Mr. Baldwin doesn't think the Dexter's will pursue a lawsuit...at least not now. They're getting a divorce so that will probably occupy them for a while. I wish I could have helped Michael."

Maxine smiled. "Don't take it so hard. We do help a lot of kids, but not all of them. You know parents enter the equation. Remember, we call parents 'the x-factor.'"

Moria gave a small, rueful laugh. "You always make me feel better. See you at lunch." She sighed and walked to her desk. *I just hope there are no more issues this year.* The rest of the school day flew by, uneventful, as most of them were.

After school Moria met Jackson at the barn. The late day sun slanted down on the horses, gray, chestnut, and spotted.

They raced to the barn, looking to be groomed and fed. Moria squinted her eyes to let the horses' varied colors and speed blur into a moving canvas.

Jackson came out of the tack room with the grooming kits and stopped to stare at Moria. Unaware that he was near, she continued to enjoy the horses' dash to the bam.

"Hey, are you okay?" Jackson dropped the grooming kits and took her by the arm. Moria laughed, "I just had a vision!"

Jackson raised his eyebrows. "Umhum, if you say so. Are you sure we need to groom the horses every night?"

"If we don't groom them pretty often, they're liable to get pasture rot from the dirt and rain."

"Guess ranch horses don't need to be pampered so much. Now, tell me what happened at school today."

Moria related Mr. Baldwin's information. "So, I hope this chapter in my life is over." Moria put Rainbow Chaser in the crossties and picked up a curry comb. "Well, let's get busy." Dust flew from the horse's coat as she scrubbed away.

Jackson agreed, took the filly Promise, and began to curry her. "Yeah, your school problem could interfere with our rides."

"Spoken like a true endurance rider," she laughed.

Moria watched Jackson's careful grooming of Promise. "You're doing a great job with her. I really appreciate it, since my time is so limited. And I've never dealt with young horses."

He scratched Promise behind the ears and then continued grooming. She's going to make someone a really nice horse. What are your plans for her?"

"I haven't thought about that yet. I've got to get these puppies to their new homes first. Don't forget to pack the puppies' stuff I forgot to put it on the list."

"Oh, the list. Guess I'd better get busy tomorrow."

Jackson and Moria fed and watered the horses, turned out the lights and headed toward the house. Putting his arm around her, Jackson asked, "Why don't we go down to the Diner for supper? Even if some of your school parents are there, it's still daylight. Is that okay?"

Moria smiled sideways at him. "Are you giving me a bad time?"

He pulled her close. "No, I just don't want you to go to bed hungry."

"Why? Because I'll be grouchy in bed?"

Jackson laughed. "A + for the teacher!"

The next morning Moria had a few minutes before leaving for school. *Just time to check my e-mails. Hmm, here's a message from Jessie.*

Dear Miss Moria,

How is Rainbow Chaser? Doris Weaver says my horse is a star.

I guess that must be good. She is making me work so hard! EVERY DAY we either do a training ride or she makes me do ring work. I just like the training rides. AND, I have to clean stalls at her barn. I hardly get to watch TV anymore!

She says I can qualify for the Championship Ride in October if I just do what she says. I would like that!

Got to go! I see Doris coming up the driveway.

Love, Jessie

Moria re-read the message in disbelief. *Jessie's coming to the October ride? Guess that means Doris Weaver's coming, too. Oh shit! I think I'll keep this to myself for a while. October's a long way off. I already have enough drama in my life!*

Packing for the endurance ride consumed the four friends during the following week. Moria met Jackson at the barn every afternoon. "We need to clean out the trailer. I haven't worked on the living quarters since the last ride in the fall." She opened the trailer door and stepped in.

Jackson came over to take a look. "What's the problem?"

Moria opened the cabinets, and assorted camping gear fell out onto the floor. She began to make a disorganized pile in the small floor space. "Order out of chaos. The American way," she mumbled, separating the paper plates and napkins from the Easy Boots and hoof picks.

Jackson backed away. "Why don't you work your magic in the trailer and I'll feed the horses?"

Head and shoulders into the lower cabinet, she answered, "Here are those new rolls of vet wrap! We can take that off the list." She continued talking to herself and throwing rugs, blankets, and towels outside.

When Jackson finished feeding, he came back to the trailer and leaned over Moria's shoulder to check her progress. Gathering up the items she had thrown outside to be washed, he said, "Come on Missy, time for a shower."

"You must be a mind reader," she laughed. "Getting ready for a ride gets me so excited!"

Pounce and Pandora watched with glittering eyes as the two people raced through the kitchen, dropping clothes along the way. Pounce followed close behind them, only to have the bathroom door slammed in his face. He growled and scratched on the door. Pandora hissed, *They're on to you. You'll never get another chance to show your anger.*

Oh no? Pounce ran back into the kitchen and peed on Jackson's boots. *See how he likes that!* In a flash of gray fur he leapt onto the back of the couch and waited for Jackson's return.

Later Moria and Jackson came back into the kitchen. Jackson wrinkled his nose and sniffed.

"Whew! Smells like cat pee." He glanced at Pounce, who gazed back, unblinking. "I think I know." Moria said as she spotted the boots and the surrounding yellow puddle. She picked up one of Jackson's scuffed, brown boots. A dark, wet stain spread across the leather. "Oh my God! I'm so sorry!" she said in horror, holding the boot at arm's length and hurrying to the door to throw it outside.

Jackson stared at the boot, and yelled, "Don't apologize for your neurotic cats. I'm telling you, these fur balls need to live outside!" With those words he wheeled back around...to face the empty couch where Pounce had sat. "I'm leaving."

Jackson snatched up his hat, shrugged into his coat and walked out, without a backward look.

As Jackson drove away, showering the porch with gravel, she took a deep breath, picked up the other boot and threw it outside with its unpleasant companion.

I guess Jackson went home in his sock feet. I hope he has some more boots! Reluctantly, she gathered cleaning supplies and began to scrub the splattered cat pee off the floor.

Early the next morning Moria went out to feed the horses. She checked the trailer one more time to be sure everything was loaded. *Jackson did do a good job. I just hope he comes to get the trailer. Otherwise, guess I'll pull it myself after school. This is why I don't like to depend on other people to help me.* She ended her thought with a slam of the tack room door.

The morning hours dragged by as Moria brought her weeks' efforts to a conclusion with tests, collecting late work, and writing a few notes to parents. Maxine looked in to say, "Jeremy called. He and Jackson are on the road." Moria breathed a sigh of relief. *Well, I guess Jackson's not too mad since he's trailering the horses. Maybe I'd better pick up a new pair of boots for him this afternoon.*

After school the two women hurried to their farms to change clothes, feed the remaining horses, leave instruction for their neighbor, Rodney, to feed while they were gone, then leave for the ride. Maxine came to pick Moria up and as they pulled out of the driveway, Moria said, "I need to stop by the tack store."

"We can't stop right now. We're late as it is. What do you need? I probably have it."

"I don't think so, I've got to get Jackson a new pair of boots."

"What? Is it his birthday?"

Moria began her tale of woe. Before she finished Maxine pulled into the store parking lot. Soon her friend returned with the boots. "Guess he can take them back if they're not right."

"I declare! He needs to be a grownup and get over being so jealous of the cats," Maxine answered. "Now let's talk about the ride."

Pavement ended and the road became gravel. Soon the camp came into view, a grassy valley between a river and the foothills of the Blue Ridge Mountains. Large oaks grew along the river's edge, a testament to nature's endurance throughout the years. "I'm glad this is not too far from home. We could even come up here and do conditioning rides," Maxine said, driving through the rows of trailers to their camping spot.

"Wow! Looks like this is going to be a big ride," Moria said, as they looked at the rigs and horses to see what the weekend competition would be. Guess some people want to ride the trail before the championship ride in October."

Maxine's cell phone rang. She put it on speaker to hear Jeremy say, "Hey, we see you. Come on down past the vendors and look to the left. What took you so long?"

Maxine laughed, "You'll see!"

Soon they parked beside Moria's trailer. Jeremy met them, giving Maxine a hug, and said, "What do you think?" waving his hand toward their camp.

The guys had positioned the trailers so that the awnings and doors to the living quarters would face each other. Chairs and tables were already set up under the awnings and the horses rested in their corrals under the trees.

Maxine and Jeremy walked back to check on the horses. Moria saw Jackson coming toward the truck. She tried to read his face. Looking at the boot box in Moria's lap he said, "Hmm, I see you bought me a present."

Handing him the box, she winked and said, "A gift from Pounce."

He smiled. "Remember, I asked you to be patient with me and the cats?"

She nodded. "Oh, Jackson, I am truly sorry for what happened."

"I know you are. They're just cats...who know how to push my buttons! Come on, let's see about these boots."

While Jackson tried them on, Moria walked over to the corrals and said to Jeremy, "Looks like you guys have it under control. Thanks. I know how much work it is to set up camp. Did Jackson help?"

Jeremy said, "Oh, yeah, he just doesn't want you to know how much. Next time, he can probably do it by himself."

Moria reached for Rainbow Chaser's halter. "Guess it's time to take them to the vet check."

"Done." Jeremy answered.

"What? They've already been?"

"Yep, their cards are on the table. They all passed. No problem."

Back at the trailers Jackson handed Moria the money for the puppies. "Their owners picked them up right away. You can see them when you have time, that is, if you want to?"

Moria forced a smile. "Thanks. Maybe I'll just let them get used to their new owners."

After dinner, the four friends picked up their packets and chairs and headed for the pavilion and ride meeting. Moria reminded Jackson, "Be sure you have the map. Getting lost is not an option!"

"Tell that to the trail goblins!" Maxine laughed.

As people settled down, the ride manager began by thanking the volunteers, district forest rangers, and the participants for their support. She announced the start times and reviewed other parameters for the event.

The head vet spoke briefly. Reminding everyone of the pulse criteria, sixty beats per minute for Limited Distance and sixty-four beats for fifty-mile riders.

Moria whispered to Jackson, "Did you write sixty on your hand?"

He turned his hand over and smiled.

The vet continued, cautioning the competitors about overheating the horses. "Metabolic problems can be caused by unusually high temperatures for March, coupled with the high humidity, and many horses still have their winter coats. If there are questions, I'll answer them after the meeting. Good luck! Have a safe ride."

The manager said, "Now, I'm going to turn the meeting over to our trail boss," as she went to the computer and a large-scale map flashed onto the screen.

The riders retrieved their copies from the packets, and with pens poised, they were ready to take notes. "Even if you've ridden here before," the trail boss said, "Sometimes the plan has to be changed, so pay attention." He explained the re-route due to a washout and another change because they could no longer cross a stretch of private land. "Most important, this year, the LD and fifty mile trails will intersect. Watch closely for directions, which will be posted on Styrofoam plates where needed. Remember, the flagging will always be on the right, except for the left turns. The meeting is over, but I am available for questions and there will be a first time riders meeting right now."

Jackson looked at Moria with raised eyebrows. "Should I go?"

She laughed, "Looks like you want to make a good impression." *For a change!* "Absolutely, go ahead. It won't take long. We're going to walk the horses to stretch their legs. I'll bring Silver Dollar. Meet us in the field near the river. See you in a few minutes."

Quite a few people brought their horses out for a walk. Most of them knew each other and chatted about the rides they'd been to recently, talked about whose horses were lame, and caught up on the latest gossip.

One of the women who lived in a neighboring state came over to Moria. "Hey, I hear you latched onto a cowboy from Wyoming! Tell me about him!"

"Well, I didn't exactly latch onto him." Inwardly, she cringed. *What to say?*

"Short version. He helped me with the horses earlier this year when I had the ski accident. Now he's at his first endurance ride." Moria gestured to Silver Dollar, who grazed nearby with Rainbow Chaser. "He's got a really nice horse." Through the twilight she could see Jackson coming her way. The horses noticed his approach and pulled Moria in that direction.

"Got to go! Have a good ride!" she said, observing the lady's speculative look. *Might as well get used to this. Maybe by the next ride, we'll be old news. But tonight I can imagine the whole camp watching at us at bedtime! Or not. Maybe Jackson's right—no one really cares.*

Moria handed Silver's lead rope to Jackson. "How was the meeting?"

He gave her a hug. "Didn't hear anything new. Gold star for my teacher!"

Upon returning to camp, the riders checked the tack and the small packs which contained such things as Kleenex, ChapStick, food bars, and electrolytes for the horses, the map, and vet card. Attached to the saddle were Easy Boots to protect the horses' hooves in case of a lost shoe, water bottles, sponges to use for cooling, and rain gear. Moria noticed that Jackson still had the large saddlebags attached to Silver Dollar's saddle. *He's going to have to learn the hard way; too much weight for his horse to carry.*

"The wind's picked up," said Jeremy. "We'd better let the awnings down."

"And be sure we have our rain jackets," added Maxine. The four said goodnight and Maxine and Jeremy went to their trailer.

Jackson looked at Moria. "Well? How long do we have to wait till we can go to bed?" He began to rub the back of her neck and run his hands through her hair.

"Umm...Maybe now?" she laughed, taking his hand and nibbling his fingers. Soon they were up in the bed, snug under the quilts.

Moria rolled over on her stomach to look out the window. One by one lights went out at the campsites. An invisible cloud of anxiety hovered over the camp, but the random movements of the horses, the lonely call of an owl, and wind blowing through the pines were comforting, familiar sounds. Jackson lay still. Moria knew he understood her need to know that all was well.

Breaking the silence, he moved over to the window to be near her. "I know how you feel. When we went on long cattle drives, we posted a night guard, but none of us slept soundly anyway. There was always the chance of a stampede."

"Pray to God there is never a stampede in an endurance camp. I've seen horses running wild, dragging corrals with them, injured horses and riders and camp sites being destroyed. I see you all put the corrals against the tree line. That helps."

Jackson closed the window and let the curtain down. "Come here sweetie. No more about chaos with the horses. I know a good cure for the jitters," he whispered.

She came into his arms. The camp and its nosey occupants became a distant thought. Snuggling close, she knew that Jackson's cure for the jitters would be the perfect end to her day.

Too soon, a voice on the loud speaker woke the camp. The Lone Ranger's theme music blared out over the speakers and the ride manager announced, "Rise and shine, you fearless riders! Coffee's ready at the pavilion."

Jackson groaned and rolled over. Moria laughed. "Just wait until tonight. You've never known pain until you've finished your first endurance ride!"

Jackson sat up abruptly, bumping his head on the low ceiling. "Oh, man! We didn't get up early to feed the horses!"

Moria replied, "Done. Come on, let's go get some coffee and donuts."

"Wow! I must be a really sound sleeper!"

"Don't worry, mister, I won't let you off the hook next time," she laughed.

Thick, gray clouds piled on the eastern horizon, burying the sunrise, as the riders prepared to leave camp. Wind blew in gusts, spooking the horses, with dry leaves scattered across the trail.

Moria took a tight grip on the neck strap but tried to relax her body so Rainbow Chaser would not sense her pounding heart. The horses danced and twirled in anticipation. The timer announced, "The trail is open! Have a good ride."

Moria and Maxine placed themselves in the middle of the pack behind some riders they knew would set a steady pace. Ahead, they could see the front-runners galloping in a frenzied pack down the wide dirt road. Most of the riders knew the trail would soon turn into a single-track through a pine thicket. The racers needed to position themselves so as not to be stuck behind slow riders and lose precious time.

Rainbow Chaser and Star Shine trotted side-by-side, snorting to each other in mysterious animal communication.

Their manes and tails streamed out in the wind and white froth blew back in their riders' faces.

The three riders directly in front of them slowed down. Maxine looked at Moria who nodded in silent understanding. Maxine called, "Heads up! Passing on the left!" The slow riders spread out, blocked the trail, bolted forward, and then galloped away.

"Well, shit!" Maxine urged Star Shine into a canter. "Next time we catch up, let's do Plan B, blow by them and keep on going. The turn into the woods is not far ahead. We don't want to get behind those dorks again!"

Trees along the roadside blurred in Moria's vision. The horses welcomed a chance to do what they did best. Run!

Moria called to Maxine, "I think we've caught up with the dorks. Let's stay behind them through the pines.

Maxine yelled over her shoulder, "Watch out! You want to lead through here? I need a buffer in front of this lady, so I don't get my knees busted!"

Moria took the lead. No one appeared behind them. She took a moment to enjoy the peace and beauty of the pine forest as the horses trotted cautiously along the twisting trail, picking their way over roots and rocks. Reaching for one of her water bottles, she drank, and then poured the rest on Rainbow's neck.

Moria said, "We're almost to the jeep trail. I think the ride is getting pretty spread out."

With a questioning look at Maxine, Moria said, "Plan B?"

"Got'cha," Maxine replied, gathering up her reins.

The two moved on without speaking and approached the group at a slow trot, staying a comfortable distance behind. One of the riders looked back, as if to say, "You're not getting by this time, either!" But Maxine smiled and said, "How's your ride today?" just as the riders came out of the pine woods and onto the jeep trail. The startled miscreants glanced back at the two women. Moria moved to the left and Maxine to the right. They increased the trot and when they were close behind, surged by on each side, calling, "Heads up!" as they passed the surprised riders. Instead of galloping away, they held the two horses to a ground-eating trot. The other riders followed, but did not try to pass, and soon dropped back to their slow pace.

Leaving the conflict behind, they followed the jeep trail to a wide, grassy, river valley. Red flagging turned the riders on to a path near the river. Packed dirt, with no roots or rocks, invited the horses to canter.

Moria noticed the clouds hung in low, dark, layers and wind swayed the tall grasses back and forth. *Dear God, please don't let it rain before the ride is over!* A shiver brushed her skin, an unseen presence warning of things to come.

As they approached a grove of trees, Maxine said, "Here's where we can get down to the river—so the map says."

The bank sloped down to a shallow spot where rocks created safe footing. The horses took a few sips of water, too nervous to drink much. Suddenly, they raised their heads and ears up, looking back the way they had come.

Maxine frowned. "Might be our friends. Let's go. We just have a few more miles back to camp and the vet check. Wonder how Jeremy and Jackson are doing?"

Moria untangled Rainbow's mane from the reins and stroked his neck. "They're probably there by now. Their first loop was short. I hope Jackson remembers to take good care of Silver before he sits down to have a beer!"

Maxine laughed, "Don't worry! Jeremy won't let that happen."

Just then. Star Shine tripped. Moria, who was riding behind, said, "Hold up! She's pulled her shoe."

"Well, I'll be damned! Guess I'd better put on her Easy Boot. We still have a few miles to go." Maxine dismounted and proceeded to secure the boot on her horse's hoof.

In the distance, they could hear horses approaching. Some riders they had not seen before rode up and stopped. "Can we help?" one of them asked.

Maxine looked up as she lifted her horse's hoof to clean it and secure the Easy Boot. "Thanks. Just wait a minute, if you don't mind, so she'll be still...and I can get this thing on." With a final tug Maxine fastened the boot latch. "Y'all go on." Then saying to Moria, "Her foot's pretty torn up, we might not even get a shoe back on her and she's cut her pastern, too."

Moria frowned. "Maybe I'd better stay with you."

"Oh, please! No need for you to get slowed down."

"Well, if you're sure..."

"I'm sure! Go!"

Moria joined the group but looked back reluctantly. Maxine and Star Shine grew smaller in the distance. Each rider took turns leading and set a steady pace. Soon they reached camp and her companions waved goodbye. Moria called to them, "Have a good rest of your ride. See you later!"

Rainbow made a successful trip through the vet check and then stood quietly at the trailer, eating beet pulp mixed with a little grain and apples. Moria looked around camp for someone who might know Jackson's status in the ride. The timer! She'll know!

"Hey, Nancy. I need to check on my buddy, Jackson. Do you know how he's doing?"

"Moria, good to see you." Nancy, the timer, looked at her record sheet to see if Jackson had vetted through and left. "Yeah, he went out about thirty minutes ago. Guess he was all right. He and Jeremy rode out together. Where's Maxine?"

Moria told of the shoe dilemma. "I have a feeling she won't be going back out."

"She'll not be the only one. Some people have decided to stop because of the weather report. The storm's supposed to be really bad." With those words, Nancy grabbed her papers as they ruffled in the wind.

Moria returned to the trailer to tack up, thinking about the timer's warning. Maxine approached, leading Star. "Guess I'm out for a couple of rides," she said, biting her lip. "The farrier trimmed her foot as much as he could. It's going to have to grow out before she can be re-shod."

"Oh, man, I hate that!" Moria answered, reaching for Rainbow's bridle. Shaking his head impatiently, the horse knew it was time to go.

"It's not going to be the same without us riding together. Actually, I was kind of thinking of not going back out. A storm's coming. Some people have already pulled."

"Don't forget your raincoat," Maxine said, as if Moria had not spoken.

"You think I should go on?"

"Does a duck have wings?"

"Yeah, water wings!" Moria laughed as she mounted and rode over to stand by Nancy, waiting for time to leave.

The chestnut gelding pawed the ground and whinnied to the horses who were trotting out of camp. Moria stroked his neck. "Take it easy, mister. We'll catch up."

"Time to go!" Nancy announced.

Dust devils blew through the camp, catching loose trash and swirling it upward. A plastic bag flew against Rainbow's head. He whirled, hitting Moria in the face. She grabbed his mane and leaned forward to reach the bag. Blood poured from her nose.

A nearby crew person ran over to the horse. Taking hold of Rainbow's bridle, he pulled the bag away and helped Moria to the ground.

Reeling from the blow, she mumbled, "I'm so sorry...I'm bleeding all over everything!"

He laughed, "Wouldn't be the first time. Shit happens...or blood. Where's your trailer?" Just then, she saw Maxine running toward her.

"Looks like help is on the way. Thanks again," Moria said, pinching her nose tightly closed.

Maxine took the horse's reins in one hand and Moria's arm in the other. "Oh my God! I knew you didn't want to go back out, but this is pretty extreme. Come on, let's get you cleaned up."

"I'm going back out?"

"Count on it."

Soon Moria and Rainbow were on the trail again. Breathing through her mouth, Moria tried not to dislodge the packing in her nose. *I know Maxine's my friend...but I don't have a good feeling about this!*

Miles flew by and the wind continued to blow in ragged gusts. Clouds hovered low on the mountain as the horse and rider team began to climb the twisting, rocky trail. Rainbow Chaser seemed to sense the urgency of their mission, digging into the rough terrain and surging upward to the ridge.

Upon reaching the top of the mountain, the two stopped to breathe. Moria checked the packing in her nose, took a drink of water, and moved on. She shivered, looking across the valley at the towering clouds.

With seeming evil intent, the clouds boiled over the far ridge, headed in her direction. I have made a really bad mistake. *Screw Maxine! I've got to get off this ridge, fast!*

"Come on, let's go!" she called to the horse. Fear of racing became eclipsed by the fear of lightning strikes on the ridge.

She squeezed Rainbow with her legs and leaned forward. Her mount galloped along the trail in ever-lengthening strides. Moria took a fierce grip on his mane and prayed that they could cover the remaining mile on the ridge and start down the mountain before the storm broke.

Suddenly, the horse skidded to a stop where the trail met the road. Moria flew up on his neck, but held on. Rainbow's ears pricked forward.

He looked down the trail and whinnied to his friends, Jackson and Silver Dollar.

Moria slid off the horse in disbelief "Jackson! What are you doing here? You're on the fifty-mile trail!"

Jackson stared at Moria. "I'm lost as hell. Which way is camp?"

"Where's Jeremy?"

"Never mind him; we've got to get to lower ground!"

A few drops of rain splattered through the trees. Moria and Jackson reached for their rain gear.

Jackson began to laugh. "You think that Barbie jacket is going to keep you dry?" He reached into his saddlebag. "Here's your poncho, again." He mimicked in a Southern drawl, "Oh, Jackson, thank you so much for my fleecy yellow poncho. What would I do without your enormous saddlebags?"

Just then, a terrific bolt of lightning flashed through the sky, splitting a pine tree and setting it afire. The horses crouched and jerked back on the reins.

"Come on, Missy. We're out'a here." With those words, Jackson left the trail, followed by Moria. Leading the horses, they broke through underbrush and went deep into the ravine. About halfway down, Jackson spotted a rock ledge overhang.

Rain poured down in blinding sheets. They scrambled under the rock ledge and huddled together, still holding the horses' reins. Their mounts stood outside the overhang, flinching at each crash of thunder. Bolts of lightning pierced through the clouds like heat-seeking missiles.

The storm roared overhead. Trees fell into the ravine. "We'll never get out!" Moria screamed.

Jackson grabbed Moria's shoulders and shook her. "Shut up! You're making things worse!"

Moria answered by putting her head against her knees, which were drawn up under her chin. "You're right. Now tell me where Jeremy is."

"I wanted to move on and Jeremy didn't. So, I went on ahead."

"And here you are," Moria finished. They sat without talking. A silver curtain of rain sluiced over the edge of the rock shelter. *This could be so romantic if I wasn't scared witless.* She reached for Jackson's hand and held it tightly.

Looking hopeful, he pulled her close. "Maybe we could have a little fun to pass the time?"

"In here? You've got to be kidding!" Then she laughed. "Tell you what? I'll give you a rain check. How's that?"

"Never hurts to ask," then his kiss electrified her world.

Wind tormented the forest. Another tree fell. Moria buried her face against Jackson's shoulder. Lightning flashed, illuminating the soaked and frightened horses. The whites of their eyes shone vivid in that one bright moment.

In a last gust of wind, the storm passed. Snuffling breaths of the horses and water dripping from the trees were the only sounds to greet the riders as they crawled from their shelter.

Moria looked at the devastation. *This must be what it's like to be the last people on earth.* Just then a jet passed overhead. Well, maybe not!

Jackson handed her Silver's reins. "You okay?" She nodded. He gave her a reassuring hug. "I'm going up to the road and see what we need to do.

Moria stroked the horses' necks to comfort them and herself, as she waited for Jackson's return. Soon she heard his scrambling, sliding approach over mud and rocks.

"Looks like we can make it out, but we're going have a lot of cutting to do." He reached for Silver's reins and started back up the steep slope.

Moria and Rainbow followed. "We should go back the way I came. We're just a few miles from camp. No use trying to finish the ride. We've lost too much time and who knows what's happened to the rest of the trail." She reached in her waterproof pack for the map. "Where's your map?"

"Well, I dropped it in the creek...but I have my camping saw! Where's your saw, Missy? Tucked in your bra?" he laughed, eyeing the small day pack tied to the back of her saddle.

She smiled, "You already know what's tucked in my bra. Or do you need a refresher course?" For once, Jackson was speechless.

The riders and horses climbed out of the ravine and pushed through the underbrush onto a small clear spot in the road. They stood for a minute assessing the damage. Fallen trees blocked the road in both directions.

"Well, let's get to work," Moria said. "Why don't you go ahead with the saw and I'll follow and lead the horses. If we get in a tough spot, I can tie them up and help."

"With what? Your teeth?"

Exasperated, Moria shot back, "Never mind! Just get started!"

The sky brightened and the clouds scurried away with the wind. The two riders trudged on, making slow progress.

Jackson looked over his shoulder. "Did you say something?"

She spoke louder, "Remember this Rossetti poem?"

> "Who has seen the wind?
> Neither you nor I,
> But when the trees bow down their heads.
> The wind is passing by."

Jackson laughed. Or, "When the trees fall to the ground. There's a monstrous crashing sound."

The horses snorted to each other. Moria laughed, "Guess they like your version better!"

Exhausted and soaking wet, the riders pushed around the obstacles where they could, waded into ditches and detoured off the road when the fallen trees were too massive to cut with a small saw. Finally, the way opened up, with corn fields on both sides. "Free at last! Free at last!" Jackson shouted. "Let's go!" The two mounted their horses and trotted away down the road.

"I have a bad feeling about this," Moria called to Jackson as they rounded the last turn into camp.

The riders dismounted and led the horses into chaos. Awnings had flipped over the tops of the trailers. Chairs and other items had blown helter-skelter through the camp. Most of the corrals were down and loose horses were being captured before they caused damage or were injured.

By evening, order was restored and everyone gathered around the fire for dinner and the awards. The ride manager, harried and bedraggled, looked over the group and said, "Thanks to all of you for your help today. I checked with 'the powers that be' and I think what will happen for those of you who did not finish because the trail was blocked—you will get credit for the miles you did, as close as we can determine.

I know many of you did not finish the ride and I take that personally, even though it was out of my hands." People laughed appreciatively. She continued, "I'll start with the hardship awards since there were so many of you in that category. You will receive a free entry to the ride next year."

The group cheered and Jackson whispered to Moria, "Maybe you'll be in Wyoming this time next year."

"Or maybe you'll be here to use your free ride entry." *And I'll never have to move to Wyoming.*

Later, Moria, Jackson, Jeremy, and Maxine sat around their own campfire, enjoying a last beer. The horses had been checked for injuries, cleaned up, and fed.

Jackson looked over at Jeremy and winked. "Guess I'd better stay with my sponsor next time."

Jeremy smiled and said, "Shit happens, man. There's always another ride."

"Well, look who's coming our way. No doubt to gloat about her win," Maxine said, as Jada came striding toward them.

"Hi, ya'll! What a great way for me to start the season—with a win!"

Maxine answered, "I heard your horse is being treated for colic. You must have pushed him through the vet check in a hurry," A sly smile flitted across Jada's face. "I waited for that new vet to check him. He hardly listened for gut sounds!"

Maxine rolled her eyes in disgust. "Someday you're going to kill your horse."

"Oh, I don't think so. He's a tough boy!"

Uninvited, Jada reached in Moria's cooler for a beer. Pulling a stool close to Jackson, she laid a hand on his thigh, and looking into his eyes said, "Hear you had a rough time today. You shoulda stuck with me! Maybe we could do some more training together."

Jackson kicked a log in the fire and sparks spiraled into the night. "You know, Jada, one of these days I'm going to dust your ass!"

She began to laugh and lurched sideways as she stood. "Sounds like fun! See you on the trail, cowboy," and staggered away into the night.

Jeremy commented, "What a piece of work!"

"'Nough said," Maxine replied. "I'm ready for bed."

Soon Moria and Jackson were in the trailer snuggled under the comforters. Jackson groaned with aching muscles and raw spots on his legs. "You poor baby," Moria teased, "Let me make you better! And, don't let that old Jada suck you into her bad behaviors."

"Yes ma'am, I'll remember that. Now, fix me, honey. I'm hurtin.' "

Later, Jackson slept soundly but Moria dozed, rousing every so often to look out the window and check on the horses. Finally, assured that the horses showed no signs of colic or other distress, she fell asleep.

Suddenly, a loud banging on the door awakened her with a start. Someone called, "Jackson, help me! I'm lost and can't find my trailer! I've been out here for hours!"

Jada! How could I miss that whining voice?

"Jackson! Wake up! Your 'friend' is here."

He sat up abruptly. "Huh? What?"

Moria pushed him with her foot. "Go help her so she'll shut up before she wakes the whole camp." Looking out the window, she could see a few trailer lights coming on.

Jada wailed, "Help me! Help me!"

"Hurry, Jackson. Get her out of here!" Moria said, giving him another push.

"Okay, okay, I'm going," he groused, pulling on his jeans.

Jackson led Jada toward her trailer, their muffled voices fading away.

Dozing again, Moria awakened to realize Jackson had been gone a long time.

Not able to go back to sleep, she left the trailer and headed into the dark with her flashlight. When she reached Jada's trailer, she could hear voices and sobbing. Moria stopped in the shadows.

Jada and Jackson stood in the circle of lantern light facing each other. Jackson's hands were on her shoulders, seeming to hold her away. Moria waited.

Jada wailed, "Oh Jackson! Please come in for just for a few minutes. Moria won't know."

"Yes. I will," Moria said, stepping into the light. She watched Jackson's face and smiled at his look of surprise. "Move over, mister. I can handle this."

Jackson stepped back, raising his hands in surrender. "My pleasure. Have at it!"

Jada wheeled around in disbelief. "You need to leave!" she screeched at Moria.

"No, you need to go to bed." With those words, Moria grabbed hold of Jada's jacket sleeve and jerked the trailer door open with the other hand. "I can't believe you're a first responder! You're the one who needs help!"

"Mind your own business!" Jada yelled. By now, lights were coming on around the camp, signals of annoyance.

"Jackson is my business!" Moria snapped back as she shoved Jada into the trailer and slammed the door. Hearing a thud, she peeked in to see the woman sprawled on the floor, passed out. "Have a good night!" she muttered.

Turning toward Jackson, she said, "Ready for bed? Maybe I need fixn' this time."

He laughed, "Wow! Guess I'd better mind my business too!"

They walked across the campground hand-in-hand as the area darkened in their wake. Moria watched the lights go off. "So much for being discreet!"

Jackson grumbled. "I was just about to put her in the trailer when you showed up."

"Hey, all's well that ends well...or whatever that saying is," she answered. "Come on, walk faster! Before we know it, the sun will be up." And, sure enough, morning came too soon.

Moria pulled the covers over her head as the first streaks of pale light became dawn, and lavender clouds edged with gold lay on the horizon. She rolled over, to find Jackson's side of the bed empty. *Where is that rascal? Surely not*....Just then she looked out the window to see her cowboy giving the horses their morning feed.

Climbing down stiffly from the bed, Moria pulled on her sweat pants, boots, and shirt. Opening the trailer door, she peered out to see Maxine and Jeremy sitting under the awning drinking coffee.

"Oh my God! That smells so good!"

Jackson limped around the corner of the trailer and helped her down. "You look like you've been rode hard and put up wet," he said, getting them some coffee off the cook stove.

She laughed, "You should know!"

Maxine interrupted, "Changing the subject for a minute, guess ya'll got Jada put to bed. We heard the commotion, saw Jada and Jackson leave and ya'll come back together, so we figured everything was alright. Was it?"

Moria winked at Maxine. "For the moment. No telling what tricks she has up her sleeve. What a train wreck! Let's pack up and head for the Cracker Barrel. I'm craving some biscuits and gravy." No one argued with this and soon they were driving away, waving to those they knew.

One guy called to Moria, "Good job!" Smiling, she returned the victory sign.

"Guess the word's out about our 'threesome'," she grinned, scooting close to Jackson. *Enjoy the moment.*

By the time the riders reached the Cracker Barrel people were waiting to be seated. Moria laughed as they walked across the parking lot, "Guess these customers don't know there's a bad economy!"

Jeremy opened the door for them, saying, "As long as biscuits and gravy are on the menu, they will come!"

Soon they were on the road again. The warmth of the sun through the windows crept over Moria. She leaned against Jackson and fell asleep.

The dreams began—blurred at first, then coming into focus. Trees and underbrush tangled with heavy vines surrounded Moria and Rainbow Chaser.

The horse thrashed from side to side, trying to free himself from the entrapment. Falling, falling, the two plunged onto sharp rocks hidden under the leaves. A voice called, "I can save you! Come to Wyoming!" Moria woke with a start. "No!" she cried.

Jackson swerved the trailer and the horses scrambled for their footing. "What's the matter?" he asked with concern. "Have a bad dream?"

"How did you know?" she asked, rubbing her eyes, wiping the drool from her cheek and reaching for a water bottle.

"You were twitching like a dog, you know, when they dream?"

Moria laughed, "Well, I'm okay. Want me to drive for a while?"

"No, I'm good for the rest of the trip. By the way, I haven't had a chance to tell you, I'm going home this week to do some things for the business. Jeremy's going with me. He's got some time off. Maybe when school's out you and Maxine can come for a visit."

Moria's heart pounded. She hesitated, "Sounds like fun!" *Not!* "We'll see what summer brings. We won't have many rides then because it's so hot. This might be a good time to check out your turf." Moria looked sideways at Jackson and noticed his satisfied smile. *Uh Oh! Looks like I've already given an inch.*

Jackson reached for Moria's hand and nibbled at her fingers, saying, "We ought to go to the Juniper Tree next weekend. Jeremy and I should be back on Friday."

"Sounds good," she answered.

Chapter Nine

*M*oria breathed a sigh of relief to be home. They pulled into Peace in the Valley Farm, and she said, "Seems like we've been gone a week. Hope the animals are alright." Just then they heard the dogs' welcome barks and whinnies from Phoenix and Promise. She and Jackson unloaded the horses and turned them out to pasture. Leaning on the fence to watch Rainbow Chaser and Silver Dollar gallop away, Moria said, "You know, the best part of this whole adventure is knowing we came home with two sound horses."

"So this is exception, not the norm?" Jackson asked as he finished unhooking the trailer then walked over to lean on the fence beside her.

"No. For me it is the norm now, but I have driven home from rides calling the vet to meet me at the barn because I'd made some bad choices and got carried away—running too hard."

"You? Out of control?" he laughed. "I can't believe it!

"Enough," she laughed back at him. "Let's feed the horses and go down to The Diner for supper."

"Sounds good. Does the invitation extend to after?"

"Wouldn't miss it for the world," she smiled, hooking her arm through his.

Later, in Moria's bedroom the two lovers shed their clothes and headed for the shower. As steaming water rained down upon them, Moria reached for the shampoo. Jackson held her as she leaned back into the spray and began to wash her hair.

"Oops, this ain't gona' work," Jackson laughed, as they slid down into the tub among shampoo bubbles and cascading water.

Pounce, lurking in the bedroom, heard Moria's excited cry, "Maybe this is the best part of our trip!"

I will get him again! Stupid fool didn't pick up his clothes! The cat leapt on Jackson's pile of clothes and peed with glee.

Jackson erupted in rage as he stepped out of the bathroom and the strong smell of cat urine wafted about the bedroom. "That damn cat! I'm gonna' clean his plow once and for all," he yelled, jumping over the ruined clothes and racing through the house in search of Pounce.

"Wait! Don't hurt him!" Moria screamed. When she reached the sitting room, she saw Jackson's bare bottom up-ended, as he searched under the couch. Moria covered her mouth to quiet her laughter.

Jackson turned around, his face red from exertion "What? You think this is funny? Get my keys and go bring me some clothes!"

As Moria opened the door to step outside, she looked back to see Jackson reaching for the TV remote and Pounce crouched on the stairs to the loft.

Dear God, please don't let him kill my cat! she prayed hastily, while running to the truck.

By the time Moria returned, Jackson had calmed down. While he dressed, Moria sat on the couch beside him. "Honey, I'm so..."

"Don't even go there," he replied. "Somehow, I've got to be smarter than a cat!" Then he noticed Pounce on the steps, Giving him the finger, Jackson growled, "I'll get you yet, you miserable fur ball!"

Unconcerned, cat lifted his paw and spread his claws, as if to say, "Same to you, buddy!"

The next morning at school Moria and Maxine had time for coffee before the children arrived. Moria told Maxine about Pounce's misadventure and ended by saying, "Guess I'll go shopping again."

"Well, you'll have time this week, with Jackson gone. Anything else going on?"

Walking over to the trash to throw her cup away, Moria said, "This is a good time to go to the ranger station and look at the new trail maps. Kam said to drop by anytime. Want to go? "

"Wish I could. I've got tons to do at home since Jeremy's gone, too. Let me know what you think after you've seen the map. This is our last chance to make suggestions."

After school Moria arrived at the ranger station, a cottage-type building surrounded by ancient hardwoods. Kam met her at the door. "Hi Moria. You must be here to see the map." He ran his hands through his sandy hair. "I'm sorry you made the trip for nothing. I took the draft home to compare it with some older maps. I'm just leaving for the day. Follow me home if you have time and we'll take a look."

Moria hesitated. *I really want to see the new map. Surely it's okay to go to Kam's house. I won't be there long. Besides, I've known him forever. He's a straight arrow guy...I think.*

"Sure. I just have to get back in time to feed the horses this evening." Moria followed Kam's green Forest Service truck out of the parking lot but failed to see Jada driving by in the other direction.

After a few miles the pavement ended and the two vehicles slowed to avoid sliding off the road on loose gravel. Her thoughts meandered like the twisting road as she thought about Kam. *I don't really know him beyond his forest work. Wonder if he's ever been married? Maybe he's gay...not that it would matter. If I had never met Jackson, Kam might have been a possibility...being a ranger's wife might be fun!* Just then, they turned into the ranger's driveway. *What was I thinking?*

"Kam, I love your place! It's so—"

"What?" he laughed, "Like the three bears' house?"

She laughed, too. "Well, yes, it's so cute!" Gray stone borders surrounded the yard. Blooming azaleas, dogwood, and lavender thrift flourished in the rustic setting. The cedar house, darkened with age, appeared to have grown from the earth.

"Who keeps your yard?"

"I do some of it and my mom comes over to help," he grinned. "Actually, she cooks and keeps the house in order when she has time."

Moria smiled to herself. *Hmm—no wonder he's not married!*

"Enough of that. Let's get a look at the map. Come on back to my office." He unlocked the door and held it open for her.

Moria got a quick look at the house, comfortable couches, guns over the fireplace, and mounted fish, bear, and deer heads adorned the pine walls. Most important, of course, a wide-screen TV, essential to the décor of his man-cave.

Kam spread the map out on a drafting table and turned on the lamp. Lost in the virtual forest on the map he began to explain where the new trail would go and the obstacles to be encountered. Moria moved closer for a better look.

The hair on their arms touched and Moria shivered.

"Cold?" Kam asked, not looking up from the map.

"No, I'm okay," she answered quickly.

After a few more minutes of discussion about the trail, Kam said in a hopeful tone, "Hey, why don't you stay for supper? I can put some steaks on the grill and I know mom made some potato salad and green beans."

"Gosh, I am hungry," she answered, looking outside to see that it was still daylight. "If it's not a bother..."

"Not at all. I don't get much company up here. Come on and sit outside with me."

He started the grill and Moria settled onto the patio swing leaning back against the soft cushions.

She patted one of the brightly-colored pillows. "Your mom's touch?" she teased.

"She knows I'm into comfort," he chuckled, putting the steaks on the grill. "Would you like a beer?

"Sure, that'd be great."

Not looking directly at Moria, he said, "Well, I didn't know...you being a teacher and all."

She laughed, "Hey, teachers are human, too!" *If you only knew!* "Sounds good after a long day." Kam went to get the beers and Moria closed her eyes, enjoying the peaceful evening.

Suddenly she heard rocks scattering down the hillside and the rustle of leaves. Startled out of the quiet moment, she looked up the hill, expecting to see a deer. No movement disturbed the trees.

Then the definite sound of a horse's hooves on the trail above the cabin reached her ears. What? Who would be riding this far from the trailhead when it's almost dark?

Kam returned with their beers and came over to sit by Moria. Casually putting his arm across the back of the swing, he said, "I'm really glad you stopped by today."

A gentle wind blew the clatter of the hoof beats from her mind as Kam slowly put the swing in motion. "What's the story with you and Jackson? That is, if you don't mind me asking." He lightly touched Moria's shoulder.

"What's the story? I don't even know... if he's just passing the time until he goes back to Wyoming or he really cares... He's asked me to go back to Wyoming with him but he knows I won't go."

Moria took a quivering breath and looked into his questioning eyes. Kam lightly rubbed her shoulder and Moria began to cry. "I don't know what to do."

He got up to turn the steaks, as they both struggled to re-group. Sitting back down, he said, "I'd like to ask you out sometime, but I don't want to interfere between you two..."

A longing for Jackson washed over her. "I guess I'd better not rock the boat until I have a better idea of what's really going on with Jackson, and me."

The ranger nodded and smiled. "Well, with that out of the way, I could give you a little preview of possibilities." He raised questioning eyebrows.

Catching her breath, she turned toward him feeling a rush of excitement tingle up and down her spine. The earth tilted as they kissed, long, and deep. The forgotten steaks flamed up as did the heat of their desire.

Kam pulled back and looked at her flushed face. Smiling again, he said, "Guess there are some possibilities!"

Stunned, Moria answered, "Wow! I guess you're right!" *What am I saying?*

He took Moria in his arms again, with purpose to explore further. Seeing her smile, he kissed her again, softly at first and then with more intensity. The clatter of stones above them went unnoticed.

Just then, a car horn blew from the driveway. The two jumped apart. Kam laughed, "Saved by the horn. That's my mom." He ran his fingers through his hair and looked regretfully at Moria. "Guess my moral compass was headed south!"

"Hey, I'm not sorry. But, you're right...I was headed that way too. Maybe I should go."

His mom came around the corner of the house saying, "Looks like you have company!" She stopped, seeing Moria. "Oh, hope I'm not interrupting anything."

"Not at all," Kam lied. "This is Moria Harris. She helps with trails and came by to see the maps. Moria this is my mom, Sadie Bryson."

Moria stood and shook hands with the older woman. "Nice to meet you. I hear you do some of the yard work. It's really eye-catching."

"Keeps me busy," she answered, nodding a thanks. "I see you all were about to have dinner." Looking doubtfully at the burned steaks, she said, "Good thing there's more food in the freezer!"

"Mom, why don't you stay for dinner?" Kam said. "We can start over."

Moria took a few steps toward the front of the house. "I really have to go. It's getting late and I still have to feed the horses. Maybe I'll see you again, Mrs. Bryson."

"Good to meet you, honey," Mrs. Bryson answered, heading toward the kitchen door.

Kam and Moria walked to her truck in silence. As she put the key in the ignition, he leaned on the open window and said, "For all sad words of tongue and pen, the saddest of these, it might have been." Then, he grinned, "Remember, I'm next in line!"

Moria gave Kam a weak smile saying, "See you on the trail."

Dusk had fallen as Moria headed down the mountainside. She switched on the headlights to chase away shadows lurking along the road. *What was I thinking? Maybe I wasn't thinking...or, maybe I wanted this to happen just as much as he did. Is Jackson the right person for me? Maybe I have raging hormones! I haven't been to the doctor in a while.*

The familiar homes of Cherry Valley came into view and in the distance the sky brightened with lights from the town. "I've got to stop for gas," Moria said aloud. "Jeez! I'm talking to myself—must be the stress!"

As she pulled into the gas station, Maxine drove up beside the next pump. "Hey! Just getting back from looking at the maps?" Then, she peered closely at Moria. "You look like hell! What's going on?"

Not looking at Maxine, Moria said, "Yeah, it took a while. Do you have time for coffee?"

"Sure. Anything's better than grading papers! Let's go to The Diner."

The two friends settled into the worn, comfortable booth and ordered their coffee.

Moria sat silently, frowning into the distance.

"So? How did the maps look?"

Moria knew Maxine suspected more than the trail project was at stake. Might as well get it over with, "Well..." she began, and the story came out in a jumble of guilt, excitement, and confusion.

Maxine's disbelieving look became one of concern when she realized Moria's distress. "Wow! I'm speechless—but what were you thinking?"

"I don't know! Maybe I'm just a slut at heart!" Moria pushed her coffee away and propped her elbows on the table, burying her face in her hands.

Maxine replied, "Look out! Here comes company!"

Just then, Jimmy Brown, one of their students, ran over to the booth. "Hey, Miss Moria!" Stopping abruptly, he asked, "Do you have a headache?

"Yes, Jimmy, I do."

"Will you be at school tomorrow?"

"Sure," she smiled, "See you then," and waved across the room to Jimmy's parents. Moria turned back to her coffee, looked at Maxine, said, "I feel sick."

"Well, you're not the slutty type—no wonder your head hurts! The question is how are you going to handle this?"

Moria reached for the salt and pepper shakers and the catsup bottle. "This is the way I see it," she began, lining up the three containers side-by-side. "Here's Jackson." She placed the catsup bottle in the middle. "This is me," she continued, putting the salt on one side of the catsup "and this is Kam," she finished, putting the pepper on the other side of the catsup."

Maxine frowned. "So you're saying Jackson stands between you and Kam?"

"Well, sort of. Jackson will be gone in the fall..."

Maxine grabbed the condiments. "Oh my God! You need to see a shrink!" She hastily rearranged the bottles. "This is how it ought to be!" She put the catsup and Moria, the salt, side by side and returned the pepper to stand beside the paper napkin holder.

"There!" she smiled, "Like it never even happened!"

Moria couldn't help but laugh. "Yuh think?"

"Trust me. Nobody will ever know. Kam's pretty close-mouthed; he's not going to talk."

"What about whoever was in the woods?"

"Hmm...well, there's that."

Maxine asked, "Did you tell Kam about the noise?"

"No, I didn't have a chance to. Who do you think it was?"

"Who knows? That's a loose end. Could show up to bite you in the butt!"

Moria looked at her watch and reached for the check. "I haven't even fed the horses and I have a ton of laundry to do...all the muddy clothes and stuff from the ride. What a train wreck this day turned out to be!"

Maxine gave Moria a hug, saying, "Guess Jackson's going to call you tonight. Better get your shit together. At least you do have a few days before he comes back. As we say, bless your heart! See you tomorrow." With that, Maxine climbed into her truck and waved goodbye.

Moria drove to the farm, dreading to hear the phone ring. Her spirits lifted as she walked to the barn and heard the anxious whinnies of the horses. The familiar task of feeding the animals soothed her nerves.

"What a beautiful evening! It's a shame to waste this full moon while I'm inside doing the laundry. Humm. Think I'll go for a ride." Moria sat down on a hay bale beside Rainbow's stall, waiting for the horses to finish eating. Soon she felt the gelding snuffle lightly at her shoulder as if to say, "Well, let's go!"

Thinking out loud, Moria said, "I haven't been down the valley road in a long time. There's hardly any traffic at night. What do you think, mister?"

The chestnut snorted his approval and soon they were on their way. Glow sticks swung from the horse's breast plate and stirrups to alert drivers of their presence. A soft golden haze bathed the fields bordering the road as ground fog mingled with the dusk.

Breathing in the smell of freshly plowed fields, tears came to Moria's eyes. *I will never forget this moment. I need to remember, my time is not always God's time. What does all this chaos in my life mean?* Taking a deep breath, her mind eased. *Carpe diem. I can do that. Is 'seize the day' a solution? Well, that's Jackson's answer!*

Rainbow Chaser trotted steadily down the dirt road. Oblivious of his owner's distress, blowing and puffing at imagined 'horse getters,' The horse began to canter. His rhythmic strides sent the message - Let me go! Moria gripped the neck strap sending a message back, "You're lucky I even let you canter!" For a moment, fear blew away in the mist.

In the next instant, a deer leapt into the road, crossing Rainbow's path. The horse skidded to a stop, slinging Moria into a ditch. She let go of the reins as she fell, hit the ground, and covered her head. Her mount turned back and came over to stand beside his unfortunate rider.

Slowly Moria reached for the reins and got to her feet. The deer was nowhere to be seen. "Oh, mister, I'm so sorry! This was stupid to go out in the night by myself!" The trembling horse pressed his head against Moria's side. Stroking his neck, she reached in her pack for a flashlight." Let me see if you're hurt."

"Well, buddy, looks like I won't have to call 911!" Mounting up and turning toward home, she reached in her pocket to be sure she hadn't lost her cell phone. "Oh, heck! I left it in the truck. That's really stupid!"

Jackson's call went unanswered and the glow from Moria's phone faded into the night.

The next morning Moria limped across the parking lot at school. She knew the scrape on her arm, now bandaged, would bring unwanted attention and questions about what had happened. Soreness from the fall had set in with a vengeance. Maxine took one look at her friend then listened in amaze-ment to the story of her misadventure.

Moria concluded with, "Well, guess that's one of my nine lives used up, as Pounce would say. The good news is that the fall wasn't as bad as I had imagined it would be, but next time it could be worse."

As expected, Moria's students wanted to know about the accident. What to tell them?

Maxine opened the divider between the two rooms. *Better get it over with,* Moria thought.

She took a shaky breath and addressed the group. "Don't worry. I'm fine. Just a misstep in the dark on the way to feed the horses."

Maxine raised her eyebrows, as if to say, "Sure you did! Just tell them the truth- even grownups do stupid things!"

Moria glanced at Maxine, as if reading her thoughts, and said to the students, "Guess it's better not to be out in the dark without a flashlight. Remember my lesson."

Later in the day, while the children had gone to PE, Maxine chided Moria for not being truthful with the children.

Maxine shook her head. "You know better than to ride when you're upset and can't concentrate. I'm not believing this! It's a wonder worse didn't happen!" She paused for a breath. "Jeez! You should be writing a Hollywood script!"

Moria's eyes blazed. "That's easy for you to say! You have an easy life with Jeremy at your beck and call!" Maxine turned away and closed the divider.

Moria moved through the day teaching her classes and speaking to Maxine only of the tasks at hand. The day seemed endless. The ache of every move and her harsh words to Maxine punctuated her bad choices.

That was wrong what I said to Maxine. But who will take care of me? Moria puzzled, dropping her head into her hands.

A sudden wind blew through the open door ruffling the papers on her desk. Startled, Moria looked up and thought she heard Fredrick's voice.

"You can take care of yourself." The door slammed shut.

Maxine opened the divider. "Who was that?"

"Nobody." Moria stood up and began to gather the students' daily papers.

"Feeling better?" Maxine asked.

"Yeah. Sorry I was such a bitch."

"No matter. You do lead a stressful life. Have you heard from Jackson?"

"I missed his call. I'm sure I'll hear from him tonight."

Maxine smiled. "Guess we'll be going to the Juniper Tree this weekend. I really miss Jeremy."

Moria turned out the classroom lights. "I miss Jackson, too.

The rest of the week passed quickly with school and tending to the horses. Moria's aches and bruises faded. In her conversations with Jackson, she stuck to news about happenings with the horses.

Friday afternoon Moria returned from work to find that Jackson had returned from his trip. Fear and elation churned in her stomach. She walked slowly toward the barn. Jackson fastened the gate and ran to her. "Oh, baby! I have really missed you!"

Moria leapt into his arms and buried her face on his shoulder. "I've missed you, too!" *I really have!*

"Come on inside and tell me about your trip. I've got some steaks for the grill."

He hugged her tightly. "I've got a little something else in mind first."

Moria delighted in Jackson's touch and her brief encounter with Kam drifted out the window along with the butterflies in her stomach.

Later, Moria, dressed only in a long tee-shirt, walked Jackson to his truck.

Smiling, he waved goodbye. "Get dressed, Missy. Remember, we're going dancing tonight."

After a quick shower, Moria searched through the closet for her favorite cowgirl shirt—dark blue with gold thread designs stitched on the collar and sleeves, and added tan jeans, soft leather boots and gold hoop earrings to complete the outfit. *Got to look good at the Juniper Tree—especially if Jada's going to be there!*

While applying her make-up, Moria faced an anxious reflection. Color seemed dull in her usually bright green eyes; eyes telling the story of her misdeed.

Is Maxine right? Put the pepper back with the napkin holder...like it never even happened? Or, should I just tell Jackson what happened and get it over with?

Jackson's knock at the door brought her mind back to the present. *We had a great time earlier this evening and Jackson didn't seem to suspect anything. Tears flooded Moria's eyes. I am such a slutty, evil person! What is the matter with me?*

As Moria and Jackson entered the Juniper Tree, the familiar musty smell of the old bar wafted through the door. Bright neon lights flashed a welcome, comforting Moria's spirit. Friends greeted the couple as they approached the long table.

I'm okay. I can do this. Moria chanted the well-worn mantra in her mind.

Searching the faces at the table, she quickly spotted Jada and her husband Richard, and at the other end of the table, and, yes, there sat Kam Bryson. He waved to Moria and Jackson, motioning them to the empty seats beside him. Jackson smiled and waved back, taking Moria's arm and guiding her to the vacant seats. *My life is over!* she thought.

After Moria and Jackson ordered their drinks, the ranger launched into an enthusiastic description of the trails project. "Moria thinks the new trail design will work great," Kam said, looking at Jackson.

"I'm sure we'll enjoy riding them," Jackson answered politely, watching the band assemble on the stage.

Kam replied, "There's a lot of work to do before we can use them." He smiled and winked at Moria. "She got a good look at the maps earlier this week."

Moria looked away and shifted uneasily in her chair.

Jackson raised his eyebrows as if to say, *You didn't tell me about this.*

Just then, the band began to play and Moria tugged at Jackson's hand, dragging him toward the dance floor. As Jackson took her in his arms, he said, "Well, Missy, tell me more about the maps. I saw Kam wink at you. What's going on?"

"Nothing." Kam's just being flirty. He's like that sometimes when he's had a few beers."

Jackson pulled Moria closer and buried his face in her hair, "I hope my cowgirl's not changing horses in the middle of the stream."

"Don't pay any attention to Kam. He's just lonely."

"And, you would know this because...?" Jackson asked, looking into Moria's face and drawing her closer.

Before Moria could answer, Richard and Jada danced by.

Smiling, Jada said, "What about changing partners?" Jackson frowned. Quick as a flash, Jada danced into his arms and Moria twirled away with Richard, relieved to be away from Jackson's suspicious questions. As she and Richard danced, Moria watched Jada's animated face turned up to Jackson and his expression of disbelief.

At the end of the song the couples returned to the table and Jackson grabbed Moria's hand. "Let's go outside for some fresh air."

Moria left the table, a lump of dread in her stomach, sensing fresh air was not on Jackson's mind. They walked out of the building in silence and over to Jackson's truck. He jerked the tailgate down and lifted Moria up to sit on it, then stood in front of her, hands on his hips. His glare could melt the strongest soul.

"Showtime," he announced grimly.

Moria flinched.

"I'll get right to the point," he continued. "Jada said she just happened to be riding by Kam's house and saw you two making out. She said she was surprised you all didn't just 'do it' right there in the swing!"

Speechless, Moria stared at Jackson. *So, it was Jada up on the trail!*

"No. that's not how it was!" Moria began to cry. Jackson turned his back and waited.

"Then, how was it?" he asked, turning back to look into her face.

"Okay, here's what happened. Yes, Kam and I probably would have gotten into trouble if his mom hadn't arrived." Moria stopped to gather her thoughts. "You're going to be gone in the fall and you said our relationship could be just a 'thing'!"

"So that's your excuse!" Jackson grasped Moria's hands in his. "Things have changed since then...for me. What about you?"

Moria looked away, not wanting to meet Jackson's eyes. Taking her hands from his warmth, she gripped the cold, unforgiving edges of the tail gate. Finally she spoke, her voice barely above a whisper. "I don't know." She hesitated, searching for the elusive answer.

Jackson threw his hands up in disgust, turning away again. Moments passed.

Whirling around, he said, "I'm done. The invitation to move to Wyoming, married or not is off the table. I'm not going to live with some neurotic head case. I know you're not ever going to leave your precious Cherry Valley, and all your friends! You can't even make the tiniest commitment toward a real relationship!"

Shocked, Moria cried out, "Jackson, I do care about you, but..."

"But, what? I have to make a living in Wyoming where the law firm and the ranch are. You could teach school and do endurance riding there! We've been over all this before! Get in the truck. I'm taking you home!"

"My purse! I need to get it!"

Jackson jumped in the truck and cranked the engine. "Hurry up, and don't cry on Maxine's shoulder. It's not her business!"

Moria fled into the bar and straight to the restroom. She leaned on the sink, shaken and distraught, the door opened behind her. Moria glanced in the mirror through tear-filled eyes. Jada's image wavered in the glass. Moria turned to face her adversary.

"You! It's all your fault, you meddling bitch," she yelled at Jada.

Jada leveled a gaze at Moria and answered calmly, "No, Moria. It's your fault. Jackson is a fine man. You should take better care of him—if you can."

Moria lashed back. "How would you feel if I told Richard how you're always trying to get in Jackson's pants?"

Fear skittered across Jada's face. "You wouldn't!"

Moria pushed Jada aside and reached for the door. "Watch me!"

"Wait!" Jada called in desperation. "Truce? I'll leave Jackson alone if you'll leave Richard out of this!"

Moria hesitated. *I'd never lay that burden on Richard. He's a really nice guy.* "We'll see," she answered. "You better hold up your end of the deal." Without looking back, Moria hurried out to get her purse. Maxine started up from her chair, seeing evidence in Moria's face of another 'Jackson crisis.'

"Don't." Moria held a hand up to Maxine. "I'm going home." She turned and walked away.

During the ride to Peace in the Valley Farm Moria glanced at Jackson's unforgiving face and then looked out the window. Silence squeezed into the truck like an unwelcome guest. Leaning her head against the seat, Moria watched the dark landscape fly by. *Is that me? A blur of darkness? Life with Fredrick was bad, but this is worse! It's easy to manage thirty kids in a classroom. Why can't I manage this relationship with just one person? Maybe we're like two ships passing in the night. Is that what I want?*

Jackson's truck turned into the driveway and Moria spoke. "Are you going to move Silver Dollar to Jada's farm?"

Jackson took a deep breath. "No, I'm not going to Jada's. I can't handle any more drama. You'd think we're still in high school! I'd like to keep the horse here and we could still ride together." He glanced at Moria and saw her smile.

"That works for me," she said. By now, they had stopped at the carport. Opening the truck door, she jumped out. "See you tomorrow?"

Jackson said, "Sure, let's ride!"

"The horses?" Moria teased.

Jackson slapped his forehead. "Oh, my God! Remember? That's my line!"

Laughing, she went inside, exhausted. The cats met her at the door and followed her into the bedroom. Dropping her clothes in a pile, she tumbled into bed. Pounce and Pandora leapt up on the scrambled covers to keep her company. Pounce crept up beside Moria's face as she dozed off. Snuggling beside her, his whiskers brushed her face.

"Jackson?" Moria mumbled.

No, it's me, Pounce, he seemed to say, digging his claws into her shoulder.

Pushing him onto the floor, she pulled the covers over her head. "Go away, you jealous cat!" Moria's last thoughts before sleep were Jackson's words, *"You can't even make the tiniest commitment toward a relationship!"*

Why can't I leave Cherry Valley and begin a new life in Wyoming with Jackson?

Pounce purred the likely answer: *You're a neurotic head case?*

Chapter Ten

*E*arly the next morning Moria struggled out of bed, wondering if Jackson would do his job and come feed the horses. After tending to the cats, she poured herself a cup of coffee, moved to the porch, and settled onto the wicker swing.

Dew sparkled on the grass and newly-woven spider webs glistened with diamond droplets of mist. A fresh morning breeze rustled the leaves of nearby trees and a few pine cones fell to the ground. *If I could just be like those pine cones, leave my home and go away to another life. But what will happen to them? Run over by the mower? Eaten by squirrels? What will happen to me?* The crunch of gravel in the driveway scattered her thoughts as Jackson's truck appeared.

The cowboy bounded onto the porch, saying, "Hey, sleepyhead! Go get dressed. I'll feed the horses and we'll get an early start. Jeremy called, and he and Maxine are going to meet us on the road." He paused for breath. "Maxine is going to ride Catch on Fire, since Star Shine is lame." He tousled Moria's hair, his eyes meeting hers. Then the fragile moment shattered as Jackson said, "Get a move on, woman!"

Startled, Moria headed for the door. "Sure. I'll hurry. See you in a few minutes." *Wow! It's like last night never happened...except he didn't kiss me good morning.*

Before Moria finished dressing, Maxine called.

"Give me the short version of last night. You looked like a deer in the headlights when you came in from the parking lot."

"Jackson said not to cry on your shoulder," Moria answered.

"Oh, never mind Jackson! What happened?"

Moria gave her interpretation of the evening, finishing with, "I'm getting about half-mad at myself for being such a train wreck."

Maxine replied, "Better to be half-mad than half-sorry for yourself."

"Humm, I guess so. See you on the road."

The four riders met in front of Maxine's house. The horses snorted and pawed, eyeing each other. Jeremy's horse, Artic Cat, stood between Catch on Fire and the other two horses, as if to say, "Mess with her, and you'll mess with me!" Rainbow Chaser edged around Artic Cat, whose ears were back. Rainbow inched forward, and touched Fire's nose. Artic Cat kicked out at the chestnut gelding, landing a glancing blow on his haunch. Fire struck out with a shrieking whinny, *I can take care of myself!*

The riders quickly separated the horses. Moria laughed, "Well, I guess that's settled!" *Maybe I should take lessons from Catch on Fire!*

As the riders did a warm-up walk down the dirt road they began to discuss the next endurance trip. "I think we should do the beach ride," Maxine volunteered. Nobody complained about this plan. She continued, "Guess we'd better do some training on the River Road. We're lucky to have twenty miles of dirt road with no gravel." Ever optimistic, off the endurance riders went, each one already thinking of a successful finish at the Sand and Waves Ride.

Later, at the barn the two riders hosed the horses down and turned them loose in the pasture. Moria asked, "Are you hungry? I can make you a sandwich."

Jackson laughed. "What? Peanut butter and bananas again? Let's go to The Diner."

"Sure, that would be great," Moria answered, turning off the tack room lights. As they walked toward the house, Jackson took Moria's hand and said, "I need to go in and wash up. Is that okay?

"Just don't take your boots off when Pounce is around," she laughed, swinging their hands back and forth. When they went into the kitchen Jackson rolled up his sleeves and turned on the water in the sink. Without regret, Moria went to Jackson, wrapped her arms around his waist and pressed against his back. The voice of desire became her own voice. "You can wash up in the bathroom," she said softly.

Jackson spun around and held her close. Burying his face in her hair, he murmured, "You are precious, you minx! The hell with washing, we can do that later!" Sweeping Moria up into his arms, he reached the bedroom in a few short strides.

Pounce scampered from the room and Jackson slammed the door with his foot. "Not this time, you fur ball!"

Moria made love to Jackson with wild abandon, a wanton wanna' be cowgirl, turned loose at last.

Later, Jackson lay sprawled out on his back with a dazed look in his eyes and a smile on his face. "Wow! What was that all about?" he asked, looking up into Moria's mischievous, shining eyes.

She answered, "Free, free at last!"

"What?" Jackson sat up and Moria knew she had his attention. "Have I missed something here?" he asked, sensing a change in Moria.

"Maybe, I've been doing a lot of thinking. You asked if I would go to Wyoming, not—will you marry me? I barely know you." A flicker of a smile crossed her face. "Even though I'm getting pretty attached to you, I'm not leaving Cherry Valley. When you have to go home in the fall, so be it. In the meantime, it would be a shame to waste having great sex and a good time together. We can be friends with benefits."

Jackson stared at Moria in disbelief. Rubbing his face, buying time for the right answer, he finally said, "I have to ask...do you love me?"

"Maybe I should ask you the same question. I do care about you. Love is a one-way street, in my mind. We both need to go in the same direction. I'm not there yet."

Jackson gave Moria a hug and said, "I'm not going back to Wyoming without you. Women! You gotta' love 'em!" Then, reaching for his boots he said, "Hey, are you hungry? We never made it to The Diner."

"Sure," she laughed, pushing Jackson back down on the bed, "Guess I am hungry...for some more yummy cowboy!"

As Moria drove to school Monday morning she thought back over the weekend: Jackson's angry words when he found out about her "dalliance" with Kam, the confrontation with Jada, and her own decision to enjoy her time with Jackson, no strings attached. *At last, I am in control of my life again!*

Moria opened the door to Cherry Valley Elementary and stepped into her comfort zone—children, lesson plans and routine. Maxine was already in the classroom when Moria arrived.

The two sat down for a quick cup of coffee and took a look at the calendar for the rest of the year. Maxine announced, "Well, I guess you see our class has the program for the last PTA meeting." She circled the date. "Just six weeks away." Moria began to bite her fingernails.

"Don't do that!" Maxine chided. "Bad example for the kids."

"Yeah, I might have to go the principal's office!"

"We will have to let Mr. Baldwin know what we're going to do for the program."

Suddenly, Moria's face brightened. "I know! We can turn the Alice in Wonderland story into a play!"

"Been done," Maxine answered.

"I know. But what if...the Queen of Hearts was a rodeo queen..."

Maxine jumped in right away. "And the soldiers could be cowboys!"

Moria grabbed a piece of paper and began to write, saying, "Instead of the white rabbit, we could have a gopher!"

Excited by this new approach to an old story, Maxine added, "The cowboys could do a line dance..."

Moria finished the thought, "And instead of having a tea party, they could have a beer blast!" By now, their gleeful words tumbled over each other in half completed sentences. Laughter filled the classroom, interrupted only by the reality of children's voices in the hallway.

Picking up her papers, Maxine reminded Moria, "Don't forget, we have to get our plan past the boss!"

"No beer!" Moria answered, going to open the door and greet her rowdy charges.

"Let's get together tonight and see if this is going to work."

"What about Jackson?"

"He'll be fine," Moria answered.

Maxine looked uncertain. "You don't think he needs a little extra attention?"

Moria gave Maxine a meaningful glance, "He needs to rest. See you tonight!"

She was surprised to see Jackson waiting on the doorstep when she returned home in the afternoon. Wow! Maybe he's already rested!

Upon getting closer and seeing Jackson's stone-like face, she took a deep breath. Then she noticed a glass vase on the step. The vase held a single rose, and taped to the door, a folded sheet of paper. Moria got out of the truck and walked toward Jackson, her mind awhirl. *Now what?*

Without a word, Jackson pointed to the note. "Looks like Smoky the Bear's been busy again."

Moria snatched the letter off the door and sat down on the steps beside Jackson.

"So, can I read over your shoulder?" he asked, scooting closer.

She ripped open the envelope and unfolded the letter. "I don't care."

Moria asked, "What I want to know is, did you make Kam write this?"

"The less I have to do with this particular ranger, the better."

Dear Moria,

So sorry I interfered with you and Jackson. I don't want you to be upset, or lose you, my best trail worker!

I guess Jackson won't be interested in working on the trails since the trouble. He is welcome if he wants to join in. The next work day is two weeks from this Saturday.

Take care,

Kam

Jackson's dark eyes portrayed a shadow of uncertainty as he captured Moria's gaze. "Question: how did Kam know about 'the trouble'?"

Moria folded the letter and stuck it in her book bag. "Probably Jada's big mouth. Word gets around—just like the Jada thing at the ride when we had to 'escort' her to her trailer. Pretty soon some other gossip will come along and this whole issue will be yesterday's news."

Jackson stood up to leave and said, "I've got to finish bush hogging the Rutherford's pasture this afternoon. Why don't you feed the horses this evening?"

"Sure. I've got to go over to Maxine's tonight, anyway."

Later in the evening the two teachers sat down in Maxine's kitchen to work on the play. Moria loved this room, with its gold walls, green cabinets and stainless steel appliances. Miniature yellow roses bloomed in the bay window where the gray cat, Tuffy, curled up among the flower pots. Maxine poured their coffee and Moria said, "I always feel like we could be a magazine ad in your kitchen."

Then looking at her ragged jeans and sweat shirt, said, "Well, maybe not! Guess we better get to work. But first, I need to tell you about Kam's letter."

Maxine's eyes widened as Moria told of the afternoon's scenario. "Sounds like you've got a handle on this, at least for today. Are you going to respond to Kam's letter?"

"No, I'm going to try and forget this nightmare ever happened."

"So be it. Denial works, too!" Maxine laughed. "Time to fall down the rabbit hole with Alice!"

Moria wrote their ideas from earlier in the day in her notebook and suggested, "Let's try to get a first draft, then we can go back and revise...just like we teach the kids."

Maxine said, "What about Alice? Should she just be a regular girl, like the original story?"

"Hmm, let's think about that. Here's an idea. We could use cardboard boxes and make a tunnel for Alice to crawl through and tumble onto the stage amongst the queen's subjects."

"Cute! Then one of the soldiers could say, "Halt! An interloper has sneaked into our midst! Call Homeland Security!"

Writing furiously, Moria said, "Then the queen could say off with her head. Do you think that's too violent?"

"Well, it's a classic story, so let's go with it. Mr. Baldwin will have the final say. Look at the computer games—off with the head happens every day! No one will even notice!"

"Okay. Why don't the soldier-cowboys use lassos instead of swords?"

"How funny! Might get a little complicated, though—all those ropes swinging around!" Maxine said, as she brought out some chocolate chip cookies to encourage their endeavors. "Take some home with you. You can have them for breakfast!"

The two women worked on into the night until Moria noticed the time. "I better go, so we can get some sleep, or we'll have a bad day, for sure. Maybe we can get this done in a couple of more days. See you tomorrow."

Moria drove slowly past Jackson's house on the way back to the farm, noticing all the house lights were out. On a whim, she turned into the long driveway, cut the lights out, parked and walked cautiously toward his bungalow. "Ha! Mister, have I got a surprise for you!" she said aloud. Creeping up to his bedroom window, she waited. All seemed quiet. She scratched on the screen. No sounds came from inside. Scratching harder, she also tapped on the window frame. Suddenly, the blinds flew up and Jackson's startled face appeared in the window. "Who's there?"

She took a step back into the glow of the security light. Smiling she said, "Hey, mister big bad wolf, it's Little Red Riding Hood! I brought you a treat!" she said, holding up a chocolate chip cookie.

"Am I dreamin'? Come on in!" He left the window and went to the front door, greeting Moria with a joyful hug. "I can't believe my luck!"

Smiling, she held out the cookie. "Thought you might be hungry."

"You got that right! I'm hungry for some cowgirl love. Feeling wild?"

"Watch me, Mister! You're going on the ride of your life!"

Much later, Moria roused from Jackson's arms. Looking out the window at the faint pink light on the horizon, she smiled to herself, remembering the time she fell asleep on Jackson's couch and thought he had taken advantage of her. Glancing on the floor in the corner she saw the pictures with the broken glass, where they had fallen when she slammed open the door. *I need to get those repaired*, she reminded herself. Then remembering Jackson standing naked, hands on hips, scowling at her and the broken pictures. *Was that only three months ago? So much has happened in my life since then.*

A tiny thought scurried around in the back of her mind. *He is leaving. Go, or let go! No, not yet, not yet!*

Moria and Maxine met in the classroom for their usual cup of coffee. Maxine opened a bag of donuts, offering them to Moria. "Guess we might need some reinforcement since we have to meet with Mr. Baldwin this morning and see what he thinks about our version of the play. They looked over the hand-written script and notes before heading to the principal's office.

Mr. Baldwin listened to their ideas about the play and a frown wrinkled his brow.

"Hmm...Ms. Harris, this sounds acceptable. I need to see the finished product." He rearranged some papers on his desk, then looked directly at Moria and said, "I know you sometimes have an unusual approach to teaching. Then he smiled. "Just let me see it before you start practice so there won't be any surprises."

"Yes sir. We'll keep in touch. Thanks for your...support," Moria said, gathering up their efforts."

On the way down the hall Maxine said, "Well, that wasn't too bad. Let's go ahead and tell the kids."

"Should we have try-outs or just assign the parts?"

"We'll cross that bridge when we come to it. Let's see what kind of reaction we get."

After announcements were over Moria opened the divider to address both classes. "Guess what? Our classes are responsible for the spring play and Ms. Franklin and I have a great idea! We're going to do Alice in Wonderland!" A giant moan went up from the class.

"No! That's for babies!"

"Too stupid!"

"It's a girl's story!"

Maxine held up her hand to quiet them. "Wait, you guys! You haven't heard it all! We're going to call our play 'Alice Goes West'!"

Silence fell and the children looked at each other, then a babble of voices broke out. Moria whispered to Maxine, "We're going to draw out of a hat for the parts, okay?"

"Works for me."

Moria regained control of the class, telling them the script wasn't finished yet and they would draw names for the parts. Then in a teachable moment she announced, "I'm going to read a short version of the story aloud and you all can be thinking of ways to make our play have a western theme! When I've finished reading the story, you can write down some of your ideas. Remember, keep your plan workable— this isn't Disney World!"

By now Maxine had found the Alice in Wonderland book and handed it to her teammate. "So much for getting Math done right now!" she laughed. The children cheered and gathered on the floor to hear about Alice's adventures. Before Moria began to read, she heard outrageous ideas flying back and forth among the children.

At the end of the day, the two teachers were exhausted. "Looks like we've started a wildfire with the play," Moria said, as she packed her book bag.

"Well, at least they're excited about something. Maybe we can work math, social studies and science into..."

Moria held up her hand. "Stop! My head is spinning!"

Maxine said, "You're right. One day at a time. Let's call the guys to meet us at The Diner. Who wants to cook after a day like this...or any day!"

Moria and Maxine entered the restaurant and Moria commented, "Looks like our guys aren't here yet."

"No wonder! They're feeding the horses!"

Jeremy and Jackson arrived and before long dishes of scrumptious country food covered the table.

"Pass the sweet potatoes," Jackson said. "This is one of my favorite things about the south, sweet potatoes and Southern Belles. Wonder if Little Red Riding Hood was a Southern Belle?" He winked at Moria.

Maxine looked at Moria."Have I missed something here?"

Moria laughed, "Yes, you did. The big bad wolf ate the chocolate cookies."

Maxine nodded with understanding. "Glad they went to good use!" she laughed.

"If I learned to cook sweet potatoes, would you stay in Cherry Valley?" Moria asked Jackson asked in her heaviest Southern drawl, looking up at him in wide-eyed innocence.

Jackson frowned. Moria realized she might have stepped over the line of their fragile relationship.

Then, putting his arm around her, he smiled. "Well, ma'am, could you cook cornbread, too?"

Everyone laughed, but in her heart Moria knew this would never happen. She would not cook cornbread and Jackson would not move to Cherry Valley.

Moria sighed. *For all sad words of tongue and pen...*

As the four friends walked to the parking lot, Jeremy said, "Hey, let's go for a night ride! Moon's full tonight!"

"Why not? Sounds like fun!" answered Maxine.

Jackson laughed, "Another endurance adventure! Let's go!"

Moria looked doubtful, remembering her recent night ride and the encounter with the deer. "Hmm...I don't know..."

"Oh come on! We'll ride in front and scare off the 'horse getters'." Maxine said.

Moria smiled, "Why not? My insurance is paid up! Let's meet on the Cemetery Road and ride to the plantation. It's just about an hour each way."

As Jackson and Moria saddled the horses, Jackson said, "Tell me about the Cemetery Road. Sounds like there's some history lurking in the shadows."

Moria laughed, "You know, our country's rich with history, but the south is decadent with stories of the past, preserved by people who keep the Southern ways alive. It's who we are."

Jackson looked thoughtful. "Yeah, like our cowboys and Indians in Wyoming. Gotcha. It's all about tradition."

"Back to the Cemetery Road—as you can already imagine, a battle was fought here during the War of Northern Aggression."

Jackson smiled.

"The cemetery was started after the battle and is still open to families of the deceased."

"Is that you?"

"Yes, my farm sits on an original land grant from the 1700's and some of my ancestors are buried in this cemetery. We'll go take a look someday, "Moria answered. "Now, let me tell you about the plantation. It's not what you'd expect...a mansion with white columns. It's a two-story weathered wood structure. The Historical Society takes care of it but the state has possession because of some long ago mix-up about the ownership. So, nobody cares if we ride on the property since it's not an official historical site."

"Can't wait to see it," Jackson said. "Maybe we'll even meet some Southern ghosts!"

The riders mounted up and left the barn, soon meeting up with Maxine and Jeremy. They trotted away in single file with Moria last.

The moon had risen above the trees and shed a soft light over the countryside. Pines, silhouetted against the gray sky, swayed in the night breeze. Nocturnal creatures went about their business, scurrying around in the bushes.

An owl hooted nearby and flew across the road with great flapping wings. The moon cast the owl's shadow onto the road, spooking the horses. Moria gripped Rainbow Chaser's mane.

"You okay?" Jeremy called back to her.

"I'm good. Go on." Moria answered.

The four horses and riders trotted or cantered most of the way to the plantation, slowing down only for the gravel sections of the road. Turning off the road onto a jeep trail, the group came to a walk because the horses were breathing heavily. Rainbow stretched his neck and relaxed, but not Moria, ever watchful for surprises in the night.

Soon they reached the back gate of the property and the riders dismounted.

Jackson, who was in front, looked through the rusted, wrought iron gates at the weathered home place, silver gray boards reflecting the moonlight. Tangled wisteria vines drooped low from the trees, purple clumps of blooms hidden by the night.

"Open the gate," Moria said. "Be care—"

Just then the rusted hinges gave way, causing the gate to fall against Silver Dollar. The gelding leapt back, jerking the reins from Jackson's hands. Jackson fell down on the gate and Silver galloped away to the front of the plantation house and down the driveway.

A moment of disbelief followed as the riders helped Jackson untangle himself from the bushes and remnants of the gate. "Oh my God! We've got to catch him," Jackson shouted, starting after the horse.

"No! Wait! We need to split up." Jeremy called to him.

Maxine agreed. "He's right. Jackson, you don't know where you're going. I'll ride back the way we came and you wait here. Jeremy can track him the best he can and Moria can go to her barn and wait. He'll either figure out how to get home, circle back, or stop somewhere and graze. Come on let's go!"

Jackson sat down on the edge of an old stone fountain, full of leaves and a broken statue. "I need to be doing something!" he said, jumping up and pacing back and forth.

Moria said, "Call 911 and tell them there's a loose horse near the old plantation. They'll know the location. Somebody might catch him and call in. Do we all have our phones? Let's keep in touch. Thank goodness we have service out here!" She looked at Jackson. "Sit tight, honey. We'll find him."

Moria and Maxine galloped away, back up the trail.

At the intersection of the jeep trail and Cemetery Road, Moria and Maxine parted company. Maxine dismounted and led Catch on Fire to the edge of the road to graze and Moria trotted away toward the farm. *I need to go faster,* she thought, urging Rainbow Chaser into a canter. "Deer, deer, go away! Come again another day!" Moria chanted in unison with the horse's three-beat gait. Soon she reached the driveway and slowed to a walk, letting the gelding cool down. Then, she turned the horse into the pasture to finish cooling. She hurried to the front porch and settled in the swing.

Restless, she called Maxine. "Any sign of him?" Moria asked.

"No. It's quiet. A car of drunks passed but we stepped into the woods and they never saw us."

"All's quiet here, too. What about Jeremy?"

Maxine answered, "He says Silver Dollar took to the pavement at the end of the driveway and ran off up the road in the direction of the farm.

"Let's hope Silver's compass is working!" And her unvoiced thought, *I hope he stays on the side of the road and doesn't get hit by a car.*

"If he didn't slow down or get off into the swamp, he should be here any minute. Will you call Jackson and update him? Thanks."

Moria did not have to wait long. In the distance she heard the faint drumming of hoof beats on the pavement. Silver Dollar tore into the driveway as if banshees were after him.

Moria stepped out into the driveway and called, "Whoa, boy! You're home now," continuing to speak to him in a sing-song voice. The horse came to a walk, limped to her, and stopped. Moria brought him into the porch light to check for injuries. "Wow! You did a number on yourself!" she said aloud, looking closely at the damage from the fallen gate.

She started walking the horse carefully to the barn while reaching for her phone.

Jackson answered. "Silver's home," Moria said. "He's pretty banged up. We'll need to check him over better when you get here. I'm going to put an ice boot on his leg and come pick you up."

In reply to Jackson's question, Moria said, "No, I don't think we need to call the vet tonight. Let's see how he is in the morning. Will you let Maxine and Jeremy know he's home? I'll meet you on the paved road at the end of the driveway in about fifteen minutes."

When Moria arrived, Jackson climbed into the truck, saying, "What is it about endurance riders? There's always some drama going on. I just wish my horse wasn't the star of the show tonight!"

Moria, who was driving, said, "Scoot over."

Jackson slid across the bench seat and Moira took his hand, rubbing her thumb in his palm. "This too shall pass, is one of my favorite sayings, followed by: I'll think about that tomorrow!"

"Yeah, Scarlett, I hear you," Jackson laughed.

Soon they reached the barn. Maxine and Jeremy were already there, tending to Silver's wounds. "Looks like he fell on the pavement," Jeremy said. "He's pulled a shoe, has a swollen knee and some abrasions, so far as we can tell right now." Then Jeremy grinned added, "At least Jackson's brand new expensive tack isn't scraped up too much."

Jackson removed the ice boot to examine Silver's knee. "I've seen worse, but he could have a bone chip or whatever else. I'm going to call Dr. Barr in the morning to get an x-ray. Let's keep him in the stall tonight. I'll sleep in the trailer so I can walk him every couple of hours."

Moria answered, "Good idea. There's more ice in the tack room refrigerator. You know, last time we spent the night at the barn was when Promise was born. Seems like just yesterday."

Moria and Jackson looked at each other, lost in the memory of that night...*the first time Jackson asked me to move to Wyoming. I do love him.*

Maxine cleared her throat, interrupting the moment. "Hey! Get a room! Or maybe a horse trailer! Just kidding. We better go. Call if you need to. See y'all in the morning."

As Jeremy and Maxine rode away, Moria said, "Guess I need to bring some things from the house..."

Jackson laughed, "It's already after three, you have to get up in a couple of hours. Maybe you should go on to bed. Not that I wouldn't enjoy your company!"

Moria opened the trailer door and smiled. "I'll just sleep in my clothes and stay with you, if you don't mind."

"Need you ask?" he replied. "I'm going to walk Silver and take the ice off for a little while. See you in a few minutes."

Later, when Jackson entered the trailer, Moria's deep, steady breathing told him no fun and games tonight! He climbed up to the bunk, Moria turned over and mumbled, "Fredrick, go away! Go away!"

Jackson took her in his arms and whispered, "Fredrick's gone, honey. It's just me - Jackson. I love you," he said.

"I love you, too," she murmured. Suddenly sitting up disoriented, she asked, "How is Silver? What time is it?"

"It's time for you to go back to sleep. I'll wake you at six. Let you sleep a little longer. Our boy's doing fine, but still stiff. I didn't give him any Bute. I'd like for Dr. Barr to see him first." Moria fell back on the pillows and was fast asleep again.

The next morning at school Moria said to Maxine, "I think we need to have an 'independent study day,' don't you?"

"Sounds good to me. I'll go check out a couple of videos. The kids can take notes and illustrate them. When they know they can draw, they'll take lots of notes, which takes lots of time!"

Moria answered, "I'll write up some library passes and also give them map work to do. They always like that. Why don't we let them make up math stories? Then we can use them tomorrow."

At planning time the two teachers decided to go out to their trucks and take quick naps. Moria let the seat back and gratefully closed her eyes, letting the sunshine cover her like a warm blanket.

She awoke with a start! Mr. Baldwin peered in and tapped on the window.

"Ms. Harris! What is the meaning of this?"

Opening her eyes, Moria stared into Mr. Baldwin's frowning face. Dreams of lying on the sunny beaches of Cancun vanished as Moria gathered her scattered thoughts. She rolled down the window.

"I wasn't feeling well and thought some rest would help me make it through the day. Maxine is resting, too. I think we caught something from the children…"

Mr. Baldwin started to walk away, then turned back, saying. "It's time for class. You and Maxine have already had 'Friday-itis' this year. It's Thursday. Are you going somewhere tomorrow?"

Moria took a deep breath. *No, thank goodness!* "No sir. I'll be here."

"See that you are."

Moria watched Mr. Baldwin's retreating back and jumped out of the truck to wake Maxine, who was parked a few spaces away. She knocked on Maxine's window, motioning for her to get out.

"Busted!" Moria laughed, telling Maxine what had happened as they walked into the building.

"Changing the subject," Maxine said, "That cowboy in our neighborhood, Rodney, said he could make some lassos for the play and wouldn't charge. I told him we'd give him a free ad in the program. He runs a horseback riding business and does summer camps."

As they entered the building, Moria looked thoughtful. "Hmm…maybe we could do summer camps at your place. You have an indoor arena, some trails and a pool… Perfect!"

Maxine shook her head in disbelief. "As if we don't have enough going on in our lives right now!" She smiled. "We can think about it."

Moria called Jackson on her way home from school. Switching the phone to speaker as he answered, she said, "Hi. I can feed the horses this evening. I know you must be worn out taking care of Silver. What did the vet say?"

"Not as bad as we thought. Dr. Barr x-rayed and didn't see any bone chips, or worse—mainly just the scrapes and soreness."

"What about going to the Sand and Waves ride?"

"I didn't ask. He's coming back in a few days. Besides, we have to get the Bute out of Silver's system. Remember? Miss Endurance Rider?"

"How could I forget? Sounds like we just need to keep medicine on the scrapes and turn him out in the paddock. I think we should cut down on his feed for a few days, too. I can take care of him tonight."

"Sounds good. Thanks. Maybe I should come over. I don't want you to get lonely!"

"You rest up!" Moria laughed, "You know I'm not going anywhere!

"Is that a promise?"

She heard doubt in Jackson's voice. *He doesn't trust me!* "Promise. See you tomorrow!"

Smiling, she pulled into the driveway. *Maybe I need to make a trip to Victoria's Secret.*

Before going to bed, Moria checked her e-mail. "Oh my God! Here's something from Doris Weaver! I hope nothing's happened to Jesse!" The two cats sensed Moria's distress and began to purr and rub against her legs. She looked down at them and said, "Well, here goes," and clicked to open the message.

Hey Moria,

Just checking on you and that scumbag, Jackson. Got in touch with your friend Jada. Looked in the membership list and saw Cherry Valley has only one zip code. Figured somebody with a horse named Blackjack would know what's going on in the neighborhood! So you're having an affair with the forest ranger? Is he as good in bed as our cowboy?

See you on the trail in October!

Doris

Moria hit the keep as new key, closed the laptop, and stared into space. *What to do? Respond and give Doris the satisfaction of stirring things up? Ignore the message? Then, would Doris pursue this juicy tidbit with other endurance riders in the community? Would she get in touch with Jackson?*

Oh shit! I need to think about this...tomorrow. But sleep eluded Moria. She tossed and turned, trying to think of a way to make Doris's intrusion go away.

The hands on the clock moved slowly toward morning. By three a.m. Moria got up. "I might as well check the weather," she said to the cats and picked up the remote. "Now I'm hungry!" Going to the freezer, she chose her favorite, mint-chocolate ice cream. Finally, Moria fell asleep on the couch until gold bands of sunlight crept through the blinds and shone on her face. She struggled to sit up as the alarm clock buzzed like an angry wasp. Exhausted and worried, Moria went straight to check her e-mails. *Thank goodness!* She breathed a sigh of relief that no "Doris" messages had darted into her computer during the night.

I'm going to deal with this right now! Opening Doris's message, she hit "reply" and wrote:

I'll be waiting on you at the finish line, bitch!

Maybe she'll back off—or else we'll go to war!

Driving to school, she smiled to herself. *Wow! I feel powerful!* But, her inner voice said, *You're out of your league, Missy! Better watch your back.*

Later in the day Moria shared the Doris message with Maxine.

"Damn her hide!" Maxine scowled. "What are you going to do?"

"I've already done it!" Then she relayed her response to Maxine.

Maxine stared at Moria. "That's the message you sent? Bet the fur's gonn'a fly now!"

Moria answered, "Also, I'm going to tell Jackson about Doris's interference. Then if he hears some rumors, maybe it won't be so bad."

"Good idea," Maxine replied. "Let me know how it turns out."

"I'm on my way to Victoria's Secret after school. Maybe that will harden Jackson to the news!"

Soon the children occupied her day, and she was grateful for the distraction.

After school Moria drove to the mall to do her shopping. I feel like such a poser, she thought, opening the shop door to a brand new world. Dazzled by the colorful and exotic choices, she stood just inside the door and then turned to leave when a sales lady appeared at her side.

"May I help you?

"Uh, sure. I'm looking for some cowgirl underwear...well, you know—more than...underwear."

The sales lady smiled and said, "Come with me. There seems to be a craze for western clothes, even lingerie."

Moria walked out the door in shock. She peeked in the bag at the few scraps of material. "I spent fifty dollars for this? I could have bought a ton of horse feed for fifty dollars!" Before leaving the parking lot she took out her purchase and smiled. The material felt soft in her hands and the red and white bandana design was just too cute. Tiny spurs with quick release snaps held the pieces together. "Bet Doris Weaver doesn't have any cowgirl lingerie!" she said aloud. Her flushed face and bright eyes signaled a new adventure!

When Moria reached home she called Jackson. "Hey, I can feed the horses this afternoon but I want you to come over this evening. I've got something to show you."

"Sounds good," he answered. "See you then."

Moria hurried out to feed the horses then began getting ready for Jackson's visit.

After a shower and use of her meager beauty supplies she looked at the final result, saying to her reflection, "Wow! I don't look half-bad!" Just then, she heard Jackson at the door.

Throwing on her old blue robe, she went to let him in. As Jackson stepped inside, she dropped the robe.

He stared for a moment and then grinned. "This is what you wanted to show me?"

Twirling around, she laughed. "What do you think?"

Jackson swept Moria into his arms and headed toward the bedroom. "Actions speak louder than words!" It didn't take Jackson long to figure out the spur snaps and the cowgirl garments fell to the floor.

Pounce waited until the two were occupied with each other. Creeping into the bedroom, he looked at Moria's discarded clothing and grabbed it with his teeth. Wrinkling his nose, he trotted into the living room. Pandora looked at her companion with large round eyes. *You are in so much trouble!*

Pounce growled, *I'm not going to pee on this, just hide it,* he answered, stalking around the room.

Pandora began to lick her paws and wash her face. *Don't be surprised if you end up at the animal shelter,* and walked over to stretch out before the fire.

Much later Moria said, "Would you like a beer? I have something else to show you."

"There's more?"

"Well, it's on the computer. Prepare for a shock."

Moria opened Doris's message. Jackson read it and sat back, running his fingers through his tousled hair. "Too much drama for me!"

"What are we going to do?" she asked.

"We?"

"I need your help. I'm afraid this rumor will get out over the Internet."

"So? You think this will damage your precious reputation and your school parents might find out? Put your boots on, Missy! Grow up!" Jackson said impatiently.

"I could lose my job!" Moria began to pace around the room and bite her fingernails.

"Hey, don't chew on your paw! Better to wag your tail!" he laughed.

"Jackson, this is not funny! I'm worried."

He took Moria in his arms and held her. "I have a simple solution. You could start a new life in—"

"I'm not moving to Wyoming!" Moria pulled away and frowned.

"Here's another solution." Jackson sat down at the computer and proceeded to block Doris's access to Moria.

"I need to know if she's doing more stuff!"

"No, you don't. I'm sure Jada will tell you if there's more. Now, go to bed. See you tomorrow. I need to do everything I can to help Silver get better so he can go to the ride. Enough of this bullshit." With those words, Jackson gave Moria a hug and went out the door singing "Oh, give me a home where the buffalo roam..." His voice faded into the night as he reached his truck.

I need to get some fresh air, Moria thought. On her way to the barn she took a deep breath. The wind seemed to whisper through the trees—*this, too, shall pass.* Welcoming whinnies of the horses made her smile. Dixie and her pup bounded over in a joyous greeting.

Moria sat down on a hay bale and scratched Dixie's ears. *Dogs always have time!* she thought. Moria cupped the puppy's face in her hands. Looking into his bright eyes, she said, "I need to find you a home. You don't even have a name!" After giving the dogs and horses some treats, she reluctantly left the barn. Walking back to the house, she thought, *Jackson's right. Too much drama. We need to get ready for the ride. It was my fault—sort of—that all this got started in the first place. Well, maybe it was all my fault! I need to get some rest so the children won't run all over me tomorrow!*

When Moria went into the house, she saw her new garments under the kitchen chair. "Pounce, you rascal! What? Were you going to give Pandora a gift?" The cat rolled over on his back for a tummy rub and began to purr loudly. Moria scooped up her pets and headed for bed.

Chapter Eleven

*T*he next morning at school the children had just settled in for the day when Jimmy Brown raised his hand, waving a letter. Ms. Harris! I got a letter from Michael! Moria looked startled, her mind flashed back to the unpleasant meetings with the Dexter's. Jimmy handed her the letter.

"Well, how nice! Would you like to read it to us?"

Jimmy stood up proudly, cleared his throat and read:

Dear Jimmy,

Thanks for the news from Cherry Valley. The play sounds like lots of fun. We're coming to visit my aunt that weekend. Do you think the teachers would let me be in the play? Maybe I could have just a small part?

Jimmy paused and looked at Moria. "Can he be in the play?" the youngster pleaded. The class chimed in, beating on their desks and chanting, "Michael! Michael!"

Maxine pulled the divider back to see what she was missing. Without a word, Moria handed her the letter and waited a moment while her teammate read it, then said, "Maybe it would be good PR to let Michael be in the play. We could find a small part for him."

"Okay by me. Guess we'll have to run this by Mr. Baldwin."

Just then, the classroom door opened and Mr. Baldwin entered the room. Frowning, he looked around and said, "What's going on? I could hear your class all the way to my office! Maxine stepped out into the hall with Mr. Baldwin while Moria got the class under control.

Later, at lunch, Moria said, "Well, let's hope adding a new member to the play is not a mistake. At least, the boss was agreeable, but I don't think he's too happy! We'll have to make this work! We can have Michael come to the dress rehearsal."

As the busses rumbled away at the end of the school day, Maxine said, "Why don't we go for a ride this afternoon? Jeremy has to do inventory at the bar, so he's busy."

Moria said, "Sounds good to me. Jackson is doing some work on the Rutherford's farm. Besides, Silver's not well enough to go out. The vet is coming today to check on his progress. Hope it's good news."

Later, the two riders met on the road behind Moria's farm. "Where do you want to go?" she asked Maxine.

"What about River Road? We can get in a long gallop. We probably need it more than the horses!"

Fear balled in Moria's stomach. *Gallop on the River Road with all the critters, real and imagined, jumping around in the bushes? Has Maxine forgotten my fear of falling? What was she thinking?*

Maxine looked sideways at Moria. "You up for this?

"I feel weak!"

"Get ahold of the neck strap and give Rainbow courage with your hands and legs. Remember what you told me Jackson said? And, your dream about Rainbow Chaser. He told you, too."

"Let's go," Moria answered.

The horses puffed and snorted, challenging each other to a faster pace. The riders moved on at a steady trot for a couple of miles and then walked over the bridge to let the horses' breathing come back down. Soon, they were off again at a trot, a canter, and into a gallop. The wind stung Moria's eyes. She took a tighter grip and prayed to her guardian angel, *Don't let me ride faster than you can fly!* The horses neared the river, began to trot, and then slowed to a walk. Moria loosened the reins and relaxed. "Thank you, thank you!" she mumbled, looking around as if expecting to see the angel hovering nearby.

"What?" Maxine asked. "I couldn't hear you."

"Endurance angels probably run marathons in their spare time to keep up with us!" Moria laughed.

Moria took a deep breath of the warm spring air and smiled, grateful to still be topside on the horse as they crossed the river and headed for home.

Later in the evening Jackson, Jeremy, Maxine and Moria met at Moria's house to plan for the up-coming Sand and Waves Ride. The four friends sat around the kitchen table with a copy of the ride flyer and a map. Jeremy rubbed his hand over the map and said, "I know the GPS will get us there, but there's just something about having this piece of paper in your hand..."

Maxine laughed, "I know. It's like comfort food! Remember the time the GPS led us right into someone's farmyard? Luckily, the guy knew where we needed to go. We only wasted two hours! Yeah, better take the map, just in case."

"I don't know if I'm going to ride yet," Jackson said. "The vet is coming back one more time. He didn't say no, but I could tell he thought I shouldn't take him." He picked up the flyer and looked at it longingly. "This will be a great ride. Guess I'll have to crew and miss all the fun."

Moria said, "We can always use extra help. Speaking of... Sarah and her boyfriend want to come and help. Actually, I think they just want to go to the beach!"

Maxine looked surprised. "A boyfriend?"

"Well, I'm not sure. He does live on a horse farm in West Virginia. Sarah's been to visit and says it's a classy place."

"Meaning, they have someone to clean stalls?"

Moria laughed, "At least he lives on a farm. That's a pass in the door!"

Soon plans were made, and as they were leaving Jackson said, "Where's my list?"

"Hang around and I'll make you one in a while. See you guys later!"

"Before we get to in a while, we didn't talk about where everyone's going to sleep," Jackson said in a concerned voice.

"Here's what I'm thinking. Sarah said Will is bringing a tent. Sarah, Maxine, and I can sleep in my trailer and you can sleep in Maxine's trailer with Jeremy or you can sleep in the tent with Will." Moria smiled. "Your choice!"

"At least I know Jeremy. Guess that'll do." Jackson said with a sigh.

Moria put her arms around Jackson, pulled his shirt up and began to rub his back.

He smiled. "Oh yeah! If it makes you happy I believe I could spend a couple of nights with Jeremy." And with those words, they disappeared into the bedroom. Jackson pushed the door shut in Pounce's face. The angry cat yowled but his tiny voice was lost amongst the moans and sighs coming from within the forbidden room.

Pandora sat nearby, watching the scene. She purred at Pounce, *You're no match for Jackson!*

*Someday...*the angry cat hissed as he crept away.

Thursday evening Moria and Jackson met at the barn to pack the trailer. Jackson put Silver Dollar on the lunge line and they watched him trot in both directions.

Moria said, "He looks sound. What do you think?"

Jackson stopped the horse and unsnapped the line. "He looks fine to me. Dr. Barr said go ahead and take him to the ride."

Moria began to load Rainbow Chaser's tack into the trailer. "Well, what's the worst thing that can happen? You'll get pulled from the ride. The vets will keep a close eye on him. Besides, you'll know if something is wrong and you'll stop—won't you?"

"I've put too much work on this horse to take a chance on making him worse. Of course I'll stop!"

Moria thought, *Wait till you're caught up in the race. We'll see!*

Early the next morning the two trailers pulled out of Cherry Valley toward the Interstate. Dreams of success rode with them as they looked forward to the thrill of galloping on the beach. As the group drew closer to the coast, the sight of great live oak trees draped with Spanish moss and flat, sandy roads intersecting the highway brought speculation about what the trail would be like, remembering that sandy trails can be deceptive, taking a toll on the horses' legs. Most important of all, who would make it across the finish line?

As the trailer neared camp, Moria pointed to the side of the road. "Hey, there are some ribbons! This must be part of the trail!" And then, the ribbon markers disappeared into a forest path. "I can hardly wait!"

Turning off the highway and onto the entrance road brought Moria back to the business at hand. "We need to find a spot near the vet check and the water supply. I'm glad we remembered to haul drinking water for our horses, even though it's heavy. I've heard some horses don't like the coastal water. Here's a perfect place to set up camp and there's room for both trailers." Grass fields stretched out on both sides of the drive, with frequent water spigots stationed along the road.

As Moria pulled in to park, Sarah ran to meet her, followed by Will.

Maxine took a quick breath. "Oh my God! He's so cute and he looks strong enough to carry the water buckets."

Moria said, "Trust Sarah to catch a cutie!"

As Maxine got out of the truck, she answered, "Guess it runs in the family!"

Jeremy and Jackson pulled up beside Moria's trailer and the two men got out. Introductions were offered all around and Sarah gave everyone a hug. When she got to Jackson, she said, "You need an extra hug for taking good care of the horses and my mom!"

Jackson looked over Sarah's head and winked at Moria, saying, "Well, I don't know which is the harder job, your mom or the horses."

Sarah laughed. "I know that answer! Guess we need to get started. I think we've got a lot of work ahead of us. Why don't Will and I take the horses for a walk so they can relax from the trip?" The horses were unloaded and the two young people walked them away to a grassy area to let them graze.

The four riders began the routine of setting up camp. Soon the corrals were in place and stocked with water, hay, and small feedings of beet pulp and grain. The trailer awning sheltered tables, chairs, and well-stocked coolers. Jackson surveyed the scene with satisfaction. "Are we good, or what?"

"We're good!" Moria laughed and looked across the field to watch Sarah and Will returning with the horses. "Before we go to the check-in let's jog them out to be sure they're sound, especially Silver, and don't forget their travel papers," she reminded everyone.

Sarah and Will jogged the horses, one by one and the riders watched each horse's gait at the trot. They all agreed that the horses appeared sound and then the group moved on to the vet check. They joined others on the driveway and it soon became congested with competitors and horses headed in the same direction. "Watch out so nobody gets kicked," Maxine said, as horses whinnied and danced with excitement, seeing so many of their kind.

The check-in line stretched down the road so Moria suggested, "Why don't Sarah and Will wait with the horses while we go register and get the vet cards?"

By now, other riders had observed the arrival of the Cherry Valley contingent. Moria smiled. *They know fit horses when they see them!*

Returning to the line, Moria took charge of Rainbow Chaser, shifting her weight nervously while waiting for his time to be examined. The horse completed his vet check easily and his flowing gait at the trot gave his rider confidence that he could be one of the horses to beat. *He would be the one to beat, if I wasn't afraid to race him!* This thought wove tangled strands of doubt through her mind.

Silver Dollar passed the check with a caution from the vets, "We're going to watch him carefully because of his recent injury. Take care on the trail and good luck!"

Catch on Fire and Arctic Cat received excellent scores, and on the way back to the trailers, Jeremy commented, "Now, if we can just finish up as well as we're starting!"

Moria reached over to rub Rainbow's neck, thinking, no storms, no lost riders, thrown shoes, and no injuries. Is that asking too much? So many things can happen!

The riders jogged the horses back to camp and fed them, finishing just in time to hear the ride manager blow the horn, to signal the meeting.

"Sarah, you and Will might want to come with us," Moria said, as they gathered up their chairs and ride packets and headed down the driveway. "There might be some rules you'll need to know since we haven't been to this ride. Sometimes they don't want us to have crews on the road. At least there aren't any away vet checks!"

The riders reached the meeting and settled down to get the information they needed. Moria dug into her pocket and handed Jackson a pen. He took it and wrote sixty on his hand to remind him of the Limited Distance pulse rate. Covering her hand with his when he returned the pen, Jackson looked into Moria's eyes and said in a low voice, "Guess I'm a slow learner!"

"Not that I've noticed!" she laughed, feeling a warm flush spread through her body.

The manager went over the usual items, start times, vet criteria, layout of the trail and any hazards that might be encountered. In closing, she stressed to the riders, "I can't say this enough times—don't take the horses on the beach except during the hours of the ride! We can lose our permit if we violate this rule. It's okay for you all to go there whenever you want, but I think it's still too cold to swim! We're done unless you have any questions. Have a good ride! Stay safe. You know my favorite saying, 'keep the steel side down and the fur side up'! See y'all in the morning."

On the way back to their camp site, Maxine said, "I'll unhook my truck so we can get our stuff up to the vet check tonight. No need for Sarah and Will to have to do this, and if we set it up ourselves we can find things quickly."

Just before going to bed, Moria and Maxine checked the horses to be sure they had enough hay and water, and gave them a dose of electrolytes. Jeremy, Jackson, and Will took a few more things up to the vet check, and Sarah set out the stove and coffee supplies, fuel for the riders. Moria called to her, "Don't leave the food out! There's bound to be some raccoons around! They've gotten my breakfast too many times!"

Jackson said good night to Moria and reluctantly followed Jeremy over to Maxine's trailer. Finally, everyone was bedded down in their respective spots. Sarah said, "Well, Mom, looks like Jackson is really fond of you...or more?"

Moria, who was up in the top part of the trailer arranging her bedroll, glanced away from Sarah and then unzipped the sleeping bag, asking, "What about Will? I noticed he hardly left your side!"

Sarah laughed, "He was a little overwhelmed. I think he wants to impress you guys. He really paid attention at the meeting!"

"What about impressing you, sweetie?"

"Well, that, too!"

"Is he a keeper?"

Sarah yawned and pulled off her boots. "We'll see. Man! I'm exhausted but I am looking forward to tomorrow. Hope all of you finish. And Mom, thanks for letting us come to help."

"Hey, it's my pleasure! Sleep well. You might not thank me by tomorrow night!"

By habit, Moria looked out the window for one last check on the horses. They stood quietly, heads low, most of them sleeping. Gazing across the road, she could see Jada's camp, visible in the lantern's light.

*What mischief will she be up to tomorrow? I always dread hearing her run up behind me on the trail and fly past with some sassy remark. Someday...*and with those words Moria drifted off to sleep, hearing phantom hoof beats in her dreams.

Early the next morning the riders mounted their horses and prepared to face the challenges of the day: the trail, the vet check, and their own competitive spirits! A cool breeze blew from the ocean, stirring the Spanish moss which draped the ancient oak trees. The first light of dawn brightened the horizon, the gift of a day without rain.

As the riders trotted up and down the driveway for the warm-up, Moria said to Maxine, "Riding on the beach will be great! That's motivation to get to the last loop, 'cause that's the only time we'll go there. "

They slowed to a walk and Maxine said, "I'm impressed that they have volunteer scoopers to clean the beach afterward. I hope nothing goes wrong."

Just then the timer called, "The trail is open!" The front-runners, who had been lurking near the start line, galloped away, their horses running like they carried no riders. Moria and Maxine circled back to the middle of the pack. When they trotted out of camp, Jackson and Jeremy waved good-bye.

Jackson gave Moria a thumbs-up and pointed to his horse's neck, reminding her of Rainbow Chaser's neck strap. She waved back and took hold of it as Rainbow launched into his steady, flowing trot, a horse on a mission.

Moria's body tensed as she gathered up the reins and looked ahead. The horses surged along the wide, sandy road, a herd of grays, bays, blacks, and chestnuts with manes and tails flying in the misty morning.

Tears welled in Moria's eyes from the wind and the 'thrill of the chase.' The riders' attire, colorful as a scattered box of crayons, blended with the muted tones of the horses' coats, to create a lasting memory.

A flock of turkeys rustled in the bushes, causing Rainbow Chaser to jump sideways. Moria's joy swirled into anxiety as she lurched to the horse's side and grabbed his mane to right herself. "Nice save!" a passing rider called to her.

"Thanks!" Moria answered, busy reorganizing herself in the saddle. She looked over at Maxine, who was dealing with Fire's reaction to Rainbow's spooky dance, and said, "Sorry."

"Not your fault," Maxine replied. "Heads up, we've got some riders coming up behind us. We're almost to the turn-off at the jeep trail. Let's pick up the pace!" Rainbow and Fire's ears flicked back and forth upon hearing the urgency in Maxine's voice and the hoof beats of the approaching horses. Without a cue, the two horses began to canter.

The jeep trail led deep into a pine forest and palmettos grew in profusion, their sharp blades reminding the riders to stay topside along this trail! They sped along the path, wanting to put some distance between themselves and the oncoming competitors.

In a couple of miles they emerged from the pines onto a paved highway. A water tank had been placed on the grass beside the road and several crew people waited for their riders. Sarah and Will jumped off the tailgate of the truck and hurried toward Moria and Maxine to see what they might need.

"How's it going?" Sarah asked.

"So far, no problems. We've got a lot of miles to go," Moria said. "Did Jackson get out of camp okay?"

"Flew away like a leaf in the wind!" Sarah laughed.

Moria looked skyward, saying, "May the force be with them!" Rainbow and Fire stared down the road, watching their competitors diminish in the distance. "Looks like they're too wired to drink right now but there are some more tanks before we get to camp."

The two young people poured some water on the horses' necks, then Maxine and Moria prepared to leave just as the next group of riders appeared. "See you at camp!" Moria called to Sarah.

As they trotted away down the side of the road, Moria cautioned, "Remember the ponies. They were one of the hazards!" Soon they crossed the four-way stop and Maxine said, "They're near here. Yep. Here they come!" A herd of Shetland ponies barreled up to the fence and raced back and forth alongside the horses. Rainbow and Fire clattered onto the pavement and the riders slowed to a walk. Soon this 'hazard' was behind them, waiting nearby to terrorize the next group of horses.

As they approached the first vet check, Moria and Maxine dismounted, loosened the girths and walked slowly down the path so the horses could begin to cool. In the distance they could see Sarah and Will approaching at a jog.

Just then, several riders ran up behind them. "Heads up! We're coming through!" The Cherry Valley women pulled their horses quickly off the narrow trail to let the others pass.

"I could see Fire's pulse jump up," Maxine commented with a scowl, looking at the horse's heart monitor.

"Me, too," answered Moria, untangling Rainbow from a cluster of vines.

Sarah and Will took the horses to the crew area and began to prepare them for the exam. Sarah looked at her mother, "I know, Mom, no electrolytes until they are ready to leave."

After the horses had vetted through with no problems, Moria and Maxine rested at the crew area and the two young people walked the horses to let them graze and relax. Soon the riders were on the trail again.

The sun rose higher in the sky. "I'm glad we trace clipped the horses. It must be eighty degrees!" Maxine said, wiping sweat from her face and leaving dirty streaks across her forehead. "I've always heard ladies perspire and other women sweat. Guess we're the other women!"

"That's got to be more fun," Moria replied, pulling her sticky shirt away from her back. "My feet are starting to burn. I thought I had this problem fixed. I bought a size larger boots..."

"We'll do some research the internet when we get home," Maxine said. "You know endurance riders always have strong opinions and some of them are actually helpful!"

The two riders trotted on in silence for the next few miles, passing four or five riders who had slowed down. Moria recognized some the front-runners. Everyone spoke in passing and Moria and Maxine continued on their journey.

The second vet check went well although the heat and humidity began to take a toll on the horses, resulting in a longer time for the pulse rate to come down.

Sarah checked Moria's water bottle, "Mom, you didn't drink on this last loop! You know what happens when you get dehydrated—we'll have to pick you up from a ditch!"

Moria hugged her daughter, saying, "You're right! I just hate to drink much water 'cause then I have to get off and pee!"

Sarah frowned at Moria. "Drink, or lay in the ditch and wait for a ride to camp. Your choice!"

"You win! Give me another bottle of water." Securing the water bottle, Moria asked, "What's the progress for Jackson and Jeremy?"

"They got out of the vet check with no problems so they're on the last loop. They were in the middle of the pack when they left but I think they're going to pick up the pace." Sarah smiled at her mom, "I think your cowboy rocks! He and Jeremy are having a great time. I wouldn't be surprised to see those two in the top ten."

Moria rolled her eyes and sighed. "He's not my cowboy! If he was, he'd listen better! That guy has a lot to learn. We'll see. At least he's got Jeremy to keep him from over-riding."

Sarah offered her mom some sweet tea, a turkey sandwich, and chips. Then, handed her some jelly beans. "You know these are bad for you!"

Moria put the zip-loc bag of candy in her pack. "I'll have them on the trail. I need a sugar spike to get through the last loop. Look out beach; here we come!"

She started toward the Porta-Potty, calling over her shoulder, "Take care of my boy—and I don't mean Jackson! Be sure Rainbow gets his electrolytes, offer him just a little feed and let him graze. I don't want him running with a full stomach and it's getting hotter."

Moria and Maxine left on the last loop. The horses seemed to sense the riders' anticipation. Salty air laced the wind and lifted the horses' manes, alerting them to an unfamiliar environment.

As they trotted east toward the ocean, the cool forest of moss-draped oaks gave way to a line of scrub pines, twisted by relentless wind. The two riders stopped to let the horses breathe. Maxine looked at Fire's heart monitor and laughed. "Glad the vet check's not here! We'd never make it through!"

Moria gazed ahead to the dunes topped with sea grass. "Well, here we go! Guess we'd better let the horses have a peek before we blast away."

Just then, four riders came cantering down the trail. "Move over!" one of them yelled. Moria and Maxine guided their horses off the trail and waited. Sure enough, as the competitors topped the rise, the crashing waves spooked their horses and flung the riders onto the dunes. Maxine tried not to laugh as she and Moria rode over the rise, to see the errant horses racing down the beach without their passengers. Fire and Rainbow trembled at the sight of the rolling waves and the sound of the escaped horses galloping away.

The two Cherry Valley riders stopped, realizing this could have been them. Even now, their horses twirled and snorted. The fallen riders brushed themselves off and Moria rode closer. "Sorry the horses got away from you. Want us to tie them up if we catch them headed to camp?"

Two of the riders had already started down the beach in search of their mounts. The other two people, bedraggled and spitting sand, looked at each other, dazed by their bad luck. One of them answered, almost in tears, "We don't know what to do. This is our first ride!"

Moria checked her phone, glad to see it had service. "Why don't you all wait here? I'll call the ride manager and they'll send someone for you. Your horses will probably beat y'all back to camp."

The disgusted girls sat back down in the sand. "Thanks. Are you sure they'll come for us?"

"You all stay put. They'll be here. See you back at camp," Moria called over her shoulder, tossing them her tube of sunscreen and a couple bottles of water.

By now, Rainbow and Fire realized the waves were not a danger and the rhythmic sounds seemed to calm them. The two horses trotted along the beach and then began to canter, in pursuit of the missing horses.

The chestnut and the bay hunkered down and galloped faster. Fans of sparkling sand flew out behind them, testaments to their racing spirits!

"Oh my God! Get a grip! There's no stopping them now!" Maxine called to Moria.

Gusts of wind whipped the horses into a frenzy. Fear pounded in Moria's heart. Soon Rainbow's pace settled back to a steady canter. Moria took a breath and began to relish the thrill she had so looked forward to—galloping on the beach!

When they left the sandy shore and took the wooded path toward camp, Moria looked back over her shoulder, glad she'd met the challenge. *Maybe I will grow up someday! Fredrick, if you'd stepped up to the plate when we were married, I wouldn't be such a wreck!* A strand of Spanish moss brushed her face. She heard his voice in her head, *You are a wreck of your own making, just like me.*

Moria started to brush the moss away, muttering, "Am I hearing voices?" then snatched it from the tree and stuffed it into her pocket.

Before long Moria and Maxine came upon the other two riders who had been dumped on the beach. They were mounted and leading the riderless horses. Moria said, "I see you caught them. Your friends are waiting for a ride back to camp."

"Thanks. I figured someone would help them. Maybe we're not cut out for this sport!"

"Well, this is not a pony ride, for sure! I've learned some things the hard way, too." *And I'm still learning...*

Ignoring Moria's comments, one of the riders asked, "How far is it to camp?"

"Not too far." Moria laughed to herself. *How many times have I heard that statement, after hours on the trail? Did that mean a mile, five miles, what?*

The disgruntled competitors cantered away. In the settling dust, Maxine looked at Moria and said, "I know what you're thinking. Let them go. Their horses' respirations were really high. Bet you a dollar they won't make it through the vet check. Come on, let's get this done." The two women trotted on through the shaded trails and into a pine forest. Wisteria vines twisted through the trees. Lavender blooms cascaded from overhead, creating a shelter of flowers. The humming of bees warned them not to linger.

"Wow! This is like being in the twilight zone!" Moria said, looking back over her shoulder.

They rounded the last bend and camp came into view. "Uh oh, here comes Sarah. She's running. Something's wrong!"

Out of breath, her daughter said, "Silver's been hurt!"

"Oh no! What happened?" Moria looked toward their trailer, forgetting about the vet check.

"It's all over now and Silver's going to recover...eventually. He slipped on some pine needles and fell up against a tree, scraping all the healing scabs from his shoulder."

"Gosh! I'm so sorry! Poor Silver! Poor Jackson! How is he taking it?"

Sarah sighed. "Not too well. Guess he's showing his true colors. What a baby!"

Without thinking, Moria quickly took up for Jackson. "This is his second ride with no completion. That's pretty discouraging." Then, thinking about the riders who had been dumped on the beach, she said. "Well he'll just have to suck it up! Shit happens!"

Sarah looked sideways at her mom as they walked across the field, saying, "Let me take Rainbow to the vet check and you can go tend to Jackson." Without answering, Moria handed the reins to Sarah. Maxine walked ahead to meet Jeremy and Will.

When Moria reached the trailer she saw Silver in the corral, dozing from his tranquilizer. Medicine and blood dribbled down his leg and onto his hoof. Her heart went out to this gray gelding. Wonder what will happen to him next? *Maybe he needs to wear a Saint Christopher's medal to guide him on a safe journey!*

She walked around to the front of the trailer to see Jackson sitting in one of the chairs, legs stretched out, hat pulled low over his eyes, and a litter of beer cans scattered around him. Anger flashed through her mind as she remembered Fredrick's drunken sprees when things didn't go his way. Without thinking, she kicked his chair to wake him. "Get up you piece of..."The chair fell over and Jackson rolled to the ground, groaning and struggling to sit up. Rubbing his face, he looked up at her, and mumbled, "What?"

Moria began to cry. Jackson jumped up and reached for her. "Honey, what's the matter?"

"Don't touch me, you drunken fool!"

A look of alarm flashed across Jackson's face. "Hey! Wait a minute!"

Moria pushed the beer cans aside with her foot and Jackson took her in his arms, saying, "What is this? A Fredrick flashback?

Moria sobbed into Jackson's chest. "I don't know! I'm so tired, I can't think straight...and I'm afraid!"

"What? That I'm an alcoholic?"

"Yes." she whimpered.

"Oh my God in heaven! Come on, let's go for a walk," Jackson suggested, as they saw Sarah and the others approaching.

Soon they were settled on the river bank. Moria's thoughts whirled around like frightened birds. "I'm sorry. This isn't what I meant to have happen!" Sniffing and wiping her face on her sleeve, she leaned against Jackson's shoulder. "I know you're upset about the accident. I came to help you...but I guess that didn't work out!"

Sarah's words tumbled through her mind—*go tend to Jackson.*

Silence spun out in webs of confusion for the lovers. Finally, Jackson spoke, "Where are your big girl boots? It's your choice."

Jackson looked down at Moria's tear-streaked face and waited for her answer.

She tilted her face to his and smiled. "Guess I better take the leap of faith!" *For now anyway.* "Let's get back and check on the horses. I need to see how Rainbow and Fire are doing and I want to get a better look at Silver. Tell me what happened."

"To make a long story short, guess I thought I was riding the motorcycle. 'Nough said."

They walked back to camp, arm in arm. When they reached the trailer Sarah ran to hug Moria. "Congratulations! Fire placed ninth and Rainbow was tenth! We went ahead and stood them for Best Condition. Their vet scores were high but your finish times pulled the score down. Arctic Cat came in fifteenth. Jeremy got off-trail for a mile or so. He wasn't the only one. Maxine reminded me to tell you the beach guys didn't make it."

"Thanks, sweetie. I really appreciate all your hard work today, and Will, too," Moria said, giving Sarah a hug.

She squeezed her mom's hand and whispered, "Jackson really is a good guy!"

"Is that a vote of confidence?" Moria asked, laughing at Sarah's change of heart.

Later in the evening, the weary campers sat around a bonfire reliving the events of this day and days past, but conversation stopped at the sound of distant hoof beats pounding on the beach. Startled riders jumped up, thinking their horses were loose. Many people dashed back to camp and others ran toward the beach.

Someone called out, "Hey, there's the rider! Oh man! No clothes on her! Looks like Lady Godiva!" A bright moon back-lit the racer, silhouetting her shapely form and long hair whipping in the wind. She leaned low over the horse's neck, a ghost rider in the night.

Moria grabbed Jackson's hand. "Come on! I know who that is! Don't you?"

Jackson grinned. "Yeah. I guess it's Jada. Who else would it be?"

Sarah and Will raced with others down to the beach while Moria ran to their camp, pulling Jackson with her. "I've got to get the camera! This is my chance to get some leverage on her so she'll back off about Kam!" Flushed and breathless, she grabbed the camera from the seat of her truck. "We can catch her if we hurry."

Jackson threw up his hands and took a step back. "Not we, Missy. I don't have a dog in this fight." With those words, he took a beer from the cooler and settled into a chair, smiling up at her.

"You're not going to help me?" Moria stared at Jackson in disbelief. "Never mind! I need to go!"

She dashed across the road and into the edge of the woods, circling around to Jada's camp. Breathing hard, rivulets of sweat running down her face and back, she waited. Standing in the tree line, with shaking hands Moria aimed the camera. I have only one chance to get this right.

In the distance she could hear the ride manager yelling, "I'll find out who did this! I'll search every camp for a sweaty horse! We'll lose our event permit, for sure! Here comes the ranger!" Her strident voice faded into the night. Like a silent movie,

Moria watched the manager and the ranger in heated conversation, both with arms waving.

Chaos reigned in the camp as riders ran from corral to corral searching for the unknown rider who may have destroyed their chances of ever returning to this beach.

Moria checked her watch. Had only ten minutes passed since their pleasant evening had been so rudely interrupted? Steady now, she pointed the camera at the opening in the trees where she thought Jada would appear—suddenly having doubts about her hasty decision to play detective. Too late now! Here she comes!

Leaves rustled, branches parted, and Jada rode up to the trailer, naked as a jaybird, and slid down Blackjack's side to the ground. Stepping out of the trees, Moria began to record the moment as her digital camera clicked away.

Jada whirled around. "What the...!" Then, seeing Moria, she growled, "I should have known it was you!" Jada let go of the horse and lunged for the camera.

Moria held the camera over her head, saying, "Better get some clothes on and try to cool your horse down. Here comes the ranger!"

"You bitch!" Jada hissed. Grabbing a towel from a nearby chair and wrapping it around herself. "You'll pay for this!"

"In your dreams!" Moria laughed.

Jogging up to her trailer, Moria held the camera high, saying, "Got it!" She stopped short, seeing the grim faces of her friends.

"What? What's the matter?" No one spoke. Dread washed over Moria, sending crashing waves of uncertainty through her body. "I got some great pictures..."

With a straight face, Maxine asked, "You joining the Mean Girls Club?"

Moria looked from one to the other at their stoic faces. "What's going on? I just want Jada to leave me alone! This is my chance..."

Jackson interrupted, "To blackmail her?"

Moria sank to her knees, placed the camera on the ground,

covered her face and began to cry. Jackson crouched down putting his arm around her shaking shoulders. "Hey, we were just teasing! Guess we went a little too far!"

Maxine handed Moria a beer. "I am so sorry! We thought we'd have a little fun and made up this plan while you were gone. We're really proud of you for capturing that priceless moment! Tell us what happened,"

Moria and Jackson sat on the ground, Jackson's arm still around her. "I can't believe you all did this to me!" Moria said, pushing her tangled auburn hair away from her face and shaking her head in wonder.

Just as she began to relate the saga of her evening, the sound of running footsteps disrupted her tale. "Uh oh! 'Scuse me a minute!" Moria grabbed the camera and locked it in her truck.

Jada rushed up to Moria, who was still standing beside the truck. Fiercely grabbing her adversary's arm, Jada said in a low voice, "Give me the camera!"

Moria jerked her arm away. "No more harassment about Kam or anything else about my life. Do not break into my house. The memory card is going into my safety deposit box for safe-keeping!"

Jada extended her hand and smiled slyly, "Why don't we call a truce?"

Moria frowned. "Hmm...Seems like I've heard that before! Remember our 'talk' in the bathroom at the Juniper Tree? I don't trust you but we'll see if you can hold up your end of the deal this time. Guess we better concentrate on what really matters—competition on the trail. "

Without an answer, Jada walked away.

Moria returned to the group. "Let's vote. If you think Jada's done with her mischief, raise your hand." They all laughed, but no one lifted a hand.

The next morning Sarah and Will gathered up their belongings and prepared to return to school. Moria stood by the camp stove and poured fresh coffee into the mismatched mugs, each one sported a label for a completion award from some endurance ride. The enticing aroma wafted up from the mugs, drawing everyone to the table.

Moria hugged the two young people and said, "Thanks for all your help!"

Smiling at Will, she said, "And, what did you learn this weekend?"

He grinned. "More than I ever wanted to know about endurance riding—and the people," he said, glancing across the driveway at Jada's trailer. "Just kidding. This was great fun...guess I learned never leave home without your electrolytes—or the beer!" Laughter greeted his assessment of the trip.

Jackson and Jeremy helped the couple carry their camping gear to the car, Maxine and Moria began to gather up items which had collected under the awning and were scattered around the trailers—clothes, mostly wet and dirty, empty cans, paper plates, a set of splint boots and a sweat-covered saddle pad. Moria laughed, "Our parents would tan our hides if they could see this mess! Speaking of parents, my mom and dad are coming to visit sometime in the summer. Guess they think it's time to take a look at Jackson...if he's still here. Seems like he's spending a lot of time in Wyoming."

Maxine shook out another trash bag for the offending clothes and said, "Good thing Rodney can watch the Rutherford's farm when Jackson's gone since Jeremy likes to go Wyoming, too. For a used-to-be city boy he's really enjoyed his visits to the wide open spaces. Hope he doesn't get bitten by the western bug," she continued, throwing the bag in the trailer. "Whew! What a mess!"

Moria said to Jackson, "Do you mind if I ride back with Maxine? We've got a lot of school stuff to talk about. We need to load Silver in my trailer and y'all can take the other two."

"No problem." Jackson said.

Moria leaned into him and stroked his cheek. "You're the best!" she purred.

"Yeah? If I was the best, you'd be riding home with me." he replied.

"Oh, well, that's a good point!" she laughed. "See you tonight?"

"Count on it if I'm still walking. Y'all have a safe trip!"

Moria pulled her rig out onto the highway and headed back to Cherry Valley. Rainbow Chaser and Silver Dollar looked out of the trailer windows, blinking into the early morning sun. Silver snorted, What is going to happen to me next? *That cowboy is a piece of work! Guess he should'a stuck to motorcycles!*

Rainbow snuffled into his hay bag. "Who knows? Maybe you'll go to Wyoming and learn to herd cows. Might be safer than doing endurance!" The trailer picked up speed. The horses rocked back and forth, mesmerized by the passing traffic, settling in for the long ride home.

The two women rode in silence for a few miles, both lost in thoughts about their one-of-a-kind weekend. Then Maxine broke the moment, asking Moria, "Would you move to Wyoming? I can tell you and Jackson are becoming more that just a 'thing.'"

Startled, Moria looked at Maxine. "What brought that on?"

"Well, would you go?" Maxine persisted. "Is it still about Fredrick? I know you cared about him, in spite of that chaotic life. He isn't coming back, you know."

Moria gazed straight ahead as if her answer would be found in the stream of traffic. "I know that. I just don't want to take a risk on failure—again. Nothing's worth it."

"Don't be too sure. I think you'll be sorry when Jackson's gone for good...without you!"

Moria didn't answer but dug into her backpack which rested on the floor between them, and pulled out the handful of Spanish moss she'd kept from the trail ride. Rolling down the window, she tossed it out. "Good bye, Fredrick! Now, is that better?" she asked her friend.

"Only if it's better for you," Maxine answered quietly.

The miles rolled by and up in the morning Moria noticed a gas station at a country exit. Hmm, good place to unload the horses. "Your turn to drive," Moria said to Maxine as they slowed and pulled off the highway.

Maxine roused from her nap and looked out the window. "Where are we?"

"Half way home. There's a grass field next to the station. Let's take the horses off for a few minutes. Oh my aching legs!" Moria said as she climbed out of the truck and went into the store.

On the road again, Maxine was wide awake. "We need to talk about the play to be sure we've covered all our bases. Rodney did a good job teaching the boys to use the lassos. Maybe too good," she laughed.

Moria said, "That's great! Lucky we have talented moms to make the costumes and some of the dads are coming Saturday to build the scenery. Jackson said he'd help, too. Also, did I tell you? Jacky's mom volunteered to coach the kids with their lines. What can possibly go wrong with all this help?" She looked ahead, to see thunderheads piling up on the horizon. "Uh oh, looks like we might be heading into a storm, only here, we hope!"

Maxine followed her gaze, "Don't go there. It ain't over till it's over!

Moria leaned the seat back and turned on the radio to hear a prophetic country song "...Desperado, why don't you come to your senses?...Come down from your fences...You better let somebody love you, before it's too late." The words tugged at her heart. *Is that me?*

She reached for the jelly bean bag and searched for the green ones, feeding them slowly to herself and thinking about her future. Do I want to grow old-alone?

What about Kam? I know he's interested in me. What if we got married? I could stay in Cherry Valley. Maybe it would be okay. I could learn to love him.

The swishing sound of the tires on hot asphalt seemed to say otherwise. She could hear Jackson's soft whispers in the night and even now feel his closeness. Are we bonded? How did this happen?

Because you wanted it to, the singing tires seemed to say. Moria fell into a light sleep, only to be awakened by the stop and go of heavy Atlanta traffic. Turning off the radio, she sat up to help watch for unexpected events on the highway and finish the last of the jellybeans.

When they reached Maxine's driveway Catch on Fire galloped up to the fence with a welcome whinny. Moria said, "Looks like the guys beat us back. Maybe they passed us when we stopped at the gas station."

As Maxine climbed out of the truck and Moria took the driver's seat, Maxine said, "Get some rest. Let me know if there's anything I can do for Silver. See you in the morning."

When Moria reached Peace in the Valley Farm, Jackson was waiting. He opened the gate and then jumped into the truck. With a big grin, he said, "I sure missed you!" He lifted Moria's hair and began to rub her neck.

Moria leaned over, giving him a hug. "I missed you too! Let's see, how long has it been...six hours? We're pathetic!" she laughed; all her anxious thoughts gone with the wind.

As they unloaded the horses Jackson said, "I've got some steaks ready for the grill. Two. Just you and me. I need some alone time with you."

Moria smiled. "I am kind'a hungry... for you! Don't put the steaks on yet!"

She reached up to unfasten the trailer door and noticed a few strands of Spanish moss clinging to the back window. Staring at the tiny fragments, she frowned. "Guess we're not finished yet." she muttered and stuffed the omen into her pocket.

"Did you say something?" Jackson called from the other side of the trailer.

"No, just thinking out loud. Let's doctor on Silver and get these guys settled. If you'll start the chores, I'll hang the wet stuff on the fence. *Why is life so complicated?* Moria asked herself as she threw the saddle pads over the fence.

Chapter Twelve

*E*arly the next morning Moria and Maxine sat in the empty classroom waiting for the children. Looking around at the peaceful scene, Moria frowned, "I can't even remember what we're going to do today!"

Maxine walked over to her desk and glanced at the plans. With a wicked gleam in her eyes, she answered, "I believe we're going to have another independent study day."

The arrival bell rang and Moria brought herself back to the moment, hurrying to greet the children and take a read on their attitudes as they began their day. Even with tumbled thoughts of Jackson and their passionate interlude the night before, she managed to get the students started on their morning work. Just then, Moria looked up to see Mr. Baldwin's face peering through the small glass portion of the door.

"Heads up, at the door," she called softly to Maxine who was on the Internet looking up ride schedules.

Maxine quickly left the computer and the two teachers began moving amongst the students.

The principal entered the room, observed the divider pulled back and the students engaged at their tasks. "What are they working on?" he asked suspiciously.

"Some of them are doing remedial work and some are entitled to enrichment activities," Moria answered, not adding they will do this all day! The children continued working, with only side-long glances at each other.

The announcements came on the video screen and the class stood for the Pledge. No matter how many times Moria said the familiar words she never failed to get a lump in her throat, wondering what future awaited these children beyond their innocent childhoods.

The principal departed and as soon as he closed the door, the children clamored in a babble of voices, "Did we do okay? We were quiet. Can we have extra outside time?" Their hopeful faces looked to their teachers for an answer. Maxine and Moria gave their charges huge smiles and a thumbs up. Moria laughed, saying, "Good dogs!" The children responded, panting and lifting their hands like paws, looking forward to their earned reward.

After school Moria and Maxine gathered their classes in the auditorium to work on the play. "Oh, I forgot the scripts. I'll just be a minute." Moria said, hurrying back to class.

Maxine began answering questions about the costumes while the children squirmed in their seats, anxious to get on stage. She shouted to the boys who were wildly swinging their lassos at each other, "Cowboys, put your ropes on the floor! The rodeo's over!"

An announcement came over the intercom, calling Maxine to the phone. "Ms. Harris will be right back," and cautioned the children, "Sit tight for a minute." She could see her teammate down the hall talking to a parent. Catching Moria's eye, she gestured toward the auditorium then continued to the office.

Very shortly, shrieks issued from the waiting children and pandemonium broke loose. Maxine and Moria reached the door at the same time, to see the entire class running around the auditorium. The cowboys chased the screaming girls, yelling "Yea haw!" and trying to capture them with the lassos. The two teachers ran into the midst of the disruptive group, snatching the ropes away and motioning the bandits back to their seats.

Teachers who were still in the building and people from the office rushed into the fray. Most of the children had resumed their seats, knowing they were in deep trouble. "Babies!" the boys whispered under their breaths, causing more crying.

As the group quieted, Moria realized there were still screams coming from behind the stage. "Oh my gosh!" she said under her breath, racing up the steps and pulling the curtain aside to discover Mary Lou tied to a chair. The boys were unsuccessfully trying to blindfold her with a bandana!

Moria stared in disbelief "Stop it right now!" She grabbed the two boys by their arms and shook them soundly, not concerned, in the heat of the moment, about child abuse or the future of her job. "What do you think you're doing?" Her agitated voice echoed into the auditorium as she shook the boys again and glared into their startled faces.

Maxine ran up the steps to assist. Her distraught face appeared around the curtain as she came to Moria's aid while keeping a close eye on the subdued class. Waving to the assorted people at the door, she called, "We've got it under control!"

But Mr. Baldwin didn't agree. He came bustling down the aisle and up onto the stage, jerking the curtain open.

"What's the meaning of this?" he roared as Moria tried desperately to untie Mary Lou. The two boys stood to one side, frozen with fright. Jackey sniffed and rubbed his tear-stained face. In a low voice he mumbled a few words. "Speak up! What did you say?" he growled to the two lads.

"We just wanted to kiss her... like in the movies. I guess it wasn't such a good idea!" Jackey finally answered.

By now Mary Lou was untied. She smoothed her skirt, and smiled, looking up at Jackey with wide, blue eyes.

"You wanted to kiss me? Why didn't you just say so?"

Moria looked at Maxine, who covered her mouth to keep from laughing, and cringed at Mr. Baldwin's scowling face. "Ladies, I assume you are going ahead with today's practice. I need to see you all in my office before you leave."

"Yes sir," the two teachers answered in unison, herding their charges back to the group.

Moria addressed the class. "If we have any more uncalled for incidents we won't be able to have the play. This is really discouraging to see such outrageous behavior the moment you're left alone." She narrowed her eyes to portray her most fierce teacher face. "Got it?" They nodded and looked truly remorseful. The rest of the practice went smoothly. The children sensed their luck had run out.

After a dressing-down from Mr. Baldwin, who warned about "lack of supervision and straying away from reasonable educational practices," he dismissed them.

Moria and Maxine crossed the parking lot to their vehicles Maxine said, "Well, just a couple of weeks till the play. What else can possibly happen?"

Moria took a deep breath and let it out in an exasperated sigh, reminding her, "There's still the Michael factor. We won't see him until the night of the play. Guess we'll just hope for the best. Why do we always get into so much trouble?"

Maxine laughed, saying, "Maybe Thoreau had the answer, "If a man does not keep pace with his companions..."

Moria continued, "Perhaps it is because he hears a different drummer."

Laughing ruefully, they finished the saying together. "Let him step to the music he hears, however measured or far away."

Then Maxine added, "Let's hope we don't have to go far away, except for endurance rides!"

One afternoon later in the week Moria met Jackson at the barn to care for the horses. The sun colored the clouds with gold and a gentle breeze wafted through the trees. Moria stopped at the gate to watch Jackson bring the filly, Promise, in from the pasture. She smiled to see Jackson chatting away with his young charge. *I've got to find her a good home...an endurance home,* she thought.

Jackson trotted Promise toward Moria and posed her as if she stood in a halter class. The filly's spotted coat shone in the lowering light, her ears perked forward, waiting for the next command.

"Wow! You've done a great job with her," Moria said, delighted with the little one's progress. Jackson stepped the filly from the pose and Moria began to rub Promise's withers. "You know, we've got to wean her soon. What do you think about moving Phoenix over to the Rutherford's with Sarah's pony? They're good neighbors to let us spill over onto their farm." As an afterthought, she said, "Their property belonged to our original land grant but somewhere along the way the Rutherford's bought it and it's been in their family for so long nobody even remembers. Ha! I'm probably related to them somehow!"

Jackson laughed. "Spare me the family trees of the north Georgia mountains! Let's decide when we're going to make the big move. We're not going anywhere for a couple of weeks. I guess in the morning is a good time to start. I'll get Jeremy to come over and help me."

Moria looked doubtful. "I need to be here."

"No, you don't. Let us handle this," he answered firmly.

"Well...You'll call me if anything goes wrong?"

Jackson grinned. "Nothing will go wrong. Remember? I'm a cowboy."

She stepped closer and leaned into him, tilting her face to his. "How could I ever forget?"

Before bedtime Moria remembered she hadn't checked her e-mails. She said to Pandora, who perched on the shelf over the computer, "It's a good thing I don't have Facebook or some other such thing—I'd never get anything done trying to keep up with everybody's life!"

The large golden cat peered down at Moria, *You're right! You have enough going on in your own life, Missy! You better help Pounce before Jackson kills him!*

Unaware of Pandora's thoughts, Moria scrolled through the e-mails. Hmm...here's a message from Jessie.

Dear Miss Moria,

How are you doing? I am fine. Well, sort of. Miss Doris says she wants me to win the Junior Championship at the October ride. My mom and dad think she's pressuring me since this is my first year to compete. They're thinking about getting me another trainer but there is no one else close. I wish I lived in Georgia!

My mom and dad can ride with me but that's not real training. Can you coach me over the Internet? I can't wait to meet you! How is Silver Dollar? I'm sorry he got hurt. More later.

Love,

Jessie

Wow! What a mess! Moria looked up at Pandora and rubbed her furry face. "You're lucky. You only have to deal with Pounce."

You say! Pandora grumbled in her throat.

Moria sat for a few moments, thinking about how to answer Jessie's note.

Dear Jessie,

Sorry you are having problems. Do the best you can. The Internet is an amazing invention but I don't think I can help you this way! Let's stay in touch. Maybe after the Championship your parents can help you and you can continue your riding. I'm looking forward to seeing you in October but if it doesn't work out, there's always next year!

Keep the steel side down and the fur side up!

Love,

Moria

The next day after school, Moria went shopping for Jackson's consolation gift—a Saint Christopher's medal for safe travels. While looking at the choices, she noticed the Saint Jude medal and looked at the tag which read, "Persevere in the environment of harsh, difficult circumstances, just as your forefathers have done before you." Guess I'd better buy that one too! I'll get some for the rest of us, just in case. I need to hurry home to check on Promise. She's probably a wreck!

When Moria arrived home, Promise's plaintive whinnies greeted her. "Poor baby!" Moria said aloud, jogging to the barn. "At least Jackson's here."

The cowboy greeted her with a frazzled look, shirttail out, and his usually well-groomed hair standing on end. "Thank God you're here! This little girl's about to do me in! We never had this much trouble weaning foals on the ranch. I've been here all day because I was afraid she'd hurt herself."

Moria looked in over the stall door. Promise pranced over, thinking to be let out. Moria rubbed her neck. "No, baby girl. Maybe you can go out tomorrow."

Then saying to Jackson, "Thanks, I know this was a hard day. No more four-legged babies for me—horses or dogs! I'll call Maxine and Jeremy to bring some food from The Diner. We can eat here and keep an eye on her a little longer. What about tonight?"

Jackson answered, "She'll be okay by dark...I think. We'll keep the other horses in, too. That'll help. Yeah, food, good idea. Don't forget the sweet potatoes!"

As they opened the trailer to get out the table, chairs and other needed items, Moria asked, "What about Phoenix? Was she upset?"

"I trailered her over to the pasture and Jeremy stayed with Promise. The mare ran into the field and greeted Sarah's pony with a squeal and kick, then they settled down to graze. She's going to be fine."

Moria said, "What would you think about riding her after the milk bags go down? She's going to need a home, too. Or maybe we should keep her for a back-up horse."

"I vote for a back-up horse," Jackson said with a grin.

Moria thought, *Well, you're not taking her to Wyoming!* But she said, "She is half-Arabian and sound. That's a good start."

Jackson said, "What's her background?"

"The rescue people said she was broke to ride they thought."

Jackson laughed, "If she's not, it won't be the first time I've been bucked off!"

Maxine and Jeremy arrived with the food and they all settled down for a good Southern meal and a re-telling of Promise and Phoenix's new life.

After dinner, Moria said, "I've got presents for you guys. I'll be back in a minute. Soon she returned with the bag of medals which were fastened to key chains. She dumped the contents of her purchase on the table and picked up one of the items, dangling it back and forth.

Jackson grinned wryly, "You're going to hypnotize us?"

Moria handed him the key chain and said, "No, even better. Now you won't get hurt or in a desperate situation because Saint Christopher is the saint of safe travels and Saint Jude has got your back. Read the tag."

Jackson looked closely at the medals as Moria handed Maxine and Jeremy theirs.

"Hey, thanks! Looks like Saint Jude must have been an endurance rider in his past life, being that he knew about harsh and difficult circumstances. Just one thing—do you think the saints will have a GPS so they can keep up with us?"

"Let's hope!" Moria said as they finished the meal. "Thanks for bringing the food, Maxine. I owe you."

"Always," Maxine laughed, as she and Jeremy left. Over her shoulder, she called, "Don't forget the trail work day on Saturday."

Jackson looked at Moria with surprise and frowned. "A work day? You didn't tell me."

"Well, I was going to..." Moria kept her eyes on the cluttered table and began to throw the trash into a bag. "I didn't think you would want to go...because Kam will be there."

"Do you want me to go? Or is this by invitation only?"

Ignoring his taunt, she said, "Of course I want you to go. Will you?"

"Can't miss an exciting day in the woods with our fearless forest ranger. Sure, I'll be there. End of discussion."

An uncomfortable silence hovered over them as they fed the horses. When they started toward the house Jackson put his arm around Moria and began to swing the key chain back and forth in front of her. In a low, soft voice he chanted, "You are getting sleepy... sleepy. You want to go to bed with me." Then, he snapped his fingers.

Moria answered, "Wow! I am so sleepy! And I want to go to bed with you! Is that how it works?"

Jackson laughed and pulled her closer. "Remember what I said, hypnotism only works if you want it to."

"So this is a scientific experiment?"

"Yeah, but we're not finished!"

As the couple approached the house, Pounce pulled the curtain aside with his paw and peeked out. Growling, he began to shred the curtain.

Saturday morning the parking area at the trail head was crowded with trailers and forest service vehicles. The rangers gathered everyone together and discussed the parts of the trail in need of attention.

"Today we'll work in two groups," Kam announced. "I'll take some of you up to the ridge on Sawyer Mountain. There's a bunch of blow-downs from last winters' storms. If you're chain-saw certified you need to come with me, plus we'll need a few others to cut face branches and move debris. Jackson and Jeremy, you guys can move the logs off the trail where we cut. We'll ride in about five miles to work and bring the horses with us as we move along. When we're done, you all can ride out the way we came or go on down the other side and come back on the logging roads. Be sure you've got plenty of food and water. This will be a long day."

With those words, the groups divided up, some going with the other ranger to work on a washed-out culvert.

Moria said to Maxine, "Let's go with Kam. We'll get the most riding this way."

Jackson mounted up on Silver Dollar, whose shoulder was improving, "This is the first time he's been out since his injury. Cross your fingers." He smiled at Moria and snapped the saintly key chains to his saddle.

Kam's group rode their horses single-file through a short stretch of woods and into an open area, overgrown with kudzu. Huge piles of brush covered with dense green, leafy vines created an alien landscape. A few dead trees, bleached silver from the weather, stood tall against the blue sky. Here on this forsaken hillside the trees were a testament to the past when the foothills of the Blue Ridge Mountains were stripped bare for timber, leaving the mountains to heal themselves. The red clay logging road, eroded with time, added an unforgiving scar to the scene.

The trail workers, familiar with the surroundings gave it no thought, other than to know reclaiming this trail would be a job for "the big dogs," requiring machinery and professional expertise and most of all—money. As long as riders could struggle through the gullies, it would not be changed.

Soon, Kam began to whistle, "Oh, I wish I was..." the riders answered in lusty voices, "in the land of cotton!" And, everyone sang out, "Old times there are not forgotten!" Kam's rich baritone echoed above them all, "Look away! Look away! Look away, Dixie Land!"

Jackson raised his eyebrows at Moria and said under his breath, "Our ranger sings, too...among his other talents?"

"Oh, I forgot to tell you. Before The Juniper Tree had a permanent band, Kam played a guitar and sang there just about every weekend."

Jackson raised his voice over the continuing choruses of Dixie. "Did you go to the bar then?"

"Sure. We could hardly wait for it to open. You know, there's not much to do in Cherry Valley."

Jackson grinned. "What about your precious school parents? Weren't you worried that they would see you at a bar?"

Moria thought for a moment. "The temptation was just too great. Anyway, everybody went. I tried not to drink too much, or dance with the dads." She smiled, staring into the distance, remembering the fun of country western dancing and getting acquainted with local guys—the wanna' be cowboys whose enthusiasm was more evident than their dancing skills!

Jackson interrupted her reminiscing to say, "Guess that was living on the edge for you!"

Moria stuck her tongue out at him and said, "Enough. Let's sing."

The horses scrambled over the rough terrain and Kam began to sing as if he were performing again at The Juniper Tree. "Oh beautiful for spacious skies..."

Moria breathed in the warm spring air and glanced over at Jackson who had raised his voice to the song. *Even riding through a field of kudzu can make me happy, or maybe it's the company I keep!* and she joined in..."for amber waves of grain."

At the top of the ridge the riders dismounted. Kam motioned to Jackson and Jeremy. "Come on with me. We can go ahead and get the trees off the trail." He pointed to a couple of other guys. "If y'all will use the machetes and cut the brush back about five feet, the ladies can cut face limbs. Throw the branches off the trail. Be sure you toss them to the downhill side. Any questions? We'll meet at the flat rocks for lunch."

Moria said to the other women, "If it's okay with everybody, I'll go first and throw brush for a while and you all can do the face branches." All agreed, so she dismounted and began walking down the trail. Rainbow Chaser followed, snatching leaves from the fallen brush and pulling it back onto the trail.

Maxine laughed, "Hey, looks like your helper needs more training!"

"Well, that's not gonna work! Come here, mister." Moria looped the reins over her arm so she could have better control. "Too bad he won't throw the brush off the trail!"

The riders continued on their way, swapping off with the tasks. After a few hours Moria could see the guys ahead at the flat rocks. Their horses were tied in the shade and the men were unpacking their lunches.

"Thanks for waiting on us!" Maxine called.

Jeremy held up a bread crust. "I saved you some!" he said, holding it in his hand as if to give a horse treat.

Too soon, the riders gathered their trash, and prepared to leave. "Wow! I could stay here all day!" Jackson exclaimed, looking out over the valley, spotted with cloud shadows, splashes of sunlight and sheltered by the hazy blue foothills.

Moria mounted Rainbow Chaser and turned away. *Yes, but would you? Stay here all day... all year...and forever?*

Kam announced, "We're done for today. You can either ride back the way you came, which is shorter, or continue on the ridge, down to the old farm, and go home that way." The endurance riders chose the long route, but some others returned back down the trail they had worked so hard to clear.

In the evening, Moria and Jackson sat in the old country swing on Moria's porch. "Wow, I'm more tired than I thought," she said.

Jackson replied, "Come over here and lean on me. I'll push the swing and you can rest up for our indoor adventure."

Pounce peeked out of the bushes and then sharpened his

claws on the wooden flower box. *You will have a misadventure!* He growled.

Looking over at Pounce's preparations for the evening, Jackson said grimly. "Not this time, buddy. I'm on to you!"

Soon the cats were forgotten as the two lovers became lost in their moments of desire. The swing creaked and rocked until even Pounce backed away.

Jackson stopped stroking Moria's bare shoulders, stood up and said, "Maybe we should go inside. I don't think this swing can take much more!"

Moria laughed as she picked up their shirts, "This swing has been here longer than I have. It's pretty sturdy and no doubt holds a few family secrets!"

The door closed in Pounce's face. Pandora leapt down from her perch in a nearby tree. *Give it up*, she purred, swishing her fluffy golden tail. *Let's go hunting.*

* * *

The school play, "Alice Goes West," consumed the time and interest of the fourth grade class, with parents in and out of the room for last minute preparations. Even Mr. Baldwin stopped by to check on their progress.

After the principal left the classroom, Maxine said, "I guess we have his blessing, for now anyway. Let's hope nothing goes wrong."

Moria folded Michael's hedgehog costume and placed it with her books to take home. Then, picking up only the costume, said, "Why am I taking any work home? I'm too nervous to concentrate on anything but the play. Thank goodness we'll have Jackson and Jeremy backstage to help us. Mr. Dexter is bringing Michael a little early to fit the costume. I'll take care of this. Can you be sure we have all the music ready?"

"Done. All the CD's are in my purse. I'm going to stop by the auditorium and check the sound equipment." Maxine closed the classroom door. "Well, tomorrow's the big day!"

Moria tossed and turned throughout the night with fitful dreams of out of control cowboys and screaming girls.

Jackson called as she dressed for school on Friday morning. "Don't worry about the horses. I'll take care of them and meet you at the school this evening. Then he laughed. "I know. No beer for us or the cowboys!"

"Jackson, thanks more than I can say. Let's go to the Juniper Tree when we're done tonight and celebrate our efforts, and hopefully our success!"

"You got it, Missy. We're gonna have a great night!"

Jackson's encouragement lifted her spirits. As she met her excited students at the classroom door she remembered the endurance mantra, to finish is to win.

After school Moria and Maxine went to The Diner for a quick bite to eat then returned to school to change clothes. In the locked classroom the two teachers hurriedly dressed for the evening. Moria unzipped her bag and pulled out a floor-length lavender skirt and white old-fashioned blouse with lace at the sleeves and neck. Digging into her bag again she found her dancing boots. A gold belt and gold earrings completed her outfit.

Maxine began dancing the two-step around the classroom, flouncing her black skirt back and forth, fluffing the ruffles on her red blouse, and shaking her silver jewelry.

Moria joined in and the two friends began to dance up and down the aisles. A knock at the door and Jeremy's voice called, "Showtime, ladies!"

Soon students began to arrive, some too early. Maxine said, "Why don't you see about Michael's costume and I'll keep these guys corralled for a few minutes?"

Just then, Mr. Dexter and Michael came through the auditorium doors. The children began to chant and stomp their feet. "Michael, Michael!" Hearing their chants, he waved and ran toward his friends. Maxine laughed and rolled her eyes, saying to Moria, "So much for keeping order! Go on about your business!"

The next hour became a whirlwind of activity with a final check on the sound system and adjustments to the children's costumes. Jackson and Jeremy stayed in the background but a stern look from the men reminded the rowdy children that real cowboys had come to their play.

At last, the lights dimmed and the audience quieted. The curtain rose on a western backdrop of cactus, blue sky, towering snow-capped mountains and, for ambience, a few cow skulls and old wagon wheels leaned against the backdrop.

Kenny Roger's song, "The Gambler" began to play. The music faded. Alice tumbled out of the cardboard box tunnel and jumped up to meet the Queen who wore a resplendent pink cowgirl costume and gold crown. Her majesty frowned at Alice's appearance—blue dress, white pinafore, and black patent leather shoes—then screamed, "Off with her head!"

The audience cheered and the cowboys scrambled out from backstage, waving their lassos. Alice leapt back in alarm as she faced her captors.

Just then, the White Rabbit, dressed in a gopher costume and top hat came to the rescue. "Stop! She is my lady love!" He grabbed Alice's hand and the two ran off stage.

The Queen stared in amazement. "That's a fine kettle of fish!" she roared.

Moria and Maxine, standing in the wings, doubled over with laughter. "I don't think that line was in the script!" Maxine said when she could get her breath.

The cowboys looked at each other with confusion, not sure what to do without their expected cue lines.

The Queen stopped and stared toward the stage wings.

Moria said in a low voice "Get..."

The Queen smiled, then shrieked, "Get those interlopers!"

The play rolled on with few mishaps, and was supported by a delighted audience.

The curtain closed on the first act. The dads switched the scenery and the moms helped with costume changes and props.

Moria held up a sign printed in bold letters, Croquet Game. The children hurriedly took their places and waited impatiently for their favorite part of the play to begin.

The backdrop now portrayed the castle and rose garden protected by the cowboy guards. Some of the students became croquet wickets, bent over in a frontward arch, wearing white shirts with card designs painted on them. Cardboard flamingos, served as mallets. The hedgehogs, dressed in furry brown outfits, could hardly wait for the game to start.

Chaos reigned as the competition began and the audience cheered for their favorite players! The hedgehogs rolled around with abandon. The queen and her subjects grasped the flimsy birds and chased after the errant game pieces. The flamingos quickly became bent and the dyed pink chicken feathers flew off in all directions.

The queen finally screamed, "Enough! Off with their heads," pointing to the rollicking hedgehogs. The soldier-cowboys rounded them up and the curtain closed to applause and laughter from the audience.

In the final act, The Trial, Alice shrunk and grew to giant size, aided by the school technology teacher who used computers to convey Alice's image and voice onto a screen. Moria and Maxine waited with bated breath as the young students filled in with their parts at the appropriate moments.

With a sigh of relief at this success, the teachers gave the class a thumbs up as the curtain closed. The cast reappeared for the curtain call, and during the standing ovation from the audience, Moria whispered to Maxine, "What price, fame?"

The two teachers acknowledged the cast members and then accepted flowers from the Queen and Alice. Mr. Baldwin came forward and thanked the townspeople for attending the play and supporting the school. "Proceeds from this event will be used to open a reading area in our library which will be furnished with a couch and additional magazine subscriptions."

The principal beamed with pride, just like this presentation had been his idea.

As the cast and audience adjourned to the gym for refreshments, Maxine said under her breath, "Wonder how long we'll be in his good graces?"

Moria muttered back, "Just till we screw up. It probably won't be long!"

The teachers stayed busy accepting congratulations and chatting with the parents. The children, released from supervision, raced around the gym, sliding on their sock feet and scattering cookie crumbs about. Moria and Maxine looked at each other, smiled, and said in unison, "Not our problem!"

Having helped with the cleanup, Jackson and Jeremy came in from the auditorium. Jackson dusted his hands and announced to Moria, "Like it never even happened! All's secure. Let's head out!"

Maxine laughed, "We've earned some play time, for sure!"

Jackson teased Moria. "Is it okay if we walk out together? You know, the parents..." nodding toward the moms and dads gathering up their children.

She winked, "I think we're safe. They've got their hands full!"

Soon the lights from the Juniper Tree came into view, welcoming customers, eager for a night of fun. Jeremy met Moria and Jackson at the door. "Guess I'm the designated driver tonight since I have to work... again," he added, reminding Moria of his duties at the play. See you guys later."

The couple settled at their table crowded with friends. Richard said, "Jada and I saw the play tonight. Great work. Maybe you've missed your calling."

Jada lifted her glass, toasting the two teachers. "Ya'll need to quit teaching and go on to Broadway! Seriously, it was great entertainment."

"Thanks. Glad you enjoyed it," Moria replied as the waitress came to take her order.

Is she for real? Being so friendly? Maybe it's because of the beach pictures I'm holding hostage. Ha! Or maybe she's wishing we would go away to New York City. Too bad, Jada. You will eat my dust...someday.

At closing time the four friends walked across the parking lot. Moria thought, *It can't get much better than this....* Fragments of their past experiences flashed through her mind—the good times and the bad—remembering the day Jackson saved Dixie's puppy, helping to birth the foal, rescuing her from the river, the endurance rides, the on-going war between Jackson and Pounce, the magic between the sheets. Moria reached for Jackson's hand. *He never lets me down. He is truly a stand-up guy! What's the matter with me?* She sniffed.

Jackson stopped and turned Moria toward him, taking her face in his hands. "Hey, what's the matter? Didn't you have a good time?"

She looked up into his face. "Too much to drink. I guess adrenaline and alcohol don't mix very well."

Maxine, observing that the two had stopped, said, "We'll wait in the truck."

I can't go down this road right now. "I'm okay. I just need to go home."

Jackson looked worried. "Do you want some company?"

"No thanks." Moria giggled, leaning into Jackson, "We would disturb Pounce."

Jackson rolled his eyes and laughed. "At least I'm not calling you a drunken fool. Remember, at the ride when Silver got hurt?"

Moria tried to focus on Jackson's words. "Huh?"

"Never mind." Jackson answered as he guided her toward his truck.

The next morning loud bells clanged in Moria's ears. Or, maybe it was the phone? "Hello?"

"Good morning, Ms. Moria, it's Michael. We're getting ready to leave town and I asked my dad if we could stop by your farm and see the horses and dogs." He stopped for a breath, waiting for her answer.

Mr. Dexter took the phone. "Hope this isn't inconvenient. Michael talks about the pictures on your desk and has always wanted to visit your farm. We won't be back in Cherry Valley for quite a while." He paused, "I know this is asking a lot."

Moria headed for the kitchen with her cell phone pressed to her ear. Putting it on speaker and starting the coffee, she said, "Sure. Why not? Give me an hour or so. I'll look forward to seeing you all. Let me give you directions."

After coffee and a shower, pieces of the night before fell into place, all except the last part of the puzzle, her Wyoming cowboy. Pounce and Pandora sat attentively on the bathroom counter, staring at Moria's face, sensing her unsettled thoughts.

Hearing the crunch of gravel on the driveway and knowing her company had arrived, she scooped up the cats with a hug. "As you so rightly said, Scarlett, 'I'll think about that tomorrow!'" Then, she opened the front door to greet Michael and his dad.

At the barn, Michael petted the dogs and Moria pointed them toward the creek, saying to Mr. Dexter, "It's not too deep."

Michael's dad watched his son romping with the dogs. "He's always wanted a dog. Maybe we'll look for one when we get home."

Moria watched the boy and dogs race toward them. "I'm looking for a home for the pup. What do you think?"

Mr. Dexter said, "Oh, I couldn't. I'm sure these dogs are expensive."

"I want this pup to have a good home," she answered.

With a broad smile, Mr. Dexter shook her hand. "Done," he said. "We have a big yard, and she'll get the best of care."

Out of breath, Michael and the dogs collapsed nearby. Moria knelt down by them and said, "Would you like to have a dog?"

"Oh, yes! My Dad said we could get one soon." He rubbed the pup's ears and stroked her coat as he spoke.

"What about now?"

Michael looked at his dad and back to Moria. "Now?"

"How would you like to have Dixie's pup?"

The child's eyes grew wide with understanding, as he threw his arms around the dog and buried his face against the soft gray fur.

Looking pleadingly at his dad he said, "Can I?"

Mr. Dexter leaned down to pet the wiggling dog. "She's yours." His voice caught. "What will you name her?"

Michael took the pup's face in his hands and looked into her eyes. After a moment he said, "I'm going to call her Rascal." And the two rolled over and over in the grass. Then he paused. "What about Dixie? Will she be sad?"

Moria laughed. "Oh no, she has a friend named Hero. She'll be fine."

As the Dexter's drove away, Moria sank onto the porch swing. Dixie sat at her feet, looking worried. Moria scratched the dog's ears. "Give me a minute, baby girl, for some more coffee. We'll round up Jackson and Hero for a walk. Guess you'll be keeping the trail hot going to visit him! You're a good mom, but no more puppies!"

Later, Moria and Jackson walked through the Rutherford's fields on the way to the creek. Hero and Dixie bounded ahead, chasing each other through the fescue grass. The tall strands bent in the breeze, weighted down by the seeds. Jackson took Moria's hand and said longingly, "We could take a break and rest in the grass. Don't you think that would be romantic?" He turned her toward him and gave her a teasing kiss.

Moria pulled away and looked across the waving grass, smiling up at him. "Not me! Have you ever heard of chiggers?"

"What? Is that another Southern thing?"

By now, they had reached the creek and settled on the smooth, flat rocks jutting out into the water. Moria said, "You will want to rip your skin off, you'll itch so bad! Then, you have to put this awful smelly stuff on the itchy places. Not worth it!"

Jackson rubbed his hand over the rock, and tipped Moria's face toward him. What about here? Do chiggers live on rocks?"

"No chiggers." She kissed him with meaning and said with a grin, "This will only happen if you put your butt on the rocks!"

Later, Moria reached for her clothes and heard a noise on the bank. Dixie and Hero peered over the edge as if to say, "Y'all done yet?" The two lovers burst out laughing and Moria said, "At least Pounce wasn't here."

Jackson cringed, remembering the painful scene, Pounce leaping on his bare back and the chaos that followed.

Moria smiled as Jackson helped her up. "Well, I guess now you'll have rock burns instead of rug burns! Jackson reached behind, feeling his butt. "Hmm...guess it was worth it! Next time, I vote for a bed! I'm hungry. Let's go eat. Didn't Maxine say she was cooking fried chicken tonight?"

Sitting around Maxine's kitchen table as they finished off the last of the pecan pie, Jeremy leaned back in his chair, propping it on two legs against the wall. Without thinking, Maxine looked at Jeremy said, "Four on the floor."

Jeremy shot her a puzzled look. Moria covered her mouth to keep from laughing.

"Huh? What?" he asked. "Oh, you think I'm gonna fall and hurt myself?" Just then, as he sat forward, the chair fell over. Hands on her hips, Maxine peered down at him. "At least I don't have to write an incident report!"

At last everyone settled on the screen porch, Maxine serving mugs of coffee, laced with Irish whiskey. Maxine leaned over to Moria handing her the cup. "Guess you could use this," she said with a straight face, reaching over to pull some leaves from Moria's hair.

Moria had the grace to blush, cutting her eyes sideways at Jackson. "Umm, uh..." she said under her breath, brushing the rest of the leaves away.

Maxine grinned wickedly. "Get it when you can!"

Jeremy stretched his legs out in front of him and savored his coffee. "Where's our next ride?" he asked, knowing this would be a hotly debated topic.

After much discussion and Maxine bringing her laptop out to check the ride schedule, Jeremy said, "I vote for the River Song Plantation ride."

A chorus of ayes met his suggestion. Jackson joined in and then said, "Now I've heard everything! I know you guys are dying to tell me all about it."

The three friends' words tumbled over each other, everyone talking at once. Jackson caught only a few words, the clothes... and food...rooms. Jackson held up his hands in surrender. "Hey, one at a time! This is an endurance ride? We're going to take the horses?"

Jeremy said with a grin, "You will forget you went to the ride, but you'll remember the trip! We usually ride only twenty-five miles so we can have time sit on the veranda and sip mint juleps. Then, we need time to dress."

Jackson looked perplexed. "We have to wear a tux?"

Jeremy laughed. "Oh no! You will wear a full Confederate uniform, complete with sword."

Moria added, "My favorite part is the dresses. Some of them are originals or excellent replicas. They are gorgeous! The staff does our hair and make-up. It's truly a premier event."

She looked at Maxine. "Changing the subject, maybe we should ride the fifty. We don't want to get behind with our points. This will be a pretty fast ride and the horses are fit. I think we'll be back in time for a mint julep. We could ride on Friday."

"You're right," Maxine answered. "Jeremy, what about you?"

"Guess I'll ride fifty, too."

"Maybe I would do better in a fifty. I could ride with you guys," Jackson said in a hopeful voice.

"Silver is barely over his injury. I wouldn't do it," Moria reminded him.

Determined not to give up, he said, "What about twenty-five?"

"Let's see how he is, closer to the time for the ride. Maybe someone would lend you a horse."

"Who would do that? I haven't even finished a ride!"

Moria smiled. "You could pay...lease a horse. Let me look around for you."

"I don't want to finish my first ride on some stranger's horse!"

"You're right. Let's be sure Silver's fully recovered. He seemed good when we did the trail work."

Jackson went out with Jeremy to feed the horses while Maxine and Moria cleaned up the kitchen. Moria said wistfully, "I want Jackson to finish a ride almost more than for myself. If we can get Silver going again, maybe it will happen."

Moria and Jackson said their goodnights and climbed into his truck. Moria leaned back in the seat and closed her eyes.

"Wear you out on our excursion to the creek today?" Jackson asked, reaching over to rub her arm.

"You wish! No, not to disappoint you...I'm thinking about the ride. I want to get our entries in tonight. There might not even be room."

Jackson replied, "Money talks."

"Not at this ride. The legacy people get a phone call to see if they're going to attend, and they have first choice on everything."

"Humph. Guess you better take care of it tonight. Sounds like it's gonna be fun."

Chapter Thirteen

*T*he last days of school unraveled like a ball of yarn in a room full of kittens. The teachers, school-wide, hurried through their tasks with dazed expressions, filling the trash can with more and more papers that suddenly lacked the importance they had held the week before. Finally, the doors clanged shut.

A TV station from Atlanta made its yearly trip to Cherry Valley to film the unusual school closing. A blur of faces looked out the bus windows as the busses roared away. Some of the teachers line-danced down the sidewalk (thanks to instructions from the P.E. teacher!) Even Mr. Baldwin joined in. They waved goodbye and sang, the wheels of the bus go 'round and 'round, all through the town.

Moria breathed a sigh of relief, saying to Maxine, "Glad we had the option to finish post-planning early."

"Yeah. Otherwise, we would have had to come back to work on a furlough day...for no pay!"

Maxine called before Moria reached home. "Why don't we go camping this weekend? The horses need a good work-out to get ready for River Song. I thought we might go to Lizard

Springs. They've got electric at the campsites and a band plays every night during the summer. We can even swim in the lake. Best of all, there's miles and miles of trails."

"You don't have to ask twice, I'm on it! I'll call Jackson. I don't think he's got a lot to do on the Rutherford's farm this weekend. We don't need much food since they have a great restaurant. We don't even have to hurry home Sunday night. Oh, joy! I can hardly wait!"

The Cherry Valley riders reached Lizard Springs by noon Saturday. The sun, high above the trees, sent shafts of scattered light through the pines beckoning the campers to unknown trails and fun in the sun.

The driveway to camp twisted up the steep hill, with hairpin turns not designed for the faint-of-heart. Moria looked out over the edge of the road at the treetops and into a deep ravine. "Humm. Maybe this wasn't such a good idea. I hope they have search and rescue nearby!" The truck crept onward to their destination. Twice, she grabbed Jackson's arm when she heard the horses scrambling for their footing.

He shook her off saying, "What are you thinking? Let go!"

"Oh, jeez! I'm sorry! I know better," she answered contritely. "It's just different when I'm not driving.

Soon they were settled at their camp sites and the horses had time to rest while the riders ate lunch. "Here are the trail maps I pulled off the internet last night. Looks like some challenging riding," Moria said, giving them the maps.

"Must be a school teacher thing—passing out papers. Are we ready for our lesson?" Jackson teased her.

"You might be glad to have this map before we get back. Guess we'd better take the GPS too, just in case. Why don't you get it from the truck and pack it in your enormous saddle bags, since you insist on having your horse lug around this extra weight!"

"'Nough said, Missy," Jackson replied, heading toward the truck.

The four riders mounted up, fortified with snacks, water, the GPS and ...the maps. The horses stood calmly, sensing they were not at an endurance ride. A steep trail led out of camp and up the mountain. "Not a good place to start with fresh horses." Maxine laughed, clinging to her gelding's mane.

The riders climbed for about twenty minutes, finally reaching a ridge high above the camp ground. They stopped to gaze at the beauty below and let the horses breathe. In the valley, to the east side of the ridge, camp appeared to be inhabited with toy horses and people. The river, a ribbon of silver, meandered through the mountains, emptying into a huge reservoir dotted with tree-covered islands.

Jackson said, "I know Wyoming has spectacular scenery but this is down-home gorgeous!"

Moria smiled and thought, *Someday you will love the South, God willing.*

The horses trotted along the ridge. Rainbow Chaser, in the lead, began to canter. Moria grabbed his neck strap with one hand, deciding to let him roll on, even though a flicker of fear lurked in her mind.

Wind blew strongly across the mountaintop. The sun shining through leaves cast moving patterns across the trail. Moria's horse took advantage of his lead and picked up the pace. Rounding a curve, the gelding skidded to a stop at a downed tree across the path. Losing her grip, Moria threw her arms around the horse's neck and slid to the ground.

Catch on Fire, following close behind, sidestepped off the trail. Arctic Cat and Silver Dollar pulled up short. Jackson jumped off, threw his reins to Jeremy, and ran to Moria. "Are you okay?"

The fallen rider laughed, "What's new? I'm fine, just facing my fears again! Why can't I stay on this horse?" She leaned her face against Rainbow's sweaty neck.

Jackson turned Moria to him, holding her close and whispered, "I would kiss you, but not the sweaty side!"

She wiped Rainbow's sweat on her sleeve, turned to him and laughed. "I didn't kiss him!" Taking Jackson's face in her hands, she said, "How about this?" Her lips locked onto his surprised mouth.

"Get a room!" Jeremy called. Looking at Maxine, he winked and said, "Or, maybe we'll join you!"

Jackson replied, "Oh, yeah, we've forgotten the mission. Get to the end of the ride so we can get a room!" Now, we've got to figure a way to get around this tree."

The large oak had fallen across the trail. A steep bank rose to the left and the tangled roots of the tree and high rock ledges blocked any chance of going up and around. The riders looked downhill into a ravine, covered with thick underbrush.

Maxine said, "I hate to go back. Let's try to go under."

"Huh?" Jeremy said, looking perplexed.

"We can cut some of the branches away, take off the saddles and the horses can get under!"

"What? Cut the branches with our teeth?" he asked.

Looking at Moria, Jackson said smugly, "Behold! I will reach into my enormous saddle bags and presto, a camping saw! Good idea, Maxine."

The men took turns sawing the limbs. After tying the horses, Moria and Maxine threw the fallen branches to the side of the trail. Moria laughed. "I never thought we'd be doing trail work on our vacation!"

Clearing completed, the riders unsaddled. One at a time, rider going first, each horse crouched down and dashed under the tree trunk. Once more, saddled up and moving down the trail, the group enjoyed an uneventful trip back to camp.

Upon their arrival, Jackson said, "I'm going to the office and tell the rangers about the tree. They'll want to get it down before there's a serious accident. We'll get showered at the bath house and meet y'all at dinner." The two men headed to the lodge.

Moria and Maxine looked at each other. Maxine said, "Looks like we're in charge of all else," and they began bedding the horses down for the night and stowing the gear away.

Moria scooped grain into the horse's buckets, saying, "You know, I love taking care of the horses. Maybe it's because they appreciate what we do for them!"

Cutting the hay bale strings, Maxine replied, "Men, they're such rascals, but how could we do without them?"

Moria agreed, thinking of Jackson's warm arms and skillful hands. An evening breeze sent a shiver down her spine, or was it thinking about the night to come?

Startled awake the next morning, Moria sat up, disoriented for a moment. Bright sun streamed into the trailer and the horses scuffled around in their corrals, banging on their feed buckets. Waking Jackson, she said, "Your turn."

He sat up rubbing his eyes. "Oh yeah, feeding." Climbing out of bed, he struggled into his jeans and tickled Moria's foot. "Have fun last night?"

She scratched his chest with her foot. "You're always the icing on the cake especially after all those hours of cowboy dancing."

He answered, Well, get up, Missy, I have another treat for you. Get your bathing suit on."

"I thought we came to ride?"

"You'll see." With those words, Jackson went out to feed the horses.

The four friends gathered for breakfast. Between bites of sausage and maple pancakes, Moria and Maxine tried to get a straight answer from Jackson.

He only laughed and said, "Guaranteed to rock your world!"

When they returned to the trailers, Jackson said, "Don't bother to saddle, and leave the jeans, we're going swimming! Y'all can swim, I hope."

Jackson laughed as Moria and Maxine looked doubtful, full of questions. "Come on, let's head for the beach!"

They mounted up bareback, no shoes, no helmets. Moria stressed, "I can't go without my helmet!"

"Ah, but you will. Let's go."

Moria's scattered thoughts brought back memories of the motorcycle ride to Drapersville last winter. *It was scary, but I did have fun. How bad can this be? I might even like it.* With those thoughts she relaxed to the rhythm of Rainbow's long-strided walk as the horses went single-file down the path to the beach. Small waves lapped gently at the shore. The horses stood and looked with caution and then, followed Silver Dollar's lead into the water.

Moria called to Jackson. "Wait! I need a tutorial. How are we going to do this?"

At that moment, Catch on Fire pawed and laid down in the shallows. Maxine jumped out of the way, knee-deep in the water. Then the horse scrambled up, shook himself and tossed his head, slinging drops of water on his rider. Laughing, she said, "Maybe we do need a lesson."

Jackson urged Silver into deeper water. "Just follow me. It's easy. Stay on their backs until they begin to swim. You can stay on, or hold the mane and swim beside them. Just keep your legs out of the way."

Moria frowned, looking across the lake. "So where are we going?"

"To the island!" he shouted, as his horse plunged into deeper water and began to swim. Catch on Fire followed, then Artic Cat and last, Rainbow Chaser.

Moria felt the horse's legs begin a powerful churning. She quickly stretched out, floating in the water, holding on to Rainbow's mane and flutter-kicking beside him. The surface of the lake broke into sparkling waves, tipped by a white froth but Moria had no time to think about the scene around her. Keeping her goal—the island—in sight, spitting water, and kicking as hard as she could, Moria and Rainbow swam on in the choppy waves.

She could see the other horses and riders swimming strongly ahead, as if this was an everyday occurrence. Almost there! Moria took a moment to look over her shoulder. A crowd had gathered on the distant shore to watch the swimmers progress. About half-way to the island a small motor boat idled in the water to ensure their safety.

Dripping horses and riders scrambled up on the beach. "Wow, that was fun! Now what?" Maxine asked Jackson. "Looks like you have this all planned out!"

"This is going to be great!" Jackson said, "Come on! Let me show you where we're going to put the horses." He led the way across the beach and through a wooded area on the way to the other side of the island.

Barefoot, the four friends walked cautiously down the dirt path, trying to avoid rocks, pine cones and sand spurs. Spying a convenient tree stump, Jeremy said, "Why don't we ride?" leaping onto the stump and swinging his leg over Arctic Cat.

Relief calmed Moria's pounding heart. By now, the missing helmet was not even a thought. Walking near the horse in her bare feet was the immediate fear but when she mounted Rainbow his wet, slick body became her island of safety.

Soon they emerged from the woods. A small grassy area surrounded by a split rail fence which extended out into the lake, awaited them.

"I can't believe this! It looks just a like a movie set. How'd you do this?" Moria asked, sliding off Rainbow, forgetting all about her feet.

"Money talks," Jackson laughed. "When I went up to tell the office about the fallen tree, I saw a brochure about the island trips, by boat. A few people swim their horses, thus the corral. There's more. Let's put the horses away and get back to the beach."

The riders gathered at a picnic table tucked into a stand of hardwoods. "Well, if this is not the cat's pajamas!" Maxine said, looking at the table surrounded by several coolers. "Let me guess, fried chicken and potato salad...and?"

"Let's take a look," Jackson said, beginning to set food on the table. "Hot biscuits in the warming bag and a pecan pie." Searching in another cooler he produced, beer, wine, water and soft drinks. "Dig in!"

Later, the friends stretched out on the beach towels provided by the lodge. Moria sighed and rolled over onto her stomach.

"Goin' to sleep?" Jackson asked, brushing her auburn hair away from her face.

"No, I'm enjoying a great way to do a training ride. Just think, if you lived in Cherry Valley, we could come here all the time."

Jackson sat up and looked out across the lake, not answering.

Moria sat up also. *Uh oh. I've spoiled our day.* He drew a line in the sand and placed a small rock on each side. Then, jumping one of the rocks over the line he said, "Let's just settle this and make plans to go to Wyoming."

Silence hung over the couple like a brewing storm.

Moria bristled, saying "I've told you I'm not leaving Cherry Valley. This is my world." She drew her knees up, rested her forehead on them, and then turned her face away.

Jackson hurled the rocks into the water. "Yes, this is your world, your tiny world. I give up! I'm going to check on the horses."

Jeremy got up from his towel. "Guess I'll go check on the horses, too." With those words, he ambled down the path after Jackson.

Moria continued to sit with her head on her knees. Maxine sat up and said, "What are you thinking?"

Moria leveled a gaze at Maxine. "I'm not going to Wyoming. I don't think I can handle this relationship. What if I fail again?"

Maxine said, "Just suppose Jackson did move to Cherry Valley. How would you feel?"

Startled, Moria stood up and shook out her towel. "What? Do you know something I don't know?"

"No, just a 'what if' question."

"Well, I don't see that happening. Jackson's already talking about going home a few weeks early to help with the cattle drives. He said Jeremy would finish out the house-sitting."

"So how do you feel about that?" Maxine asked, folding her towel and going over to get a drink from the cooler.

"Who are you—Dr. Phil?"

Maxine laughed, "Sometimes I feel like it!"

"So what would you do?" Moria asked.

"I don't have to make that decision. Hey, here come the guys with the horses. Guess we're leaving."

Jackson rode Silver Dollar and led Rainbow. Jeremy followed on Arctic Cat, leading Catch on Fire. Jackson announced, "Ladies, your mounts a wait." He jumped down and handed Moria Rainbow's reins. "Want a leg up?"

Moria searched Jackson's face for a clue to his mindset. *Is he mad? Does he really care? Are we done talking?*

"Sure. Thanks."

The horses plunged into the water and swam toward the distant beach as if they did this every day. The setting sun colored the waves orange and pink with touches of gold. Just like swimming in a kaleidoscope, she thought as mauve and gray washed through the colors. *That's my life, always changing. Maybe it's time to be a grown-up. But, what does that mean?*

Rainbow snorted water from his nose, seeming to say, "It means put your boots on, Missy!"

Moria looked closely at the side Rainbow's face. "Did you say something?" But Rainbow did not answer, swimming steadily on toward shore.

The horses and riders reached the beach, chilled and hungry. At camp Moria and Maxine gathered up their clean clothes and headed to the showers. "See you at the lodge!" Maxine called over her shoulder.

Later, seated on the terrace to a meal of barbeque and all the trimmings, the four friends relived the day, carefully omitting Jackson and Moria's disagreement. Maxine brought up the River Song Plantation ride and they discussed the logistics of when to leave, what to take, getting the horses shod and hiring their neighbor, Rodney, to tend to the horses that would not be going to the ride.

By the time they returned to camp stars shone like beacons across the sky. *An answer to my life?* Moria wondered. *Which way do I go?*

The couples reached the trailers. Jackson took Moria's hand, saying, "Want to call it a night?"

Grateful for the warmth and strength of his hand she answered, "Sure. See you guys in the morning."

Settled in the bed, Jackson took Moria in his arms. "Sorry I upset you today."

"Well, it was my fault, too."

Jackson answered, "Let's call a truce and go back to being friends with benefits like we started out. No pressure."

"I can do that." Moria traced her fingers up and down Jackson's arm. "When is your next trip to Wyoming?"

Jackson sat up abruptly, bumping his head. Looking at Moria curled up beside him, he asked, "You want to go with me?"

"If it's not too much trouble...I'd like to."

"I'm leaving in a couple of days. Is that too soon?"

"No. That's fine. Will you check with your mom? I want to be sure it's okay."

"First thing tomorrow! I'm almost afraid to ask—what brought on a change of heart?"

"Not a change of heart...just trying to be open-minded...I really care about you."

Oh my gosh! What am I saying?

Before she could answer her own question, Jackson's lips closed on hers and the beacons of stars flashed before her eyes.

The next morning at breakfast, Moria announced, "I'm going to Wyoming in a few days!"

Jeremy looked at Jackson. "Huh?"

Maxine shrieked, "To live?"

"No, just a visit. Seems like a good time—while school's out," Moria answered as if it was no big deal.

Maxine looked hard at Moria, finally saying, "Hope you have a good trip. Remember, Dr. Phil will be around when you get back."

"Well, I was going to do some yard work and painting this week, but that can wait. I am looking forward to seeing Wyoming and the ranch. Guess we'd better get home so I can pack."

Maxine shook her head in disbelief and grinned at Jackson. "Your magic wand must be pretty powerful!"

Jackson winked at her, "We'll see!"

Upon reaching Cherry Valley, Maxine's parting words to Moria were, "Don't forget to take St. Jude and St. Christopher with you," reminding Moria of the medals she'd bought for everyone earlier in the year.

"Oh, them. Yeah, guess I better."

"Where's my suitcase?" Moria said aloud to the cats, digging into the storage closet, flinging Christmas decorations, skis, cast-off boots, horse blankets and various other items aside. Finally, she pulled her bag out and looked the attached tag. *Colorado seems like so long ago. I never would have met Jackson...enough already! I need to get packed.*

Morning sun streamed through the windows as she set the suitcase aside and shoved the other stuff back into the closet. "I've got to clean this out...someday!" she said, continuing her one-sided conversation with the cats.

Pounce growled to Pandora, *I've got a bad feeling about this!*

Pandora jumped onto the window seat and stretched out in the sun, saying, *You're just jealous because she's probably going away with that cowboy.* The yellow cat began to lick her paws and wash her face. *Give it up, Pounce. I'll bet you a mouse he's here to stay.*

Not if I can help it!

Pandora flicked her tail and taunted the disgruntled cat, *You better hope she never has to choose between you and Jackson.*

Pounce followed Moria into the bedroom. While her back was turned, dragging clothes out of her closet, Pounce curled up in the suitcase. Moria turned around, dropping the clothes on the bed. "Oh, Pounce, do you want to go to Wyoming? I have a cat carrier. I bet Jackson wouldn't mind!"

The sleek gray cat sat up in horror. Moria scooped him up with a hug and a kiss. "Just kidding! You need to stay here and take care of the farm. I won't be gone long."

You say! he meowed plaintively and stalked away.

Moria's phone rang. Looking at the caller ID she thought, *Sarah. What to tell her?*

"Hey, glad you called. How's your summer going?"

Sarah responded, "Just more of the same. Maybe I should have taken a break from classes. Oh, well, too late now. What's going on at the farm?"

"I'm going to Wyoming for a few days."

"What? With Jackson? Why?"

"Because I need a vacation."

"And?"

"Why don't we talk about this when I get back?"

"Okay. I'm going to come home for a few days and catch up on your life!"

"That sounds good. See you soon. Take care."

Moria set the phone down and laughed aloud, "I can't even catch up on my life!"

Searching through a pile of papers on her dresser she mumbled, "Where's my to-do list? I've got to make a trip to Walmart."

The day became a whirlwind of last minute tasks: be sure all the animals had enough food, emergency numbers in place, take out the trash, wash the dishes, make the bed, sweep the grit off the kitchen floor. There! Done.

After a restless night, Moria sat in the kitchen waiting for Jackson. Pounce came up and put his paws on her leg. Staring into her face he seemed to say, "Please don't go."

"Oh Pounce, you'll like the West, lots of critters for you to catch." *What am I saying? I'm only going for a visit!*

Jackson's truck pulled into the driveway. Moria took a deep breath. "Well here goes."

Pounce bounded away to the loft, glaring down at Jackson as the cowboy entered the kitchen.

Jackson took a look at Moria's large suitcase. "We're only going to be gone a couple of days, you know. Our jet might not be able to carry this weight," he teased.

"Our jet?"

"Yeah. The company jet is stopping for us. The pilot delivered one of our attorneys to Washington; so now we can get a ride home. We have to get to some airport outside of Atlanta." He dug in his pocket for the information. "I better set the GPS, since we won't have any trail markers to follow."

"A private jet? Hey, I could get used to this!"

Jackson gave her a hug. "I'm counting on it!"

The jet lifted into the sky and Atlanta's skyline faded into a distant haze. Stone Mountain became a small rock and the Chattahoochee River unwound through the towns and the countryside to the Gulf of Mexico. Moria pressed her forehead against the window and gazed down at the landscape below, saying to Jackson, "When I fly I love watch the ground for trails." She tugged on Jackson's arm. "Hey, there's a power line with four wheeler tracks and in the woods you can see jeep roads. So many places to ride..."

"You'll have to entertain yourself some other way soon. We're going to be too high to see anything but clouds."

Moria continued to peer out the window, saying, "Do you imagine pictures in the clouds? We're right in the middle of all those dogs and horses I always see!"

Perplexed, Jackson took hold of Moria's shoulders, turning her toward him. "Did you get enough sleep last night?"

"Well, no, not really. I was too excited. Are you sure it's okay for me to visit? Did you ask your mom?"

"What if I said no? Would you parachute away?" he joked. "Here, have a Coke. You need some sugar and caffeine. We'll be home in time for lunch. Maybe you can get your head out of the clouds by then. In the meantime..."

Moria wrapped her arms around Jackson's neck and began to rub in all the right places, saying, "We could join the Mile High Club today."

Jackson responded, "Maybe you don't need that Coke after all!

Later Moria awoke to Jackson's excited voice saying, "Wake up! There's the ranch!"

At that moment Moria knew it would be hard to channel Jackson's love for the home he'd always known...toward a new home in Cherry Valley.

Moria gripped the arm rests, saying uncertainly, "We're landing in a cow field?"

Before Jackson could answer, the plane settled on the dirt runway and came to a stop with clouds of dust engulfing it.

Jackson reached for Moria's hand. "Remember, you're in the Wild West now!"

In a moment she could see clearly out the window. Jackson's parents waited beside a jeep, smiling and waving. The stairs let down and the door opened to a magnificent view of mountains, stark and enduring, encompassing a valley of lush grass.

"Oh my God! This is beautiful!" Moria exclaimed.

Jackson smiled. "There's more."

They stepped down from the plane and the older couple came forward. Jackson hugged his mom, saying, "Mom and Dad, I'd like you to meet Moria Harris. Moria, my mom and dad, Molly and Ben."

Ben nodded approvingly, saying, "Welcome, Miss Moria." His blue eyes twinkled in his weathered face. "I hear you're a pretty good rider. If you're going to see the ranch you'll need a horse with some get up and go. I've got just the one picked out for you."

Jackson looked hard at his dad. "Not...?"

"No, I would never put her on Thunderfoot! What are you thinking?"

Moria laughed. "I can hardly wait to ride, even Thunderfoot!"

She winked at Jackson. "I brought some of my equipment with me in case I need it."

In answer to Jackson's puzzled look she said, "You'll see."

Turning to Molly, "Thanks so much for having me visit. I hope it's not an inconvenience, showing up on short notice."

Molly hugged Moria. "Honey, we're glad you're here. Welcome to Morningstar Ranch."

"Thank you. What a lovely name for your place!"

Jackson smiled. "Wait until tonight. You can almost touch the stars."

They climbed into the jeep and Molly said, "Lunch is ready. Afterward, I can take Moria on a tour of the ranch and our little town. Son, I know you have a lot to do while you're here. But, maybe in the morning you'll have time to take Moria for a ride up to the old home place. I'll pack y'all a lunch."

"That sounds great. A ride in the mountains with my girl and your picnic lunch—I'll make time."

The jeep crested a hill and on the opposite ridge the ranch house nestled into the hillside, landscaped with rock formations and natural planting. Stone, glass, and huge timbers created a perfect western home.

Moria said, "That's the ranch? Wow! I was expecting... well, not this."

Ben laughed. "What? A sod shanty? Wait 'till you see the home place. It was built in the early 1800s. This house was built in the 1900s and we've updated it from time to time. Most of the materials came from our land."

"Except the interior—that was my doing," Molly said. "Ben thought I got a little carried away! You're welcome to stay in the main house, but Jackson likes the cottage. It's pretty much where he stays when he's here."

"The cottage sounds fine. Thanks."

Jackson took Moria's bag, saying to his mom, "We'll be over for lunch in a few minutes."

He opened the door to the guest house. "Take a look around. I need to turn on the computer and the air. I'll just be a minute. Make yourself at home." He pointed down the hall. "There's the bedroom in case you need to hang up some of your stuff."

"Jackson, this is so charming!"

"Charming? Sounds like the three bears will step out any minute."

"Oh, you! I'm starving. Your mom said lunch is ready."

Jackson held Moria close. "What about an appetizer before lunch?"

"We had an appetizer on the plane, remember? You have some crackers and cheese around here?" she teased.

Laughing and giving her a quick kiss, he said, "I know you have a one-track mind when you're hungry. You win...this time, Missy!"

Later at lunch, Molly talked about furnishing the house and her travels in quest for the antiques which were displayed throughout their home.

Ben gestured toward the sprawling ranch beyond the window and smiled at Molly. "You're a keeper, even with your spending habits!" Then, turning to Moria he said, "So I raise lots of cattle and keep going to the office every day!"

"Speaking of the office," Jackson said to his dad, "Guess we'd better get down there. I've got some paperwork to do."

Moria glanced at Jackson. *Paperwork? Why are you still in Cherry Valley if you have so much work here? Seems like you're making a lot of trips back home.* Moria's thoughts vanished when Molly said, "Ready for your tour?"

The afternoon passed in a blur, visiting small town shops and seeing the schools Jackson had attended. Molly enjoyed telling stories of her son's escapades during his youth.

Moria could see the handwriting on the wall. Molly wanted her son's girl to fall in love with their home and way of life.

Molly pulled into a parking space in front of a coffee shop. "Let's take a break. I hope I haven't worn you out."

"Oh, no. Not at all. Jackson doesn't talk much about himself. Sounds like he was a rascal!"

They entered the shop and Molly commented, "The coffee's good but the scones are better. Here, let's sit by the window."

Molly excused herself to the restroom. Moria propped her chin in her hands, gazing out the window at the passing traffic and people shopping. *Could I live here?*

Molly returned to the table. "You look tired. Are you okay?"

Moria smiled, saying, "I think the altitude's getting to me. I'm really enjoying myself. A good night's sleep will help."

Molly raised her eyebrows. "Yes, a good night's sleep will do wonders."

The two women chatted easily for a few minutes then Molly asked about Silver Dollar and why Jackson hadn't finished any rides.

Taken off guard, Moria said, "Well, things happened. It was something different every time."

Molly looked hard at Moria. "Aren't you his trainer?"

"Sort of. I've just tried to help him get started. You know he's going to do it his way. I think the sport's harder than he thought. I'm doing longer distances than he is, so he's on his own when the ride starts. Sometimes he just does stuff without thinking, but I know he loves the horse and would never hurt Silver on purpose."

Molly's steely-blue eyes captured Moria's troubled face. "Do you know Doris Weaver?"

Molly had Moria's full attention. *I don't need this!*

"I know who she is," Moria replied cautiously.

"Did Jackson tell you they were engaged?"

"Yes, he did." *Don't say any more than I have to!*

Molly continued, holding Moria's gaze, "I don't want my boy's heart trifled with. What are your intentions?"

Moria burst out laughing. "That sounds like what my dad should say to Jackson!" Then, placing her hand on Molly's, "I'm so sorry. That was rude. You took me by surprise."

"That's me," Molly laughed, putting Moria at ease. "I usually say what's on my mind."

Moria stirred her coffee, buying a moment to sort her thoughts then looked at Molly. "I haven't known Jackson very long. I realize he'll be moving back here soon. In spite of those circumstances, I've come to care about him and I've told him so. I think he feels the same way about me." She hesitated. "We both have deep roots where we were born... and we've both weathered some storms...He probably told you I'm divorced." Meeting Molly's eyes, she continued. "I don't know what will happen. Right now we're just enjoying each other's company, one day at a time."

Molly's only reply: "You're always welcome here."

Moria smiled and reached for the check. "Thanks so much for your kindness. I'll get this." Picking up the check, she turned away with relief and a better understanding of Jackson's ties to home.

Molly softened at Moria's apparent honesty. "Let's go back to the last shop we visited. I want to buy you that beaded belt you admired...a memento of your western visit."

After dinner Moria and Jackson walked back to the cottage, arm-in-arm. "How was your day?" he asked.

"Your mom is so precious and...so direct. She loves you very much."

"Yeah. Sometimes too much, but I wouldn't trade her," he grinned. Maybe that's why I'm house-sitting and resting the rodeo horses.

"Seems like a lot of trouble to be running back and forth every few weeks."

Jackson stopped and tipped Moria's face to his. "Don't you know why I keep returning to Cherry Valley?"

"So you can take Silver Dollar to rides?" she joked, breaking the moment.

Taking Moria's lead, he said, "Well, that, and I miss Pounce and Pandora."

"That'll be the day!"

Jackson opened the cottage door and stepped aside for Moria to enter, announcing, "News flash! Goldilocks is now entering the three bears' home. She spies the porridge on the table. Oh, Wait! Maybe she wants to try out the beds first."

Caught off guard, Moria took a moment to recover. "No, Goldilocks wants to check out the Jacuzzi. I think she noticed it on the deck."

By now, Jackson's clothes lay in a heap on the floor. "Papa bear will help Goldilocks remove her garments!" Moria's scrambled out of her jeans and all else as Jackson took her hand and led her to their trysting place.

The bubbling water and Jackson's warm body soothed her troubled mind. Cherry Valley became a distant thought, waiting to be reclaimed. The closeness of the stars seemed to bind her to this time and place. She turned into Jackson's arms, comforted by this cowboy she had come to love.

Early the next morning Moria and Jackson arrived at the barn to find their mounts already saddled. Moria looked closely at the two horses, a dark bay and a palomino. Both animals stood tied to the hitching post, staring out toward the mountains. "So, which one's for me?" *I hate getting on strange horses.*

As if reading her mind, Jackson gestured toward the palomino and said, "I know you don't like to ride unfamiliar horses, but you'll like Golden Air. She's a good ride—smooth and well-trained." Untying the mare, he said, "Here, let me give you a leg up."

"Thanks for adjusting my stirrups," Moria said to Wylie, the stable manager. She pulled the neck strap from her pocket. Would you please put this around Golden Air's neck?"

Jackson raised his eyebrows and smiled at Moria, saying, "Remember, you're not on an Arab today." Then, they walked the horses out of the corral into a perfect Wyoming day, bright sun, cool, with a light breeze blowing across the hills.

Moria took a deep breath, "What smells so good? I need to bottle it into my shampoo."

"You already have it available. It's the sage brush. Next time you buy shampoo, look for it."

"I'll remember that." Moria relaxed and lengthened her reins. You're right. Golden Air is a great ride." Just then, a rabbit leapt out of the underbrush into the trail. The palomino pricked her ears and Moria grabbed the saddle horn, remembering Rainbow's giant spook when confronted by a rabbit.

Jackson laughed, saying, "See, I told you!"

The two rode on in silence, climbing higher into the hills on the steep, rocky trail. Moria looked out over the valley where blue haze obscured the horizon. *What's over the horizon for me? Now I know what it's like to be between the rock and the hard place. I've got to make a decision—but not today. I want to enjoy this time with Jackson.* Her thoughts were interrupted as her cowboy stopped his horse and pointed ahead. "There's the home place," he announced with pride.

Moria stared at the ramshackle house. Weathered boards and a wooden shingle roof leaned in on each other as if to shelter the past lives of those early pioneers. In a brief moment, the yard seemed to be filled with people from the past going about their daily tasks. Moria blinked, gasping in surprise.

Jackson studied her face. "You saw them?"

"Oh my God, what was that? A vision?"

He smiled. "I guess you could call it a vision. Not everyone sees them...only those who belong here."

Moria dismounted with shaking legs and tied Golden Air to a fence post. "I need to sit down." She looked cautiously about as if expecting Jackson's ancestors to come forward and invite her to stay.

"This is too weird. I thought only Southerners were acquainted with the ghostly past."

"Not so." Jackson replied, taking the picnic items from his saddle bags. "Come on over here. We'll eat and I'll help you recover!"

"If you think we're going to have sex in front of your ancestors—that's not going to happen!"

Jackson gave a look of mock surprise. "Actually, I've barely recovered from last night! Anyway, I want you to see the Indian graves."

"Just the graves?" she asked.

"Yep. No ghosts...that I've ever seen!"

Later, the riders packed up the remains of their lunch and prepared to head back to the ranch. Jackson dug into his pocket. "Hey, wait a minute! I've got something for you."

Moria looped the mare's reins over her arm and walked toward him. "What? An arrowhead?"

"No, something better. Come here. Hold out your hand."

Moria took a deep breath. *Uh oh. Here it comes. I'm not ready for this. She held out her hand and Jackson took it in his.*

"Close your eyes," he said, stroking the palm of her upturned palm.

Moria felt something heavy in her hand as Jackson curled her fingers around the object. Eyes still closed, she asked, "A gold nugget?"

Not answering her question, she heard Jackson's voice, tense with excitement. "Open your eyes."

Moria opened her hand to see Jackson's class ring—from high school. Speechless, she stared at the gold ring, set with a green stone. Picking it up, she looked closely at the lettering and date. *What to say?* "Wow! I'm going to wear your class ring?"

"Seems like it suits our activities...goofing off, having sex, hanging out with friends..."

Before he could continue with his perception of their relationship, Moria interrupted, "You're right. That's us," and slipped the ring into her pocket. Laughing, she said, "I'm honored to be your girlfriend. Can I ask? Where is your college ring?"

Jackson gave Moria a leg up on Golden Air, saying, "It's back in Cherry Valley with my stuff. Why? Do you think you're ready for prime time?"

"Jeez, sometimes I feel like I'm not even out of kindergarten!"

Jackson mounted his bay gelding. "We'd better go. Dad said the plane's leaving at six. We need to get back in time to pack."

In the golden light of the setting sun goodbyes were said by all. Moria and Jackson climbed the steps and turned to wave. Ben and Molly stood close together, Ben's arm across his wife's shoulders. Molly shielded her eyes against the light, blew the couple a kiss and put her arm around Ben.

Settling into her seat, Moria said, "Your parents are the best! I really enjoyed my visit...all of it."

"Mom and Dad really like you. You'll always be welcome. No pressure...next time!" Jackson said, giving her a lingering kiss. With those words, he let the seat back and closed his eyes to further discussion about the future.

He must know I need some time to gather my thoughts. Taking Jackson's ring from her pocket, she held it in her palm, closing her fingers on it. She felt the ring begin to warm, as did her heart. Maybe I could live here. *Dear God, you sent me this cowboy. Please help me make a decision.* There was no answer. Outside the window, Morningstar Ranch faded in the distance, as the plane headed south into the darkening sky.

Sun streamed through the bedroom window. Moria awoke to the insistent ring of her phone. Squinting at the display screen, she answered, "Good morning, Maxine. Would I like some coffee from Dunkin' Donuts? Oh yes!"

Soon the women were seated at the kitchen table. Moria began to fill Maxine in on the highlights of the trip, including her vision.

When Moria stopped her story, Maxine said, "So what's changed?"

Moria smiled. "Jackson and I are going steady." She reached in the pocket of her robe and handed Jackson's ring to Maxine.

Maxine stared at the ring and then at Moria. "Huh?"

Moria began to laugh, saying, "His high school ring. Jackson says I'm not ready for prime time yet...the college ring or more."

Maxine recovered from laughing, to say, "Well, I never— You two beat all I've ever seen! So, what else?" she asked, laying the ring on the table.

"Well, at least I've met Ben and Molly and I've seen the ranch. Now I have a better understanding of where Jackson's coming from—his roots run deep. His love for Wyoming and his life there rivals my love for Cherry Valley—and my life here. What will happen I don't know. I guess I could live there."

Maxine looked closely at her friend. "You guess? It's a long way back from Wyoming, baby girl. You better think this out."

"I know." Moria looked wistfully out the window at the horses, the fields beyond and the hills that enclosed the valley. Propping her chin in her hands, she continued, "There's just something about this place...I know it sounds silly but I feel responsible for this land, what little there is left. I don't know if Sarah would ever live here. Probably not. Anyway, if I left, I could deed it to the state, never to be developed. I wish we hadn't sold fifty acres to the Rutherfords."

Maxine asked, "What could be done with your place... such a small piece of property?"

Moria laughed ruefully, "Maybe it could be a dog park! Wouldn't be my worry." But uncertainty in her eyes said differently. She gazed out the window again at Peace in the Valley Farm. "This is my home, but I would share it with Jackson. Guess that won't happen."

Maxine looked skeptical at Moria's pronouncement then stood up to leave. "Enough looking into the future. I'm sure you have a lot to do today, but maybe we can go for a ride later."

"Well, I was going to work in the yard and do some laundry—but riding today sounds better! Jackson's busy at the farm so he can't go."

"And, Jeremy's working...so let's saddle up!"

Soon the two women met on the dirt road and trotted toward the hill trails. Rainbow Chaser snorted and puffed, trying to engage Catch on Fire in a race. The bay gelding leapt sideways to the challenge but Maxine took a firm grip on the reins, saying, "Hold on, buddy."

Moria glanced over at her friend with trepidation. "We're going to race today?"

"Yep. Remember the Championship ride? You're going to race. End of discussion."

Moria's heart pounded, imagining Rainbow galloping to the finish line and spooking enough to send her flying through the air and crashing into a tree, or worse. She pulled her horse up short, whirling around in the road to face Maxine. "Maybe I don't want to race!"

"Oh, my God! Enough already. Stop whining! You've got a fine horse with lots of potential. You're obligated to race him—or sell him and get a pony!"

"No. I'm not obligated! He's my horse and I can ride him however I want to!"

Startled at Moria's outburst, Maxine took a deep breath and said, "Why didn't you tell me this before? I thought we were training so you could race."

Moria said, "For me, racing's an option not an obligation. I want to train with you and the guys. Maybe I will race one day...if I have to." Turning Rainbow down the road, she said, "Come on, let's ride."

For once, Maxine was speechless. The two riders trotted on down the road. A web of silence hung between the two friends, each caught in her own thoughts.

Finally, Moria said, "Maxine, I didn't mean to hurt your feelings—I know you've tried hard to help me get over this phobia about falling. Maybe I never will. Guess it's a blessing we can't see into the future!"

"It's okay. I overstepped the bounds and got into your space. I thought I was mentoring you! No hard feelings?"

Moria shortened her reins as they reached the edge of the ravine. She looked over at Maxine.

"I'm okay, too. "

"One more thing. When you train with us and we race in the training rides—you race, too."

"I can do that."

The two riders descended a steep trail to the river. The horses waded out belly deep into the tree-shaded water and drank, pushing their noses playfully into the water and sending sparkling sprays into the air.

The two women looked longingly at the cool depths of the river. Maxine said, "Are you thinking what I'm thinking?"

Moria answered, "Oh, yeah!" and guided Rainbow up the bank and into the edge of the woods. "Nobody will be around this time of day and in the middle of the week."

Soon the horses were tied to the trees beside two piles of clothes. The riders paddled in the river, splashing like playful otters.

Moria pointed to the posted signs: NO SWIMMING $50 FINE "Wow! This is like forbidden fruit! We could get fined for this, you know." She laughed and swam downstream to sit on an outcropping rock warmed by the sun.

Maxine joined her, saying, "Hope the horses don't get spooked. We couldn't get over there in time to stop them if they broke loose. It's a long way home on foot!"

A motorized vehicle sounded in the distance. Moria and Maxine looked at each other in shock. "Busted!" Maxine laughed, diving into the water. Moria followed, swimming her best speed stroke toward the bank where the horses were tied and more important—their clothes!

Before they reached safety, a four wheeler appeared at the top of the ravine. "Well, well, what do we have here?" Kam

Bryson drawled in his best official voice, and reached for his camera.

Seeing his intent, Moria yelled, "Don't you dare!" sinking into the water, up to her neck.

"Ha!" Kam chortled, "This is the most fun I've had in a coon's age!" and started down the bank on foot.

Hearing the horses scramble, the women looked over their shoulders to see the saplings swaying as the horses pulled back, startled by the approaching ranger from across the river.

Moria said under her breath, "We've got to get the camera!"

Maxine replied quietly, "He's just trying to make trouble—probably because he couldn't win you away from Jackson. Come on. I've got an idea."

"Well, we are breaking the law."

"Never mind that. Remember, to finish is to win."

Moria had to laugh, in spite of their perilous position. "I don't think that's exactly what AERC had in mind with this motto."

Maxine called, "Hey, Kam, let's make a deal."

"What?" he asked, pointing the camera across the river.

"We won't report you for stalking if you'll erase the film you just took."

"Stalking! By God, I'm just doing my job! You're the ones breaking the law!"

Maxine whispered to Moria, "Let's go," and the two started swimming toward Kam. They arrived near the bank and waited, their bodies shimmering in the shallows. Kam stared, mesmerized by the scene before him.

Breaking the silence, Maxine said, "Not only stalking, but enticing us to the bank with threat of arrest if we don't come ashore—naked. I'll bet your camera doesn't have audio. So who would know what was said? It would just show us getting out of the water." With mock fear on her face, Maxine started to stand up.

Kam looked pleadingly at Moria. "We've been friends for a long time. Can't you stop...this farce?"

Moria replied with a smile, "Your call."

The ranger gave one last try. "I can make it hard for you all to have access to the trails. I'm sure there's some endangered thing out here or an environmental no-no."

"Do that, and you'll have Jackson on your back. Remember? He's an environmental lawyer."

Kam threw up his hands. "I give up! You bitches are a hard case!"

Moria and Maxine stared unbelievingly at the ranger. Gathering her wits, Moria said, "Whatever. Now, we need to hear you fade away into the distance. One more thing, lay your phones and the camera on the bank. We'll leave them at the ranger station later today. Don't try to report us. Two against one is poor odds for you."

"Bitches! Kam yelled as he roared away, throwing the phones and camera into the weeds. "Your guys will hear about this!"

Moria said to Maxine, "Not if we get there first!" They swam back across the river, dressed and headed home, returning the way they had come to pick up the forest service equipment.

On the trail back to the farms the two friends discussed the drama as it had unfolded.

"Guess that was a little extreme," Moria commented. "Maybe we should have a dinner meeting tonight and break the news, before Kam does."

Maxine answered, "Why don't we put the horses away, go by The Diner to pick up supper and stop by the ranger station?"

Moria turned Rainbow toward home, saying, "We can eat at my house. I'll call the guys."

"See you in a few minutes," Maxine said over her shoulder, and trotted away.

Soon the two women were in Maxine's truck, headed out on their errands. At The Diner they ordered quickly, the usual— wings, potato salad, and key lime pie. Moria said, "We'd better get some extra cash…"

Maxine looked over at her friend. "That's no surprise. I figured you'd want to take Kam some money."

"Yeah, so he'll feel lucky with the outcome and forget his encounter with the mermaids!"

"We can only hope."

When they reached the ranger station, Maxine said, "Guess we can get an envelope inside. What kind of a message should we leave?"

"Humm, let's say, Trails donation. Have a nice day! And draw a smiley face."

The ranger at the desk took the phones, the camera—minus the memory card—and the envelope. With a puzzled look he said, "Kam's not here right now."

Moria said, "He's expecting these things. They were accidently left in the forest."

On the way back to Moria's farm Maxine said, "Just exactly how will we spin this story to the guys?"

"Guess we'd better tell it straight. They'll probably get a good laugh out of this."

After the tale was told that evening, the four friends sat on Moria's porch. Citronella candles burned nearby to ward off mosquitoes. The soft light reflected a spark of mischief in Moria's eyes as she thought back over the day. Jackson rocked the swing and put his arm around Moria. Leaning her head on his shoulder, she said, "Guess we won't be welcome at the trail volunteer days anytime soon."

The others agreed, but Jackson said, "You wait and see. He's gonna' want all his help to show up. I'll bet you he'll act like nothing ever happened."

"You may be right," Moria answered. "Besides we won't be doing any work 'til it cools off. I've got to get some stuff done around here before we go to the River Song Ride. School will be starting before we know it."

"Tell me some more about this ride," Jackson said.

The three riders began to talk at once. Jackson held up his hand. "Wait a minute. Just tell me how it's going to work so we can still get to the dance. That seems to be the most important part of this trip.

"Since we have plenty of time, we should probably ride on Friday and help out on Saturday. That's my thought," said Maxine.

Everyone agreed on the plan and Moria reminded them, "The ride starts before dawn because it's so hot. We'll need the second day to recover!"

Jackson looked puzzled. "How is the trail marked?"

"There'll be plenty of glow sticks at the turns and the ride is always held on or near a full moon. The horses do great."

"Going in the dark energizes them—or maybe it's us!" Jeremy added. "Besides, it's only an hour or so that we need the extra light.

Reflecting for a moment, Jackson startled the group by saying, "If you all are going fifty miles, I'm going to tag along. Maybe I'll finish this time."

"It would be good if you could finish a twenty-five first," Moria replied.

"Well, if I'm not going to finish, I would rather it be on a fifty. Maybe we can do some of our training rides at night so Silver can get used to this new plan."

Looking at Maxine and Jeremy, Moria said, "You guys okay with this? But no night training rides."

"Fine with me," Jeremy said. "If we get separated during the ride, one of us can take Jackson, depending on how the horses are doing."

Jackson shot back, "Hey, I'm not a baby!"

Jeremy grinned, "No, but maybe a pre-schooler!"

Jackson stopped the swing abruptly. Jumping up, he said, "By God, I've herded cattle all over Wyoming. How hard can this be?"

The others laughed and Moria said, "Seems like we've heard that before. Now, let's work on the list—plenty of bug spray, electrolytes, Emergen-C for us..." She looked at Jackson, who had resumed his seat in the swing. "If you'll load the hay and grain, I'll wash the saddle pads and whatever else."

Maxine nudged Jeremy with her foot. "Same for me," she said, rising from her chair.

Jeremy pulled Maxine into his lap. "I know the drill," he answered, nuzzling her neck.

Maxine got up reluctantly and tugged Jeremy to his feet, "See you guys tomorrow. Maybe we should do a night ride. Jeremy, why don't you ask off from work?" she suggested as they left.

Turning Moria's face toward his, Jackson said, "Oh. Yeah, that reminds me, we need to check on the cats... in the bedroom. No telling what that shithead Pounce has been up to."

The gray cat peered through the screen door at his arch enemy. *Just wait 'till you get to the bed...I'll fix you!* Pounce growled, scurrying away on his disruptive mission.

Moria and Jackson hurried through the house, turning off lights and dropping clothes as they made their way to the bedroom. When they reached the back of the house, Jackson pinned Moria against the wall. "Maybe we don't need the bed," he panted. In the darkened hallway the two shadowed figures did not notice Pounce staring at them. Breathless, Moria whispered, "We're almost to the bed! You're not the one against the wall!" she laughed, pulling loose and stepping quickly into the bedroom.

"Oh my God!" Jackson yelled as the two fell into the bed soaked with fresh cat pee.

How'ya like them apples? Pounce hissed and made a run for the loft and his hiding place.

Moria screamed, "The bedding's ruined!" She leapt up to strip the covers off before Pounce's mischief could sink into the mattress. "Oh, Pounce, why are you so bad?" Moria muttered, but deep in her heart she knew the cat was jealous.

Jackson tore through the house. "I'm going to kill that devil!"

Moria raced after Jackson, "Stop! Don't you dare touch him!" she yelled.

Jackson stopped mid-way of the living room, and spun around toward Moria. Taking hold of both her arms, his nose a few inches from hers, he said grimly, "It's either me or the cat!"

Moria burst out laughing, "You're such a baby! Pounce's brain is the size of a peanut! How is it he always gets the best of you?"

Jackson blew his breath out and collapsed on the couch. Running his hands through his hair, he answered, "Never mind, I'm going home." With those words, the cowboy began to gather up his clothes, examining each item to see if Pounce had done any more damage.

Moria stepped ahead of Jackson at the door. She leaned against it, blocking his way. Brushing her fingers across his cheek, she said softly. "Sorry this happened. Guess I was a little distracted. Next time I'll put the cats outside...if there is a next time."

Jackson gave her a hug and grinned. "There will be a next time. Somehow, I'm just not in the mood right now!"

Pounce observed the two humans and listened to their conversation. *You're right,* he whined. *There will be a next time. I'll get you yet! Someday you'll be going to Wyoming— without us.* The cat peered out of the loft window at Jackson's retreating back. Turning away, he sharpened his claws on the carpet to punctuate his wrath and stalked back downstairs.

A few days later, Moria and Maxine's trailers headed out of town, tightly packed with all their needs for the weekend. Grateful to have Jackson driving, Moria leaned her seat back. "Are you sure you want to tackle fifty miles on this ride?"

He answered, "Remember? I played football. I can do this."

Moria reached up to turn on the radio. "You know, we've got your back if the goin' gets tough." *And it probably will.*

"Thanks. Even cowboys need a wingman once in a while."

In the early afternoon the trailers pulled off the interstate onto a sand-packed road lined with giant oaks draped with Spanish moss. Thick clumps of palmetto growth covered the ground.

"Looks like that beach ride we did," Jackson commented, glancing to the side of the road.

"Actually, we're not far away from there. Too bad we can't combine the rides. I don't think riding a hundred miles on the beach will happen in our lifetime!

They turned into the driveway leading to a spectacular plantation house, white painted brick, two-stories, faced with balconies and comfortable rocking chairs on the front porch. Their drive continued past the main house to a rustic cottage set back in the pines and surrounded by a split rail fence.

"You know, we were lucky to get a place with paddocks for the horses. The management said the cabin's unlocked. We can pick up the key when we register. More privacy. You'll like it," Moria winked and rubbed Jackson's leg.

He laughed. "Do we need to stop on the road?"

"Better today than tomorrow after you've ridden fifty miles! But there's no time now. Sorry I brought it up."

Jackson tugged at his jeans. "Yeah, you brought it up. You minx!" he answered, ruffling her hair.

At sunset, light filtered through gold and lavender clouds illuminating the plantation garden. Tables set with china, silver, and candles greeted the riders for the evening meal. For a moment Moria felt herself in another world, one of grace and elegance. Japanese lanterns swayed in the breeze and reflected points of light sparkled from the table settings. She smiled. *Now I know why I come here*, and reached for Jackson's hand.

Jarred to reality, she heard the ride manager yell to the crowd, "Meeting in an hour, right here. Go light on the bourbon and branch water. Remember, you're not going to get much sleep before the ride."

Jackson said under his breath, "I have a flask. Maybe I'll just bring it along."

"You do that," Maxine answered. "We'll wait while you throw up in the woods."

Jackson rolled his eyes, "I can hold my liquor!"

"We'll see. While you're moving along in the dark and the horizon is playing tricks on your eyes your stomach will not be happy!"

Jackson did not reply. By the set of his jaw, Moria could see he planned to prove Maxine wrong.

At the riders meeting, the manager announced the start time for fifty milers—four a.m. Everyone groaned. "You'll be glad, come sun up. Rest when you get back...better for the horses, too." She went on to describe the trail, marked with glow sticks and said a couple of spotters would be at the creek crossings...some a little boggy.

"How deep are the bogs?" one of the riders questioned.

The manager hesitated and looked over at the trail boss, "You tell them," and she stepped aside.

"Who's riding a pony?" No one answered. He laughed. "You'll be fine," and sat back down.

"Any more questions?" the manager asked. "See y'all in the morning at check-in time. Don't be late. You know that upsets the timer!"

The Cherry Valley friends walked back to the cabin, checked on the horses, and organized their gear for the early rising time.

"What about feeding the horses?" Jackson looked doubtfully into the corrals at the resting horses. "The ride is only a few hours away."

"Well, there's different opinions," Jeremy said. "They just ate before we went to dinner. Maybe we should wait 'till the first vet check."

"That's a good idea," Maxine answered.

"Works for me," Moria said, and Jackson nodded in agreement. "Let's get some sleep or it's gonna be time to tack up the horses."

Under a rising moon, quiet settled over the camp. Deep in the forest an owl cried, who, who, who—questioning the outcome of the day ahead. Coyotes howled in the distance. A camp dog barked in reply. Moria looked out the window at the horses whose watchful gazes were alert to the nighttime sounds. Checking the time, she said aloud, "Jeez! I've got to get some sleep!" Jackson reached out to snuggle Moria into his arms.

The next thing she knew, he awakened her, saying, "Put your boots on, Missy. Time to ride."

Darkness embraced the land and a damp breeze met the riders as they walked to the staging area. Jeremy commented, "No rain on the radar, guess it's always humid down here."

Moria stroked Rainbow's neck. "He's already sweating. Hope I've given him enough electrolytes." She looked over at Jackson. "Did you..."

He glared, "I have learned a few things, Missy. I know about electrolytes."

"Just checking." He's really nervous. To lighten the moment, she asked, "What about your flask?"

He grinned. "Left it...for now."

The Cherry Valley riders approached the timer, gave their numbers and began to trot up and down the driveway. After a few minutes, they pulled off to the side because the horses were already breathing heavily. Moria wiped her face on a sleeve, saying, "Let's get in the middle of the pack and try to keep a steady pace. The management's put out plenty of water for the horses and us...if these suckers will just drink!"

Over a hundred competitors started the fifty mile ride. Some riders raced ahead, others held back, and those with young, old, or fractious horses waited to start. Jada disappeared with the front-runners, galloping around the bend.

Catch on Fire bounded forward, showering Rainbow Chaser with sand. The chestnut raced up, eye-to-eye with the bay gelding, and tossed his head as if to say, "Bring it on!" Silver Dollar and Artic Cat pounded close behind. Jackson called out, "Is this the steady pace for fifty miles?"

"Not for our fifty," Moria shouted back, struggling to get Rainbow under control. "We need to watch it. We're almost to the pavement crossing."

The horses settled into big-strided trot and the friends took turns leading. Now other riders mingled into the pack and the tight foursome became separated. The middle group surged on, and soon the paved road came into view. The front-runners were already bunched up, waiting to cross. Sherriff's deputies manned the crossing where riders had to wait for the signal to go ahead. Moria could hear the scramble of hooves on the pavement as anxious riders tried to keep their places in the ride.

Jeremy moved in front to wait his turn to cross and the other three came up behind him. He glanced at Jackson's sweating face, wrinkled with stress. "Don't worry. Some will pass us here, but we'll catch up—and get ahead."

Jackson grimaced and fought with Silver Dollar. "No problem. I just don't want to become road kill!"

Soon after crossing the road, a large pack of riders forged from behind, in roiling, shifting waves—horses and riders on a mission. Maxine called. "We'd better get a move on!"

After a few more miles a spotter appeared in the road, turning riders into the woods on a twisting single-track trail. Glow sticks marked the way through a leafy, green tunnel of kudzu-covered trees. Ahead, Moria could see a glimmer of light. The trail opened onto a washed out, red clay road winding through an abandoned farm. The riders, distracted by hoof beats close behind, barely glanced at the vines strangling the weathered buildings—their inhabitants, victims of the past.

Pink clouds fringed with golden light streamed across the sky on a welcome breeze. Encouraged, the riders moved on. Levees surrounded weed-choked fields, once filled with crops of indigo and rice. Today these banks had become bush-hogged paths for horse-rider teams jockeying for a valued position before reaching the bog.

"Pull up!" Moria called to those behind her as they left the road at the washed-out bridge and skidded down the bank onto a narrow trail beside the creek. The riders walked cautiously through the newly-cut path to the ill-fated crossing. "Uh oh, this doesn't look good," she announced, watching the rider in front of her slide into the creek—a morass of thick, sucking mud. The horses and riders waiting their turns, watched quietly. But no one walked away.

The horse in the creek struggled for his footing, slipped, pitched forward on his knees, and threw the rider onto his neck. The girl grabbed his mane, slick with mud, and slid off into the mire.

A rider waiting on the bank turned and headed back to the road. "Screw this!" she called to the others. "I'm going to find another crossing!"

The spotter on the opposite bank threw a rope to the hapless rider in the bog and helped her up. The horse recovered his footing and lurched up the bank on his own.

The spotter yelled to the departing rider, "You better stay here! We've looked all up and down the creek, a mile in each direction. You won't find another crossing! At least here, you've got some help! Besides, you're gonna be disqualified anyway, for leaving the marked trail." The rider disappeared through the trees and was soon out of sight, to who knew where.

Moria looked over her shoulder at the other riders and said, "Guess I'm next!" With those words, she grabbed the back of the saddle with one hand to steady herself. Rainbow sat down on his haunches and slid gracefully into the creek. The horse, belly deep in mud, searched desperately for his footing; struggling a few feet further, he clamored up the bank. The waiting spotter handed Moria a fistful of paper towels. Grinning, he said, "You might want to wipe your face!"

The others in her group made it safely across the hazard, climbed back to the road and continued the journey. The riders presented a woeful, dirty picture as they trotted and cantered down the country lane to the first vet check.

Moria mourned, "My new boots! They're barely broken in! Wonder if my homeowner's insurance covers this?"

Maxine said, "You did good on the crossing! Treat yourself to another pair of boots—we'll probably all need them after this! Wonder where that other rider went? Maybe she turned around and went back to camp,"

Wiping Silver's reins with his bandana, Jackson asked, "Speaking of camp, we must be getting close, right?"

Just then, they saw a sign saying, TWO MILES TO CAMP.

"Thank God! This mud's beginning to dry and it ain't feeling too good! Hey, something's going on up the road. Hope no one's hurt." Several riders had stopped at a farm house. The Cherry Valley riders approached slowly. Three young boys had set up a crew station in the yard, energetically hosing off horses and riders. Some people stood beside their mounts and others stayed mounted for the pause that refreshed.

"Is that allowed?" Jeremy questioned.

"Sure." Maxine answered. "Just the same as having your crew meet you on the road. We're lucky! Hey, guys. Where'd you get all this stuff?" she asked, pointing to the hoses, squeegees, towels, and large electric fans.

Without missing a beat on their tasks, one of them answered, "The ride manager brought it to us, said we'd be well-paid!"

"Wow! Talk about going above and beyond!" exclaimed Moria.

"Now I've seen it all—Southern hospitality—at its best!" Jackson laughed, dismounting to enjoy his shower.

Deputies guarded the return pavement crossing and wished the riders good luck. One of them removed his sunglasses to wipe his face and called out, "Glad it's you, not me!" The rising sun beat down on wet horses and riders, creating a sauna effect. Most of the competitors slowed down and dismounted near the vet check.

Stopping at the timer's stand, Moria suggested, "Let's drop the saddles and check the horses' pulses." At the crewing area, organized chaos reigned. Riders and crews worked to cool the horses, present them for the exam, and be designated "good to go." Two large box fans hung in the trees over the vet line, an extra perk for the participants.

Moria noticed quite a few competitors had not pulsed down. "Now that we've cleared the check, let's get the horses settled with some food and water. Maybe we'll have time to make it down to the cabin and change clothes."

"Works for me," Jackson replied, limping along in his wet jeans.

Jeremy grinned, "Forget to wear your bike shorts?"

"Yeah. At least I remembered to bring them."

Soon, the riders were back on the trail. Moria said, "This should be an easier loop. It's mostly dirt roads and a pass through town."

"That's a new one," Jackson commented, riding up beside Moria.

"It's pretty interesting," she continued, "how the town reinvented itself around the plantation—just like in the old days. They cater to corporate groups all year long. Most everything they need for the events comes from right here in the village—food, repairs, maintenance of the property, and extra employees. Full-time people mend and clean the costumes we're going to wear tomorrow. There's a staff on the road all the time looking for jewelry, authentic clothing, furniture, dinnerware and silver place settings..." Moria urged Rainbow forward. "I'll tell you more later. We need to catch up! Maxine and Jeremy are moving on—without us!" They cantered up behind their friends and the group took advantage of the wide roads to gain some time.

Up ahead, a few people were walking their horses but galloped away when they saw the riders approaching. Maxine said, "Ha, guess we're going to have to push them along. Let's see what happens. I know them, they're the 'hurry up and wait' ones. We're not in the top ten, so it won't matter if they get in ahead. Let's not get sucked into their pace."

The sun climbed higher, its rays zeroing in like lasers, seeking out the least hydrated horses and riders to bring them down. Clouds of deer flies and no-see-ums joined in, engulfing the riders and their mounts. Maxine said to Moria, "Tell me you brought some bug spray with you!"

"Actually, I did. A small can, but maybe it'll be enough to go around...once." Continuing the pace, the riders sprayed the horses' ears and themselves.

Up ahead the erratic group by-passed a water tank which the manager had placed in the shade of a huge oak. Rainbow Chaser and the other three horses dunked their faces in the tank to wash the bugs away and managed to get a drink amidst the splashing. Grass grew nearby and the horses grazed for a few moments, then all were on their way again. As they approached the second vet check, Jeremy said, "Only ten more miles and we're done. Halleluiah!"

"Amen!" Jackson shouted.

Again, their horses cleared the vet check and the riders left out on the last loop. Moria said, "Looks like we'll be back in time for lunch. I hear they have a great buffet on the patio." These words encouraged the riders to 'git er done'...remembering the last few miles always seem the worst. More abandoned farms and fields became a blur from the shimmering waves of heat and the hastened pace.

Entering a woods trail, they walked the horses to let the pulse and breathing come down. Maxine reminded everyone, "The creek's just up ahead. This will be the last one we'll cross before camp. Better sponge good." Soon they reached the shaded stream. Swift running water swirled knee-deep around the horses.

Swatting insects from his face, Jackson said, "Except for these damn gnat things...this is great!" He unhooked his sponge and began to drench Silver with water.

"Don't forget to squeegee the water off," Moria commented.

"My God, woman! I know that!"

Moria laughed, "What's the matter, heat gettin' to you?"

"You better watch it, Missy," Jackson retorted, slinging a

sponge full of water on her. Soon the creek became an arena for a water fight. The horses danced around as their riders battled it out with soaked sponges.

A waiting rider called from the bank, "Any time now! We need to get in!" The annoyed voice reminded the combatants that playtime was over. Reluctantly, they left the sparkling sun-dappled water to the next riders and the weary group trotted away.

When the finish line came into view, Jackson said, "Let's race!"

"No!" his companions yelled in unison.

Jeremy looked over at his friend, saying, "It'd be a shame if you rode fifty miles and didn't finish the ride. Silver's barely over his injuries and don't forget, you want to be sure you can get his pulse down. Better not take any chances."

Disappointed, Jackson answered, "Yeah. You're right. I'd be pissed off if I didn't finish." Dismounting, he loosened his horse's girth and patted Silver's neck, saying to the horse, "Not my choice, buddy," and looked wistfully at the finish line.

Moria's group stood with their mounts waiting for the final check. The horses reached for nearby grass, never knowing the anxious heartbeats of their riders.

Jackson hung back, waiting for the others to go. His usual swagger missing as he faced the moment of truth.

Jeremy and Artic Cat went first and passed with flying colors. Next Maxine and Catch on Fire presented to the vet. The bay gelding stood perfectly still to be examined, ears forward, and nostrils flared, anticipating the trot-out. At the command, Fire bounded away on a slack lead rope with Maxine running hard beside him. Returning to the vet, she laughed, "Better check me first!" Then she heard the welcome words, "You have completed!"

Moria took a deep breath, looking at the short distance to the vet—only twenty feet away. The longest walk...the fewest steps. Saint Christopher, I hope you're with me now! Rainbow arched his neck and nickered softly, recognizing Dr. Barr.

The vet laughed, "Looks like he's trying to gain a few points here."

She grinned, "Yeah, it's part of his training."

"Jog him out," the vet answered, "Let's see how he's doing."

At last, Moria accepted Rainbow's vet card with the coveted word, "completed" scrawled above the vet's signature. She breathed a sigh of relief, forgetting about Jackson, until Silver gave an anxious whinny, calling to Rainbow Chaser

"Hey, stay close!" Jackson called in a tense voice. Moria stood her horse at the end of the arena, facing toward Silver. Now the gray settled down and walked quietly beside his owner but kept his eyes on Rainbow, then trotted away at a brisk clip with Jackson sprinting to keep up.

Approaching the orange cone positioned at the end of the arena, Jackson heard Moria say, "You got it! Looking good!" and blew him a kiss.

Jackson stumbled. "Oh shit!" he cursed under his breath. Silver jerked his head up, steadying them both.

Dr. Barr checked Silver's vitals and handed Jackson the vet card. Smiling, he said, "Congratulations on completing your first endurance ride. Silver looks like he could do another fifty miles!"

"Not with me!" Jackson laughed, then added, "Thanks for your hard work today."

Moria hurried to the out gate and gave Jackson a hug, saying, "Good job!" *Oh, my gosh! Sounds like I'm talking to my students!* But Moria realized Jackson didn't notice as Maxine and Jeremy added their good wishes.

Leading the horses back to the paddocks, they talked about ride and especially Jackson's success. The cowboy reached for Moria's hand, saying, "Let's face it—I just drafted along behind you guys. I never would have kept the pace if I'd been out there by myself. Thanks."

Jeremy grinned, "Yeah, I wondered when you'd figure that out!"

Jackson shot back, "Well, sometimes you just need a little help from your friends. Maybe I'll pay it forward...someday. Enough of this Winnie the Pooh stuff. Where's the beer?"

Moria's heart skipped a beat, thinking about 'someday' and her life without Jackson. *What will he do? Back to Doris Weaver? Back to Wyoming? What will happen to Silver Dollar? I wish I'd never met you, Jackson Durant! You've turned my world upside down.*...Dust blew off the road from the horses' scuffling feet and settled on the roadside bushes. *That's me...dust blowing in the wind.*

"Hello? Anybody there?" Jackson grinned, waving his hand in front of Moria. Blinking, she pulled back from her restless thoughts and looked up at Jackson's face, streaked with dirt and sweat from the day's effort to reach his goal. She squeezed his hand and replied," I was thinking about a hot shower. What about you?"

"Need you ask?" Quickening his step, he added, "I know. Take care of the horses first."

During the afternoon, Maxine and Jeremy went shopping in the village and toured some of the plantation homes open to the public.

Moria and Jackson collapsed on the bed. Jackson said, "Have any energy left?" Moria answered, "Don't even think about it!" The ceiling fan whispered softly...enjoy the day...enjoy the day...enjoy the day.

Chapter Fourteen

*T*he awards meeting brought riders, crew, volunteers and other support staff together to hear about the "thrill of success and the agony of defeat" which defined each rider's day.

Maxine said in a low voice to Moria, as the two women settled in their chairs, "I heard that Jada's horse has a bowed tendon and couldn't finish the ride. She's already been on the phone calling all over the country trying to find another horse for the Championship ride."

"Poor Blackjack! On second thought, maybe he's lucky. At least she won't be riding the crap out of him anymore. Hope she'll give him decent care...he still might be okay for pleasure riding. Wonder who'd be stupid enough to lease her a horse? She'll probably have to buy one."

Maxine replied, "Well, shit happens. It could have been one of us. There might be a hole out there with your name on it. Better not get too smug!"

"What? Are you taking up for her?"

"No. I'm just saying sometimes it's the luck of the draw. I've seen people do all the right things and the wrong things happen. Look at Jackson and all that's happened to him—and you're his mentor!"

"Yeah...well...Jackson's a hard case."

Maxine grinned, "What? Are you taking up for him?"

"Nooo, I think he'll always be a loose cannon like Jada. You're right. Who am I to judge? Besides, he's on his own now. Soon he'll be riding away into the sunset." Her voice caught. "I am glad he finished today...since I am his mentor."

Maxine looked sideways at Moria. "Is that what this is all about—you being a good teacher? You better get over yourself before the best thing that's ever happened to you walks away—into the sunset."

Moria did not answer.

Dusk settled over the endurance group gathered on the patio to enjoy the lingering ambience of the evening. Twinkling lights and the attendance of white-coated waiters serving dessert and coffee added to the feel of long ago and far away. "I'm going to miss you," Moria said to Jackson. Then, squeezed his arm, adding, "You did good today, mister."

He grinned. "I know. Thanks for all your help. Guess this is the end of the Southern road for Silver and me." He stared off in the distance.

Moria waited.

"Maybe Silver will become a ranch horse. I think he would like that," Jackson continued in a quiet voice.

"No more endurance?"

"I'm gonna' quit while I'm ahead. There's gotta be more to life than endurance riding...besides, I don't think it would be much fun without you and Rainbow."

"What's this? A guilt trip?"

Giving her a teasing smile, he answered, "Yeah. I guess so."

The ride manager called for everyone's attention and conversations came to an end. She offered the usual thanks for help from staff and volunteers—a few funny stories and hard luck tales were recounted, ending with the announcement, "By the way, one of our riders decided to find her own way back to camp. The rescue unit is still looking for her." In the distance they could hear the thump, thump, of a helicopter, flying low in search of the errant rider. "Let that be a lesson. Stay on the trail! Now for the best part of the day—the end!"

The guy in charge of handing out t-shirt awards came forward with the completion list. Each rider received a round of applause as their name was called. When Jackson's turn came, Moria was startled to realize the group was giving him a standing ovation. On her feet, with tears in her eyes, she thought, *He's earned this...he never gave up. I should learn something from this.* She could almost hear Jackson's voice telling her, "Better put your boots on, Missy!"

The group quieted. Jackson unfolded the blue shirt designed with silver and black running horses, Holding it high in a moment of triumph, he announced, "This shirt is now my most valuable possession!" Everyone laughed, perhaps remembering their own first completion awards and the thrill of success.

Early the next morning, after caring for the horses, the four friends headed to the check-in table to see where they would be needed for the day. Jackson and Jeremy were assigned to the boggy crossing and Moria and Maxine worked at the vet check. The day flew by as competitors came and went, each chased by his own bright tiger. The sun rose higher, insects gathered about people's faces and sweat drenched their colorful ride shirts.

Moria moaned, "I don't think I can drink one more bottle of Gatorade!"

Maxine tossed an empty water bottle in the trash and agreed. "Wonder how the guys are doing? Think I'll call them." Reporting back, she said, "They're hanging in there. Jackson is getting to use his lasso. That's keeping him entertained!"

The last rider finished in mid-afternoon. Awards were handed out soon after to give participants time to recover from the day and prepare for the evening. Dinner would be an elegant affair in the mansion. Some people would choose to play cards in the game room. Others planned to enjoy the evening relaxing and being served refreshments on the patio.

Moria's group headed to the cabin for showers and then back to the dressing rooms upstairs in the mansion. Jackson hesitated on the stairs as he and Jeremy turned to their dressing rooms, saying to Moria, "And why are we doing this? Remind me again."

Poking his chest with her finger, she looked up into his puzzled face and said, "Tonight you will be a true Southerner. Just wait! This will be a night to remember!"

The dressing rooms were attended efficiently by employees who had done this job many times. Moria's dark blue gown with puffed sleeves and a full skirt fit as if made for her. Tiny crystal beads sparkled on the folds of her dress, catching the light with every step. A gold comb gleamed in her auburn hair and antique jewelry completed the outfit. Moria glanced in the mirror and smiled, saying under her breath, "And I am a Southern girl, now and forever—amen!"

Maxine waited at the top of the stairs, wearing a peach-colored gown inset with a darker shade of lace. "Man, I'm glad we could wear our own shoes. "Hey look! There are our gentlemen!"

The two women peered over the balcony to see Jackson and Jeremy standing with a group of Confederate soldiers. Music began to play and the gray uniformed, sunburned endurance men turned as one toward the stairs to escort their lovely ladies to dinner.

Moria walked slowly down the stairs to meet Jackson, her eyes locked on his. *I am going to keep you—somehow!* His hand reached out for hers at the last step. She took his arm and he smiled, saying, "Welcome to my home. Shall we go to dinner?"

The night became a kaleidoscope of changing colors. Bright dresses coupled with flashes of gray turned the ballroom into a fantasy world. Candles lit the scene, casting shadows on the wall—perhaps reflecting ghosts of the past.

Jackson turned the trailer into Moria's driveway and stopped. Shaking her awake, he said, "Looks like you've got company."

"Huh?" Moria roused herself up and looked out the window. An unfamiliar black SUV sat parked in the shade. "I don't know that car. Maybe it's the IRS!"

"You're expecting them?" Jackson asked with a sly grin on his face.

"Well, you never know..." Moria's face paled. She gripped Jackson's arm. "Look! There on the porch! It's..." She stared in confusion. "It's Fredrick! Oh, I hope nothing has happened to Sarah." Moria jumped out of the truck and ran toward the house, stopping a few feet from him.

"What are you doing here? Is Sarah okay?"

Jackson pulled the trailer slowly down the drive and stopped beside them, saying with authority, "I'll put the rig and the horses away. See you in a few minutes." Then gave a nod and drove on toward the barn.

Fredrick waved to Jackson and turned back to Moria, "Sarah's fine as far as I know. I'm passing through and came by to visit. Come over and sit with me." He gestured to the steps. When Moria didn't move he kept talking. "Looks like you've been on a ride...and I see you've got some help," he added, glancing in the direction of the barn.

"You came to visit?" Moria asked skeptically. She looked him up and down when he didn't meet her eyes. "Why are you really here?"

"Sit down. I want to talk to you." He waited while Moria finally made up her mind to sit down with him. *He looks so much older,* she thought. *Well, I guess I do too.* Recovering from the shock of his sudden appearance, she relaxed a little bit knowing that Jackson was within shouting distance if things went south. "So...what's goin' on?"

Fredrick propped his elbows on his knees and looked out across the yard, then turned to Moria. "I'll get right to the point. I came here to apologize for disrupting your life during the years we were married."

"I'm sure I didn't help matters any," she replied honestly. *Maybe some of the trouble was me.*

Moria looked into Fredrick's earnest face and saw truth in his eyes. *Does he want to come back?*

He did not respond to her admission. "I've quit drinking, been a few years now. I need to make amends for the hurt I caused. I am truly sorry."

Moria's heart softened. "Wish I could have been more helpful. I'm glad things are better." She pulled a tall piece of grass from the edge of the steps and twisted it around her fingers, thinking of what else to say.

"You were helpful, actually, because you didn't enable me. I left—to find somebody who would. My life was all about the next drink. You can imagine what happened—I hit bottom. But, by the grace of God and some good friends, I have a new life."

Moria began to laugh.

"What?" Fredrick frowned.

"I'm sorry to laugh. This situation sounds like a tearful end to a 'happily ever after' movie."

Fredrick smiled and immediately looked ten years younger. "Yeah, I guess it does. Except this is not the end, it's just the beginning. I'm on my way to Nashville to be with the lady who'll be my wife."

"You're getting married? Wow! Congratulations. Does Sarah know?"

"Yes. And before you ask—I want her to be a part of the wedding party, so I checked with her to be sure our plans won't interfere with the championship ride where she'll be crewing. We chose another date." He laughed ruefully. "Guess some things never change."

Fredrick got up to leave and Moria walked with him to his SUV. He opened the door and to the ding, ding, ding, of the door chime, he gave her a hug. "Thank you for giving me a beautiful daughter." Then, tapping her gently on the nose, he grinned, "I'll always remember the good times." With those words, Fredrick drove away, calling out the window, "Good luck at the ride!"

Moria stood in the drive until his car turned onto the road. A gentle breeze blew through the pines and ruffled her hair. *A part of my life, gone with the wind, perhaps gone forever.* Her heart felt light as she smiled to herself and headed to the barn.

Jackson greeted her at the gate, "Well? Are you two getting back together?"

"Oh, please! But I'm glad you asked." Propping her foot on the rail, she looked across the gate at him. "Fredrick's getting on with his life, but not in Cherry Valley."

"So...that means you're ready to go to Wyoming?"

"No. It means that I can put part of my life behind me. And, I'm thankful that out of all of this, Fredrick and Sarah have managed to forge some kind of bond. You'll never guess what..." she said.

"What?"

"They had tentatively set the date for the same weekend as the championship ride, but they've changed their plans so Sarah can crew for me at the ride and go to the wedding."

Jackson took her hand as they left the barn. "Looks like you'll have to send a wedding present," he joked.

When they reached the house again, Moria said, "I need some down time. This has been an overwhelming few days—especially today."

"No problem. I could use a little extra rest myself. See you tomorrow?"

"Sure. We need to unpack the trailer."

"Most of it's done. Maybe we can go to dinner." He gave her a tentative hug.

She caught his face between her hands, kissing him, and said "I'll miss you."

He grinned at her. "You are a piece of work," and strolled away whistling Dixie.

Moria could hardly wait to call Maxine. "You'll never believe who showed up on my doorstep..." then told her about Fredrick's visit.

"Well I declare! What will happen next? So how do you feel about all this, Missy? Maxine asked.

"Well, Dr. Phil, I don't know how I feel. Why don't you tell me?" Moria kidded.

"You know my answer already: you can't control the circumstances but..."

"You can control how you react." Moria finished for her.

"'Nough said. Why don't you get that information tattooed on your arm? Then we wouldn't keep having this conversation. I'm glad Fredrick's life is better. Now, maybe you can get on with yours. On to matters at hand—we have a couple of school meetings soon, pre-planning, and then we're back in the saddle again."

"I wish!" Moria answered. "I'm exhausted. See you tomorrow!" Her cell phone rang just as she hung up with Maxine.

"Hey sweetie! How's everything going?"

"That's what I called to ask you. Dad seemed fine when we talked. Was everything okay?"

"We're good, honey," Moria smiled. "I'm actually glad he stopped by."

Sarah hesitated then asked, "Are you moving to Wyoming now?"

"Now what?" Moria questioned with sudden irritation.

"You know...now that dad's not in the picture."

"Sarah, help me out here. I'm really tired. Let's talk about this later."

"Okay mom, I'll call you in a few days."

Moria grumbled to herself while she fed the cats, turned off her phone, and fell into her bed.

* * *

The next few weeks passed in a frenzy of school plans, keeping horses legged up, and attending to the daily chores of life. Moria and Jackson were closer now than ever before, but still, something seemed to be missing. Moria's heart wavered when thinking about taking the leap of faith that meant she could make Jackson hers.

One evening the two were sitting on the porch talking about—what else—the horses, Phoenix and Promise's future, Silver Dollar's successes, and Rainbow Chaser's enduring spirit on the trail. Dixie and Hero sniffed around in the yard, rooting out chipmunks and mice. Pounce and Pandora leapt onto the swing, eyeing Jackson.

"What's that all about?" Moria studied the cats' odd behavior.

"Watch this," Jackson replied, digging into his pocket for a bag of catnip. Pounce began to purr with vigor and placed his paws on the cowboy's shoulders. Pandora snuggled into Jackson's lap, rolled on her back, and reached for the bag.

Moria burst out laughing, "When did you accomplish this?"

"All those days you've been at school. Didn't take too long. Shoulda thought of it before." He fed the treats to his new best friends, finally scattering the remainder on the floor. Treats consumed, the cats sat on the steps watching the dogs on their nightly hunt.

Pounce said, *All that attack on Jackson's getting old. Catnip is better. Besides, he's not going anywhere.*

Pandora twitched her whiskers skeptically, *How do you know?*

Because he wouldn't have made friends with us if he was going away. Pounce answered, and jumped off the porch to prowl into the bushes, followed by Pandora.

Moria watched the cats wander away, "Now I've seen it all."

Jackson grinned, "Guess they're not so bad after all...for cats."

* * *

September brought cool mornings but afternoon heat held summer in its grip. Leaves drooped on the trees, grass withered, and the sky showed no promise of rain. Golden rod, Queen Anne's lace, and purple asters lined the roadsides, their petals thick with dust.

One evening after school, Moria and Maxine took the horses out for a conditioning ride. Moria wiped the dripping sweat out of her eyes, "Maybe this wasn't such a good idea."

Maxine checked Fire's heart monitor, "His pulse is already high. We might as well go on at a slower pace, since we're out here."

The horses sensed the lack of enthusiasm of their riders and plodded slowly down the road toward the mountain trail. The women legged the horses into a trot, steadily working their way up the mountain.

They reached the ridgeline and Maxine said, "Maybe we should get off and lead them a ways."

"Huh? Get off? That's pretty extreme."

"You'd better get it together. If you don't give this next race all you've got, you'll be sorry later."

Moria dismounted and said, "Maybe I'm getting too old for this."

"Come on, girlfriend! We've got at least thirty years of riding left in us."

Moria followed Maxine down a trail, resolved to capture this time in her life, the horses, and her friends; gifts freely given.

Later in the ride Moria looked into the ravine and said, "I wish we could use the river tail and cross the covered bridge. Guess Kam's not going to put that on his priority list since we pissed him off with our swimming adventure and ruined his fun. We're lucky he got mad and left."

Maxine replied, "Well it's not over 'til it's over. There might be a way to get this done. Remember we have the GPS maps we made, the only copy of the trail plans, and the environmental report in my computer. We never got around to sending all that to his office since I'm the unofficial secretary for our group. It would take a long time for this work to be done and over."

"Hmm...so you're thinking maybe he would be willing to trade opening the trail again and getting the bridge repaired to get the information he's supposed to have anyway?"

"What do you think?" Maxine asked, shifting in her saddle to look over her shoulder at Moria. A misguided squirrel took that moment to leap into the trail and Catch on Fire spun sideways. Maxine grabbed his mane and lurched onto his neck.

"Hey, good save!" Moria said, grabbing the neck strap in case Rainbow followed suit. "It's a stretch to get Kam to cooperate, but I guess it's worth a try. Why don't we go by the ranger office after school tomorrow and have a little chat with our boy? We do still have the camera film from the river escapade plus the trail plans—he owes us."

"Good idea. You know, another thing; we need to tell Mr. Baldwin we'll both be gone on the same Friday to the ride. We better line up a couple of good subs. Thank goodness the kids are manageable, being it's the first of the year."

"Maybe we'd better buy a box of his favorite chocolates."

Maxine asked, "Have you noticed it seems like we're always bribing somebody?"

The riders reached the ford that crossed the dirt road and paused to let the horses drink. Moria replied, "Whatever works!" The horses perked up and trotted briskly down the road. "Guess they're not so tired after all, the rascals."

The next morning, the two teachers met in the classroom to plan how to approach the principal, who frowned on people taking time off unless it was an emergency. "Maybe we should cry?" Moria suggested.

Maxine picked up the box of chocolates. "This'll work better. Trust me. He's hardened his soul to us, but not to his sweet tooth. Besides, we haven't used our personal days and we did get good subs."

They knocked on the door and entered. Mr. Baldwin eyed the candy Maxine held in front of her and gave the two women a stern look. "I see you are already up to mischief. Let me guess...you want to take a personal day only a few weeks after school's started."

Maxine offered the candy and the principal nodded, indicating to put it on his desk, and said, "Now that I have accepted your gift, tell me which day you want off."

"Uh...Moria needs to go too," Maxine replied quickly.

"Both of you on the same day? Not acceptable. Moria glanced toward the candy and handed Mr. Baldwin a piece of paper with the subs names.

Saving face, he continued, "These two are excellent. Go ahead. Don't have any accidents and be sure you're back on Monday.

Moria and Maxine thanked their boss—as if he were doing them a favor—and left, closing the door behind them. Moria looked back through the glass portion of the door to see him reach for the chocolates. "You were right," she laughed. "At least we know that's done. Guess we'd better plan an independent study day when we're gone. No group work."

The children worked quietly most of the day, while their teachers made lists for the ride. When the last bus rolled away, they prepared to leave and Moria said, "Sometimes I feel a little guilty when I'm not engaged with the kids...like I'm not doing my job.

Maxine replied, "You do more than your job every day. Their test scores prove it. We're good!"

"I'll feel better when I hear our boss say that. Why don't we make a trip to Kam's office on the way home?"

When they reached the ranger station, Moria said, "Let's hope we don't make matters worse."

"I think we've got Kam's attention, at least right now." Maxine replied, opening the door and asking the desk attendant if it was convenient to see Ranger Bryson.

They were ushered down the hallway to Kam's office. The attendant knocked on the door. "Some people to see you," she announced and walked away.

Maxine opened the door and strode in with more confidence than she felt. Moria followed close behind.

Kam sprang out of his chair, overturning it and yelled, "You..."

Moria put her finger over her lips and nodded toward the hallway, closing the door.

"Bitches! What are you doing here?" he finished, his face flushed with annoyance.

The two women took seats, uninvited. Moria waited a moment and said, "We need a favor."

He stared at her, snatched his chair upright and collapsed into it, head in his hands. "What? You've decided to blackmail me?"

"No." Moria said, ignoring Kam's outburst. "We're interested in helping get a project started—the river trail and the bridge."

"We don't have any extra money for that."

Moria continued, "We can have some fund raisers apply for grant money. You know, a lot of the work has already been done—the GPS maps are ready and the environmental report is finished."

He replied, "Where is that stuff? Did y'all ever send it to me?" He turned his chair around to search in his computer.

Moria and Maxine looked at each other and waited, not answering.

After scrolling through some of the files he said, "You must still have that work."

"We do." Maxine answered. "We want to make a trade. We'll give you all the information we have if you will at least get some kind of authority from the forest supervisor in writing, to make completion work on the river trail and bridge a priority. You know, it could be a feather in your cap."

Kam pondered this statement for a moment. "I'll see what I can do. You'll have to return the information now. I'll need it when I meet with my boss."

Moria looked at Maxine, who nodded in agreement, "We are counting on you to do what you say. Word gets around."

"Hey, wait a minute! What about the film?" the ranger asked with worry.

In all innocence, Moria answered, "What about it? End of discussion."

Maxine added, "Don't screw around on this with us."

"That's a scary thought." Kam said, walking to the door and ushering them to the hallway. "See you on the trail," and waved them goodbye.

That evening at Moria's barn, she shared the day's events with Jackson as they fed the horses.

"Don't count on getting any results from Kam. He'll probably weasel out of it with some excuse," Jackson commented.

"Well I know he doesn't want our meeting out in the public domain, especially since he let us hold information that never should have left his office."

Moria began filling the water buckets and said, "I can't worry about this anymore right now. I've got to focus on getting ready for the ride. We're leaving in a week. I'm so glad you'll be here to crew for me. And, can you come over in the morning when the farrier comes? I forgot to tell you."

"What about getting your truck serviced? I think it's been a while."

"Could you..." she asked, shutting off the water.

Jackson took Moria in his arms and held her close. She relaxed and the day's struggles faded away. *How can I do without you? You are my soul mate.* Aloud she said, "Would you like to help me grade some papers?" She smiled up at him, rubbing her hand against his thigh.

"My pencil's sharp. I'm ready."

Chapter Fourteen

L ater in the evening the phone rang. Moria sat up in the bed and reached for it. *Jessie.* "Hey, sweetie. How are you?" Moria could hear tears in the child's voice. *This is not good.*

Jessie blurted out, "Miss Doris had an accident and broke her leg. Now she can't come to the ride. Will you sponsor me? We have transportation for my horse and my parents will be there." The young girl paused, took a quivering breath and continued, "Doris says she's going to call to see if you can help us."

Be careful what you wish for, remembering her statement to Jackson a few days ago.

"Sure. I'd be glad to and look forward to it. What happened to Doris?"

"Her horse slid into an arroyo and fell on Doris's leg. The horse ran home and she called someone from her barn to get help. I stayed there until the EMT's came. Luckily, we weren't too far from the road. It's going to take a while for her to get better. So, I'm glad you and I can ride together. I need to tell you one more thing. I am one of the top three juniors nationally. I have to race."

Nooo! But Moria said, "I know you need to do the very best that you can. I'm not sure I'm the one to sponsor you."

By now, Jackson was awake and listening to Moria's end of the conversation. He touched her shoulder and pointed to her, mouthing, "You do this."

Jessie said in a desolate voice, "Then, who would sponsor me?"

"Maybe my friend, Maxine, would help you out. She has a fast horse, Catch on Fire."

Jessie answered, "Rainbow Chaser's fast. Miss Doris said a lady in your neighborhood, I think her name's Jada, told her you were afraid to race. That's not true, is it?"

And, a little child shall lead them..."Not exactly, I'm just cautious. Jada injured her horse at the last ride. I want to be riding Rainbow for a long time. To answer your question..." she glanced at Jackson and smiled, "Yes, I will sponsor you, and we will race."

"Oh, thank you! I'm so excited! I've got to go pack. See you real soon!"

Moria fell back on the pillows and let out a deep breath. "Well, I'm glad my insurance's paid up.

Jackson laughed and said, "Don't underestimate yourself, Missy. You'll be amazing!"

Moria tossed the covers aside to get up and said, "Maybe now's the time to try some hypnotism—you think?"

"I have a better idea. Come here."

Moria turned around, "I'll bet you do!" Jackson worked his magic—fear, uncertainty, and indecision drifted out the window on a gentle breeze.

On the way to school Moria called Maxine. "Guess what?"

"You're sponsoring Jessie at the ride."

"What? You already know?"

"Three guesses..."

"Facebook? Tell me!"

"If you would get your own page, you would know these things."

Moria turned into the school parking lot with Maxine right behind her. "I know you'll keep me up-to-date. It's more efficient to let you bring me the important stuff—so?

As the two teachers walked into the school, Maxine said, "Jessie's one of my friends. She couldn't wait to let everyone know, especially her competitors, that she's still in the hunt. Another little nugget of information—Jada did get another horse. She'll have to ride open, but she'll be on the trail. You better watch your back. She's calling the mare White Trash."

"Oh, my gosh! Am I even surprised? What will happen next?"

And soon she knew. Late in the afternoon her mom, Claire, called. "We're coming through Atlanta tomorrow and wanted to stop by the farm, just overnight. We can stay in the RV and won't be any trouble. I know you're getting ready for the ride. We do want to meet Jackson, too." She paused for a breath.

"You won't be any trouble, at all. The house is a mess. At least I have an excuse this time!"

Claire replied, "Maybe I can help you. I'll cook a chicken pot pie, do your laundry, wash the saddle pads or whatever else."

"I'll appreciate your help. I do want you to meet Jackson, although he'll be going back to Wyoming soon. I wish you could stay for the ride."

Moria could hear laughter in Claire's voice when her mom said, "You know your dad. We have to stay on schedule! See you tomorrow."

Jackson was already at the barn when Moria arrived home. *Guess I'd better get down there and be sure everything's in order. I know that's the first place my dad will want to go.*

"Got some news for you," Moria announced, opening the gate and petting Dixie and Hero, who bounded up to greet her.

"What?" Jackson set the wheelbarrow down and reached for his water bottle.

"My parents are coming—tomorrow."

"Great! I'd like to meet them. What do we need to do to get ready?"

"Mostly be sure the barn looks good and the horses are groomed. I can straighten up in the house tonight."

The next afternoon her parent's motor home rolled into the driveway. Moria rushed out to greet them. "I'm so glad y'all made Cherry Valley one of your stops," she teased. "Jackson's here. Come on in."

Moria's dad, Roger, and Jackson shook hands and Moria could see her dad taking Jackson's measure. "Let's go take a look at the horses," Roger suggested, and they departed, chatting like old friends.

Claire got busy in the kitchen, one she had worked in for many years. "Maybe I'll go down to the barn with dad and Jackson," Moria said.

"Why don't you stay here with me? Let those two get acquainted. Catch me up on your life—and especially that handsome cowboy." She winked at Moria as if the two shared a secret about their men.

"Well," Moria began, and burst into tears. Claire came over and put her arms around her daughter.

"Come on, honey. Let's sit on the porch a while," and poured two glasses of sweet tea for them.

Moria wiped her face on a paper towel and followed her mom outside. They settled in the swing and she remembered with comfort, all the times they'd sat together, sorting out problems in Moria's young life.

"Sorry. Guess I'm just stressed out. I called you about Fredrick's visit. That's enough by itself. Then, coping with the beginning of school, keeping Rainbow in peak shape..." She hesitated, "But most of all, Jackson's leaving after the ride. He wants me to go with him." Moria searched her mom's face for an answer.

Claire put her arm around Moria's shoulders, saying, "I know you want your life packaged all neatly, with directions to guide you and a buzzer to sound if you make the wrong choices."

Moria smiled ruefully, "Yeah, I really could use that buzzer right now."

"Tell me more about Jackson. I know we've talked and e-mailed about the horse activities but I want to know what you think about him."

Moria took a deep breath. "I love him but I can't go to Wyoming. My home is here on this farm and in Cherry Valley. I can't imagine living anywhere else." Then she frowned, "Guess that sounds pretty wimpy, doesn't it?"

Without a word, Claire left the swing and went out to the motor home. Returning, she handed Moria a package. "I made something for you. I've been doing a lot of cross-stitching during those long hours on the road."

Moria could feel a picture frame inside the paper wrapping. She ripped it loose, to see a familiar saying, *Home is where the heart is.* Below the words Claire had sewn two running horses—a chestnut and a gray.

"Oh, Mom, thank you so much!" Moria ran her hands over the stitching. A quick thought flitted through her mind. *God sent me a message on a beer sign, 'Go for the Gusto!' Now, He's into cross-stitching?*

Just then, Jackson and Roger returned from the barn. Moria laid the cross-stitching on the swing and went to meet them, "So, Dad, what did you think?"

"Everything looks like it's in tip-top shape. Your Jackson has a handle on what's going on down there. I wish we'd never sold that fifty acres to the Rutherfords. You need some more land. Jackson showed off the filly's training. Looks like she has promise.

Moria laughed, "That's her name!"

"And Phoenix is a great mare," he said. "Are you keeping them?"

Reading her dad's thoughts, she said, "I'm planning to give Promise to Jessie. The mare? I don't know..."

Looking wistful, he said, "Too bad I don't have a place to keep her." Then looking at Claire, he said, "Hmm, maybe I do. You know that farm right down the road from us? Bet they could use another border."

Moria hugged him. "Consider Phoenix an early Christmas present. I would love for you to have her. Maybe we could do an endurance ride together one day."

Roger rolled his eyes at her and said, "Life holds lots of adventures for me yet, it seems. I'll see about getting her shipped down when we get back."

"I can trailer her for you. Don't hire anyone."

He answered, "You'll probably be pretty busy after the ride. Don't worry about it."

"I'm always busy. I'd like to come visit, anyway."

"We'll see. What's for supper? Smells good."

Moria got up at daybreak to make coffee and say goodbye to Roger and Claire. As their motor home pulled away, Moria said aloud, "I might as well feed the horses, since I'm up." At the barn she fed the horses. Then fastened Rainbow in the crossties, groomed him and examined his legs for swelling and cuts. Looking into his face, she said to him, "Who says horses don't have expressions?" His bright, knowing eyes told her the answer—I'm ready to race.

Walking back to the house, she pulled the checklist from the pocket of her jeans. *I've got to get some more duct tape on the way home today and shop for food. Thank goodness Jackson can help me finish packing.* I need to call and let him know I've fed the horses.

At school Moria and Maxine were on a mission to have the day run smoothly while they were gone. Addressing the class, Moria said, "Be on your best behavior and we'll have a fun surprise for you." She raised her eyebrows and gave her teacher look. "If there are issues there will be another surprise. Your choice." The children looked sideways at each other and one of the boys raised his hand, speaking in his most serious voice. "You can count on us!"

"Oh, yeah." Maxine said under her breath, but answered, "I know you guys will make us proud!"

The rest of the day passed without event and soon the classroom was empty. "Well, guess we're down to the wire. Let's get out of here. I've still got packing to do." Maxine said.

"Jackson had a to-do list today. Hope he got everything done."

"You're gonna miss that cowboy when he's gone. Not just because he's a 'fetch and carry' guy. You know there's more."

"Don't start," Moria snapped. "Sorry. I just can't handle one more thing right now." Softening her voice, she continued, "Too bad we have to take so much stuff. We could trailer together since Silver Dollar and Arctic Cat aren't going."

"More is better at an endurance ride!" Maxine laughed. "See you in the morning. Good thing the ride's not but fifty miles away. I'm glad they picked the Ridge and Valley ride site since we know the trail."

"Me too," Moria answered absently, her mind already home.

Jackson was at the barn when Moria got there. "All the heavy stuff's packed. Take a look and see if we're missing anything."

Moria stepped into the back of the trailer to double-check the needed items. She heard Jackson's phone ring and his voice, becoming agitated as the conversation progressed.

Getting out of the trailer and walking over to Jackson, she could see distress on his face. "What's the matter?" she asked, coming closer.

He disconnected the call and said, "Come here. I need to tell you what's going on."

His worried face frightened her. "Are your mom and dad okay?"

Jackson led her over to the tack room steps and they sat side by side.

"That was Wylie, our head wrangler. Some of our cattle have strayed over the mountain onto the next ranch. That old buzzard is laying claim to them because they weren't branded and he cut the ear tags off, knowing they're ours. Right now, he's sitting on a lot of our money. If we don't get those cattle to the railway on time, we'll have to keep them another year. I need to get back there right away—tonight."

"Tonight?" Moria's head spun with this unexpected turn of events. "Can't you wait till the ride is over?"

"Listen, Missy, I have to go. You don't get it, do you?. You'll have plenty of help at the ride. What does it really matter to you, anyway?"

Alarmed at the tone of his voice, she answered, "Of course it matters. It's just..."

"That's it damn inconvenient for you. Is that it?"

Moria stood up and walked away, crossing her arms and gripping them to stop her shaking hands. "Are you going to fly or take everything tonight? I could watch the horses for you until you can come back for them."

"I'm not coming back. When I roll out of here tonight, I'm gone—for good. I'll pick up Silver when I leave in a few hours and try not to disturb you."

Moria stared, unseeing, out into the darkening night. *Disturb me? You've turned my world upside down—again!*

Jackson came over and put his arms around her. "I love you. I'll always remember our time together. You're a special girl."

Tears rolled down Moria's cheeks. "What's the matter with me?"

Jackson tipped her face to his. Smiling, he said, "You just need to put your boots on, Missy."

She sniffed and through her tears, said, "Where are those boots? I can't seem to find them!"

"Let me know when you do. Good luck at the ride. Be safe." Kissing her goodbye, his hand lingering on her cheek. Then, the cowboy strode away without a backward look.

Moria sat back down on the tack room steps, stunned beyond measure. She leaned her head against the door and closed her eyes. "Maybe this is just a bad dream," she said to Dixie, who laid her chin on Moria's knee and whined for Hero, who had disappeared into the dark with his master. Looking across the pasture, she saw Jackson's truck pull into the Rutherford's driveway and back up to his trailer. "Too late to call Maxine. What can she do, anyway?"

Dixie continued to whine, looking at Moria, sensing that all was not right in their world. "Come on girl, you can stay in the house tonight."

Sleep eluded her and hours later she heard Jackson stop on the road. In a few minutes, Silver's hooves crunched on the gravel drive, the sound growing fainter as the cowboy and his horse left for home.

The next morning Moria trudged to the barn, took care of the horses, and left Rodney a message about their care. With a heavy heart, she loaded Rainbow in the trailer and pulled up to the house, going inside for a final check. Pounce and Pandora sat on the table but Moria didn't notice their disobedience. "Oops, almost forgot my phone," she said, looking to see if Jackson had called.

Pounce meowed, looking for his new best friend. *Where is he? Have you run him off?* The cat growled to get Moria's attention.

She took his furry gray face in her hands and as if reading his mind, "You know, we might be making a mistake, here."

Pounce meowed again and Pandora crept closer to Moria. "Oh, my gosh! You two! I'll be back in a couple of days. You miss Jackson, don't you?" *So do I.*

On the way out to the truck, she picked up the cross-stitching gift off the swing, planning to put it in the living quarters of the trailer. Then, laid it on the seat with an assortment of all else that didn't get packed.

Before she left Cherry Valley, her phone rang. Maxine. "Hey, where are you?"

"Almost to the interstate."

"We're ahead of you a few miles. Jeremy said Jackson left last night." Maxine paused for a response.

"I've turned the page," Moria replied.

Puzzled, Maxine asked, "What does that mean?"

"Never mind. I've got to go. See you at the ride." She disconnected and dialed Jackson's number.

His voicemail was her only answer. Laying the phone down, she stopped at a rest area and rolled down the windows. Hot air rushed in to greet her. *That's me—a bunch of hot air. What was I thinking? I can live anywhere. It's who you're with that really counts. And dialed Jackson's number again.*

"Hi, this is Jackson. Leave a message. I'll get back to you."

I hope so. "Hey, it's me. I've found my boots and after the ride I'm packing to move to Wyoming—if you'll still have me." Moria rubbed her fingers over the cross-stitching. *Thanks, Mom.* "We can have a good life, no matter where we are. It's true. Home is where the heart is. I love you."

Soon Moria arrived at the familiar ride site, light of heart, and drove to the parking space Maxine had saved. Her friend rushed over to the truck, motioning Moria to roll the window down. "Are you okay? You didn't sound like yourself while ago."

Moria answered, "Maybe I'm not myself anymore. I'm going to Wyoming. That is, if Jackson will still have me. We belong together. I know it's meant to be, or he never would have been in Cherry Valley when I needed help."

Maxine stared at Moria in disbelief. "Did you talk to him?"

"No, I left a message," she answered, getting out of the truck. Maybe I'll hear from him soon."

"Well, I never...you're a piece of work!"

Jeremy walked up. "Enough girl talk. Let's get to the vet check. I've got a bunch of stuff to take up there."

Moria looked around their immediate area. "Is Jessie here yet?"

He nodded in the direction across the road and answered, "They're across the way. Jessie's been over to our camp looking for you. I think they're in the vet line. She's a cutie, and her horse looks great."

When they reached the vet check, Jessie ran to meet them. The young girl had grown taller, and no doubt wiser, during the months of tough endurance training. Moria handed Rainbow's lead rope to Maxine and opened her arms just in time to catch the youngster as Jessie gave Moria a fierce hug.

"Miss Moria! I'm so glad to see you!"

Standing Jessie at arms-length, she said, "Wow! You've really grown!"

"Yeah. Miss Doris worked me hard and my mom stopped buying chips and sodas." She wrinkled her nose. "I had to eat vegetables." Tugging at Moria's hand she said, "Come on over and see my horse!"

Moria looked at Maxine. "Do you mind holding Rainbow for a minute? I'll be right back."

They walked across the grass to Jessie's contingent, and the child, remembering her manners, introduced her dad, Paul, and the two girls who had hauled the horses, both women were tall, slim, and tan, and looked like they could give you a run for your money. *Why do the California riders always look like Barbies and Kens?* "You've already met my mom at the doctor's office." Jessie added, smiling at Ruth.

Moria greeted everyone, then asked the girls, Chris and Tara, "Why don't one of you sponsor Jessie?" glancing at their two fit Arabs. Chris said, "We would love to but neither of our horses are qualified. We've never been to the southeast and wanted to see what it is like, so at the last minute, we agreed to haul Jessie's horse and ours. Man, is it always so hot and humid here?"

"Yep. This is pretty normal, even in the mountains. I hope you have plenty of electrolytes."

"We're going back by the vendor's and get some more," Chris answered, wiping her forehead on her sleeve.

Ruth said, "We've brought extras. Doris said we would need them." Looking at Moria she continued, "Doris is having surgery on her leg in a couple of days. She sent you a message." Ruth dug into her pocket handed Moria a crumpled piece of paper.

Unfolding it, Moria read:

You better race your Rainbow Chaser! Get Jessie through the ride to first junior—where she belongs. And, don't let her get hurt! The girls will keep me posted during the ride. My spirit rides with you.

Doris

Moria read the note again and stuffed it in her pocket. *Wow! That's a pretty tall order, Doris Weaver. We'll see how fast our guardian angles can fly!*

All the horses cleared the vet check and Moria noticed many of the endurance riders checking out the California girls and the juniors took a good look at Jessie and the dapple gray Arab she called Friendly, knowing that was the pair to beat.

After dinner and the rider's meeting Moria suggested everyone come over to her trailer so they could make plans. Paul and Jeremy had set the crewing needs in one spot so they could work together. Five competitors going out and coming in at different times would keep them busy.

Chris and Tara were amazed at the elaborate set-up in the crewing area. Water buckets, feed for the horses, coolers filled with drinks and food for the riders, chairs, clean saddle pads, fly spray for horses and humans, and an assortment of grooming tools were efficiently arranged under a pop-up tent. Jeremy's rule for the riders: don't move anything! We've got you covered.

Tara said, "We usually carry what we need with us and hay and water are provided at the checks. I could get spoiled with this," she said, waving her hand in the direction of the tent.

As the group walked toward trailers, Moria checked her phone. *Where is he? Why hasn't he called?*

Maxine glanced over at her friend and teased, "Hope you're not a day late and a dollar short."

"This is not funny! I've put the rest of my life on the line. You'd think he'd at least call!"

"Maybe he doesn't have cell service," Maxine.

"Oh, please!"

Moria pushed thoughts of Jackson aside as the group made a plan for the ride. It was decided that Moria and Jessie would start in the front-runners pack. *I feel like an imposter!* she thought. *I've got to get Jessie through this ride and help her win. If she doesn't, I don't want it to be my fault.*

Maxine would ride her usual pace, perhaps with Moria and Jessie. Chris asked Maxine, "Who are the consistent winners? Will you point them out to us in the morning? I think we'll draft along behind them—or you," she said. "What about Jada?"

"We don't know Jada's new horse. She's supposed to be a pretty nice mare. Hope she stays that way," Maxine answered.

Everyone departed for the night and Moria said, "I want to check on the horses. Be right back."

Rainbow and Fire stood quietly in their corrals but vigilant to the night sounds. The horses' ears perked forward when Moria approached with an armful of hay, followed by Jeremy with fresh water and electrolytes.

As they tended the horses, Moria asked, "Have you heard from Jackson today? I left him a message, but he hasn't called back."

Busy giving Fire the electrolytes, he answered, not looking at her. "Uh, no, I haven't. Guess he's half way home. I think he was pretty much driving non-stop."

Moria replied, "Let me know if you hear from him."

"Will do."

Moria climbed the steps into the trailer and tried not to think about Jackson's presence. But she couldn't help looking around, missing his boots, his doeskin hat, and his rodeo bag of clothes.

Have I waited too long to open the door for the rest of my life? Enough of this! I've got to focus on the ride. I can't let Jessie down.

She began to set out her clothes for the next morning. "Where are my boots? I know I put them in this cabinet just a couple of days ago," she said aloud, digging deeper into the small, dark space. After a thorough search in the trailer and her truck, Moria ran her fingers through her hair, muttering, "Guess I'll have to wear my tennis shoes. If that's the worst thing that happens to me tomorrow, I'm lucky," and placed her well-worn shoes nearby.

Autumn leaves swirled across the dirt road as riders warmed up for the National Championship Endurance Ride. Bays, chestnuts, grays, blacks, spotted, and gold blended into a mosaic of moving colors, but riders working the horses up and down the driveway did not notice.

Moria mounted Rainbow Chaser and looked around for Jessie. Just then, Paul came toward them, holding a lead rope with Friendly prancing beside him. As they reached Moria, Jessie said, "Let go, Daddy! I'm okay!" He did so, and the gray and his rider darted into the driveway with the other riders. Moria moved onto the grass and watched the young girl handle Friendly. At the end of the drive Jessie turned and came back. Moria said, "You're good to go, honey. It's almost time. Let's show 'em what you've got!"

Maxine and the California girls joined them and Maxine said, "We've got your back for the first few miles and we'll see what happens at the first vet check. This should be an interesting project!"

In spite of the chaos around her, Moria could not keep her mind from returning to Jackson, his whereabouts, and lack of response to her calls. *Where are you? Why won't you call? How could my life have fallen apart in just a few short months? Me—who's always had control of my life—since Fredrick left anyway. Seems like just yesterday, Jackson, you came to help at the farm. So much has happened since then. How could you walk away, and not come back?* Gathering her reins a little tighter, she came to the moment. *I know Scarlett; guess I'll take your advice and think about that tomorrow.*

Just then, Jada cantered by. "Hey, pussy cat, see you at the finish line," she jeered. Moria shouted back, "I'll be waiting for you!"

She looked over her shoulder at the young rider close behind, and motioned her forward, saying to Jessie, "You set the pace. Ride like you've trained."

"Miss Doris says never look back."

"Sounds like a plan. Just think of me as your guardian angel." And don't ride faster than I can fly!

Moria's fingers brushed over the saints medals, fastened to her saddle. Who would have imagined a ski accident would lead to this day?

The front-runners bunched at the starting line. Moria placed Jessie and herself just a few horses back in the cluster. Jessie watched the group in front of her. She did not look back.

Thank you, Doris Weaver. And a little child shall lead me...

"Three, two, one! The trail is open. Have a safe ride!" called the timer. A cloud of dust floated into the trees and with the dust, flew the dreams and misfortunes of the day to come.

Moria had cautioned Jessie about the sharp turn into the woods, but reminded her again. "We're almost to the turn. Get a grip!" Jessie did not look back. Moria took hold of Rainbow's neck strap as they flew into the knee knocker pines, scattering sand behind them. Maxine, Chris, and Tara followed close behind.

Moria could hear Tara's voice over the thudding hooves and wind in her ears, "Oh, my God! Where are my wide, open spaces?'

"Not in Georgia, cowgirl!" Moria called back. Just then, Moria's knee took a hit. "Oh, shit!"

She glanced down and called back to Tara, "No blood. Guess I'm okay."

Jessie barreled along behind the five riders. Moria had dropped back a few lengths to check on her knee. "Uh oh, come on, buddy," and put a leg on Rainbow, who surged forward, closing the gap. Moria caught up just as Jessie took the turn onto the jeep trail. The youngster and her gray never looked back.

One of the front-runners slowed down. "Passing on the left," Jessie called. The rider moved over. The four front-runners who were still in the lead slowed down to a trot. One of them said to Jessie, "Want to pass?"

"No thanks," she answered.

Good girl, Moria thought. *Chase them all the way to the vet check.*

The four in front paced at a slow trot. *They're trying to spook her.*

Jessie stayed behind them for more than a mile. Moria could see the older riders look at one another and then move on out. *They know the rest of the pack will be closing in, then there's Catch on Fire and Maxine, consistent top-ten competitors, and the California girls—the unknowns. Good choice, ladies!*

The jeep trail led to the wide, grassy, river valley. Moria knew they were coming up on the water stop. *What to do? The riders in front know I will offer Rainbow water. Bet they're not going to stop.* She looked back at Maxine, who shrugged her shoulders, as if to say, "Jessie's call."

Sure enough, the leaders bypassed the water, and Jessie followed on their heels. Moria looked longingly toward the shaded water hole but the chestnut gelding never slowed down. Maxine, Tara, and Chris turned off the trail to refresh the horses. Behind her, in the distance, she could see another pack of riders closing in.

Shortly, the trio rode up behind Moria and Jessie. "The horses wouldn't drink," Maxine said. "Another bunch was right behind us. Not too much further to camp."

The four riders in front of them jumped off, dropped their saddles and went straight to the vet check. Their crews ran beside them with water and sponges to squeegee the water off before it became hot.

Paul, Ruth, and Jeremy were waiting at the crew area. A quick check of the pulses for the five horses indicated they were ready to go for the exam. As their horses got in line, Ruth said, "I can take Friendly, Paul will take the girls' horses and Jeremy can take Catch on Fire and Rainbow Chaser, if that's alright with everybody."

The grateful riders headed for the porta-potty and then food table where Ruth had outdone herself with fruit, sandwiches, chips, cookies and drinks. The women and Jessie grabbed some sandwiches and drinks, then hurried over to see how the horses were doing. One of the front-runners was over in the shade with her horse, trying to cool it down.

"Guess the pulse was too high," Moria commented. "Too bad the ride manager didn't borrow the fans from River Song."

Ruth jogged Friendly and then stopped by the vet to complete the check.

"Wow, your mom looks like she's a runner. She makes it look easy."

Jessie laughed, "Well, she is now. She and my dad run almost every day. They're going to do a half marathon later this month."

Moria ruffled Jessie's hair. "I hope you appreciate your parents. You're a lucky girl."

"I know," Jessie answered. "Miss Doris is always reminding me!"

Chalk another one up for Doris. Just then, her phone rang. *Oh, my gosh! It's her!*

"Hey, Moria, Chris called me. Looks like you guys are doing okay so far. Sounds like one of the fronts is not going to make it back out, not right now, anyway. Don't back off! You hear?"

Moria replied, "Sorry about your accident. Don't worry about Jessie. You did a good job. I've got to go. Talk to you later."

"Wait! Let me speak to Jessie."

Moria handed her phone to the youngster. Jessie's eyes lit up and she laughed when Doris spoke to her. Moria sensed a bond between the two, and a twinge of jealously pricked at her. *Get over yourself,* she thought. *You've got a job to do. Get it done!*

Jessie returned the phone saying, "Miss Doris said I'd better not be spoiled when I get back. What does that mean?"

"It's a Southern thing, honey."

Smiling up at Moria, she said, "Maybe we could move to Georgia and I could be your junior rider and be spoiled."

Moria's heart melted. "I would love that! Come on, we need to go help with the horses."

Soon they were on the trail again. Three front-runners were still in the mix. Maxine said, "I guess they've decided we're not going away. They're setting a pretty steady pace," then she grinned. "They could always drop back!"

Two foothills with long ridge lines took the riders away from camp and into a valley on the opposite side of the hills, back through a gap, and onto a long dirt road which finished the next loop. By now the sun was high and the humidity higher. At the vet check, Chris and Tara decided to back off the pace, wanting to be sure they finished. "This is a long way to drive and not get a completion," Tara said. "We'll just mosey along and still finish in plenty of time."

"Ten miles to go," Moria told Jessie, as they started out on the last loop. Fear began to cloud Moria's mind. Now the three fronts had dropped back, letting Moria, Jessie and Maxine set the pace.

Moria said to Jessie, "Don't let them push us."

Jessie fretted and said, "Miss Doris wouldn't like for me to get behind."

"Well, honey, Miss Doris isn't here. Don't you worry. We're going to turn you loose pretty shortly, now. Your other junior friends are only a wish in the breeze. You stick with us. When we tell you to run, you go."

"I know. And, don't look back."

"You got it."

At the river crossing the horses waded in, splashing and drinking. Moria eyed her competitors, who were inching their way toward shore. Nodding to Maxine, she said, "Let's go." Just then, one of the front-runners' horses went down in the water. The rider screamed as she pitched forward, headlong into the river. The horse thrashed about, going under, and bobbing up again.

Moria yelled to Jessie, "Get to the bank!" The frightened child obeyed and moved away.

Maxine shouted, "I'll get the horse. Y'all help her."

Moria and the other two women pushed their horses against the current to the spot where the rider struggled to gain her footing. Moria glanced toward Maxine, who had caught the horse and was headed toward shore.

The fallen rider took hold of her friend's stirrup to steady herself and climbed out, to see her horse rolling in spasms on the ground. "Is he dying?" she sobbed, wiping muddy water from her face.

Maxine said, "Calm down. He may have just gotten a cramp from the cold water. We need to get him up and try to walk him."

The dazed rider and Maxine urged the horse up. He stood shivering and heaving, then fell to the ground again. Jessie had backed out of the way, trying to settle Friendly down. The friends of the unfortunate rider said, "We'll go for help," eyeing the open trail ahead.

Moria heard riders approaching the river crossing. "Uh oh," she said under her breath. "There come the other juniors who are looking for a win."

Maxine said to the grounded woman, "Here, let's get him up again and you walk him until help comes. If he goes down again, I'd leave him be."

By now the two fronts were hightailing it up the road and the juniors and their sponsors were fording the river.

Maxine mounted Fire and said to Moria and Jessie, "We can catch them! Let's go!"

Moria finally understood the thrill of the chase and set Rainbow on course for the last two miles. Bright sun sifted through the leaves of the trees arching overhead—red, gold, bronze, and yellow, creating a whirl of shadowed patterns on the road.

Moria looked ahead at Jessie's racing figure, autumn leaves flying up behind her. Fear flew away like the leaves as Rainbow dug in and ran faster than he ever had before.

The riders with the juniors were close behind. "Come on, mister. We've got to stay with Jessie, or she'll be disqualified if we get separated."

A mile to go. Moria yelled, "Go, Jessie!" Maxine followed Moria and they closed the distance to the two front-runners. "Oh my gosh! We're going to pass them!" The women looked startled as Jessie, then Maxine and Moria galloped by. Jessie and the gray became a cloud of moving dust.

Maxine called to Moria, who was now beside her, "Put the hammer down, or I'm going to beat the socks off you!"

"Not today!" Moria shouted back and turned Rainbow loose. She could hear cheers as Jessie crossed the finish line. Rainbow nosed out Catch on Fire by a few feet as they neared the end. Cheers erupted as the two dashed past, still running, out of control.

Maxine passed Moria, as she fought for control of Fire. Rainbow had other ideas. Seeing the turn into camp, he scrambled around the corner.

Unprepared, Moria was slung off into a stand of saplings full of briars and undergrowth. The small trees bent with her weight and she slid deeper into the underbrush. Stunned, she lay still, but could hear urgent voices, sounding far away. In a moment, she felt hands helping her from the bushes.

She mumbled, "I'm okay..." her voice trailing off as she sank to the ground and closed her eyes.

Smelling salts, offered by a rider whose trailer was nearby, helped Moria struggle back to reality. Trying to make sense of what happened, Moria's wavering voice asked, "Did Jessie win? Where's my horse?" and attempted to get up.

Maxine and Jeremy knelt beside her. "Be still," Maxine ordered. "The EMT's are coming. They're just down the road."

After the medics cleared her, Moria settled into her trailer. She managed to take a shower and apply medications to her scrapes and bruises. Looking at her beat-up face in the mirror as she brushed out her hair, she aloud, "Jackson, where are you?"

Maxine knocked on the door. "Are you okay?"

"Yeah. I'll be there in a minute."

She stepped out of the trailer to be met by her friends and other riders she barely knew, who came to offer congratulations. Overwhelmed by their greetings, and her exhaustion, tears welled in her eyes. Looking at them and giving a stiff smile from her bruised face, she said, "Wow! I should fall in the bushes more often."

Jessie came forward, saying, "I would hug you, but it looks like it would hurt." Smiling, she continued, "Sorry you fell. Miss Doris said you did good."

"That's a lot, coming from her," Ruth added. "Come here a minute, honey. Miss Moria has a surprise for you."

Jessie came over to sit beside her mom and Moria. "A surprise?" The child looked around expectantly.

Moria answered, "Not here, Jessie. I have a filly at my barn that's going back home with you. Her name is Promise. In a few years she'll be your new endurance horse."

The young girl stared in disbelief. "You're giving me a horse? Oh, thank you! Thank you! When can I see her?"

"'You all can pick her up in the morning. My farm is on your way home. Good thing you brought a really big trailer!"

Jessie gently took Moria's hand, saying, "You have made this the best day of my life! I'll take good care of Promise—I promise," then laughed at her words.

Moria sat down with her friends and the day was re-hashed from everyone's experience. Amid all the chaos, Tara and Chris had finished, along with Jada. "Why was she so far back?" Moria asked.

Jeremy laughed, "Richard crewed for her. He said he came to protect his expensive investment...the new horse."

That evening, after the awards, most of the riders sat around the camp fire, savoring the day. Moria said to Maxine, "I've got to go to bed. It's been a long day. I'm done in."

Maxine looked at her watch and replied, "Why don't we stay a few more minutes? You won't be able to sleep. The sun's barely down."

Moria looked at the sunset, streaked with lavender and pink cirrus clouds, called by some, the mares' tails. "Okay. A few more minutes."

In the distance she heard a horse's shrill whinny and Rainbow answered. Startled, she looked at Maxine. "Will you check on the horses?"

"No need," Maxine said, "Here comes your cowboy."

In the gathering dusk, Jackson rode into camp on Silver Dollar. The remaining riders stepped aside as he came closer and dismounted, handing the reins to Jeremy.

Reaching behind the saddle he said, with a big smile, "Hey, I brought you something," and showed her the missing boots.

"Jackson?" Staring at him, she stepped forward and reached out, saying, "Why do you have my boots?" And then she knew.

He held the boots behind his back and said, "Sit down, Cinderella."

Flushed and teary eyed but with a huge smile, Moria eased back into the chair and Jackson knelt in front of her locking her gaze into his dark eyes.

Wordless, she looked into his face. All the pieces of the puzzle fell into place and she knew her life was changing forever.

He unlaced her tennis shoe. "Here, hold this," he said, placing the other boot in her hands.

Glancing at it, she reached for the strings, which were tucked inside. Her hand closed around something small and cold. She pulled the strings out to examine the item. A bright diamond sparkled in the firelight. "A ring? You brought me a ring?

Jackson took her hands in his. "I believe you're ready for prime time, Missy. Will you marry me?" His question hung in the air, unanswered for a moment.

Looking into his hopeful eyes, Moria lifted her hands to his face. The world, the camp, her friends, and even the horses seemed to stand still in time, waiting for her answer. "Yes, I'll go with you to Wyoming or to the ends of the earth. I love you."

Applause and some tears greeted the two as Jackson helped Moria from the chair. "Let's go to the trailers. I believe we've got some champagne waiting for all of us.

After all the well-wishers had left, Moria sipped the champagne and said in amazement. "I don't understand? How did all this happen? Why didn't you call? How did you get back so quick?"

"I never left."

"What?"

"I hid out at Maxine's. I didn't want to be half way to Wyoming when you called me."

"How did you know I would call?"

"Pounce and I had a little talk and your dad and I came to an understanding, that he would hunt me down if I didn't take good care of you."

"Oh, you!" she laughed. "That's my dad!"

"It was all I could do not to come sooner, when you fell. Jeremy kept me up-to-date during the day. By the way, congratulations. Just don't be racing anytime soon," he joked.

Surprising herself, Moria said, "Hmm, I don't know. "Racing can be addictive!"

Maxine laughed. "Looks like we've unleashed a monster!"

"First things, first!" she answered, smiling at Jackson.

Jessie's family and the California girls bid their friends good bye, saying they would stop by the farm in the morning.

Jackson said to Moria, "It's only fifty miles to Cherry Valley. Let's go home, Missy."

Not believing Jackson's words, she said, "Home? To Cherry Valley?"

"Peace in the Valley Farm is our home. "You might need to stay in that chair for another surprise. I'm moving here and opening an office."

"In Cherry Valley? Are you kidding me?"

"No kidding." Jackson's pleased look said it all.

Moria stared at Maxine and Jeremy, not believing Jackson's words. "It's true?"

Maxine grinned. "For sure. Jeremy's going to work with him and manage the office."

"You knew about this?" Moria asked, looking accusingly at her friend.

"Yeah, I did." Maxine replied with a big smile. "We can talk more tomorrow. Jeremy's bringing Jackson's trailer back. See you all at The Diner for breakfast?"

Moria stood up to go and said, "Sounds good. I am truly amazed at this day! How did all this go on around me and I didn't even have a clue! Fill me in on the back story!"

"Will do," Jackson answered, "On the way home. Oh, one more thing. Here's your wedding present. He handed her a plain manila envelope.

"You've already got me a present?" She carefully opened the envelope and pulled out an official looking document. Unfolding the paper, she scanned it and said, "The Rutherford's fifty acres? You bought it? It's...ours?"

Jackson took Moria in his arms, saying, "Forever and ever—amen!"

"I'm almost afraid to ask, what will happen next?"

Just then, Kam walked up to their camp. "Hope I'm not interrupting anything. Meant to get over here sooner, but since this ride is in my district, I've been pretty busy today."

Shaking hands with Jackson, Kam said, "Congratulations. The word is out that you're staying around. Guess we'll be seeing a lot of each other, you being an environmental lawyer, and all."

"Remains to be seen," Jackson said, smiling, "Maybe not, if all goes well in the forest."

Kam handed Moria a folded letter. "Here's your wedding present."

"Wow! I've got another present?" she asked, unfolding the paper.

"Oh my gosh! Permission to start work on the river trail! Thanks so much." Moria got up from the chair and handed the paper to Maxine. Then, limped over to Kam, "We really appreciate this. We'll be by your office next week."

"Thanks! Surprising her with a hug, he whispered in her ear. "Just remember, I'm next in line."

Moria smiled, saying "In your dreams!"

Later, Moria and Jackson drove down the gravel road through camp. She looked out the window, watching the riders caring for their horses. Lanterns glowed in the dark as the campers settled down.

Jackson glanced at her, "Hey don't get homesick for the endurance camp. I looked at the schedule. There's another ride in two weeks. Want to go?"

"I love you, cowboy," Moria laughed, joy in her heart for the ride home and her new spirit for the adventures ahead.

About the Author

_A_ nn Cofield is a proud mom, grandmother, horse lover, retired teacher, and passionate endurance rider.

While spending her early childhood years in Oxford, Mississippi near William Faulkner's plantation, she was taught to ride by Faulkner's daughter, Jill, who let her ride up and down their driveway.

Ann has had horses in her life, for as long as she can remember. She would ride for hours at her home in Rome, Georgia, be gone all day traversing fields and woods, but would always be home before dark.

She has experience in hunter-jumper and Tennessee Walking horses, as well as managing several endurance rides and clinics. Ann was the last rider to finish the Tevis Cup in 1987. Currently, she teaches English/hunt-seat riding to youngsters at The Riding School and writes instructional materials for young riders.

Ann lives in Buford, Georgia where she writes horse-related articles and poetry, and spends time with her two dogs and her horse, Timex. This is her first novel.